The Sacrament of the Goddess

Joe Niemczura

Plain View Press
1011 W 34th Street, Suite 404

www.plainviewpress.net
Austin, TX 78705

ISBN: 978-1-63210-002-3
Library of Congress Control Number: 2014937267

Cover art permission of Exotic India Art of Delhi, India, purveyors of fine metalwork and art objects
Cover design by Pam Knight

Acknowledgements

Epigrams quoted at chapter beginnings are used within Fair Use and attributed to the author as they appear.
Lyrics quoted by Ram to Matt on arrival in Beni are from the song "Against the Wind" copyrighted by Bob Seger. Used under license from the artist's management company.
The news article about the March 2004 Battle in Beni is copyrighted by The Associated Press.
The excerpt from the Lonely Planet Guide to Nepal is copyrighted by The Lonely Planet company.
Lyrics from 'Be Still My Soul" are from the Lutheran hymnal and are believed to be in the public domain.
Words to the prayer uttered by Ranjit are from Thich Nhat Hanh, the zen Buddhist master, and are believed to be in the public domain.

to

Julie and Amy

and the

Women of Nepal

Contents

San Francisco, USA, The Last Big Sendoff

"**Y**ou could be lying in a ditch, bleeding to death, like last time."

"It ain't gonna happen, Mom."

"Did you even once consider the idea that if you did, it would just break your poor mother's heart?"

"I can see how it might upset you. That's not the point of going to Nepal this time, I assure you."

"You're being selfish. Selfish! And you need to be in better contact this time."

"You're exaggerating. If I had bled to death, would I be here today? No." He put his hands on his thigh to cradle the scarred spot where the shrapnel was removed.

"But you came home practically a cripple. And your poor mother nearly had a nervous breakdown," she said. "You're lucky they didn't amputate."

"Mom, I can walk just fine, I don't even need crutches or a cane."

Barbara made a loud sigh.

I'm glad I didn't tell them everything, Matt thought. He looked around to measure the invisible zone where diners at nearby tables cocked their ears to overhear the conversation. Several couples held their napkins against their faces to hide the fact that they were whispering back and forth in low voices. *We're making the usual dramatic scene,* he thought, *it's free entertainment for every patron of the Top of the Mark.* He didn't often go out to dinner with his parents and now he was reminded yet again why that was so. But it was better than if they ate at home. *I'm glad John and Barbara flew all the way here from Boston, it's not quite so embarrassing that way. Nobody knows us. These people are human shields. It would turn into a real spectacle if they weren't here to remind us to be civil.*

Matt reminded himself that his mother was secretly proud of him. She would go back home, and Barbara would remind her friends that her son the doctor had just completed his surgical residency at Harvard and would serve the world's poor by volunteering in Nepal for a year before returning to join his father's group practice in surgery. *Harvard. Doctor. Humanitarian. Now there's a triple crown.* And every week at Saint Catherine's Church, during the prayers of the faithful, the whole congregation would pause while she solemnly asked everyone to pray for her son, the Catholic Missionary

Doctor in a far off land. *Barbara the martyr would be the star of the church's coffee hour. She will be on everyone's prayer list.*

But right now, she was a simmering pot of random, fearful thoughts, each one splattering into the air as soon as it bubbled to the surface, from across the table. Barbara was worried in that peculiar way of hers, which was to squirm and shoot sparks from her eyes until everyone around her was walking on eggshells, waiting for her to blow up. *Her anxiety is getting the better of her. Saint Barbara of Perpetual Worry. Thank God I never told the whole story. There are simply things you don't tell your parents.*

He felt like blurting out the naked truth. *Yes, Mom, all those good intentions are true, but the real reason I am going back to Nepal is because I was passionately in love with a woman when I was there as a college student. Not just any woman. A Goddess. A Buddhist Goddess.* He smiled to himself at the thought of how to bring it up, exactly. Matt was retracing his steps to find her. He worried that she might be dead. It was more than just a remote possibility, and he needed to know for certain. But since he never even hinted about the existence of a woman before, it was too late to tell his parents now.

Matt wanted to keep things calm. He looked over at John, his father, who was trying to make the best of it. *Their lives don't quite intersect the way they used to,* Matt thought. *Thank God for her church friends. They take the pressure off John.*

Matt braced himself for the continuous dose of Catholic guilt, drop by drop. It was enough to produce numbness and paralysis but not quite enough to be fatal to the recipient.

"I promise I'll write. And there's email. There's even a paved road that goes to Beni now. It's not so isolated anymore, and the civil war is over."

"I know you claim to be an adult and everything, but just remember your poor mother back home, worried sick. My poor heart. You can't count on those people to look after you."

He wanted to say, "They saved my life last time," but thought better of it. "I hear you, Mom. I'll be careful."

He looked for a way to distract her. Maybe he should bring up John's proposal to Barbara. It took place at this very restaurant back when John was a dashing UCSF surgical resident. *Nothing wrong with conjuring happy moments from the past unless, of course, there aren't any. I wonder if they were ever happy.*

"Look at the bright side, Mom. I'll be back in a year. Would you prefer to send me to San Quentin State Prison Monday?" Matt said, "Or would you feel better if it was Alcatraz Federal Penitentiary?" He pointed out the window. "Isn't that Alcatraz out there in the bay?"

John chuckled. Barbara slapped her knife and fork on the plate, with a jarring motion. The sound jolted the serenity of the place. John suppressed his laugh and sat up straight. She glared at John.

"At least if you were incarcerated, I'd know where you were and that somebody with some sense was looking after you. You could end up lying in another ditch in Nepal, bleeding to death again, maybe even the same ditch as last time. Except this time no one would save you. You don't care. You don't care about how you're abandoning the people who love you. You're going to give your poor mother a bleeding ulcer."

"I'm not abandoning anyone. The parties in Nepal have signed a peace agreement," he said firmly, "We. Have. Been. Through. This."

He reflexively straightened his leg. "See, the knee is fine. The leg is fine. I'm fine."

"You think it will be just fine?" she pointed with her finger, "Do you?"

"Do you?" she repeated for emphasis, louder this time.

Yes, Mom, the leg is fine. It's a piece of my heart that's missing. O God I wish we could talk like real people for once.

Now it was clear that nobody was conversing at any of the adjacent tables. Every diner within thirty feet stared down at their food. There was an awkward silence while Matt, Barbara, and John looked out at the twinkling lights on the hills and valleys. He wished things could have been more relaxed. Barbara demanded togetherness. "Quality face time" was the exact phrase she used. Her intent generally translated into taking hostages and beating them into submission. She couldn't bring herself to actually express her feelings, and this whole discussion was the exact opposite of what she wanted. *She wants to be sentimental, but she doesn't know how.* He looked at John. Barbara was on the edge right now and even if she held it together, she was destined to erupt after Matt made his getaway. He tried to reassure her.

"Mom, at Mass General I led the surgical team as we dealt with life-threatening emergencies. When a life is on the line we need to perform at our highest level."

"What does that have to do with anything?"

"Plenty. I know how to work under stress. Success in a crisis requires clear speech. You may have difficulty with this. But I want you to know that even if you pull my arm out of its socket and beat me over the head with it, I am your son, and I still love you with my whole heart. If it makes you feel better, lay on the guilt. But nothing you can say or do will change that fact. I love you, Mom. Now can we please get on with the meal?"

She looked down at her silverware and fidgeted with the fork and spoon. She made a soft sound, like the cluck of a hen. *She still can't look at me and say, 'I love you' back,* thought Matt, *but I know she does. It's not easy to be Barbara.*

John decided to talk about surgery. He was bored by literature, film, books, and current events, but he could talk endlessly about the technique of anastomosis or some new surgical gadget. *Least of all, John never dealt with the elephant in the room. Not the one in this room, anyway.*

John ordered two shots of Templeton Rye. The waiter poured and John raised his glass in a toast. "I guess it's time for me to reveal to you the last frontier, the last algorithm applied in surgical decision-making. You were never old enough, never mature enough until now. I feel as though it is time."

Matt refused to raise his glass and said, "Wait a minute, Dad. I'm thirty-two years old. I thought you already told me everything."

John set his glass down and cleared his throat. "My own father didn't tell me this until I was forty. Your comment about stress in surgery reminds me. Never allow yourself to be empty-handed. Bare hands are dangerous for any surgeon. If you are ever at a loss for the next step in surgery, never just stand there and think. Don't waste time. Time waits for no man. Sometimes even the best surgeon is at a loss. In that case, get - the tool."

"The tool? Which tool?" Matt thought about the hundred or so surgical instruments he used on a regular basis and the other five hundred or so more specialized instruments he could identify by sight. *This can't be…*

John leaned forward, "The universal surgical implement. The one that fits every situation when you don't know what to do next."

"There is no such thing."

"Yes there is. You just didn't know it."

"They would have taught me at Harvard."

"No."

"Why?"

"Because they don't know everything at Harvard."

"Yes, they do."

"No, they don't."

"Will we discuss this or just contradict each other all night?"

10

"I am a Fellow of the American College of Surgeons, and you should not argue with me."

"I will when you are wrong."

"You shouldn't."

"But I will. Simple fact."

"Who is contradicting whom?" John enjoyed the verbal fencing. He held up an apple from the fruit bowl on the table. "Work with me. Let's postulate for just a moment that this is the earth, Matt."

"O Lord, save me from a geography lesson."

"I'm serious. Harvard is – here. And Nepal is – here. They are one hundred eighty degrees apart."

"And your point is?"

"God made them opposite, because it was ‑ the divine plan. He intended them to be opposite," he said with glee. "It logically follows that the rules they teach at Harvard do not apply to Nepal. Now do you want to hear this or not?"

They both looked at Barbara. Her face glowed. She was quiet now, after two glasses of wine, looking at her husband, blue eyes shining in the candlelight. Barbara showed more gray hair at the temples than Matt remembered. *This is the woman who brought me to my first day of preschool. I looked at the other moms, and I knew my mother was the best of all*, thought Matt. *That was back when she used to smile.*

He laughed when he looked back at John. "It's not the one grandfather invented, is it?"

"No, of course not."

"Give me a hint. There are four categories of surgical instruments – dissecting, grasping, clamping and retracting. Can you at least tell me the category it belongs to?"

"It's the universal tool. It falls into all the categories."

"I give up then."

"Good. Show some humility. Now, as you know, the general public likes to think that surgeons are omnipotent and invincible, so this is not ever to be discussed except with other surgeons. Never. You must be sworn to secrecy."

"Okay. Tell me," said Matt, with arms crossed.

"First you must promise."

Matt made the sign of the cross. John leaned forward and whispered into Matt's ear.

Matt looked back with new eyes, "You were serious."

"Yes."

"I thought you were full of bull. But it is very handy to know that one little amazing factoid. I can already think of a couple of times I could have used that little pearl of wisdom on a trauma case."

"I knew you would appreciate it. Time to give your father some credit."

"Okay. You win. Now – when was the last time you needed it?"

"I do mostly elective cases now, so it's been awhile. I've waited to pass it along. You young cowboys need this. Just remember, I'll be dying to know whether you use it, yourself. I wish you the very best, son. Go get 'em."

"I solemnly swear to note every possible detail when that time comes."

He turned to Barbara and asked, "Remember when we picked blueberries in Maine, Mom? I will be in Nepal for mango season. When I have one, I will think of you. You taught me to enjoy fresh fruit."

Barbara now rejoined the conversation. "Look at the fresh strawberries on the dessert table. And apple pie."

The wicked spell was broken and the rest of the meal was pleasant. Matt and John toasted.

"To The Universal Implement."

"And every surgeon who needs it."

In the blustery early morning, his parents accompanied him to the plaza in front of the hotel. Across the way, Grace Cathedral reflected the rays of the rising sun like one of the Himalayas. Matt stood by the taxi for a big hug from Barbara. She whispered in his ear, "Don't come home with a tattoo."

The taxi pulled away, and he watched from the back window as she turned to John, stamped her feet, and wagged her finger at him. Matt said to himself *I know you love me, Mom.*

December 2006 – Part 1

On the plane, he looked at the right hand of the woman seated next to him and said, "My mom has one of those claddagh rings."

Her blue eyes sparkled and she said, "Oh, is your mom Irish?"

"Boston Irish. Catholic. Picture of John F. Kennedy in the living room. "

"I'm from San Francisco. Never been to Boston but I always meant to go. My name is Maureen, of course. "

He looked at her red hair and freckles and said, "Saints be praised you'd blend right in. So what will you do in Nepal?"

"Our group will do the trek to Everest Base Camp. When they go back to the states, I will spend two extra weeks at a Tibetan Monastery in Kathmandu and take a retreat to learn about Buddhism. I'm a hospice nurse, and mindfulness meditation is a big part of the program every day in my job. Going back to the source of spiritual practice is a good idea."

"We have something in common. I'm in the medical field myself." He looked down at his hands. He was about to play the doctor card. He hated to be cynical about it, but it was a sure way to get a woman to talk.

"Let me see – pharmaceutical salesman."

"What? You think I sell Prozac? Or Oxycodone? Guess again."

"Brain surgeon?"

"Nope, those guys are depressed all the time. You're getting warm though."

"You better not be lying. Let me look at your hand." She took it in hers. "Hmm, I can tell a lot by looking at a person's hand."

"O God, a nurse who also reads palms. How is my lifeline?"

"Would you do things differently if I told you the answer?" She closed her eyes and traced her fingertips over his palm. "Every doctor I know has soft hands and nice nails. Yes, you probably are a surgeon. You have big strong fingers. Orthopedics?"

"Nope, not happy-go-lucky."

"Obstetrician?"

"Not my cup of tea. I'd be too embarrassed. Probably not outgoing enough."

"General surgery."

"You are an amazing guesser."

"I have a sixth sense about these things."

"Good. Let's get down to shop talk. How did you end up doing hospice?" It was obvious that she'd been checking to see if he had a wedding ring or the telltale lack of tan where one should have been.

"Death can be orderly," she said, "When it goes well, we help the patient achieve a sense of peace and serenity by the time they check out. We tell the patient you can choose to die from cancer or you can choose to live with cancer. We help them live as well as they can."

"What counts as 'orderly?' "

"Using the time to say goodbye and to make amends with people in your life. Getting in touch with your spirituality. Looking for new horizons."

He thought of Kali at that moment. *We did none of those things. I wonder if it's too late.*

They talked for awhile, then he dozed off even though she still held his hand.

The low hum of the engines lulled him to sleep. Ten years gone by since Matt's first trip to Nepal during summer break from Dartmouth, but he still remembered the smell of that first plane and the way all the other passengers seemed larger than life. He was a seasoned air traveler now, but this same sense of wonder came back to him this time. The trips blended together in his mind.

He closed his eyes, half expecting that when he opened them again, he would be seated once again with the other 1996 summer students, and of course, unaware of the fate that lay before him. He tried to recall the names of the other kids, all from colleges in the Northeast. He couldn't remember a single name, but somehow the faces looked similar to the ones around him today. Young, intelligent, ready to conquer the world, parents far behind. His 1996 trip to Nepal was the first solo travel of his life. *How can you learn about serving humanity unless you see how people live in the poor countries of the world,* his father had said. *This will help you get admitted to medical school. And The Annapurna Circuit is one of the legendary hikes of the world. The scenery is stunning and the culture of the people is fascinating.*

June 1996 – At the Hospital in Beni, Nepal

"It is not safe to walk back to Pokhara and your leg is too weak. This is monsoon now," said Doctor Ranjit. He and Doctor George Fergusson used their bare hands to palpate the raised red ridge on Matt's thigh at morning rounds. Matt was weak. He lifted his head to see the eight-inch scar on his thigh as they examined it.

"We reconstructed part of your quadriceps when we took out the shrapnel. Thank God the femur and the knee are intact. And if it had hit the main artery you would clearly be dead. As it was, we nearly lost you. The wound does not seem infected. You will be able to walk eventually, but for now, it's too arduous to walk the path to the paved road. You are weak from blood loss. And your kidneys need to rest.

"You can recuperate right here in Beni. Maybe three to five weeks before we can organize a way out. You are too big to carry in a pack basket." Ranjit saw that Matt was crestfallen. "You planned to stay two months anyway. Five weeks may seem like a long time, but you must learn patience. Your wound will not heal over night. And you lost so much blood. There is also more to Nepal than trekking."

"What happened? I don't remember anything other than being carried here."

"Nothing?" said Ranjit. "You were on a trek to Dhauligiri Base Camp. The police said you were in a landslide along the way. Your two porters were killed. You should never have set up camp there."

"Prakash and Taramunyi dead? That can't be."

"You may not think so, but it happened. That was bad, but it became worse when the Maoists ambushed the police patrol as they carried you back. The ambush caused the long delay. If the police hadn't sent a second patrol, you would be dead now. You are a very lucky man. Those fools didn't even follow basic rules of first aid. And now three policemen and five PLA fighters are dead. That makes ten dead in this one incident. The civil war has come to Beni, and you are a casualty."

Doctor Ranjit continued, "We will get you safely to Pokhara and home. You must gain strength for the journey. It may be awhile. Until then there is a young woman who helped save your life. She wishes to improve her English. You will tutor her in conversation."

Noon came. The pungent fragrance of curry awakened him first. *Food. Good food.* He was aware of his hunger, then he became aware of the faint scent of some kind of perfume. He slowly opened his eyes. *Is this real? The morphine must have done a real number on me* his mind told him. And then he realized that this sensual creature, with the long braid of shiny black hair cascading over her shoulder, was real. She walked as if she were stepping from cloud to cloud. Her skirt made a swishing sound. She got closer and into his line of vision. He almost forgot to breathe. *She has the biggest brown eyes I have ever seen, and she is looking at me.*

He's a kuire, but he's not as pale as he was the other day, she thought. *Dr. Ranjit can perform miracles.* Yellow hair, blue, piercing eyes, freckles. She took him in from head to toe and noticed the muscles of his arms and legs. *Maybe he plays soccer or cricket.*

He heard a sweet, soft voice say, "Here is your lunch."

Eyes half closed, he woke himself up from this reverie, wanting the moment to last and yet not wanting to embarrass her.

This time she called his name. The Westerner opened his eyes and saw her waiting. He sat a little higher in the bed and pulled the sheet over his chest. She watched him as his eyes journeyed from her face to the lift of her breasts and down to her belly, along the edge of the skirt which revealed only the tips of her toes.

He sees right through me with his eyes, she thought.

"Here is lunch," she said again, louder. "The hospital does not provide fooding, and from now on, I will bring fooding for you." She removed the cover to reveal a dozen momo, a small dish of achaar, some boiled greens that looked like spinach, and two hardboiled eggs.

"Doctor Ranjit says all Americans are meat eaters and we must feed you protein."

"Namaste. My name is Matt. Thank you for this. And what might your name be?" *Here is one more episode in my dream. Today this is a pleasant dream. How long does it take to grow a braid like that?* She wore a traditional outfit. She looked fit and healthy; her skin was dark, too dark to be Chinese. She had a glow about her, and Matt was captivated by the way she carried herself. Her blouse accentuated her figure even though it was loose on her frame But most of all, he was drawn to her eyes – big brown eyes like a doe. *O God, this is one beautiful woman.*

"Matt Sar. My name is Sushila. Ranjit dai sent me here. He says you English language teach. Let's go."

She gave a musical laugh and showed flawless teeth. Her eyes moved and danced to the words as she spoke, scanning his face for his reaction. All this made Matt nervous – he was normally shy around women. *Here is the prettiest woman I have ever met, and she is talking to me. Oh my God, what a voice.*

"In Kathmandu, my high school teacher sayed she teach us King's English." She sat on the small stool by the bed. She pronounced "school" with a kind of hiccup in front. Every word that began with "s" started that way. Matt cocked his head to concentrate.

"My friends call me Kali," she said. "It means 'dark-skinned one.' "

"I thought Kali was not a good name. Somebody told me that Nepalis don't like to be reminded that they are dark."

"But I am dark. 'Din me raat, raat me dat.' "

She translated. "In the daytime you see my skin, at night all you see are my teeth."

Matt replied, "If you said that to a dark person in USA you might get a punch in the nose."

"We are in Nepal. Kali is fine name, and I like my color. My father was Chetri caste, warrior caste. Because of him I was born with a tan even though my mother is Gurung. Just remember never call me 'po-Kali;' that is bad name. I like name of Kali. She is patron Goddess of this city because of river. Galeshwori temple here is famous."

"The food smells great."

"My mother cook this fooding. The hospital gives no any fooding for no any patient. Too many castes. Unclean to eat fooding of lower caste. Doctor Ranjit said Westerner have no any caste and no any family. You get good fooding from us while you here. Evening fooding I am also bring."

Matt was mesmerized by the sound of her voice. The word *caste* sounded like "*cahhhste.*" He tried to look away but couldn't. *I can't move my eyes away from her.*

Matt replied, "What if you didn't bring this? Does that mean I would go without food? What do the regular Nepalis do if they are sick?"

"Each caste have small hotels nearby, each hotel have kitchen. Each patient pay for own fooding and lodging. Family will fix money for fooding. "

Cahhhste again. *Try not to stare,* he told himself. It took effort but he finally broke away.

"Kali, your English seems perfectly fine to me," said Matt. He knew it was a lie. Sushila could say the words well enough and had an enviable vocabulary, but she retained the high-pitched music of the Nepali language and spoke too rapidly. *Like a Bollywood actress.* In fact, it was this very imperfection that Matt found to be irresistible. *She is a songbird when she talks. She speaks the beautiful language of songbirds.* She had a nervous way of moving her eyes when she spoke in English. *Just like a bird perched on a branch of a tree.*

"Am I the first American you have met?"

"No, there are other foreigners that come here, and since child days I talk them," she replied. "Past days at Saint Mary's in Kathmandu I never speaked with foreign boys. We go Thamel we see them but no talk. Keep walking."

She continued, "Beni people speak many local languages. I speak four, and English is five. I want to go further study in the U.K., but first I must do good on language test. Exam I already took once, but test score no good. "

"Bummer. How many times can you re-take it? and how old are you anyway?"

"I have nineteen years. My mother says once more I can take. You help me, okay? Economy of Nepal is no any good, all my friends are go abroad for further study. I don't wanna be only one here."

Matt thought he heard a note of desperation in her tone. "I will help you but only if you also teach me some Nepali," said Matt. "That way we can help each other."

"And how many years do you have, Matt Sar?" she asked. Kali smiled when he requested to learn Nepali. *He is different. A Nepali man would never ask a woman for help. What does this mean?* "I am happy to teach you Nepali," she replied. "Tell me, Matt Sar, what is your further study?"

"I just passed twenty one. I have one more year of college, and when I finish, I will study to be a doctor like my father and his father. They are surgeons, like Doctor Ranjit."

"So you are in caste of surgeons?"

He laughed, "Yes, I suppose. You should come to USA and be at University with me."

"That would please me so much," she laughed.

That night, Sushila went to the puja room when she arrived home. Her house was small, with only a few rooms, but there had always been a puja room as long as she could remember. It was in the northeast corner of the house, and Sushila once asked her mother why they did not have a fancier bigger puja room.

"We are small people and we will be happy with small gods. It is not the size of the space used for worship that matters," said her mother. "It is the size of your heart that matters. You can learn the lessons of Buddha and the Goddess in a prison, you do not need even this humble puja room. There are people in this town who are happy with much less than what we have."

Two people could kneel there and contemplate the family gods. Sushila meditated with her japaa beads and began with a hundred and eight mantras to the Goddess.

She could not seem to clear her mind. Vajrayogini was the family Goddess, and her statue was the centerpiece of the puja room. When Sushila was little, the lama told her to pray to the Goddess to protect her. "Vajrayogini is dark, and some call her Kali. You are dark, and you are meant to seek guidance from her," the lama said. "Kali will be your *ishta devi*, your personal connection to the divine."

Sushila closed her eyes and asked her *ishta devi*, Kali, to appear to her; but this evening she only heard the sound of Matt's voice. She wanted to cleanse herself of worldy thoughts, but instead she found herself remembering the sound of his laughter and the way he smiled. *Such a good man, such bad karma…..*

"O Vajrayogini, please guide me in the way of releasing my fellow sentient beings from their pain on earth," she prayed. She meditated on the spirit of the Goddess. "I take refuge in you and in dharma. Come and give me wisdom and compassionate light for sentient beings, who do not know the teachings of Buddha." As she prayed this, she pictured herself walking with Matt, hand in hand, conversing about the world. She would make him tea and share the joys of the day.

She decided to dedicate herself to the study of her English lessons. Late into the night she repeated every new word over and over again. She fell asleep and dreamed of Matt helping her with her English and in life.

"I will be your fooding didi," she laughed the next day as she uncovered the tray with the morning dal-bhaat. "We start by teach table manners. You eat like Nepali now." She showed him how to eat with only his right hand. She watched him. At one point he forgot and she made him tuck his left hand behind his back. *He is watching me.* She used just the tips of her fingers to roll a little ball of rice mixed with lentils and place it in her mouth neatly, the perfect model of etiquette. Afterwards, she brought a small mirror to show Matt how the turmeric in the lentils had stained his mustache and chin. "Don't worry, you will develop skill. We have time. "

Matt watched her closely. *She has such elegant gestures and yet she is so down to earth. I feel as though I could talk to her about anything.*

After lunch, they reviewed the notes from Sushila's English class, and Sushila read aloud from the *Kathmandu Post*. Matt listened, stopping her and making her repeat the problem words several times.

After the first week, Matt finally asked, "Kali-ma'am. Doctor Ranjit said you saved my life when I came in. What happened?" He lowered his voice. "Can you tell me?" *Here I am*, he thought, *and I owe some kind of debt to a person who could pass for a Goddess.*

"Ranjit asked me not to speak of this, but I think you deserve to know. It is quite simple. Army men brought you here, and you were pale and dying. Ranjit was angry. Sticky pool of blood when peons lifted you off stretcher. Ranjit said you were bathing in pool of your own blood. Very bad, Ranjit very angry. Ranjit said you would die unless you had a transfusion. I never see him so angry before, as he shouted at Army captain. You and I have same same blood. Only one other with same same blood. You got my blood while Ranjit fixed your leg. I get dizzy so we stop. It was like magic. You were white skin, then you were pink skin. You woke up and Ranjit said you would live. "

"Thank you for this. I just don't know what to say."

"No thanks needed. It is my karma to do this. I did it to help Doctor Ranjit. He told me no talking. Big secret. Don't tell him I said to you."

Matt wondered about her request. *Why is this such a big secret?* He didn't understand but agreed. It was the least he could do. *She saved my life.*

John Smith – 1996

Later that week, an American walked in the door to Matt's room in the hospital. He introduced himself as John Smith, an attaché from the embassy. Mr. Smith was a wiry man with a military haircut. The horn-rimmed glasses immediately reminded Matt of an archaeology professor. Matt looked at the bowtie and tweed jacket and quickly became more alert. *Indiana Jones.*

"Hi, you're the first American I've seen in weeks. It's ninety degrees. Aren't you hot?"

Mr. Smith removed the jacket and said he was here to ask some questions and to expedite the process of obtaining an emergency passport. "Your passport may be in the hands of the Maoists, a terrorist organization. That is a serious matter."

Smith opened a file and shuffled the papers from it. "So you study pre-med at Dartmouth, eh? I am from the University of Virginia, myself. A Cavalier," he said as he took out a notepad. "What's Dartmouth's mascot?"

"We don't have one," said Matt, "We're just 'Big Green.' "

Smith smiled and said, "We don't often travel outside the Kathmandu Valley these days since the Peace Corps pulled out of this country. It's a damn shame they left. That leaves just a few missionaries, and, of course, the climbers and trekkers. The goal is to prevent the kind of 'accident' you had."

"Why are you phrasing it that way?" asked Matt.

"Two porters dead. That part is understandable," said Smith, "The Himalaya is a living mountain range. It's still moving. Usually the landslides are worse during monsoon. But – there are just a few questions here. The police were escorting you when they were ambushed by the People's Liberation Army. Your injuries were caused by shrapnel from the firefight, not by the landslide. Three policemen died. You are one lucky trekker. You still have some shrap inside. They don't always remove all of it."

Then he asked, "Are you sure you can't remember any of the events?"

Matt's mind was blank. "I remember sitting around the campfire with everyone, passing around a flask of raksi. They were singing. Prakash played the sirangi. Reshum Firiri. You know – the folk song. The one they all sing."

"Were you using drugs?"

"No. Of course not."

"You also had a guide, Mr. Thul Pun. Have you any idea what happened to him?

"Thul… No, I remember him around the campfire, but… I can't recall anything else…"

"Did he have a weapon? A handgun maybe?"

"Why are you asking this? No, he didn't." Matt now focused on John Smith's face.

"Are you sure? Bullets were fired. We didn't find his body."

"What are you implying? Is he wanted for something?"

"We are interested in him. How did you come about hiring him in particular?"

"He was recommended by the guy at the Hotel Himshikhar. I didn't really know him. "

Mr. Smith looked long and hard at Matt, and decided to soften the approach. "Okay. Let's leave it at that. I guess my report will be very simple."

Mr. Smith took a new passport photo. He would help arrange the travel out of Beni. "The People's Liberation Army is still out and about, active around Beni," as Matt knew all too well. "Normally they leave the trekkers alone. We are worried as to whether you will be the first indicator of a new trend. We'll get you out with an Army helicopter to Pokhara. The only problem is when. The military helicopter might arrive with just a moment's notice."

"Am I that special?"

"You've had enough problems. From here on in, we'll stay on the marked trail until you are back in the USA. Oh, and by the way, we have taken the extraordinary step of not notifying your family while this is still under investigation. We would appreciate it if you would refrain from sharing the details just yet. No need for them to worry. Things are delicate and the embassy needs to handle this a certain way."

"I'm cool. My dad knew I would be out of contact when I left. They didn't expect to hear from me for another month. Thank God my mom doesn't know about this. She gets kind of anxious. I told her 'there are no pay phones on the Annapurna Circuit.' She didn't want me to come to Nepal in the first place. She is going to hit the roof when she learns about this."

Mr. Smith returned to Kathmandu the next day.

Matt tried to ask Doctor Ranjit about the accident, but Ranjit said, "Focus on healing now. Eat and exercise your leg. You are alive. That is all that matters."

Matt asked for his clothes. "No. We burned the ones you were wearing." They gave him some jeans and a shirt to wear, though they didn't quite fit.

"You can use crutches to get around, as long as you don't put any weight on your leg."

Matt noticed that Sushila always arrived early. Earlier and earlier every day, and staying later. He looked over her shoulder at the notes and it looked like she wrote on them between sessions. *When does she have time to study?*, he wondered.

"You are really taking this seriously, aren't you?" he asked.

"Matt Sar, I make puja to Goddess to help me, and you appear. When Goddess favors you, you must be loyal to her wishes. It is not our culture to spend time with kuire, but Goddess gave me karma."

"I know about karma. But what is a 'kuire?' "

"Oh, I said bad thing. It is 'white person.' More polite to say 'videshi' – means 'foreign person.' "

Her voice trailed off, and she sat for a moment, staring at his hair. She ran her fingers over her braid and brushed the end against her cheek.

He wondered what she was thinking. *This is some kind of signal*, thought Matt. *She wants to touch my hair.*

That evening in the puja room, Sushila could not meditate nor could she clear her mind. She decided to think about Matt and to ask the Goddess for advice. She closed her eyes and pictured herself with him, sharing their life. This time she felt free to let her thoughts wander and drift where they may. She no longer resisted the idea of Matt. As she meditated, the heat rose to her face and she felt her heart race. She rocked back and forth and said his name a hundred and eight times. She focused on each *chakra* of her body, in turn. She acknowledged the power of compassion and love in the world and felt better afterwards. She had not thought of herself as a person who could summon love from a man, not thought of herself as person who was the object of love in her own right. Until now, the teachings on love were so theoretical. It was easy to be a good person by simply not doing anything bad; now she thought about ways to show love that went beyond passive restraint. Today she searched for practical aspects of the teachings to use in her own life. Her life with Matt.

She began to bring two meals each time. On the walk to the hospital she thought about the phrase: *My life with Matt.* One meal for Matt and one for herself, so that they could eat together. *Like a married couple.* For every family she knew, only the family members ate together. If you were a male guest, you ate first with the men. A female guest ate later with the women. At school, the boys and girls talked and sat together when they ate, but they were children. Now she was in Beni, where everyone followed the old ways. Sushila knew that men and women talked while eating, but right now she just ate. To talk would be too daring. And Matt did not talk. He was trying hard to master the Nepali manners. Matt imitated the way she used just the tips of her fingers to eat without being messy.

Kali also taught him to drink water from a shared pitcher, not a cup. "Very important. Don't touch spout with lips, is unclean. All castes share water pitcher but only when everyone follow rules." He held the pitcher and poured. Water dripped down the front of his shirt, soaking it. They laughed.

"You are enjoying?" she asked. His warm glowing smile was answer enough for her.

August 1996 – English Lessons

Lekhala bhavi metala ko?/Afno afno lahana ho. –
("What's plotted can't be blotted; so each one to his own lot.")
– Gurkha proverb

Monday was always the day of fasting ever since Sushila was twelve. "You will be a woman soon, and that means you will fast on Mondays as I do," said her mother. Monday started with puja like every other day, but in the summer, the women of the town would gather at the temple to pray for their husbands. Pray for his health, pray for the man to be hardworking and kind.

"There is time for you to pray. You are unmarried. Pray for a vision of your future husband," Sushila's mother told her. From that moment, Sushila prayed to the family gods for a husband and tried to picture a kind man, a hardworking man, and yes, a handsome one.

"Pray that you will have discipline to follow your husband and that he will not beat you too severely," the women at the temple said.

"Why should a man be allowed to beat a woman?" Sushila asked.

"That is the way of men," the women replied, "Someday you will understand."

On this particular Monday, Matt was outside the hospital when Sushila appeared with just one food tray. They sat on the low stone wall of the chautara, in the shade of the tree.

"Do you know this tree?" she asked. "The Buddha was born under just such a tree. His mother held onto a branch for strength."

He looked up at the leaves. They caressed the bark and he drew her hands to his.

"I want to learn about Buddhism from you," he said, "I don't know much, but I do have a simple test to see how Asian you are," he said.

She furrowed her eyebrows. "Of course I am Asian." She smiled and drew a bit closer.

"Yes, but not every Asian person acts the same. This is about eye contact. Sometimes Asian people are taught from birth never to look a stranger in the eye. Stand in front of me and lean forward," he whispered, using his teasing voice. "It's very simple. The rules are to look deep into each other's eyes. No looking away, no laughing and no smiling."

She pursed her lips to wet them and leaned forward. She needed to crane her neck upward just a bit. She looked straight into his eyes, not blinking.

Matt felt his leg ache as soon as they started, and he thought he made a mistake by standing on it. He gazed into her eyes, overtaken by thoughts of desire. *Oh my God, what would it feel like to hold you in my arms? I want to kiss your neck,* he thought, but he did not dare say it aloud. *The salt of your skin mixed with the perfume of your hair.* He needed to concentrate on her eyes and ignore his own breathing. *I want to gaze into your eyes just like this, while we hold each other close. Forever,* he thought.

He also felt unmistakable stirrings of arousal. The plan had backfired, and he was embarrassed. He hoped she hadn't noticed.

The warmth of his breath so close to her face made her blush at first. His eyes were so blue and she smelled peppermint. *His chewing gum is making me feel dizzy,* she thought.

It was a sunny day. She had fasted since the evening before and walked a mile uphill to get to the hospital. They held that position for ten, then twenty, and then thirty seconds. She swayed forward. The heat, the exertion, and the fasting all came together and she started to wobble, but held her gaze. Sounds dampened around her, and she fell forward.

Matt caught her in his arms. For a moment, they froze in an accidental embrace, before he sank to the ground. His good leg was not strong enough to hold them both. Now, just for a second, her limp body lay on top of him. He caught his breath when he broke her fall, partly because of the surprise, but also because of the unexpected lightness and softness of this woman. *I have wanted to hold her in my arms but not quite yet. Not this way.*

Some women who sat nearby came over to help. They sat Sushila up and gave her water. She waved them off. "Today is the day of fast," she told them, "No problem. I'm okay." Matt hobbled to a seat and crossed his legs. *She didn't notice. Or did she?*

She told Matt about the fasting and he said, "You must eat something. You can't walk home like this. You won't get far." He made a small ball of rice with his fingers and brought it to her lips. She looked at him while she chewed. *His fingers had touched her lips. And she felt his body against hers.*

She helped him to his room and decided to go home. There was no lesson that day. Matt lay in bed and thought about the way he felt her muscles move when she was in his arms.

That evening, Sushila sat in the puja room and meditated. *I fasted and the Goddess gave me a man.* She touched each of the places on her body where Matt was holding her when she regained consciousness after she fainted. All she could think about was the actual feel of Matt's body when he caught her. And how gentle his fingers were.

The next day she brought two lunches as usual. The lesson took place indoors. Matt looked through the notes and said, "Now repeat after me: 'Would you wander through the woods?' "

"Ould you awnder through the oods?"

He laughed.

She frowned. "Something bad?"

Just like a Bollywood actress. "No. it is beautiful. Watch my lips and repeat."

She tried again.

He laughed.

She blushed.

"Woo. Woo woo. Go like this," he said.

"Oo. Oo. Oo."

"No. Try wuh. Wuh. Wuh." He knew his mouth looked like a fish out of water.

"Uh. Uh. Uh."

"Woooooooo." He drew her closer to him, making the sound again as their lips were just inches apart.

She repeated it again and he felt her breath on his cheek, felt the electricity of this beautiful woman standing in front of him.

She tried again. Closer this time. *This was what I thought about since the day we met.*

"This is an important part of learning English," he said, "Pay careful attention."

Then their lips touched. He was still making the motion, it was a tentative kiss, and they both knew it.

She laughed and pushed away, then returned. A full kiss this time, just caressing the lips, not yet having the insistence of a full mouth. She closed her eyes, and he could feel her body yield to the pleasure. She blushed. She pressed herself against his chest.

She lingered right there, not wanting to part from what just happened. *It is not the culture.* Knowing at the same time, *it feels so good.* There was a long sigh and the language lesson ended that day with a long, lingering touch of the hands, enjoying the sensation of the fingers as if they could also use the tips in a lingering finger-kiss.

Matt longed for more.

Looking in the mirror as she brushed her hair, she pictured how they would look together in a formal portrait. She stood a little straighter, with the solemn face of a new bride. She braided her hair and brushed the end against her own face, reliving the day.

They worked on the "w" sound every day for a week. They both knew that it was a game. Would Matt start, or would Sushila start? First the flirting. Which of them would lean forward with shining eyes, then back off at the last minute? After a few days, her "w" was markedly improved, but still they practiced. The door to the hospital room was open, and a couple of times, the didi almost caught them.

"Matt, I am so happy to learn the secrets of English," she said one day.

"You are a fast learner," he replied, as they looked into each other's eyes.

"I am stronger today. And you do so well with eye contact now. It is your blood that flows through my veins, Sushila. Maybe you should feel how your blood strengthens my pulse." He took her hand and placed it on his own wrist to take the pulse, caressing the back of her hand as he did so.

Whispering, he said, "Your blood is pulsing through my heart. Listen to my heart beat." He took her hands and invited her to unbutton his shirt, slowly. Her hands trembled. *I have never touched a man here before.* She looked for cues to stop, but he offered none, and it was clear that he was breathing deeply. She ran her hand over his ribs, smooth because he did not have chest hair. She stopped to hold her palm over his heart and looked at the contrast between skin tones. *He is kuire,* she said to herself. She thought about what it would be like to be unclothed in his presence, touching all of her naked dark skin against the paleness of his body… And the thought made her pulse race… As a young child she had gone to the river to swim with the neighbor children, boys and girls together naked in a pool or under a waterfall, but that was the innocence of long ago. She sometimes saw porters and workers naked to the waist, but they were low caste. Kali averted her eyes and hurried past when any such man was nearby. She put her ear to his bare chest and listened.

He stroked her hair and whispered, "I love you."

She put her finger on his lips, to silence him.

Unspoken words hung in the air as he refastened the buttons on his shirt.

"I will give you my heart, Sushila," he said. "You also have a beating heart." He reached for her, cupping her breast with his hand. This time they kissed as he gently massaged her breast. She could feel her nipples respond to his touch. *More. I want more.*

"I heard a song on the radio in which the man sang 'Maya ke hola.' Is that the right way to say 'I love you' in Nepali?" he asked.

Kali blushed. *That is the song to ask for marriage.* The heat rose to her face and she wondered if he noticed. "A man only sings that song when marriage is planned. That is not the way to say it. Maybe you should just say 'Ma timilai maya garnchu.' It means 'I love you' in better way."

"I like that song and I wish you would teach me the rest of the words."

"Maybe. We have time to learn. But tomorrow will be a special lunch since you are getting better. Noontime you be ready go outside. You will see Beni for first time. I will be guide." He agreed, and she gave a little jump like a child, with a quick giggle. She thought, *I will bring him to my house,* but she did not say it out loud. Just the thought of being with him excited her. *It was wrong,* but somehow when that thought came she was more excited.

Maya Ke Hola, she thought to herself. *A song that married couples sing.* She knew that people would talk, but it was a good idea to use a tour of Beni for an excuse. All she could think about was to spend time alone with the man who loved her. She imagined her life in USA as a university student. Matt would study with her and help with her English. Maybe she would work also, and send money home to her mother.

That evening, Sushila prepared a puja plate with a lotus flower, uncooked rice, water, incense, fruit, and coconut. She went outside and picked mango leaves to add to the offering and brought it to the puja room to meditate on her life. She began the small ritual by contemplating the humility of water and asking to serve like the water. She lit the incense and contemplated the lotus flower. From the altar, she took the dorje in one hand and the hand bell in the other, ringing to focus her mind. She was the bell, she was the dorje, she was the incense, she was the lotus flower, unfolding petal by petal. *All these, for the Goddess.*

"O Goddess, I praise you for bringing Matt here and for teaching me the meaning of love." Her consciousness flew far away from the simple life in Beni. She thought about the feel of his skin and the muscles underneath, and the taste of his mouth.

She lit the small candle on the altar and prayed to the Goddess. "Please, help me stay on the path of Dharma and to save us from impurity." An answer came to her from the Goddess, an unspoken thought. *Have courage. You can enjoy the pleasure of togetherness, and you will be able to stay on the pure path.*

Sushila thanked Kali for clarifying the thing she worried about the most, and repeated the mantra a hundred and eight times in praise of Kali. She finished her puja by dressing the Goddess in a small kata scarf, and cleaned the house to prepare for Matt's visit.

The town of Beni had no automobiles or motorcycles on the streets. Someday the road would come there, but for now, all the supplies of the town arrived on the back of porters who hauled their loads over the last six kilometers from the paved road. Still, there were rickshaws, easy to summon. One or two always waited for fares at the hospital.

The Third River – 1996

And the day came when the risk to remain tight in a bud was more painful than the risk it took to blossom.

– Anais Nin

That noon, Matt hobbled outside. Then she came, Sushila in a rickshaw to collect Matt for a field trip to her mother's house in the Bajaar. For lunch. She wore a dark blue sari with silver stars. Maya Ke Hola played in her head and she hummed along.

This rickshaw sported a convertible top, a blue canvas awning with hoops of bamboo. Today a piece of blue plastic tarp shaded the driver from the sun or the rain. The streets were empty even though the rain had stopped for now. The cab was painted a darker blue, laden with old garlands of marigolds. The length of her thigh touched his when they squeezed to sit side by side. Matt tried to cradle her in his arm as they rode, but Sushila pushed it away and looked straight ahead. The sun beat down, and the streets were bare as people waited for the cool of evening.

The driver was an old man, complexion like black coffee, missing his front teeth, but that did not stop him from smiling. He wore a blue plaid skirt with a stained white long-sleeved shirt and sang a Hindi tune as he pedaled. The turban he wore accentuated his origins in the Terai. He pedaled slowly at first to gain momentum. They rode downhill to the Bajaar and soon the driver switched to the hand brakes. Sushila translated for Matt, "He says he slow us, but we will end up in river if he can't stop us. Both brakes he squeeze with all strength of hands."

At the bottom of the hill, they coasted across the playing field to the brick temple of Bhagawati that overlooked the spot where the rivers met. Sushila gave the old man a hundred rupees and asked him to wait. The driver took the note in his right hand, using the other to hold his elbow in a formal gesture, and then touched the hundred-rupee note to his forehead three times, as he blessed Sushila.

"You will leave Beni soon, but before you go, I thought it would be nice to show you where the rivers joined."

She led him down a short stairway to the riverbank. "There are three rivers that join here, it is said in this town."

He looked up and down the riverbank. The KaliGandaki River tumbled milky and opaque from the north. The Myagdi River came from the west, past a steep bank, already undercutting some houses perched there. A sheer cliff stood on the other side. Matt saw how the river gnawed away at the bank, leaving a soft cliff of soil and houses waiting to fall in. They now stood on a spit of sand that jutted out into the very spot where the waters mingled. Two Buddhist monks bathed in the cold river, up to the knees, stripped to their underwear, splashing water on themselves.

"I only see two rivers."

"Nobody see third river with two eyes. It exists in spiritual dimension. At this location, the third river is sacred to Devi Durga, the Goddess. We call her many names. Vajrayogini. Ugra Tara. Green Tara. The Hindus also call her Kali, and she is feared by some. In this town, Devi Durga is a nurturing and loving Goddess where her river joins the Myagdi and KaliGandaki. She protects us and brings wisdom to the town. If you call upon Kali, she reveal third river to you. "

"Kali?" he asked. He now made the connection between the visions of the Goddess as she formed in his mind, and the flesh and blood woman who stood at his side looking at the water.

"Yes, I know what you are thinking. Kali is my namesake. I take refuge in Kali. This is another reason I like my nickname…"

As Matt watched, a butterfly passed overhead, then another and another.

"So beautiful. Sushila, do you think Kali can take the form of a butterfly? " Matt whispered, "Look."

The butterflies were brown with blue streaks and dashes of red, and they looped like small kites whose strings were tangled together, small tight circles, sometimes touching, sometimes so close to the ground they were in danger of crashing into the surface of the water. The butterflies clustered right at the edge of the water and the wet sand. He had never seen so many butterflies in one place in all his life.

"Close your eyes and put out your hand. I will catch one for you," he said. She gave him her outstretched palm. He traced the lightest possible touch over the lines of her open hand, a lingering sensual tickle. She opened her eyes just for a second then pulled her hand away.

"It is now your turn," she said, "Close your eyes, Matt, and focus on third eye, the second chakra of your being. Open third eye and you will feel energy of other river as it flows. And energy of Goddess."

He closed his eyes. He could sense the energy of the woman next to him and the power of desire. He felt warmth and a sense of belonging here. But that was all.

"I don't know which muscles open the third eye."

They knelt and scooped out a small hole in the sand. Sushila placed incense sticks in the hole, sheltered from the breeze, and then lit them. She waved her hand to wreathe the smoke into their faces as they knelt. "And now we shall eat."

The driver waited and brought them back across the parade ground after lunch, making a long speech in Hindi when he dropped them off. Sushila laughed and tipped him again.

"What did he say?"

"He wants to drive pedicab at wedding of us."

Matt laughed. "Maybe he will. If he doesn't get a heart attack pedaling that thing up hill."

Sushila lived in one of the oldest houses in the town, made of dry-laid stones, with a corrugated tin roof. Matt noticed the garlic drying in braided bunches under the eaves. He stooped to enter the low doorway. Inside, the ceiling of the room hung just an inch above his head.

His eyes adjusted. The thick stone walls of the house kept the inside cool. It was Matt's first time in a Nepali home. It was simple and uncluttered. The floor was made of flat stones. The walls were the same stone as the outside of the house. He expected them to be dusty, but the joints seemed clean. He wondered how often they were swept. Through a half-opened door to a small room, he saw a low table where a single candle cast a warm glow as it quivered in front of the metal statue of a Goddess, surrounded by offerings and incense. He kept silent while Sushila closed that door, hiding the altar from view. She showed him the thangka, a Buddhist painting on silk cloth, hanging on one wall. There was little else in the room beside a couch and coffee table.

Sushila took his hand. "Nobody is here but us. My mother is in Pokhara."

She brought him to the mirror in her bedroom, posing as if for a photograph. *He is just the right height. We are a handsome couple.*

He stood behind her and reached around to gather her in his arms, first just with hands on her waist, then encircling her from behind. He inhaled the perfume in her hair.

"I've been meaning to ask. What is that scent?"

"Is called Elisar. I bought in Kathmandu. You like?"

She held his arms for a second and leaned back. She twined her fingers between his and looked at the contrast between this kuire and herself. She turned to face him. He felt the cool silk of her sari, and now her compact breasts pressed against him through the soft cloth. He reached his hand into the part of the sari over her shoulder. He let it fall away and touched her blouse. Her skin was silky to the touch. His finger traced the line from her shoulder down to her chest, grazing against the edge of her nipple, unexpectedly a different texture.

He was hesitant, surprised that she did not push him away. He cupped her breast and she looked up at him, with her mouth open.

Now it will happen, he thought to himself, and he felt the blood rise to his cheeks. He felt the pulse of blood throughout all his body as if his heartbeat was the only clock in the world. Her breast was warm to his hand.

Sushila took deep breaths. She wanted to stay calm, and thought about her *ishta devi*, the Goddess Kali. She said a silent prayer for Kali to give her strength and felt suddenly more confident, as if she were not herself, but a new person, part-Kali and part-Sushila. *Of course. Now I learn the real reason a woman prays to a Goddess. For strength in moments like this.* And she surrendered that part of her that was Sushila to become Kali. It was Kali whose hunger could only be satisfied with a man, with the sensual flesh of a man. It was Kali that thought of the next step, wanting him, wanting to hold him so close that their bodies melted together like wax on a sunny windowsill. Her skin glistened with anticipation. It was Kali that followed his hand with her own, reached in to lift the blouse over her head; Kali's hand touched his and guided it back to her breast. He held his breath as his hand touched her. It was as if energy was being transmitted through his hand into his body. The silk of the sari was all that covered her now, still warm where it cradled her body, and she pursed her lips to wet them before speaking into Matt's ear.

"Matt. I have never brought a man to the house. You are the first."

"Kali. I don't do this very often, myself."

Which meant *never. I never have.*

"You said my true name out loud," she said, "Teach me."

"Kali. I can't. I – I don't know how. You are the first. My first."

She laughed and whispered in his ear. "Matt, I wanted to tell you, but I was worried what you would think. You are also my first. Come."

Kali pushed him away, took his hand and led him to her bedroom—the one place in the world where she felt truly comfortable and relaxed. In one corner was a tall pile of quilts, and an electric heater now unplugged. The bedspread was printed with an elephant design, and she turned it down then lit a small candle. "I feel better to know this. We have no secrets from each other. I have prayed to the Remover of Obstacles, even though I am Buddhist."

She and Matt made eye contact, and she held his gaze while she reached his waist, pulling on Matt's shirt, loosening it, pulling it up as he raised his arms, stopping as it came over his head, kissing his chest, putting her ear to his chest to listen to his heart.

They lay down next to each other on the bed. He was not conscious of thinking. He suspended everything from his mind except to be with this beautiful woman who loved him, enjoying the feel of her long, raven hair flowing against his own bare skin, listening to her soft accent as she whispered in Nepali. It sounded like a spell being cast, and he tasted her lips while she spoke as if he was eating each word. He was intoxicated by her perfume. They lay together face to face, tugging at the remaining clothes, which formed only a superficial barrier between them. She was afraid to look at him as she unbuckled his belt, gazing into his eyes.

The pleats of her sari came apart, and now Matt touched her legs, stroking her thighs as she moved them apart. She wore silver anklets with tiny bells that tinkled. His pulse quickened as he struggled with the very idea of touching her, a feeling heightened by the realization that Kali was inviting him to do so. He had never given much thought to the idea that a woman, too, could feel carnal desire, and now this thought revealed itself. He became bolder and found her most intimate place, feeling the warmth. They explored each other for the first time. All the moments of stolen glances and touches faded into their passion. Their embrace grew stronger, tighter. His as he dove deeper. Hers as Kali guided him in to the essence of her being. Neither expected the other to be so willing, so trusting…

They stood as he brushed his hand against her hips to feel the soft muscles below the curves as she moved to a silent pulsing music. He heard only the sound of their breath, soft kisses, and the ringing of the tiny bells of her anklets. Kali pulled him on top of her and widened her legs in the final surrender, her feet touching his hamstrings as they wrapped around him and drew him in. He kissed her lips, but now he was throbbing and sensitive, finding his way in, gently at first, then stopping as if pushing against a heavy door that now swung open to him. He entered with a force that surprised both of them. Their two bodies became one. He lay still for a moment, and they looked into each other's eyes, whispering the words that two lovers share. He began to thrust again and she could feel a fullness in herself, that approached and gathered in force like an ocean wave coming to shore.

For Matt it was like the weight of the summer sky as it darkens before a thunderstorm, or the first rains of monsoon. First a dark line that was only seen far off, and he remembered as a kid, standing outside in the yard, waiting for the skies to break so that he could smell that sweet just-rained-here smell afterwards. Now he lay, stretched out and heedless, with a goddess on a hard bed in Nepal, beginning to move inside her, then faster as he knew that the weight and the power of a lightning bolt was building up inside him, an electricity that filled his thoughts. He resisted at first, but he looked down at Kali, the beauty of her skin as she lay there, overcome with the wonderment that her skin was just as dark under her clothes as it was on her face and arms. He took pleasure in the sight of his own pale skin against her darkness. "Kali… Kali," he murmured.

At that moment, Kali was as soft and beautiful as a red lotus flower in the morning sun. She, too, felt the electricity of desire, moving her hips. She had felt this feeling of love, of losing herself in the eternal when worshipping the Goddess, but never knew its true power, the true name of it, until now. Laying all her thoughts bare for *ishta devi* and thinking of how beautiful it was to actually *be* the Goddess at this moment, fearless and straining for her desires, taking what she needed for herself. She held him and moved her body more urgently, focusing on the pleasure. Matt tried to prolong it, but was swept away in a river of love that came from heaven to earth, overcome as it took hold of his body, shaking the very firmament of the earth upon which he travelled with Kali, the embodiment of every woman who ever lived and delighted the heart of a man. The release felt like a lightning bolt, traveling to another place of consciousness, if only for just a short time. Kali, too, was wet with desire, using every ounce of strength to focus on the feelings of this moment, inviting the passion to overtake her until her whole body became a sacred offering to the Goddess, and she herself was one with the Goddess.

They both cried out, Matt in the agony of lust and Kali in the surprise of awakening her body to unexpected pleasure.

And it was over. He was still in that position, still on top of her, stroking her hair, not knowing what to do or say now, listening to her breathe heavy as if she'd run a footrace. Her face was red; the skin on her chest blushed with fire and glowed with heat. Neither of them wanted to move. Tears came to Sushila's eyes and ran down her face.

Matt was confused. He stroked her cheek and whispered, "What's wrong? Did I hurt you? I tried to be gentle.… I love you so much…"

He reached out to wipe away the tears, and she kissed his fingers.

He wondered at the mystery of Sushila. A woman who could worship a Goddess and who became one, with desire and passion. Sushila and Kali both, in the same body. A woman who could surrender to passion, yet cry softly. And he wondered at his own innocence, now lost. For some reason, the brown and blue butterflies at the river came to mind. *I have never understood butterflies until today,* he thought.

"Sushila, you are so special to me." He searched for the words. "You're like one of those butterflies." *You are so beautiful when you move. Up to this point in my life, I have not understood butterflies. In USA, they make museums to display butterflies. My life has been like learning about them by going to a museum. That is not the truth of a butterfly. Now I have seen them in the air, in twilight along a riverbank in Nepal, going from flower to flower. And I shared the vision of their flight with a person I love. That is the truth of butterflies.*

"Shhhhhh," she said. It was an effort to speak. She sighed. His voice sounded far away. She saw herself under a clear blue sky, not a cloud in sight, and the edges of her body dissolved into the entire world. She lay spooned against his side and allowed the feeling of bliss to overtake her. She felt a twinge of sadness thinking about the butterflies, and for the first time she thought of her meditation with the Goddess. *I was able to show courage. But I was not able to stop when the time came. What would that mean?*

"But that is the truth of this," he persisted, "My eyes have been opened. I guess I am trying to say, I love you so. The fact that you exist, completes my life."

And now the spirit of Kali within her faded as she came back to her own body. "Thank you. I love you so." It was her own voice that said the words, but her mind was in a different place. *Butterflies? It was God that I saw. I have been one with my lover. I have been one with Kali.* At the same time, she thought of her Buddhist teachers who said *it is not our culture.* She felt distant and wanted to talk about so much more, but a sense of fulfillment pulsed through her body and stopped her. *There will be time. We will have forever to talk.*

They lay together and whispered the words of love, dozing, then seeing each other in the dim light that came through the shuttered windows. She wondered what Matt's mother was like and hoped that she could get along with her when they met. Later, they made love again, slower this time, exploring more, first twining their fingers together and loving the sight, then each feeling the muscles and motion of their partner, discovering the human body as if for the very first time it had ever been discovered on planet Earth.

Outside the house, Beni came to life in early evening, now that the sun was behind the mountains. Sushila knew that it was daring for a single woman to invite a man to her house, let alone a kuire that might come when nobody but her was home, but she had thrown caution to the wind and used a rickshaw driver even though he might spread rumors. Now, the idea of having this kuire, this foreigner, after dark, slid out of control. She enjoyed the warmth that flowed over her body, but Sushila hadn't planned to go as far as she did, and she wanted to be as discreet as she could even though it was late. Matt dozed, but she shook him and told him to dress. Matt opened his eyes and smiled to see Sushila there. *Did it happen?* He smiled when he realized that *none of it was a dream.*

She dressed and went out to find a rickshaw. Matt needed to go back to the hospital. He found his clothes on the floor, then while dressing himself he counted the buttons that were now missing. At the door, they shared a last lingering kiss as he caressed her long black hair.

Tears came to her eyes and she pulled away. "Matt, it is not our culture. You must go."

"I will be back. I will not leave you."

She gave him a gift, a small handkerchief with some of her perfume on it. He stepped outside the door, greeted by the same driver and rickshaw. He clambered on and Sushila gave the driver another hundred rupees.

The driver labored uphill with the weight of his passenger at the end of a long day. Matt saw the summit cone of Dhauligiri through the notch of mountains north of town, shining in the red glow of the setting sun even as the town lay in the afternoon shade from the hills to the west. There was the mountain, clad in shining glaciers even though this was August. Matt thought to himself, *I am twenty-one years old and I have found true love.* He replayed the scene from the afternoon in his mind and once again felt the warmth of Sushila's hands and body, the sound of her voice as she called his name, the sight of her naked breasts, and the unexpected delights of a woman. He held the handkerchief to his face and inhaled the heady scent of her perfume. He realized that he would marry this woman. He replayed the afternoon in his head and felt the surge of desire once again.

Then he thought about his dad. When nobody was home, Matt would sometimes sneak into his dad's study and look through the reference books. He knew he was breaking a taboo when he found the textbook of gynecology. Matt never read *Playboy* or *Hustler* in high school, unlike the other boys, and the one time somebody shared a *Playboy*, he was too shy to look at the pictures.

My dad is a surgeon and my mom is a nurse, he thought, *but they never taught me anything. Dad never did have a birds-and-bees conversation with me.* John was a formal man, and Matt realized now that he was too embarrassed to explain sex. But it wasn't just the mechanical act of intercourse. Like the medical books, his father never explained the communication that happened in an actual relationship between a man and a woman. John made sure he took piano lessons, learned to juggle and play table tennis, and sat by his side teaching him to tie a fly-fishing lure. They did woodworking together in the basement, and John encouraged him to get his Eagle Scout. John would do anything that might help Matt's eye-hand coordination. *John gave me plenty of face time, but he never used it to talk about relationships. He didn't know how.*

Now Matt confronted the one big flaw in his concept of the "real world." *Until now, I thought that an actual life belonged to somebody else. This is probably why I never had a real girlfriend until now*, he thought. *I was always preparing for the future. Today the future finally happened.*

Two large birds soared overhead, and the stream of wind above the surrounding hills carried them at just the right speed to create the illusion that the birds were stationary. There were no clouds. The sun shone on the hills but here in the valley it was still cool and shaded. There was not a butterfly in sight.

1996 – At the Hospital

The next morning Matt's first thought was about Sushila. He asked himself again, *did it really happen?* He was in a dreamy state as he put his clothes on, remembering why the buttons were missing from his shirt. This time he thought about how he could share this news, this twist in his life, when he returned home to the USA. His parents didn't even yet know about the accident, let alone this woman. *Mom will pitch a fit because Kali isn't Catholic*, he thought. *I bet the religion will matter to her more than the fact she's so dark-skinned.*

He laughed. *How crazy that is. I am no longer here for the sole purpose of pleasing my mom.* He knew he would miss a semester of schooling because of the surgery to his leg and flirted with the idea of staying in Nepal until then. *No. I need to go home to the USA sooner or later.* He finished dressing just before Doctor Ranjit came to the room.

"There is excellent news, Matt. The Army helicopter just landed on the parade ground. It leaves in one hour. You need to be on it. Gather your things. You are going home."

He froze. He opened his mouth to tell Doctor Ranjit he needed to see Sushila, then thought, *Oh no, she didn't want to tell her mother yet.*

"Like, now?"

"Yes. Hurry. I'll be back in five minutes."

I don't have time to say good-bye. He had a moment of panic, then scribbled a small note for her and left it on the stand near his bed. *That's the best I can do. I need to figure this out later.* When Doctor Ranjit came back, Matt was ready. A rickshaw waited outside, pedaled by the same old man who returned him from Sushila's the previous day. They exchanged glances, and Matt wondered if Doctor Ranjit noticed.

Ranjit said nothing. The two of them glided downhill to the parade ground, where a Royal Nepal Army helicopter awaited, a Russian-made Mi-17. The sound of the rotors and the dust they sent up made it difficult to speak. In this deep canyon, there was a peculiar echo to the whump-whump-whump of the chopper, low-pitched and throbbing. He was helped aboard, seatbelt now fastened in the cargo bay, holding tight with both hands as the pilot took off at an angle. Soon, Beni looked very small and distant. Suddenly, he saw Dhauligiri and the entire Himalaya as it stretched across half the horizon, glaciers shining in the sun.

A taxi brought him directly to the American Embassy when he arrived in Kathmandu. He expected to meet John Smith, but a female consular officer met with him instead.

"Where is Mr. Smith?" he asked.

"You must have mistaken the name. There is no person by that name who works here. I am here to give you your new passport and a ticket home later today."

The photo was the one John Smith took. The consular official watched, expressionless. She brought Matt to a private room to use an embassy phone to call his parents. His mother was in hysterics to learn that he was injured and hospitalized in Nepal.

"I'm fine, Mom. Really."

"You can't possibly be fine. First you say you were lying in a ditch bleeding to death and now you tell your mother you are fine?"

"Maybe I didn't phrase it quite the best way."

"And this surgery – O my God, my son is coming home as a cripple."

"Mom, the doctor says I will be walking just fine in six months."

His mother's crying went up an octave and became louder. He listened to a stream of barely comprehensible words on the other end of the phone. She blamed him for everything. He tried to tell her that he did not cause the things that happened, but it was no use.

"You're going to give your mother cerebral apoplexy."

He held the phone a bit further from his ear.

"Honest to God, Mom, I'm fine."

"This is your mother on the phone. You're not fine until I tell you you're fine. Is that clear? And you're the one who wants to be a doctor? If you keep up this way, you will be a worthless bum."

With horror, he realized that she would use this against him for a long time, maybe forever. She would throw it in his face whenever he hinted at the slightest failure in any arena. *If there is even one rejection letter from any medical school, I will never hear the end of this. Mom will engrave this on my headstone. But only after she tears me limb from limb and digs the grave by hand, cursing all the way.*

He wanted to tell her that he had met the love of his life in Nepal. He could not get a word in edgewise, between recriminations. He decided to save this for later. *It was just too much, and besides, no harm done in waiting for the best time. I will break the news sometime in the future.*

To tell her now would make her go over the edge if she wasn't already there. Dad was more businesslike. Matt knew his father would spend a day or two with his mother, probably making her laugh. She would calm down somehow.

He wouldn't cry in front of his mother. Not ever. *The less she knows, the less she worries.* Her reaction to the accident was proof that he shouldn't tell her anything. That was how John made it through his day. But Matt did cry after the phone call was over. *What if I never see her again? What if I lose her? I need her.* He had discovered the power of love. He was going to be far away, with no practical way to contact her. *This hurts worse than my leg ever did.*

Twenty-four hours after leaving Beni, he was on a plane to Delhi headed home to Boston. He held the handkerchief she had given him in his hand and enjoyed the slight hint of perfume it carried. Elisar. He wanted to memorize that scent and the feel of her hair. The small bit of cloth was the only physical proof that she existed. *I will write her when I get home,* he thought.

December 2006 – Part 2

"Where are we?" he asked. The plane engines still hummed.

"You're alive. You slept so soundly I checked to make sure you weren't dead. You must have been to some kind of party last night."

Maureen let go of his hand while he slept, while he dreamed. He shook himself awake and smiled as he always did when Kali came back to him in his dreams. Kali was his first. First true love. First ever. She held a magical place for him. These thoughts floated in his mind. He wanted to travel back in time.

"In my dream I was having flashbacks about my first trip to Nepal, nine years ago."

He rubbed his eyes. It was 2006 now, and he was on a different plane with different people. He was no longer twenty-one. He still had the scar on his leg that ached every now and again, and the shrapnel still caused the metal detectors to sound an alarm at every airport. He also had a medical degree and a surgical residency under his belt. He never remembered any details of the actual firefight between the PLA and the Nepal Police, only the long jostling as they carried him back to Beni. He remembered Doctor Ranjit and Doctor Fergusson.

He leafed through *The Lonely Planet Guide*. Maureen asked him to show her the section on Beni. There was no section on Beni, just two sentences.

"Beni is a bustling market town on a plateau overlooking the KaliGandaki and Myagdi rivers. Long an important staging post, the village has lost much of its importance with the establishment of the new road."

She said, "You know you are off the beaten path when your destination only gets two lines in *Lonely Planet*."

Maureen wasn't exactly star struck by his medical degree. Maybe she worked with too many doctors to be impressed by the title, but now she asked a few more questions. Finally, she said, "I do have one day off before our group goes away. I was hoping to find a guide in Kathmandu." He looked at her. *Yes, playing the doctor card works. She's bright and kind of funny. Nice to talk with. I don't have plans either.*

"What about me? I'll do it. I'm not an expert but it would be my pleasure. Sure, why not?"

Matt studied *Lonely Planet* for the umpteenth time, then looked through his wallet to pass time. Now there was no driver's license, just a photocopy of his passport page. Just two credit cards and some American cash. No other cards. A wad of hundred-dollar bills, ten of them, stuck in a back fold. He missed the weight of keys in his pocket. John took them back to Boston. Matt pictured the big roll top desk in John's study at home and knew the exact drawer John would choose to keep them.

For the tenth time, he took out the small packet of colored index cards, one for each of the dozen or so most-often-performed surgical procedures. He sorted them and reviewed the list of standard instruments for each tray when they were organized. He put the cards back in the passport holder around his neck and made sure to zip it tight. Right over his heart.

One Day in Old Kathmandu

Maureen met him in the lobby of her Guest House in Thamel the next day. She wore a wide-brimmed hat; flannel shirt over polypro t-shirt; hiking boots; web belt and khaki pants with six cargo pockets and zippers that circled each thigh so that the trousers could be converted into shorts. She wore a skin diver's watch with a luminescent dial and around her neck hung a passport pouch where thieves could not get to her money. A pair of aviator's sunglasses hid her bright blue eyes. Matt surveyed this and reflected on his own casual clothes, a bit crumpled. *Maureen is living out a fantasy of what she expects travel to be. Nothing wrong with that. Everybody needs to find his or her comfort zone.* Normally, Matt wore sandals, but there were occasional heaps of garbage and some of the street gutters here included puddles of raw sewage. Shoes were the order of the day, and the weather was a bit cool anyway. He knew he was still a videshi, a foreigner, but his clothes sent the message that he was *not a trekker.* Maureen seemed oblivious to this subtlety, or maybe she didn't care.

For Maureen, every other word was "amazing." Her enthusiasm shook Matt out of his sense of worldly sophistication. Her bright eyed and bushytailed demeanor was infectious. She started to flirt as soon as they found a rickshaw and clambered behind the driver.

He tried a feeble compliment. "Are you channeling Katharine Hepburn?"

"Pardon?"

"You look very mysterious. The hat. The glasses. Do your plans include a trip on The African Queen?"

"No. I do feel like I am in a movie though," she said with a grin. "Please Doctor Matt – can you tell me - does a city have a personality?"

This is an obvious flirty line, thought Matt. *She is inviting me to play.* He decided that if she wanted to play act Kate Hepburn in *The African Queen,* he could certainly channel Humphrey Bogart, and in an equally grand manner he replied, "You're asking, 'If Old Kathmandu were a woman, who would she be?' " Matt thought for a moment. "Well, it would certainly be a she, and she would have to be very colorful. How about Phyllis Diller?"

"No. Kathmandu is more like my cousin from Baltimore. Theresa," she replied.

"Who?"

"Surely you must also have a Theresa in your family. She's the distant relative you only see about once a year, at holiday parties. One time she shows up with a low-cut dress, lots of gold jewelry and a new boyfriend, smoking too much and with a gold molar you didn't notice before."

He said, "Yes, but if she is the embodiment of Kathmandu, she must be glamorous. Like a stunning beautiful Hollywood actress that everyone watched from a young age but who is now about forty; maybe she's had a well-publicized divorce and alcohol rehab but she comes out of nowhere to win the Oscar…."

Maureen said, "Yes. You've seen every movie she ever made and you realize she's the one you wanted to grow old with… You've known her forever… Maybe Judi Dench? Certainly not Julia Roberts or Gwyneth…. They're too wholesome. Somebody who still turns heads when she walks in the room… Speaks with an accent."

It was fun to flirt this way, but Matt thought of that other woman from long ago. *Of course Kathmandu has a personality. Everything about this place reminds me of Sushila.* Talking with Maureen took Matt's mind to a nice place, some place he didn't often let himself go in his professional life as a surgeon. *God, it's nice to not need to be politically correct right now,* he thought. He allowed himself to have a pleasant daydream about Maureen, then realized that there would always be something missing.

Soon they were distracted as the rickshaw entered the plaza at Indra Chowk. Matt gallantly helped her disembark. At first, it was total chaos with the sheer mass of humanity. A spider web of alleyways diverged from here, not wide enough for a car and each alleyway meandered between buildings five stories high. Even at mid-day, these alleys were cool and dark like a maze of river canyons.

Maureen made a beeline to the vegetable sellers. Matt helped her ask the price of onions, tomatoes, and eggplant. He pointed out the bitter gourd; she didn't know what it was until now. On another side of the chowk, throngs of people shopped for red velvet slippers or aluminum pots and pans or sledgehammers. A thin young man walked by and brushed Matt's shoulder while muttering "hashish" under his breath. Matt ignored him.

Through a low arch, they saw kids playing cricket in a brick courtyard. Shopkeepers sprinkled water from a Pepsi bottle onto the street in front of their door to keep the dust down. Two old guys sat on the edge of a rest pavilion playing bag-chaal, a board game. A square held thousands of red clay pots, heaping piles in myriad designs. Down one alley, a dozen shops sold pillows and bedding.

At one end of the spice Bajaar, a collection of tables held heaps of dried fish. Crusty, small ones piled in baskets as big as the hoop a pair of arms could make.

"Where do they get these?"

"We're eight hundred miles from the ocean. I sure hope they don't get them from the river here."

"Agreed. It's not a snack food," he said, "Tell me: How did you choose this trip?"

"My friend Veronica brought me. I like to hike, but I also know that Nepal is a very spiritual place, and my plan is to learn about Buddhism while I'm here. Every day I practice mindfulness meditation in my job at hospice. I wanted to be in a land where everyone was so gentle and peaceful. I also like yoga."

"For me, I enjoy just exploring a city like this. Walking is good."

"Yes, I'm glad you're my guide," she said, "The exercise is good, and it makes up for missing my Pilates class. You are limping – are you okay?"

"It's nothing."

At this moment, he felt older than Maureen though she was about his same age. He wanted his own experience to be uplifting and spiritual, but he knew from bitter experience that Nepal was a land of surprises and that things didn't always work out.

Matt led the way down a narrow alley. Steam wafted out from behind greasy curtains covering a low entryway where the lintel was shiny from the touch of a thousand hands steadying themselves as they stooped to enter. Inside, a Tibetan lady in a black wool skirt and a knit ski cap tended a large momo steamer. She waved her ladle at the spot for Matt and Maureen to sit. Maureen's eyes adjusted to the dim light coming from a single bulb on a wire hung from the ceiling. She looked at the grimy calendar from three years ago, hanging askew on one wall. Two families already sat and ate, with small children in their laps.

She looked at him and said, "Yeah, right."

He pointed at the cook, ladling the momo straight from the steaming kettle to the plate. She agreed to stay. The Nepalis all smiled as they slid along the bench to make room at the old, creaky table. Maureen pulled out a Steri-wipe and rubbed it over her hands, then on the table while Matt laughed.

"You have thought of everything," he said.

"That's my job, I am a hospice nurse," she said, "Want some hand sanitizer? You should see what I brought with me. I planned for months so I could have a real medical kit, not just a first aid kit."

One of the children reached out to touch her hair. She squirmed a bit and caught the child's hand by the wrist to show Matt how dirty it was. "This town needs a good scrubbing."

"Good luck with that."

"I'm not just a clean freak," she said, "I love my job."

"I bet you do."

She warmed her hands on the hot chiya that came in a clear glass. She talked nonstop, and he nodded again. "Hospice is very rewarding. People think it's depressing but it's not. I get to help people move to the next phase. And bereavement too."

"Just by the way you talk, I can see that it's a calling, not just a job."

"Exactly. And you don't have to be religious to use hospice either. God is more than just Jesus, you know."

"Aren't you Catholic?" he asked.

"I was, but these days I put my faith in a higher power. 'Let go and let God' is a good rule. Death is a natural process and there is nothing to fear," she continued, "Of course, I need to take time for serenity. That's why I'm here in this beautiful place, even though I've never travelled anywhere like this before. This trip is self-care for me."

Matt nodded.

As she spoke, Matt reflected on his time in the trauma surgery rotation, where the surgeon did his job, then handed the patient to the intensivists. Then on to the next case. "I'm spiritual, too," he said, "but I just can't seem to talk about it as well as you do. I pretty much stick to the prayers from Mass."

She beamed. "Oh Matt, I am so happy to help you learn. So often, you meet a surgeon who doesn't even want to talk about this. Your patients must love you."

"I dunno," he said as he dipped a momo in the sauce and put it in his mouth.

"Oh no, I believe it. You seem so sensitive. I've been with other surgeons and the only thing they think about besides surgery is sex."

Matt choked. He coughed forcefully and covered his mouth with his hand to catch the fragments of momo he sent into the air. He looked up to see whether she noticed, but she continued. He managed to say, "That's terrible," while he reached for the water.

She leaned back in her chair and looked at him. She folded her arms across her chest and said, "I thought so."

"Thought so about what?"

"I have just one question for you, Doctor Matt."

"Okay, ask it."

"What's her name?"

"Whose name?" he stammered. He felt the blood rising to his face and wondered if it was obvious.

"The name of the Asian woman you are mooning over."

"What? - How? -"

"You heard me. The name of the woman you are stuck on. And I can tell she's not your mother or your sister."

"What – how – "

"I'm a hospice nurse, remember? My whole job is to find out what bothers people and help them get things lined up before they check out. All day you have been looking at these Asian women as if you expect somebody special to come around the corner. I know that look on a man. You've got it bad. Here I am, flirting with all the skill I can muster, and you don't take the bait. I thought there was something wrong with me. Now I see. That's not it. You are as willing as they come. She must be worth waiting for."

"Her name is Sushila, and – it's a long story. I don't even know where to begin."

"Well, I want to meet this Sushila. She must be something special."

"It's not likely. I don't know what happened to her. She seems to have disappeared. Can we change the topic?"

She took his hand in hers for an instant.

"I'm sorry. That was too blunt. I stepped in it didn't I?"

He looked away.

She took a deep breath and started again. "Let's reboot. Umm, maybe when you are working with the missionaries you can start a daily meditation. I'll bet you they are all so dedicated and spiritual, like Mother Theresa. Those Christian hospitals must be so nice. Ask them if they need hospice nursing, when you get there. I bet they could use a course in bereavement."

"Good change of topic. Let's talk about death. Something safe. Something clinical. Orderly. Not quite so messy. Neat. Neat and clean."

Matt and Maureen now sized each other up like boxers in the ring. They looked straight into each other's eyes.

"Do you know about the cremation temple?" he asked.

She was the first to look away.

"People have told me about it," she said, "But I have no urge to go there. I am on vacation. And who ever said death was neat and clean?"

She's wounded too, he thought.

"A hospice nurse who doesn't like death," he said.

"It's not about death. It's about the people left behind and their reaction. The cremation temple? Yeah, right. Western tourists taking pictures of the spectacle and making comments about the barbarity of it. Let's have some dignity. I think the Nepalis are doing the best they can. It's the voyeurism of the Westerners that I'd have trouble with."

"You're more prepared than I gave you credit for."

"Ha. Now it's me that wants to change the subject," she said.

Before he could say anything she continued, "If you want to develop your spiritual side, all it takes is a candle. And journaling and yoga. Did you know that they invented the lassi, right here in Nepal?"

"Do you want one? I think I saw a lassi place in Indra Chowk across from the bead bajaar. They're cheap too."

"Um, not right now," she leaned forward, "I heard that the milk they use is not always pasteurized and it might harbor TB. You can never be too careful. You need to protect your health," she said, not wanting to be overheard.

"What about an apple then?"

"I only eat things you can peel."

"No problem." He took out a small jackknife. He started near the stem and took the skin off in a single continuous piece. It lay on the table in a spiral heap and he presented her with the apple.

"I don't think I have ever seen anybody peel an apple that way," she said.

"You didn't grow up with surgeons. We like to do clever things with our hands. I can do a potato faster than my dad can. We time each other."

After the apple, she offered him a Tic-Tac. They wandered through the labyrinth of Old Kathmandu, exclaiming and sharing each interesting sight and smell. Soon they held hands. She helped him buy a hat, a wide-brimmed one like tourists wear, "Rum Doodle Trek" embroidered on it. A shopkeeper showed her how to drape a sari, with the pleats at the level of the bellybutton. Maureen did not buy it because her mother had often told her that red haired people should never ever wear red clothes or even pink clothes.

The streets filled with shadow and they returned to the hotel. In her daypack, she now carried a small treasure trove of bargains, including a singing bowl and a necklace of green beads.

As they walked he said, "Maureen, today has helped me be – a person. I just finished a six-year surgical residency. Every minute of every day, they made me a robot. I've been molded, standardized, and socialized into a product. I'm trying to find out who I am when I am not doing surgery."

"Matt, I know it takes a lot for a guy to say that."

"Yeah, well – sometimes it's easier to tell the truth to a total stranger. Funny how that works. Thanks for just listening."

"Matt – if things don't work out – you know how to reach me," she said in a husky voice.

They exchanged email addresses and he promised to stay in touch. He reached for a tentative hug, and she responded with a short peck on the cheek. Then on impulse, she held him closer and gave him an actual kiss. Her blue eyes sparkled. He felt the softness of her against his chest, and they kissed again. They held each other, not wanting to let go.

"I'll give you credit," he said, "You're pretty good at reading a surgeon's mind."

At that moment, her friend Veronica and another woman came out the door to the guesthouse. Maureen broke away. She introduced her friends and then the three walked back into the lobby. She gave him a quick glance over the shoulder as the other two put their arms around her. He watched her disappear.

In the taxi, he thought back to the question regarding which American actress Kathmandu would be, if a city were a person. This time, the answer came to him. It was obvious. Kathmandu was a woman. The closest was Kathleen Turner. Sexy, alluring, and mysterious. Too late to tell Maureen.

The Interview to Grant Medical Credential

The credential interview plodded along. The members of the Medical Board passed around each paper document in turn and discussed them in low tones. Matt sat during long periods of silence.

The in-charge said, "So you know Doctor Ranjit Basnet? He is my senior. A colleague of mine since college days."

The next doctor chimed in, "Be careful on your travels. There was another road traffic accident on the road to Beni in the news today. An auto went over the cliff and six people died."

The committee held a formal show-of-hands vote to approve Matt's license as a doctor in Nepal. They took a certificate from the filing cabinet, and wrote the number on both the certificate and the Register. Each member of the committee reached over to shake Matt's hand after adding his signature. The official seal was applied. The committee stood up out of their chairs and came to his side of the interview table to watch as Matt countersigned the Register and applied his thumbprints in the appropriate column. They stood close, resting their arms on his shoulders, and he felt their breath on his ears while he wrote. Each member countersigned the Register to indicate that the fee was paid; then he finished. He thanked them and went on his way.

Matt's flight was uneventful. After an hour, Fishtail Peak, the Annapurna range, and Dhauligiri came into view, as well as the lake, Fewa Tal. He wandered out of the Pokhara airport terminal and looked up at the machine gun nests in green sandbags on the roof. Next, he saw the shuttle, a white vehicle with the NGO logo on it. The driver leaned against the boot and acted like the essence of cool, wearing sunglasses as he smoked. Matt took the seat in the front.

In the back seat of the Land Rover sat a family of four, two small children on the laps of their parents. The fifth person was a young Nepali woman in a brown and yellow kurtha suruwal who wore her shawl like a hood to protect her face from the sun. She also wore sunglasses that made her eyes look large. Matt recognized her from the plane and wished he had spoken to her then.

"Namaste."

The children stared at him until the parents helped them make a Namaste with little hands. The young woman laughed, a sort of squealing musical laugh, and said, "Hello. It's great that we'll have such a big strong man with us." She poked his arm.

"Who, me? Big? Are you joking? And you have an American accent," he said, "what's up with that?"

"Manju at your service," she said, "I went to nursing school in USA, but I work in Beni now. I do a lot of community projects, and I've been marketing the ski caps knitted by our women's group. You will love the town." She took her seat in the back, and one of the children sat in her lap. They cooed and pointed out the window.

The driver spoke to Matt. Manju translated. "He says you need to keep your arm inside the vehicle at all times. I think that's about all the conversation you will get from him."

After two hours, the Land Rover slowed when they came upon a bus stopped in the middle of the road. A mob of passengers gazed over the cliff. They were at the location of the road traffic accident from the day before.

The Rover belched a black cloud as the driver brought it to a stop. They all got out and joined the crowd at the gap in the brush on the riverbank side. Here the doomed car clipped off the leafy tops as if with shears when it vaulted into eternity. First, they saw the river. At this time of year, it was well within its banks. The vehicle lay on the rocky moonscape of the exposed riverbed, upside down but with the doors removed.

"Looks like they already recovered the bodies. I think its two hundred meters at least. Maybe they will leave the car there forever," said Manju.

Matt stooped to pick up a pebble and tossed it over the edge while the driver frowned. "Twenty feet would have been fatal enough. And no guardrail. Would have taken three seconds to hit the bottom. What went through their minds, I wonder," he said.

"Who knows? Every now and then, an entire busload goes over a cliff somewhere. Do you know why people ride on the bus roofs here in Nepal?" she asked, "They say it's so they can jump free in case of a road traffic accident."

"It's a country of superlatives. Highest mountains, most spiritual people, worst maternal-child health, and now, worst road traffic accidents," he said.

"Aren't you a bit cocky? You sound so cynical and you aren't even there yet."

"You really did live in the USA, didn't you? It's gallows humor, I suppose. We need to laugh or else we will cry. And anyway you started it."

"Ha. I suppose I did. It's just that you don't act like the typical, humble missionary."

"I don't know what that is."

"Serving the poor. Don't they have enough poor people to serve back in USA?"

"Of course they do. That's not the point of me doing this. I'm here to help Doctor Ranjit."

"I know who you are and why you are here. I just think you shouldn't take us for granted. I get a little tired of people who refer to us as the 'third world' and treat Nepal like its Disneyland for adults."

"Fair enough. I'm not here to be entertained. We'll just have to see how it works out. In the meantime, how does a Nepali nurse with an American accent end up in Beni?"

"When she has nowhere else to go."

Everyone stretched before getting into the Land Rover, and the driver walked a polite distance away to relieve himself. He wanted to talk with Manju, but she stuck with the children. She looked at Matt when she thought he couldn't see her, but looked away when he turned his gaze.

It was dark when the Rover coasted into the courtyard by the vehicle gate of the hospital. The Chowkidar greeted them, wearing a uniform that made him look like a Gurkha. He swung the gate open and the hinges squealed, crying out for oil.

Manju slipped out quickly and ran behind the line of the Welcome Committee, scooting behind for a place at the tail end.

"All this just for me?" asked Matt as he surveyed the formal group. He made a formal Namaste as each spoke in turn. First in line was Ranjit, now with white hair that accentuated a contrast with his dark coppery complexion. Ranjit placed the garland of marigolds as Matt said, "Guru-ji." *He doesn't look any different than he did ten years ago.*

Then Ranjit introduced the three others – Sara the administrator, with whom he had exchanged letters and emails. She looked like her picture in the NGO newsletter - pale and freckled, flecks of gray hair and a proper British accent. "So pleased, at long last. We'll meet tomorrow to go over your orientation."

Next, a young man, lanky and fair skinned. A few wisps of hair on his chin and the round glasses gave him the look of a beatnik. Alok announced, "I am from Kathmandu. I learn from you while you in Beni. I am MBBS."

"MBBS?"

"Yes – MBBS means I am medical student. Soon I apply for internships in UK. So glad to see you. I hope there is enough work for you here."

The third man in line made a theatrical bow. He sported a potbelly and a gold chain dangled over a hairy chest. He was dressed in scrubs and a lab coat, wearing a surgical cap at a jaunty angle. He smelled like curry, with a stain on his mustache the color of turmeric.

"Livingston, I presume?" he asked. "Welcome to the land of Shangri-La. It is not far from this very spot. I am called Ram. I went to medical school in Delhi. When you go to Operating Theatre, I will be the one passing gas." Ram shook Matt's hand, stubby fingers with arthritic joints. Ram draped an ivory-colored kata scarf over Matt's shoulders. "You will join us at Guest House for dinner, and we will get to know each other, Doctor Matt."

Manju was still straightening her clothes and brushed her hair aside as she said, "Hi. I am the nurse in charge of the AIDS hospice. I am sure we will talk."

Matt wondered about the one person in Beni who was not here.

Sushila. The love of my life. Why was I expecting her to be here?

He followed Ram to the flat. Matt was silent, thinking that Ranjit has been very formal and a bit distant, more than he expected. Ram filled the silence and apologized for the accommodations. "Whatever you do, don't drink water from the tap – there is typhoid in the water system but no matter how much bleach we add, it seems to survive. There will be a small bottle of clean water by the sink – use that to rinse your mouth when you brush your teeth. It is inevitable that you will have acute gastro enteritis sooner or later, but let's get some other things organized before that time arrives."

Ram unlocked the padlock on the door and said, "A man's home is his castle," as he handed Matt the key. Light came from a bare bulb that hung from a wire. *There isn't even a propeller fan in this flat*, Matt noticed. In the corner stood a long-handled shovel near a small placard of instructions in case of an earthquake.

Ram was ready to leave, but Matt said, "Ram-G, I was so glad that you survived the battle between the army and the PLA. Was it bad?"

Ram stiffened and scratched the stubble of his face. His hand moved to his throat as if he was measuring the folds of skin there. He surveyed Matt for a moment.

"Matt Sar, welcome to Beni. We will do whatever we can so that you can practice surgery to the fullest extent of your skill. But I must give you some advice."

Matt waited.

"This is a very polite and indirect culture. Our culture is based on coexisting with uncertainty. For that reason, there are topics we never discuss. They are too painful. The battle is one such. You would do well to never bring it up. Cultivate patience. Think of the wise person who said, 'I wish I didn't know now what I didn't know then.' "

"Wait a minute. That's a line from an American rock-and-roll song. You listen to Bob Seger?"

"I seek wisdom from many sources. In my opinion, the man who wrote that song was very wise. In Nepal we would call him a Buddha. Buddha will appear in your life in many ways. Listen to Buddha wherever he may appear. Until wisdom comes by, don't ask any such kind of a question unless you are truly ready to hear the answer."

"But will it hurt to just answer one question? There is a specific person I was wondering about."

"Matt Sar. Those are the most painful questions of all. Maybe not for you, but for the person who must answer. It is the exact kind of question I am telling you not to ask."

Ram left with one more Namaste as he backed out the door.

Matt was alone except for the gecko on the ceiling. *There is an elephant in the room, here in Beni, Nepal.*

Day One

When the student is ready, the teacher will appear.
– Gautama Buddha

Matt was relieved to see a Western-style sit-down toilet in the apartment, because the Asian squat- toilets required a degree of knee flexion that aggravated the old injury to his leg. He made a mental note to buy toilet paper in the Bajaar.

Matt headed over to the hospital before dawn. Ranjit was already at the nurse's station, in scrubs and a surgical hat, talking with the night didi.

"So you thought you would outwork me?" Ranjit said. "You are an hour late. Come. There is a caesarean delivery to perform. We need to get started."

Over the door that led to Theatre hung a large wooden cross, the only one in the hospital, one of the few physical reminders of the history of Christian mission work that brought this hospital to this place. The door was unlocked, and Matt heard a woman moan. He peeked into the room. The woman sat on the side of the Theatre table, legs dangling as she embraced the nurse. Matt saw her swollen fingers and heard the circulating nurse whisper encouragement as she hugged the teenaged woman. Ram was giving a spinal, his stubby fingers holding a long needle as he felt the landmarks with his other sterile-gloved hand. Ram was unshaven and still wore the same scrubs as last night.

Ranjit stopped to say some words of encouragement to the patient then joined Matt to wash hands and don sterile gowns. He recited the details of the case as they went along.

Matt interrupted him to say, "I need to tell you that I have never done a Caesarean Delivery."

Ranjit already wore his surgical mask. *Five years of surgical residency, including a rotation on the thoracic service and a trauma fellowship, but he never did a basic procedure like this, Ranjit thought. Sara wants me to work with him, but he can't speak Nepali. And this was Sushila's lover.*

Matt tried to ascertain whether Ranjit smiled or frowned behind the mask, but only the eyes showed.

"Your real medical education starts today then," said Ranjit. "I knew this would be the case. Those residency programs in USA no longer produce surgeons. They teach you to be a technician, not a doctor. Come. "

Ranjit's hands were fast. He used a technique of caesarean developed in Israel, explaining the differences in technique as he went along. Matt took the role of assistant surgeon, tying off any bleeding vessels encountered along the way. Ranjit talked all the way, interrogating Matt as if he was still a junior resident. Matt knew that he was being watched and evaluated. He was determined to be a good team player. There would be a process of proving himself. Ranjit would not accept him simply because he was American. He needed to be competent.

Matt only asked one question, as Ranjit grasped the first scalpel.

"Cautery?" he asked.

"We have a machine but it is broken. Perhaps you will repair it." Then as an afterthought, "Pray to Lord Agni for the gift of fire, my Christian friend."

Not even cautery is available here, thought Matt. Cautery was an indispensible technology in the USA, an electric sparking device on the end of a wand that allowed the surgeon to make an incision and to staunch bleeding simultaneously.

Matt looked around and counted the people in the room. Two surgeons; the scrub and circulating nurses; and Ram. The patient made six. Matt realized that in the USA at least ten staff would be present. *Maternal hypertension. Risk of fetal respiratory distress. Risk of hemorrhage.* Matt tried to remember the elements of an Apgar score, but gave up after a moment.

The team reached the moment where everything else in the universe stops while the surgeon does something clever with his hands. Now, Ranjit made the incision and reached his arm into the uterus almost to the elbow. He disengaged the baby's head from the mother's pelvis and lifted.

The baby cried as soon as Ranjit held it up. It was a boy and there were smiles all around. Ranjit clamped the cord and cut it, then handed the baby to Ram, who rubbed it with a towel to dry it off then wrap it for the mother. Ram moved the drape to allow the mother to watch the baby as it lay on her chest, freeing one arm so she could hold it there. It was quiet in the room as the baby sucked his mother's breast. The mother cried too, tears of joy, and Ram praised her for how brave she was and what a wonderful mother she would be. Matt watched the mother and baby, but then Ranjit clicked his tongue as if calling a dog, which brought Matt back to attention.

Ranjit closed the incision, layer by layer. As they worked, Matt listened to the new mother whimper and exclaim, crying with tears of joy about her new son. Matt was an unemotional surgeon, very analytical and calculating, and he was robotic at times in pursuit of the best surgical technique. This one time he allowed himself to be sentimental. *This is why I went to medical school*, he said to himself. *This is the reward*. Ranjit noticed Matt's reaction but said nothing as he finished the procedure. They put the bandage on the woman's belly and left the nurses to move the patient to the obstetrical ward.

Matt's back ached across the shoulders. He'd worn a sterile gown that was too small, the whole time. He stretched his upper body to relieve the tension.

"Doctor Matt, now you act like a woman whose bra is too tight," said Ram, "Maybe now you will have some sympathy."

Ranjit said, "And as an added bonus, the father will be pleased. This young woman was able to bear a boy, and not a girl."

"Come. It's time to take bhaat."

Only an hour had passed. The incision-to-baby time was only five minutes. Another forty minutes to close. He decided he would work with Ranjit several more times before doing one on his own. *I wonder if I can do it as quickly as Ranjit. Only time will tell.*

They exited the doors from Theatre back through the Gynae Ward, where Ranjit took Sara aside. They spoke while Matt waited out of earshot.

"Sara, some days I wonder if I am getting too old for this."

"You know as well as I do that we need the help and nobody else has volunteered since the battle."

"He seems to be a competent surgeon," Ranjit told Sara, "I will not object if he stays. He has the right attitude. But remember, it was your idea to accept his offer. And I just don't want a lot of drama."

"Thank you. We need a second surgeon to help you. I will talk with him. Send him my way after he takes rice."

Morning chiya was at a small restaurant just down the street that led to the Bajaar. Matt felt as though the hospital was airy and realized that there was no wall around the complex of buildings. This was in sharp contrast to every hospital he had seen in Kathmandu. There were chowkidars and a chowkidar station, but the only gate was the one in front of the Land Rover and anybody could walk around it. The individual buildings could be secured, but the campus could be accessed from any direction, and the only barrier was the waist-high hedge on one side. Matt surveyed the crowd - an assortment of women in colorful costumes. Ranjit waved his arms as he walked through the crowd of people on the grass. Ram smiled and welcomed them. Matt followed, aware of being the only white person in sight.

The entryway to the bhansa was narrow and the cook blocked half of it, focused on a large vat of boiling oil, scooping out samosas with a screened ladle, piling them on a greasy newspaper. The boys squeezed past. The shop owner poured chiya in small clear glasses without being asked. Ram spooned chini into his. They ordered samosas along with maize soup. The food came and the two Nepalis broke up each samosa and mashed them into the soup. Ranjit ate with a spoon as he spoke, staring down into the bowl.

"We do have a cautery machine, but it is broken. You need to look at it if you want to use it."

"What's wrong with it? Does it work at all?"

"That is the very heart of it. It turns on and it activates with the foot pedal as designed. The wand feels the same in your hand. The problem is the rheostat. We are unable to adjust the amount of current. I am afraid it is not very sensitive."

Ram interjected, "Ranjit is too generous with an inanimate object. In fact, the cautery machine puts out only one setting – full on. It lights the night. We could scorch the sky. Lord Agni himself does not wield such a flame. It is Arjun's Chariot."

Ranjit chuckled. He held one finger up in the air in a gesture that recalled the ancient mudra of knowledge and waved it at Ram as he said, "But it is not supernatural. Puja to the cautery will not result in bending it to our will." He turned to Matt and said, "Yes, I am afraid it malfunctioned during surgery and I thought we would start a small fire in the Operating Theatre. It sizzled and created a small crater an inch wide at the very first cut. I knew something was wrong. It seemed that the subcutaneous tissue melted like frying the fat of a pig, due to the heat."

"Maybe the manufacturer created such a setting so that we could make the skin incision on an elephant," said Ram, with obvious glee.

"Yes, but I am not a veterinary surgeon," replied Ranjit. "Fortunately I am expert tailor, and we stitched from that moment on. These hands have never failed me in suturing. I think I have Damai in my background." Matt did not get the joke until Ranjit explained that the caste of tailors is named Damai.

"I am learning, but I do not understand all of your banter."

"Perhaps you know Agni," said Ram, "The God of fire. As Doctor Sara would say, the prophet Elijah never called down such a flame on his altar to the Christian God."

"And Doctor Sara would also say, Elijah was not a Christian." Ranjit countered.

"Elijah and Jesus are the Christian Buddhas. Let us learn from them," said Ram, with an air of finality.

The two Nepali men were enjoying themselves at Sara's expense. Matt offered to look at the machine. They finished their breakfast. Ranjit fished out some dirty ten-rupee notes and paid the cook. The plaza outside the hospital filled with more people and chaotic activity as they crossed the space and returned to the hospital.

By this time, more blankets covered the grass. An enterprising cook now sold chiya-and-samosas from a makeshift kitchen in the open air outside the building with the large Red Cross painted on the roof.

He surveyed the Gynae Ward from the door. In Boston, Matt walked with the swagger of a surgeon, accentuated by the sure knowledge that he had completed his medical studies at Harvard University and a residency at The Massachusetts General Hospital. But in Beni he hesitated, thinking about Ranjit in Theatre. *MGH - 'Man's Greatest Hospital.' They've never heard of it and they aren't impressed. Nobody here cares about my credentials. I need to bring my A game if I am going to contribute here. Rural Nepal is the Big Time.*

Gynae Ward was one large room with eleven beds, wooden and non-adjustable. The sheets were sky blue and the blankets were dark blue. Nearly every patient was accompanied by a woman or two or three, and most visitors wore red saris and blood-red shawls, a colorful contrast to the blue linen. Some of the women squatted in the bed as they ate. The smell of porridge wafted through the room.

Just above Matt's head, a system of wires stretched three feet below the very high ceiling, from which the between-bed drapes hung. Right now, all the beds were visible and a large neat overhand knot tied in each drape kept it out of the way before it was thrown over the wire. At the end of the room was a rusty and dust-covered oxygen cylinder with white paint splashed on the top. A separate set of wires strung across the room served to support the greenish oxygen tubing that looped around the wires. Two patients were tethered to bottles of intravenous therapy, suspended from the same wire by loops of gauze bandage. Finally, there were two large ceiling fans, rotating slowly.

Matt finally stepped over the threshold. He said nothing while Sara dictated instructions to the didi. The didi smiled at Matt but neither she nor Sara said anything to him. Sara finished speaking to the didi and turned to

Matt. "So I hear you have started work. Have you taken bhaat?" To Matt's untrained ear, it sounded like she had just asked him if he had bathed, and he looked at her for a second before realizing the intent of the question.

"Oh… yes. Quite happy with breakfast, thank you."

"My rounds are finished. Come with me." Matt followed Sara outside, letting her go through the door to the administration building first. They passed the crowd waiting at the cashier's windows. Next, up the stairs to the office, passing the faded mural of scenes from the Bible.

"Matt, meet Bimla, my secretary. She is my right-hand person. She knows everything about administrative duties." Bimla smiled and gave the "Namaste" gesture. Finally, Matt and Sara were in her office.

I would get depressed if I had to sit in this office, thought Matt. There were hardly any personal touches, just a couple of framed diplomas and photographs by the door. Matt tried to picture Sara as a young woman. He glanced at the photos where she stood at a beach pavilion with her family. It was a black and white photo, and they all stood stiffly. Sara grasped the electric teakettle from the small table in the corner and poured herself a proper English tea, white china teacup with a rose design on it, complete with matching saucer. She used a pair of delicate tongs to spoon a cube of sugar, not the rough crystals of Nepali chini, and topped it off with a slice of lemon. Matt declined.

She warmed her hands on the cup and started, "I remember you from 1996, although I don't expect you recognize me. You were Ranjit's project then, and there was a Doctor George Fergusson from Oz who helped." He looked at her more closely. She was a very pale woman with faded freckles and an up thrust jaw that reminded him of Nelson at Trafalgar. *Chin up, full ahead*, he imagined her saying from the poopdeck. *She looks about the same age as Ranjit*, he thought. *Was she there then?*

"In those days, I was not the only Christian missionary stationed here. The civil war had not really reached us, and the Scandinavians and Ozzies were still here with their families. The ambush that brought you here was the first salvo, I am afraid." Her voice trailed off. *Surely, she is thinking about the attack. It must still be fresh in her mind.*

"Yes, I was trekking. The Dhauligiri base camp route. I don't actually remember anything about the ambush."

"That's not surprising. In the last ten years, bandhs are a way of life here, and we discuss them as if they are a natural phenomenon like weather. The same with small terrorist attacks. By the time the battle happened, it seemed as though we already practiced our response for five years. What do you remember about the hospital?"

"Not much. The five weeks I spent here are a blur to me now, and I can't separate the reality from my memories. Since then I have wondered about many details. I spend time telling myself that things did not happen as they did. I don't know. I have recollections of that time that are very clear, others not so much." *Maybe this is the time…*

She smiled. "In those days we had hundreds of trekkers each month; it seems odd that you became one of the few that came to the hospital. What we have all learned around here is that some events are too painful to revisit. You may want to think of that." There was a hint of warning in her voice.

"Sara, I admit, I was curious to know about some of my –ah, friends from last time."

Her tone became very serious. "That is exactly what I mean. Don't go mucking about."

He thought of all the questions he brought, and Ram's warning from the evening before. *I will save it for another time. Or never.*

After an awkward pause, the talk turned to the orientation. A translator named Prakash would accompany Matt on rounds and at the clinic. The Theatre schedule began every morning at eight; the Theatre didi would show him how to book each surgical case. For minor procedures, he could use the small Theatre next to Casualty Ward without booking in advance. First come first served if it was not already in use. He was to be on call for surgery from Sunday to Wednesday, opposite from Ranjit who would now be on call from Wednesday to Sunday. Somebody would show him where the Guest House Dining Room was. Tea with biscuits at four o'clock every afternoon; Medical Staff dinner was always at six PM; there was a signup sheet. A servant woman would take care of his laundry and other cooking needs. He was free to exit the compound, and they could find him a guide whenever he wished to see the Bajaar or perhaps hike on his day off.

"Let's be honest here," said Sara. "One thing we always find with young surgeons is that they think they are in New York when they are not. One of our other western doctors compared it to life in the trenches. You will find the imaging and lab to be a challenge. Also, there is no formal system of referral here as you might have become accustomed."

Sara continued, "In the West, an internist often makes the diagnosis and does extensive imaging. The case is elegantly laid out when you walk in the door, before you are called. The surgeon comes in and confirms the workup that has already been done. Here, the Medical Assistant will call you based on a guess as to whether it's a surgical versus medical problem, but it is up to you to do the workup from there. We have no C.T., no ultrasound, and no scans of any kind. Our x-ray machine is fifty years old. We'll all put our heads together when a problem arises, but you will need to be clever and have your wits about you."

Matt took a deep breath. Sara continued, "Let me give you an example. Somewhere along the way, Doctor Fitzmaurice will make his annual volunteer trip to help us. He's from the Outer Hebrides of Scotland, and I think he is at least 80-years old by now. A delightful man, trained in the old way and working in a village on an island for 50 years. The older men do not rely on imaging so much before doing such a thing as an appendix. Given our limitations, he's a perfect match."

Matt tried to picture a surgeon operating at eighty. *I wonder if I will still hold a scalpel at that age. Fifty years from now.* He knew better than to ask that question aloud.

"I understand. I hope I am up to the challenge. I have one last question. When the Christian NGO left, how was it that you stayed?"

She looked beyond him. He wanted to turn around to see what it was that now caught her attention with such focus. After a moment, she looked back at him.

"I was here twenty years before that decision was made," she said, "The NGO left, but God did not abandon this town. I was here to manage the transition. There is a Christian church here. A shepherd does not always choose their flock and must manage with the flock they are given. There were many reasons for me to stay. You are here for a year. We will have plenty of time to share. In the meantime, don't listen to Ram and Ranjit. Sometimes they have a laugh at my expense. They may yet come to Christ. I pray for them and so should you." With that, she laughed, but Matt wondered what she was thinking. *Everyone has a history here.*

Sara phoned the Theatre *didi*. Matt would go there that day and hand over his set of preference cards. Within a day, his instrument trays would be organized and ready for inspection. Very simple. As he exited the office, he took one more look at the pictures just inside the door. A diploma from Oxford University Medical School. One picture showed Sara with long hair in a braid and a peasant blouse with flowers embroidered on it. There was a flower behind one ear and a stethoscope around her neck. *So Sara was a hippie. How did she get from there to here?* He wondered. Matt smiled at Bimla the secretary as he left, then closed the door behind himself. He looked again at the painted murals of biblical scenes. The paint was peeling, but the mural depicted a shepherd with a flock. The shepherd in the mural wore a Nepali costume. The crowd at the cashier stations was still there as he walked down the steps.

They clearly do not want to talk about the one thing I want to know.

He decided to walk through the town. To the Bajaar of course. It was easy to find Sushila's house; the cobblestone streets and stone houses were familiar as if remembering a dream. Finally, he was there. It was the same door and same windows. The stoop was unswept. He cleared some dust from one windowpane and tried to look in – it was too dark to see. *Shuttered up and abandoned. Maybe she will never come back from the UK. It would be awkward to meet her husband anyway. But why won't they talk about it?*

The tree that grew out of the temple roof was bare of leaves. He looked at it for awhile and tried to recall how he felt the last time he was there. Then left.

Matt's First Appendix in Beni

"In the beginner's mind there are many possibilities, in the expert's mind there are few. Cultivate beginner's mind."

— Shuryu Suzuki (Zen Mind, Beginner's Mind)

Matt joined the team for dinner. Everyone was very serious at the table. *They seem to be waiting, but for what, I don't know.* Matt was not the kind of person who needed to speak and fill the silent void. He was comfortable with silence at dinner, but he was feeling a bit isolated. *Will it be like this for a year?*

At dessert, Ranjit announced, "Now that Matt is here I will go to Pokhara for a few days. I will take the Land Rover in the morning." There were knowing glances around the table.

Ram smiled. "I will watch over our young man and the surgery department will still be here when you get back."

Alok admitted a man to Surgical Ward at five in the morning. On rounds, Matt went to that bedside as soon as he received the report. *Nice that he let me sleep an extra hour,* thought Matt. Here was a 47 year-old man with a bellyache. His history and age pointed to appendicitis. The patient's exam was very ambiguous, and when Matt tested for rebound tenderness there was only the merest hint - the patient's belly was pretty soft. *So this is what Sara meant about being clever. This is not a clear call.* Matt decided to go for it, though, without any other lab tests. At the spur of the moment, he invited Alok to scrub in with him.

He called Ram. Within fifteen minutes, the man lay on the table in Theatre, with two nurses beside him. Matt said hello to the patient then went with Alok to scrub his hands and gown up. When they returned, the patient was intubated and asleep. Since Ranjit was gone, Alok could tie off incidental bleeders and help in the actual surgery, while the scrub nurse passed the instruments. Matt prepped the patient, and they started the case.

He realized that he was nervous, and looked over at Ram, who smiled as usual. *Thank God he's here.* It was Matt's first laparotomy at Beni, and he wanted God to look over everything. He needed to prove that the appendix was inflamed. *I'd hate to have to find a normal appendix on my first real case. I need to show that I can do this without the tests we'd use in the West.*

There was fluid in the peritoneum, and he breathed a sigh of relief because it was a sure sign of an infected appendix. He dug the appendix out from behind the intestines, sweating a bit because it was stuck. It came into view and he smiled to himself because it was bright red and friable. He put a small surgical clamp on the main artery and asked Alok to hold the clamp while he tied it off to prevent bleeding. Alok fumbled with his grip on the clamp and pulled on it, tearing the tip of the artery. The wound filled with blood. Matt reassured Alok and realized that he, too, was nervous, working with Matt the first time. It was easy to find the artery again, all he needed to do was to look for the blood spurting an inch into the air, and he clamped it again.

Alok took the clamp and once again, pulled too hard. The scrub nurse raised her eyebrows as she looked over at Matt. Here in the place where emotions were tightly controlled, it was a universal sign of the severest disapproval. She did not need to say anything aloud.

"No problem, Alok. We'll go over how to do this, later when we have more time," Matt repeated through clenched teeth.

Now the artery retracted into the tissue, and Matt did not see it anymore. It lay there like a time bomb. *I need the damned cautery,* he thought. He found the bleeder and tied it off himself. *This is taking too damn long.*

Matt and Alok stumbled through several more arterial ties. He tried to be diplomatic about asking Alok not to pull so hard. *There are only so many ways to phrase it,* he thought. Matt was getting testy. At last, he tied off the appendix and finished the surgery. In USA, Matt routinely completed far more complicated surgery than this, but he was conscious of the fact that his first few cases here would set the tone for the future. He was relieved that everyone saw the inflamed appendix. Nobody would question his judgment. He closed the skin incision with a sutureless scar.

Then he ran through a mental checklist of his work. *Because there was no cautery, I could not truly prevent the appendiceal mucosa from oozing after surgery. Dammit, I should have placed a penrose drain. In the USA that would be old-fashioned but here, it would be a good idea. I hope there will not be a mucocele,* he thought. He clenched his teeth again as he thought about this impending complication of a simple surgery. *I would not worry about this if I had a cautery machine that worked.*

He did not let his frustration show. He smiled and thanked everyone, especially Alok and the scrub nurse. He wanted to create a positive vibe in Theatre in order to get good results, and he thought for a while about the language barrier. The staff spoke English, but he needed to make sure he, himself, spoke at a level that enhanced communication. *I need to keep my mojo. I need some help to bring it here. The zen of surgery. I need to stay in control—be the coolest head on the team.*

He did a couple of other minor cases that day, but did not ask Alok to help for those. *The ice is broken. I'm back to doing the thing I know how to do.* Ram was cordial and attentive.

That night he dreamed he was four years old and home in Boston. He opened the door to his playroom. Instead of his toys, there was an Operating Theatre. In the dream, he wore pajamas as he stood on a footstool. He was at the right height next to an anesthetized patient in Theatre. Nobody noticed or commented on his youthfulness or diminutive stature. All the people were the same as in Beni, except that somehow Mister Rogers was also there, explaining the steps and tying off the bleeders. In the dream, he used craft supplies from elementary school art class, instead of instruments. The only instrument in the dream that resembled a real instrument was the one his grandfather invented, full-size, too big for him to grasp with four-year-old hands. It was very shiny and he didn't know what it did but it was magical somehow. There was a full range of sutures from which to choose, but Mister Rogers told him in a very reassuring voice that it was okay to use Elmer's Glue and construction paper to rearrange body organs that looked like the ones in his science kit. At the end of the dream, he took the inflamed appendix home back to the living room where his mother sat curled up on the couch with a cup of tea, reading, as if this was a school project. His mother praised him as she looked over the top of her glasses. She smiled and hung the appendix on a Christmas tree like an ornament.

He slept soundly otherwise, but he remembered the dream with his first sip of coffee and chuckled to himself. He often had these vivid dreams after he was exposed to inhalation anesthesia during a long surgery. *Did I get a snootful?* He reminded himself to double-check the way the anesthetic gases were vented here. And he decided that he needed to go through the actual instruments of every tray that were set up according to his preferences.

The next day, Matt did a gallbladder removal and two hernia repairs. In the afternoon, he met with the Theatre didi. Sure enough, all the instruments were there. Just like on the preference cards. But it was the individual instruments. The needle driver slipped out of grasp on each throw. He felt as though the forceps didn't actually grip anything, whether it was tissues or the needles. *Maybe these needle holders were meant for elephant surgery.* The surgical scissors, a precision instrument in the hands of a surgeon, were dull. *I just didn't think stainless steel ever became old and tired.* He decided he would use the large mayo scissors to do such things as hernias, because the Metzenbaum scissors were like the kindergarten kind used to cut construction paper for a craft project to bring home to mom.

Then he decided to open every tray, grasping each instrument so he could sort them into two piles, the good and bad. *I will only use the ones from the good pile.* But there were fewer trays now, because so many instruments were rejected.

The Theater didi looked on with distress. Matt told her not to slip the discarded instruments back into circulation.

"I have memorized the feel of every single one," he told her. *I am being a control freak,* he said to himself, *but I need to do whatever it takes to be confident.*

Sara came to check on progress. Matt knew she was tallying the cost of replacement tools. She sorted and re-sorted the pile of rejected tools as if she was a crime scene investigator sifting through a pile of old bones freshly exhumed from a shallow grave.

"The didi told me you were doing this. Are you really sure they are unacceptable?"

"I can't do an exploratory lap with just my bare hands."

"We're going to spend all night resterilizing these now. And I think this is five thousand Euros to replenish, at a minimum. We can't simply buy an Army-Navy retractor in the Bajaar. Surgical quality stainless steel instruments are specially made by hand. And fewer sets means we need to have the shortest possible turnaround time."

They looked at the pile for a bit, and Matt wavered.

"Sara, if there was a working cautery machine, I might not need such a quick turnaround time because there would be fewer instruments in each set."

"I see your point about the cautery. I am not an expert in the care and feeding of these devices. Why don't you also have a look at it and see exactly what is wrong? Maybe it's something simple, and easy to repair. See what you can do about it."

She turned to go, but Matt stopped her. "Sara, I do have one question left over from orientation."

"Yes?"

"Maybe I am putting my foot in it, but – I need to say the name out loud. Do you remember a girl named Sushila who was in Beni when I was here last time?"

Sara took a deep breath. Matt noticed immediately how she crossed her arms and set her jaw.

"Yes. Quite well. Quite."

"What became of her?"

"Matt, I thought you were alluding to this when we spoke the other day, and Ram also said you were inquiring. I'm glad we are having this talk while Ranjit is away. Maybe we were too subtle. Let me make it plain. Never mention that name again. Ever. Not to me. Not to anyone."

Uh oh. I didn't think this would be such a sore spot, thought Matt. His ears were ringing.

"And the battle. The battle is too fresh to discuss. Please respect the trauma we all went through. You'll just stir up our collective PTSD. For no purpose," she said.

"But – I just want to know…"

Now Sara's face was flushed. "Matt. Please. I know that Ranjit wrote you to say that she married after you left. She is gone from here. None of us are in contact. That is your answer."

Matt looked at her and listened to her tone of voice and thought, *This is not a person I want to cross.*

"Okay, so you know what happened between us. If you feel so strongly, why did you encourage me when I volunteered to come here?"

She softened her tone. "Matt, I am not here to judge you. You were a young man back then. People grow and learn over the course of their life. You are not the first person who ever asked for a second chance. We Christians know a few things about the path of redemption."

"Thank you," he nodded.

"But while I am being blunt, I might as well tell you. Since the battle we have simply not been able to attract any other surgeons. Not a one. Oh, we can cobble together some short-term men, but you are the only one who offered to come for a period of longer than a month. Ranjit has been carrying the burden by himself. He needed persuasion before he would agree to have you, but here you are. If you insist on upsetting the apple cart, we might need to make other plans."

"In other words, you were desperate."

"One might say that."

"Okay." His ears were stinging with blunt feedback. "I hear you. I promise never to discuss these things. I am here to serve." *She thinks I am the bottom of the barrel. I'm just going to have to prove to them that I am worthy of trust, that's all. I will take this challenge. I will work harder than they do.*

She smiled and said, "Thank you. In the meantime, I will work on getting these instruments up to par. I invite you to have a look at the cautery machine. Do what you can do. There is so much you can contribute here."

Part 1: Gurkha Camp at Church Crookham Hampshire, The United Kingdom –1999

Holding on to anger is like grasping a hot coal with the intent of throwing it at someone else; you are the one who gets burned.

– Buddha

The clock struck seven and Sushila waited for Captain Gurung to come home. *How did I get into this pattern?* she asked herself. *This is my life now.* She held her son and read to him. He reached out his hand to touch the book, and she snuggled him close. She was proud that the boy seemed so attentive at such a young age. Baby Arjun had already taken rice for the day, and as soon as the motorcycle pulled into the driveway, she would put him in bed so that he would be out of the way during that first five minutes of Captain Gurung's arrival.

Sushila ran through the list of possible things that could go wrong today, nervous as to what he would find this time, what would cause him to rage when he came through the door. The house was clean. The dishes were neatly stacked. The laundry was neatly folded and stacked. The three kukri knives on the shelf were polished until they gleamed. His uniforms were pressed just so. *It will never be enough. This is my life now. Still, I will do this for Arjun.*

She sat and waited. She looked at herself in the wedding photo with the Captain. They both wore the green-fringed wedding collar. Side-by-side on two golden thrones, with red curtains in the background, waiting as the line of guests presented them with small presents of nuts or money. *How young I looked. That was only three years ago.* She looked more closely. It was obvious that she was not smiling. In the photo, her eyes were downcast and she looked thin.

August and September 1996 – Beni, Nepal

Sushila was singing as she walked to the hospital, until the rickshaw with Ranjit and Matt passed, going in the opposite direction. Then she knew why the helicopter was there. She dropped the food she was carrying and ran to the Tundikhel. She was too late. Her life and her future had flown off into the sky like smoke from a funeral pyre. The helicopter became smaller and smaller until it disappeared. She hurried back to Matt's room at the hospital. It was empty, as she knew it would be. She found Matt's note, and held it to her chest as she cried.

She took the note home, thankful that her mother was still away. She lay on the bed where she had made love to her future husband, the man who would never leave her.

She smelled him on the pillowcase and wept. She read the note a hundred times. She found a loose button on the floor and knew she was never going to sew it back on his shirt, not now. Her mother returned from Pokhara and saw that she had cried. Sushila would not say what was wrong.

Two weeks later, the morning started with a queasy feeling in the stomach and became worse from there.

"A nineteen-year-old girl does not simply start vomiting for no reason," said Sushila's mother. She squinted at her daughter with a cold eye, "You had sex with him, didn't you?"

Sushila froze. *Every bad thing is coming true.* The look on Sushila's face told her mother everything.

"Tell me. No, don't tell me. I already know. Why did I think I could trust Ranjit to watch you? 'Learning English,' he said. What a fool I was to allow you to spend time at the hospital. Giving blood was bad enough, but now this. And – the boy – a videshi. You knew it wasn't our culture but – you helped him plant his *bijju* anyway!"

"Mother, it wasn't like that..." Sushila wanted to explain about the love and belonging and she wanted to tell her mother that it got out of hand and she didn't expect things would go as far as they did. She wanted to find words to describe the bond she shared with Matt, and the tenderness. But her mother was quick to speak her mind, and the story unfolded in a different way.

"I don't want to know what it was like. If I knew you were going to get pregnant at the age of nineteen, I wouldn't have bothered sending you to school," said her mother. "Why did you bother to learn English?"

"You admit that my father was a married man. You are not an example of chastity yourself," retorted Sushila.

"I did not raise you to be a rundi."

"Why do you talk to me that way? If you don't want me for your daughter, go get somebody else."

It seemed as though the argument would never end. It was punctuated by bouts of nausea. Sushila was having morning sickness, unable to hold anything down. She was desperate to avoid the topic – but it was impossible. The vomiting weakened her ability to defend herself. But the morning of disappointment and recrimination continued.

That night, her mother went into the puja room. Sushila never heard her mother weep before then. Lost in the recrimination, Sushila wanted to tell her mother about the new part of her spiritual life she had found, with the guidance of her ishta devi, because she had so many questions about becoming a woman in this new way. But hearing her mother cry was like the closing of a door.

One week later, her mother brought her to Uncle Ranjit's house to meet Captain Gurung. He was home for the celebration of Dasain festival. He was posted as a Gurkha in UK. Captain Mahendra Gurung was the son of Uncle Ranjit's sister.

"We have arranged your marriage. The ceremony will take place tomorrow." Captain Gurung smiled and bowed as he shook her hand. She thought his gaze lingered over her body too much, and she could not look him in the eye. Everyone knew why she was getting married. Sushila cried that night. This was not the wedding she planned. Maya Ke Hola, the song, now had new meaning. *What is love?*

Her new mother-in-law was quiet on the wedding day and tried to be friendly. *I hate the way she looks at me.*

The wedding night was another matter. In high school, somebody once whispered to Sushila that all Gurkha soldiers had paid for sex with prostitutes in foreign countries. Captain Gurung had never been married, but she was sure he was not a virgin, just by the way he looked at her. Sushila looked in the bathroom mirror as she prepared to join him in the bedroom. She cherished the idea of losing her innocence to Matt, and she couldn't bear the thought that now, the Captain might compare her with some prostitute in Hong Kong. She spent an hour to adjust her makeup.

Sushila finally came out of the bathroom, quaking like a leaf. She lay down, on her side, facing away from him, curled up in a ball. He was tender and patient at first, then on the third night of married life, he decided to get it over with, in hopes that things would improve with time.

She lay awake afterwards and cried.

Part 2: Gurkha Camp at Church Crookham Hampshire, The United Kingdom –1999

Once more, she looked at the wedding photo. There she sat with the red and green bangles and the sindoor of a married woman. He was fifteen years older than his bride, and in the photo he sat erect befitting a lifetime of disciplined service as a mercenary soldier for Her Majesty, Elizabeth the Second, Queen of England.

Even now, she was only 21-years old. *Maybe there is time to become the person who would please him, after all.* Then a more realistic thought: *My body may be here, but my mind belongs to the Goddess. Nobody can own my thoughts.*

Then Sushila's gaze moved to the small shrine that held a photo of her mother, trying to feel her mother's spirit even though she was far away. She thought of the puja room in Beni, and she meditated to the Goddess, a silent thought to feel the peace and serenity she used to feel in Beni. *There are others who live with less than you have, but they are happy.* She thought back to her mother's visit when Arjun was born and wished that her mother were here now in the U.K. She wished that she could have friends, any friends at all, but the Captain was suspicious of the other wives on the Gurkha post. "They are of low caste and not adequate to the station of the wife of a Gurkha officer," he would say.

The minutes clicked by and turned into hours. She looked out the window to a damp English evening. Outside it was dark, the trees were leafless and the grass was dead. No stars were visible. She double-checked everything that was already checked. She checked to make sure the phone was working and whether there was some message she might have missed. No messages. She looked at her husband's liquor cabinet and was tempted to pour a drink for herself, to surrender to her fate and allow it to unfold into the future, but she thought of Arjun and couldn't bear the idea of what her son's life would be like if his mother abandoned him. *I will be responsible.* And she refused to give the Captain another reason to shout, another reason to lash out like a wild animal. The Captain had rejected Arjun and did not hide his feelings about the boy.

Nowadays, Sushila made love willingly. *Our body is what we have. We only experience the world through this body.* She used her body to develop a sense of focus and then to achieve that sense of release into great bliss. She knew that this came from within her. She gave thanks to the Goddess, because she could only find it when she spent the day meditating with Vajrayogini. Her body was with Captain Gurung, but during the act of lovemaking, Sushila would dream that it was her blond lover from USA that held her so close. She dreamed that Matt whispered words of love and encouragement to her. A *Dakini* would occupy her body and transport her to that land of bliss, where a clear blue sky shone over everything and she was speechless with delight.

Sushila looked in the mirror and pictured the time that she saw Matt's reflection as he stood behind her. She could call up the memory, but she was worried that she would forget his face. She worried that Captain Gurung might know what she was thinking when she brushed her hair. These days, the Captain had lost his enthusiasm to make love, and she wondered if he was faithful. *I created this life, myself*, she thought. *I will not allow his anger to rule my life.*

She knelt in front of the small puja altar and contemplated the image of the Goddess that occupied the central spot. She lit some incense and meditated on patience. *Angry people are there to teach us patience.* This did not seem to console her. *I will be patient.*

Eight o'clock came and she put Arjun to bed, dressing him in a fresh napkin, singing to him, and telling him a story. She looked at Arjun's face and hands. He was much lighter skinned than she was, like his father. There was something about his eyes that kept his father's face alive in Sushila's mind. She stroked his cheek as she said, "Maya garnchu." He was a good boy. He did not ask for this life.

At nine PM, there was a stumbling at the door. She noticed the slight lurch and the need to put a hand on the wall to be steady. She did not need to be close to know that there was alcohol on the Captain's breath. His eyes were red.

This time he did not lash out at her physically, he just muttered something under his breath. He glared. She returned his hard gaze. He hung up his jacket. Neither spoke. He went to bed without eating. This was a small victory. One more day had passed. She lay down next to him and waited for morning.

Deep inside, Sushila knew that it would never stop. *The Buddha tells us that we are here to learn from all persons, even from those who are angry and who hurt us.*

One night there was rain on the windowpane and Captain Gurung was late. Instead of a lurching at the door and the scratching of a key trying to find the lock, there was a polite knock that roused her as she rested her head on the kitchen table. The police came to tell her that her husband was dead. His motorcycle collided head-on with a truck on a wet road. She was silent at the news, leaving the policeman confused. Sushila knew she was supposed to cry but she could not. *I will not miss the shouting; I will not miss the punishing silence. My body will be my own. I will not be a prisoner,* she thought.

She laughed, a high-pitched nervous laugh. *My body was always my own. I belong to myself, I always have. And to the Goddess.*

She told the bewildered policeman, "Yes, it's terrible."

After the policeman left, she went to the mirror. *I am a widow now,* she thought. *The lowest of the low.* She took the red and green glass bangles from her wrists, breaking them and throwing the pieces in the trash with the same sense of reverence she would have used to collect pieces of orange rind after a snack. She went to her clothing drawer, and found the little box of mementos from Nepal. In it was a faded note from her time in Beni, the only proof that there once was another life for her. She had not dared to look in that box for a long time. She unfolded the note.

Kali —

I didn't have time to say goodbye, but I love you. Come to USA. Doctor Ranjit knows how to contact me.

Love, Matt

Now she wept. *I have had so many lives, and they have all gone from me. I have been left to my fate. Nobody has the time to say goodbye, but they still leave me. That is my karma.*

She was a widow at the age of twenty-one. Sushila wondered what to do now and thought about going back to Beni. She wondered about the widows of the town, women who retreated to the edge of life, invisible to most, always in the back row. *Is this my karma? To watch others have the life I wanted?* She wiped the tears and rejected the picture. *I am still alive, and Arjun is now safe. I have made a passage to some new land, one more place I never thought I would go.*

A few days later Ruth from Plymouth came to visit. Ruth was the sister of Sara the Christian missionary doctor who worked with Ranjit. Ruth relayed the message that everyone in Beni sent their love. Also, a job waited for her at the hospital. They were planning to open a hospice for women who were living with AIDS, and Sushila would be just the person to run it. Sara invited Sushila to come back to Beni.

Sushila did not know what to do. Her time in UK was over. She could not separate her memories of Beni from her memories of her mother, who passed while she was gone. She missed her mother and thought back to the time when they were close, before she became a woman. Maybe things would be better in Beni.

Beni, Nepal – 1999

Sushila resumed the daily routine of life in Beni. The neighborhood well was only fifty meters from the house, and the day began with a trip there to get the day's water, carrying the jug on her hip. She remembered all the trips to the well with her mother, who used to stop and talk with the shopkeeper's wife and the other neighbors. It was a deep well, and the inside was cool, lined with green moss. Together they would pull the rope to bring up the water. During busy times waiting at the well, the women laid their jugs out in a row. When Sushila's mother was alive, she could look at each jug and tell the name of the owner, though none were labeled.

"Take this Pepsi bottle with us, it is just the size for a young girl to carry."

"It is the lot of women to carry water every day," said the women at the well. "Soon you will carry your brothers and sisters and babies of your own, on your hip."

"Shush," said her mother, "Sushila will not have brothers and sisters. And she will be a great scholar. She will not live by carrying water every day."

Now I am the mother, she thought, looking at Arjun. *We will play our game pulling on the rope to bring the bucket up from the bottom of the well, the way my mother played with me.* In the puja room, the picture of her mother was in a place of honor on a shelf next to Vajrayogini. Arjun was too young to carry anything, but he walked behind her, holding a fistful of her skirt. The women of the neighborhood whispered when she approached. *Widow. No husband. Widow. Widow. Widow.* They always stopped when she approached.

Sushila prayed to the family Goddess, and looked again at the picture of her mother. *O mother, help me find a new sanga, new friends, here.*

She decided not to let the women bother her. Sushila devoted her time to the work of starting the AIDS hospice. Sara's secretary Bimla helped her with childcare and soon they were friends. Bimla always greeted her with a smile and a kind word. Sushila's friends were the women of the hospice and the nurses. Sara always took time to talk and dandle Arjun on her knee.

2002

As years passed, a time came when Arjun was old enough to carry his own water back to the house. She picked out a Pepsi bottle that would be the right size. "I am so proud of what a hard worker you are. You will be the man of the house."

The second day of helping his mother, they encountered the dog. It was an average-sized dog. Normally this dog lay near the shade of the temple in the Bajaar, the one where the tree grew out of the roof. Nobody owned the dog, it was just there, hanging around the butcher shop, where the butcher gave bones and offal to the neighborhood dogs. Normally this dog was mellow. This day, the dog jumped up, ran to Arjun and bared its teeth with a fierce growl. Arjun was frightened and dropped his water bottle. She shooed the dog away then carried him home.

He had a bad dream about dogs that night. She brought him to her bed and held him close.

"Here is the secret of dogs," she whispered. "The dog in your dream was not a real dog. That was an imaginary dog. Dreams are like TV. You can change the channel on a dream, just like changing the channel on a TV. And in your dream, you can control the dream dog. The fear of the dog is worse than the actual dog," she told him. "So it is with the actual dog. We can tame that dog. You are in charge of your fear, it is not in charge of you."

In the puja room, she prayed; *O Buddha, thank you for teaching me how to deal with fear. I will teach my son the ways of Buddha, dharma and sanga*

She told him a bedtime story about a boy and a dog. In the story, the boy fed the dog until it depended on him.

The next day he stayed home. Later that morning she went to the butcher shop to buy some tidbits of meat. Every day, she supervised while Arjun gave the dog a treat. Soon he could give the treat himself. After a few weeks of this, the dog wagged its tail every time it saw Arjun approach, and began to follow him around

She named the dog "Lychee." *Prickly on the outside, sweet on the inside.*

Sushila took Arjun to the temple on the parade ground and showed him the image of Bhairav over the door. "Bhairav looks like a mean dog. Bhairav guards every temple. But that does not mean that he wants you to stay away. It only means that he wants you to release your fear before you cross the door and go in. It will be beautiful inside."

Now there was always a bedtime story about the adventures of Lychee. And the life of Buddha. And Green Tara. And Milarepa, and Dharma, and every story she ever heard from childhood.

Finally, Arjun joined her again on the trips to the well every morning. Now he was the one who fed the dog. Some mornings the dog waited at Sushila's house, wagging its tail when they came to the door. When the Tihar

Festival came, Arjun gave the dog a tika and put a garland of marigolds around its neck.

"You are a hard worker and Lychee will guard you wherever you go, even if you can't see him," she told Arjun.

Bimla told her about Santoshi Mata, the Goddess of Satisfaction, and gave her the little storybook to read. *She is a Hindu Goddess, but she is a sister of all Goddesses,* thought Sushila. *The story is about a man who goes away from his rightful home only to come back.* She bought the picture for ten rupees, and placed it in the puja room. *O Vajrayogini, do not be jealous. I need to think about your sister-Goddess now and again.* Sushila avoided eating or drinking anything sour on Friday. At the end of the sixteen weeks, her wishes were not fulfilled. So she started another sixteen week cycle of fasting. After the second cycle, she decided to continue weekly fasting with no end date. Every Friday, she read the story and offered the puja.

Ranjit took an interest in the boy and taught Arjun to play Bag-Chaal. He was always very formal around Sushila, and she wondered if he would ever be friendly now that her mother was no more. Arjun told her he wanted to be like Ranjit when he grew up.

At night, in her bed, she dreamed that Santoshi Mata would fulfill her wish: *My lover will return from USA. Someday I will again have the joy of a man to share my life.*

March 2004 – Boston, The Massachusetts General Hospital

Monday morning. Matt sat with a cup of coffee, awaiting morning conference with the surgical team where he was doing a fellowship. One of the other surgical residents handed Matt *The New York Times*. It was refolded to highlight one particular story from the world news.

"Isn't this where you were?"

Matt read:

NEPALI STRIFE KILLS HUNDREDS

KATMANDU, Nepal, March 21— *Nepalese government forces and Maoist rebels have fought one of their fiercest battles since the collapse of a cease-fire more than seven months ago, officials said Sunday. At least 18 police officers and soldiers were killed, while the army said it had killed hundreds of insurgents. Hundreds of rebels entered Beni, 168 miles west of Katmandu, the capital, around midnight and battled security forces for 12 hours before reinforcements chased them away. The rebels attacked the Beni jail, bombed the district administration office and ignited the police station.*

He refolded it to look at the front-page headline. It seemed as though every story on the front page was about the war in Iraq.

I hope everyone is okay in Nepal, he thought. *I have to write them a letter.* He looked at the Nepal story again. *Just one paragraph? That's it?* Then he flipped back to the Iraq stories.

There were a dozen articles, covering every aspect of the escalating war in Iraq. He skimmed them and re-read the article about Beni.

Matt wondered about Sushila. *In Doctor Ranjit's letter that said she was married, I think he wrote that she moved to U.K. - Thank God. I wish I kept in touch with her, but Doctor Ranjit was so emphatic about how happy Sushila was in her new life and that I should not interfere. She's married now. I wonder if she remembers me.* He remembered how soft her hair was as she held her ear to his chest. He remembered that one afternoon of passion that overtook them. He remembered the way he felt when she looked at him and smiled. He remembered talking with her about going to college together. The discussion about making a life together. Even today, he pictured what it would have been like to listen to her laughter across the kitchen table. *The love of my life. Kali - the sexiest woman I ever met. The standard by which everyone is judged. A voice like the singing of birds at dawn. I wish there was a photo of her. I still think of her when I see a butterfly.*

Then he remembered the stinging letter from Ranjit. *Stay away from her now.*

Don't kid yourself, Matt. She may have been the love of your life, and there hasn't been another woman like her since that day. Not one. But she got away. And she's giving all her love to some other guy.

He closed his eyes and pictured what their life would have been. After a long day at work, she'd meet him at the door and they would talk and laugh, recounting the day with humor and affection, creating the kind of safe zone only two lovers could share. She was the kind of woman who'd sneak up behind you when you were studying and rub your shoulders. Or maybe dance to the radio in the living room when a favorite tune came on. Maybe even have kids together, and she'd be a great mother.

But she's sharing every bit of all that with somebody else. Not me.

Son of a bitch. He cursed his life.

It was time to start the schedule for the day.

On the scale of things, the battle in Nepal seemed manageable. And it was already over. The end was known. One small village in the foothills of the Himalaya. *Surely, the hospital was a safe zone. Isn't there some kind of Geneva Convention that applies to hospitals?*

Beni, Nepal – January 2004

Harald and Malena Svenson were a married team, two doctors from Finland, on a three-year mission commitment to do surgery and orthopedics. Their three blond-haired children ran underfoot at the videshi gatherings, squealing with delight as they played hide-and-seek in a forest of grownup legs. The family frequently shared dinner at the Guest House with the team, accompanied by the Finnish missionary nanny who home-schooled the children.

In October 2002, the King of Nepal disbanded parliament and declared that he would assume all authority in the country. Widespread protests shook the country. The political tension grew, and the team often discussed the possible impact. Harald and Malena grew quiet at these times, exchanging ominous looks and shaking their heads. One evening in January, they announced their decision to depart. Within a week.

"We hope the team will understand. We have prayed about this decision and offered it up to God. We just can't take the risk for our children."

Ranjit replied, "I did my residency in Belfast during the troubles between Catholics and Protestants, and every day we passed through many checkpoints. The gunmen always asked 'are you Catholic or Protestant?' and I would reply, ' I'm a Buddhist,' which always made them stop and think. Then they would let us through. Only one time did a militiaman follow up and ask, 'are you a Catholic Buddhist or a Protestant Buddhist?' but he still let us through. What I am trying to say is, nobody in Nepal will target you as a foreigner." Ranjit was certain that he had applied every available power of persuasion.

"Everyone in Beni has been wonderful to us. But you have told us of the small battle you call the shootout, and we are worried that if a bigger battle happens, our children will be at risk. If something happened to our children, it would break Malena's heart," said Harald.

For once, Ranjit's charm did not produce the desired result.

Sara found herself thinking back to some vague time in the past. *The 'Good Old Days' were never so good*, she told herself. *You are smart enough to know that.* In the old days, there were ten missionary doctors, with children and a mission school.

Sara remembered the Svensons and the other Scandinavians on a midsummer's eve, children dancing around a maypole with flowers in their hair and then the whole mission community enjoying cider around a bonfire in the evening. The circle became smaller as families left, not to be replaced, until there was no bonfire.

Sara remembered the weekly prayer evening just for the missionaries; now Malena and Sara would no longer share time to bake desserts for it. The prayer meetings would continue with her Nepali friends, but she would speak in Nepali not English.

Sara counted out in her mind the seats at three tables when the whole group shared a meal. Now there would be just one table. It was going to be quiet at dinner.

Sara thought of long conversations in the sauna on cold winter evenings. From the very beginning of the hospital, the Scandinavians built it and stocked the firewood. Now the sauna would be padlocked.

There would be no missionary children, and another padlock would hang on the door to the school building. No special plays or recitations. The swing set would be idle.

Now if she set up the tea service, there would just be Bimla and herself. Maybe Sushila. Only a few cups and saucers to wash.

The sweet chaos of preschool children underfoot at every celebration. To be replaced by order and solemnity. I can hear the silence now.

And who will replace the Svensons? The need for expertise was great. The local Christian community embraced foreigners. Beni was enthusiastic about the Good News. But none of these would put Beni on the list of pakka locations for recruiting. *Without a school, nobody will come.*

Sara told herself to focus on orderly things that needed to be done, gestures to be made in gratitude for service to the Lord. Sara took the time to organize a sendoff.

On the following Saturday morning, at the Emmaus Christian Church, time was set aside to say a proper goodbye to the Svenson family. Sara hit upon the idea for the praise band to play *Finlandia,* the Finnish national anthem. The guitars kicked in, and it almost resembled the intended tune, though the singers onstage overlaid a few Bollywood-style harmonies when they began the lyrics, adding the exotic element of mystery. It was Sara's idea to sing the alternate lyrics from the Lutheran Christian hymnal.

Be still, my soul; the Lord is on thy side;
Bear patiently the cross of grief or pain;
Leave to thy God to order and provide;
In every change He faithful will remain.
Be still, my soul; thy best, thy heavenly, Friend
Through thorny ways leads to a joyful end.

Be still, my soul; thy God doth undertake
To guide the future as He has the past.
Thy hope, thy confidence, let nothing shake;
All now mysterious shall be bright at last.
Be still, my soul; the waves and winds still know
His voice who ruled them while He dwelt below.

Be still, my soul, though dearest friends depart
And all is darkened in the vale of tears;
Then shalt thou better know His love, His heart,
Who comes to soothe thy sorrows and thy fears.
Be still, my soul; thy Jesus can repay
From His own fullness all He takes away.

Be still, my soul; the hour is hastening on
When we shall be forever with the Lord,
When disappointment, grief, and fear are gone,
Sorrow forgot, love's purest joys restored.
Be still, my soul; when change and tears are past,
All safe and blessed we shall meet at last.

Though dearest friends depart, she thought.

When she chose the hymn, she only skimmed the words. Even though she knew it was coming, when Sara reached that line and sang it out loud, she thought, *that's me they were writing about. Somebody knew I was going to need strength. Somebody knew I was going to be alone. This song itself is a prayer.* The words came out. Sara's voice cracked. Her singing stopped.

Though dearest friends depart...

When they go, they will take with them every bit of fun I have had for five years. Bimla is a dear friend, but she is not a substitute. It doesn't matter whether there are ten thousand other women in this town. I just don't know if I can cope with being lonely. Sara blinked back tears. *Chin up,* she said to herself.

The sending-away service moved to a climax. Here, Harald and Malena sat in two chairs, with children on their lap or standing nearby, and everyone crowded around as the Svensons were lifted up to the Lord. Members of the community offered prayers, starting with the pastor, some in English and some in Nepali. Sara's prayer was for the Svensons to find peace in the transition and to know that they had served God.

A reception followed. People talked about the Svensons, but they also looked at her from a distance. *One more aspect of being the last.* After a while, one of the men asked Sara if she was going to leave as well.

"No. I will be here. I have placed my faith in the Lord. He will provide." *Yes, I will stay. I don't have any place else to go.* Sara reminded herself not to be selfish.

The Svensons gave their furniture to anybody who claimed it. When they were finally ready, they showed up at the Land Rover with just one day pack apiece. There, the family was greeted by Sara and everyone else for the final sendoff. The children waved from the back of the Land Rover as it disappeared down the road.

Two surgeons taken off the roster on short notice, the civil war is escalating, and no further help in sight. Oh God, she prayed. *We praise you for your wisdom in bringing us here to serve these people with our hospital. We can't do it without you, Lord. Be present with us. We seek your guidance. You have given us a burden; please give us the strength to carry it. Please God, I am afraid of the dark. Send us your Light. We're not asking for superhuman strength; but just enough strength to get through this. Even when dearest friends depart…*

February 2004 – Beni, Nepal

What the horrors of war are, no one can imagine. They are not wounds and blood and fever, spotted and low, or dysentery, chronic and acute, cold and heat and famine. They are intoxication, drunken brutality, demoralization and disorder on the part of the inferior… jealousies, meanness, indifference, selfish brutality on the part of the superior.

– Florence Nightingale

Sara looked at the young backpacker in the exam room and smiled. An embroidered yarmulke floated on his curly hair. A thick beard with long curly sideburns. He wore hiking boots and fatigue pants. *Israeli Defense Force. Newly discharged from compulsory service. On sabbatical. He can't be called back if he's out of the country.*

"Shalom," he said, "My name is David."

"Shalom, Da-veed," mimicking his pronunciation as she laughed, "We haven't seen that many Israeli vagabonds this year. What can I do for you?"

The young man suffered from a nagging cough that wouldn't go away, and the treatment was easy to prescribe. Sara reassured him that it was simple bronchitis and not pneumonia.

"I coughed like this when I was in Gaza last year," he said. "I just finished the Annapurna Circuit and I was hoping to get back to USA for Burning Man."

"You are certainly getting experiences checked off the list. It is an honor and privilege to vicariously enjoy the eternal exuberance of youth," Sara said with a smile. "Been to Macchu Picchu yet? Will you run with the bulls in Spain?"

"I'm definitely going to Campostela this summer. I just think I need to get out of here."

Sara felt a bit defensive. "Are you talking about Beni, or Nepal in general?"

He looked at her and said, "Beni. The Notebook is full of warnings. Don't you know?"

"Know? About the Notebook? Of course I know about the Notebook." The Notebook was an underground system used by young Israeli vagabonds to share useful tips and to alert each other when travelling the world.

"Does Beni still have a Notebook? I thought that today's youth would have all migrated to the internet by now."

"No, in Beni it's still written by hand. You wouldn't be able to read it unless you understood Hebrew. Anyway, most of my friends decided to stay away because of the attack."

"Here? In Beni? There's been no attack."

"There will be."

"I beg your pardon?"

He said, "I love Nepal but I dislike violence. I did village patrol in the West Bank when I was in IDF and I hated it when the Palestinians threw stones. Riot response sucks. We often deployed tear gas and rubber bullets."

Sara bit her lip. "How can you speak with such certainty? Regarding the attack?"

"I'm Israeli. I was in the IDF. We know such things."

He left and Sara reflected on the trekkers. True, the spring 2004 trekking season was slow compared to previous years. In past years, the number of trekkers grew each week, like a wave gaining in height before crashing on shore. This year, the flow of trekkers dripped, like water from a broken faucet. *Maybe Dave was right. Maybe they do know such things.*

Ranjit went to the weekly lunch meeting of the Lions Club. All the men around the table worked in the tourism industry. The guides and the owner of the river rafting company greeted him.

"We are losing our place as a trekking destination," lamented a hotel owner.

"What is this about the Israelis staying away?" Ranjit asked.

"It's not just the Israelis, it's the whole group of young people from the West who are staying away. The bandits aren't helping the situation," said another.

"What bandits?" asked Ranjit.

"The Maoists have set up checkpoints on all the routes where they extort their own trekking fee at gunpoint. It's getting so common that the guides are calling them 'Mao-bandhis.' Why, the bandits have taken to giving receipts for the money they take."

Thul Pun, one of the guides, interrupted. "The Maoists are doing no such thing," he said, "I've been guiding treks, and I have been to those checkpoints. Those guys pretend to be Maoists. They wear uniforms so people will blame the Maoists and PLA, but in truth, they have no political motivation. They use the money to buy food. Call them 'khou-bandhis.' "

They all laughed at the joke, Thul most of all, showing the gap between his front teeth. Heads nodded around the table.

"I admit, the effect is the same, no matter who is doing it. People are choosing to go elsewhere," Thul said. "Who can blame them?"

In early March, there was bad news on the front pages of the *Kathmandu Post*. The Maoists attacked Jajarkot, the major town of the Rukum district. The police station was set on fire after a street battle involving hundreds of troops in uniform. The PLA destroyed the air control tower and left the airport runway full of deep craters. The PLA did not occupy Jajarkot but kept moving.

It was still the beginning of trekking season, and the air was clear and crisp. Daily temperatures were cool and most everyone in the town wore a sweater. At night, the stars were out, and the entire Milky Way twittered above. Delightful weather for a trek. Every evening at the Guest House, dinnertime talk turned to the rumors of what the Maoists would do after the Jajarkot attack.

Meeting the Maoist

Sara and Ranjit shared what Dave and Thul said. Everyone shared his or her opinion.

"The Maoists have no reason to come here," said Ranjit. "They will go south, get on the Trans-Nepal Highway, and go straight through the Terai, laying siege to Bharatpur and Hetauda."

"Why Hetauda?" asked Sara.

"Because Kathmandu is deep in the mountains and depends on just two highways to be supplied with everything. Food, petrol, machinery – everything. These are the only land routes to Kathmandu, and if the Maoists can keep a roadblock there, it will paralyze the city," he replied.

Ram said, "Nonsense. We are in Asia, and though the Maoists and their People's Liberation Army have nothing to do with the Chinese, surely they have read *The Art of War* by Sun Tzu."

Ranjit rolled his eyes. "Did you study Sun Tzu at Saint Javier's School? When does a doctor in Beni, Nepal, have time for such intellectual meandering?"

"Ranjit dai. There is more to life than surgery. He who can read is able to transport himself around the world at will. If war were not so evil, Sun Tzu would be acknowledged as a great Buddha. A thousand years ago Sun Tzu wrote that is it folly to fight on flat ground."

Ram wagged his finger in the air as he spoke, drawing a map in the air. "To go south, the PLA would have to cross six mountains ranges up-over-and-down, and then when they arrived at the Terai, they would be out in the open flat ground where the RNA helicopter gunships will find them like grazing goats and shoot them at leisure."

He shot an imaginary gun when he said this. "The Maoists want the Royal Nepal Army to think that the Terai is their destination, but they will keep an element of surprise."

He continued, "There is a straight line from Rukum to Kathmandu. They must send their army across Jalja-la Pass, which is more than three thousand meters in elevation, but then the route follows a river valley. Everyone goes that way. We happen to be located directly in that path. No matter how well armed, the PLA must stay in the hills where the terrain is favorable to fight the helicopters. They can't drive here, but they can walk here with more ease than if they tried to trek to the King's Highway in the Terai."

Through this, Ranjit sat in rapt attention. Then he pantomimed Ram's imaginary map, using his finger to draw a different diagram in the air, impossibly complicated. He ended with the "ke garne" gesture. The team laughed.

"Stick to anesthesia. It is more profitable than cartography," said Ranjit. Ram laughed the most of anyone in the room.

Sara said, "The whole western edge of this town is hemmed in by a bluff, and the hill across the Myagdi River commands the whole town. Whoever made Beni the district capital was not thinking about the possibility that anyone would ever attack us. Until now I have thought that we were simply too remote. There is nothing here worth taking. Quite simple, really. Now I am not so sure."

Ram said, "You have a point. We are at the bottom of a deep river valley. The PLA used mortars for the battle at Rukum. We are sitting ducks."

Ranjit said, "If you are correct, we are fortunate that Jalja-la pass is ten thousand feet in elevation. It's still covered in deep snow. Until it opens, no army will get from Rukum to Beni on foot."

"Maybe this is God's way of giving us time to plan," said Sara.

The next morning she asked the maintenance crew to repaint the large Red Cross on a white background that graced the roof of the largest building. She also composed a letter to a worldwide faith-based sending organization, asking them to find a surgeon.

The next evening, the team talked about whether they would need to take sides. Despite many incidents over the years, the hospital always treated everybody. Sara recalled the time years back, just as the last six kilometers of paved road to Beni were finished. Within a week, the new bus park nearby was the target of a bombing. Six casualties came to the hospital, and a police patrol pursued the fleeing PLA fighters. That same night, a group of armed Maoists came to the door with two wounded, as if they were wandering holy men seeking a handout of rice. On that occasion, they posted an armed sentry while Ranjit operated, then refused to allow their comrades to stay overnight. They grew anxious and demanded some IV supplies and antibiotics. The Maoists loaded these into a doka. They disappeared into the darkness and the two wounded men were whisked away on motorbikes.

Other times, the Army would send a patrol looking for Maoists. The Army always made their presence seem more ominous than it needed to be, rifles at the ready, going from ward to ward in groups of three or four, asking questions of patients and ignoring anything that the doctors told them, shouting orders as they went.

"When was the shootout? I can't seem to recall the date," Sara said.

Ram piped in, "How could you forget? That was right after the attacks of Nine-Eleven in New York, the day the police decided to lay in wait a block from the hospital, knowing that the Maoists would bring their wounded here after an ambush." He continued, "We were very lucky neither side was able to prepare for that one. I am glad they have not tried it again. Let's hope both sides stay away from us."

After dinner that evening, Ranjit took Sara aside. "Call him and ask."

"The Maoist? Are you serious?"

"Yes. Call the Maoist."

Sara replied, "He knows that I know who he is. But what if there's a battle? I'm worried. What if he decides to kill me? I only found out who he was by accident."

"He would have killed you by now," Ranjit replied. "If you were going to turn him in, you would have done that by now, as well. You have already collaborated with him simply by not handing him over to the Police so they could kill him as soon as he was in custody. They have orders to shoot suspected Maoists on sight."

"But I have never talked about it openly with him. Not once."

"Sara, are you waiting for an invitation to tea? You British really are too formal."

He continued, "Surely the People's Liberation Army will not seek retribution on a videshi. Nobody will shoot a Christian missionary. And maybe we can learn something that will help us."

Sara agreed and arranged to meet The Maoist at the Hotel Himshikhar in the Bajaar.

"What can you tell me about the attack?" she asked, "We need to know. Especially since there will be casualties."

He looked at her.

He took off his hat, rubbed his bald head, and spat on the ground.

He lightly pinched the skin of his neck over the voice box, rolling it between two fingers, and then blew on his hand through pursed lips.

Sara recognized the body language; it was the gesture the Nepalis often made when they were contemplating whether to spare someone from news that might be unpleasant.

"Doctor Sara," he said, "You have been in Nepal many years but you are still a Westerner. There are formalities to be observed. That is a very direct question. Who told you that I would be an expert on these matters? I am not in control of the plans of the PLA any more than I am in charge of the weather. Prachandra does not tell me his plans."

"It will help us to plan."

"I cannot confirm or deny. Is anybody ever neutral in these matters?"

"But surely you must have heard rumors."

"Doctor Sara, the past is gone and tomorrow may never come. My rumors are no better than your rumors. The only sure knowledge is that we must struggle to make a better Nepal. You know my wife. You know my daughters. We all want to create a Nepal where women are treated as equals."

You are speaking in riddles and it's clear you are toying with me, she thought.

She reported her conversation to Ranjit and Ram. "Here we are, talking about this as if it's a clinical problem on par with cholera, or TB."

"All we can do is the best we can do. If there is a battle here, we need to work as hard as we can, and put all emotions aside," said Ranjit. "It is our karma."

"Time to contemplate Bhairav," said Ram. "If we allow our fear to overwhelm us, we will surely suffer. We must overcome our fear."

"Easy to say. Some fears are entirely logical. My days in Belfast have been coming back to me. I was lucky in those days. I want to remain neutral." said Ranjit.

Ram took Ranjit aside. "Ranjit dai, I will go to Sushila's house and make sure she has a plan in case of attack. We need to be prepared."

"Thank you. That boy is the light of my life. Do what you can."

Early March 2004 – Rukum District, Far Western Nepal

Comrade Barood took chiya and brought the glass cup to the pavilion to survey his work. *There it was*, as he lit the lantern in the room. *The model of the battlefield.* The model was based on his own photos of Beni, and he was proud of it. Comrade Barood looked again at the sand that was sculpted into mountains, the little toy bridges, the little toy houses, and especially, the little toy version of the Army Post, the CDO and the Police Headquarters down by the toy Tundikhel. *This is a mandala of future success,* he thought. *I like Beni. Someday I will return there in peace.*

The rivers were painted in blue; there was the river junction. The model showed the ridges and the approach routes in every direction around the town. After this attack, this model would be dismantled. The sand would be shoveled away and the toy buildings would be recycled and used to create a model of the next military objective. Comrade Barood wished that it would be made permanent somehow, as a piece of Nepal history that would show the skill and glorious victory of the People's Liberation Army. *We will tell the tale of this battle when the People's Parliament meets in Singha Durbar,* he thought.

He laughed about the fat hotel owners who only knew him as an occasional trekking guide. *Comrade Barood is a name I like much more than Thul Pun,* he said to himself, *it is how history will remember me.* He thought back to joining the latest trekking group and worrying about leaving his handgun behind, knowing that if anyone in Beni suspected he was Maoist cadre, he might be shot on sight or tortured. He accepted that danger, though he was glad his family in Kathmandu didn't know about his role in the People's Liberation Army. *They think I am still taking further study in London. This will help Nepal far more than a doctorate in engineering could ever do. And I am using my skills as a teacher.*

Thul thought about the Maoist leader in Beni who guided him as he reconnoitered the town and said to himself, *there is a true hero. He takes risks every day. That ridiculous hat he wore and the vanity of covering his bald head.*

Revolutionary music played while the soldiers gathered for the briefing. Comrade Barood sang along with the words:

In one night the earth is shaken by the tempest of struggle; slums and barrios have been awakened by the Great People's War. By shaking heaven and earth, the bugle of the Great People's War has sounded. While slums and barrios are awakened, enemies are uneased. Hoisting the invisible flag of Marxist-Leninist-Maoism, the people have arisen like waves of the seas!

The music finished. He started the briefing. "We will strike a blow against U.S. imperialism. You are the bringers of justice and prosperity to the people of Nepal! A death is only a death and a victory is immortal!" Then he began the day's lesson on tactics.

"Think of Beni as a triangle, with the right angle where the rivers meet. The brick temple at the parade ground is the first corner of the triangle. The longest side curves around the base of the mountain. Here are the rivers, too cold and deep to cross. Here is the bluff, too steep to climb. We will put teams above the bluff. A small detachment will guard the only road to the top. It will be impossible for them to counterattack our teams atop the mountain."

The soldiers nodded, and Comrade Barood saw that this group was mostly women fighters. "The sapper teams will go in first to lay the bombs against the police barracks wall. We will achieve the element of surprise. Then we attack in force."

He pointed to the police barracks right near the parade ground. "The main force from the north will get to the old Shiva Temple with the large tree growing out of the roof. Use that as a landmark. Don't get caught in the parade ground, you will be in the open. We will have a mortar team trained on the parade ground in case the helicopters come.

"The police are not as heavily armed as the Royal Nepal Army. The wall of the police barracks is eight-feet high, with guard towers and barbed wire on top. It encloses a large courtyard with four buildings in it. We will breach the wall and sweep the area with fire to prevent the police from going between buildings.

"On the second point of the triangle is the Royal Nepali Army garrison. Two hundred men in the barracks at the west end of town, where the mountain squeezes the river. We will rain fire down on them from above. We will attack them, too, but it is mainly to hold them down and prevent them from helping the police.

"Over the past few weeks, our friends in the town secretly pre-positioned a cache of forty-thousand rounds of ammunition, as well as grenades and bombs. We hid those in a house near the police station. On the night of the battle, you will go there to get additional supplies.

"Do not kill the officers. We will take them hostage. They are more valuable that way. We intend to exchange them for our fighters the Army now holds as prisoners. The houses in Beni are made of stone and the people will stay inside.

"The ground forces who actually take the town will gather in the last of the three corners, the one that points north. Here is the bus park and the route to the Annapurna Circuit. The road to Jomsom. This end of the town is not guarded at all. They will never expect an attack to come from that corner."

The scale model of the north end of town was accurate. There were no walls, or any machine gun placements, or sentry posts. About a thousand troops, the main attacking force, would assemble there.

At each session, Comrade Barood said, "I will personally lead the group that attacks the town on foot. I pledge my life to this cause. Never forget your heritage of bravery. Not even the British could conquer Nepal. We will create a new Nepal and you will be proud of the day you helped win this glorious battle."

Just before the session ended, Comrade Barood and the fighters stood and gave the salute.

"Down with Monarchy and Feudalism!"

"Long Live People's War!"

"Political power grows from the barrel of a gun!"

Then he reminded them, "We will gather at this spot and attack from there." Everyone looked at the model and nodded their head. The end of the pointer stick landed squarely on the courtyard of the hospital.

March 20, 2004 – 10 pm

Red sky in morning, means blood has been spilled this night
– Nepali proverb

In winter, the sal tree planted in the rest spot at the hospital was bare of leaves. The circular stone wall around the tree, filled with soil, was like the ones along the roadsides where porters stopped to lay their burdens down while they took a break. Ranjit was the most frequent visitor here, smoking his pipe and looking at the stars through the skeletal branches on a brisk winter night.

At ten p.m., Sara joined him at his perch, watching as he pulled out his pipe and performed all the little steps to prepare a bowl of tobacco, under the tree. Nepali pop music played in the distance, a mournful *gajal, a* love song about separation and longing.

Ranjit was always approachable at those times, and Sara often stopped for a chat when she found him here. He was always considerate enough to sit downwind. Sara enjoyed the way his clothes carried a sort of manly scent, like earth turned over under mouldering leaves in autumn.

Sara started out very businesslike. "How are the road traffic victims?"

"One died in casualty, we treated four others. They were admitted. I actually like doing surgery on Saturday, it's not so busy here when the Bajaar is shut down."

Dogs barked in the distance, maybe a little more than usual, but still –not as much as other times, Sara thought.

She swatted the pipe smoke. "Rather disgusting habit."

"And I was just about to offer you some. That just leaves more for me I suppose," he replied. "I agree. It is disgusting and dirty. I learned how to smoke a pipe from the British in Belfast." He blew a smoke ring, "One of many bad habits I picked up there."

"Oh, dear." She laughed at the good-natured teasing. Ranjit was moody lately. *He wants to talk,* she thought. Sara would never admit that she thought of her father when she smelled pipe smoke, let alone that it was a pleasant memory. Somehow, it brought her back to family time around the coal stove in the evenings, her father reading the newspaper and reading the best bits aloud for her mother to enjoy with a cup of cocoa.

He was a true professional colleague. She thought back to when she first considered mission work, with only a vague idea of the people she was going to serve. In those days, she possessed an incomplete idea of their lives. Ranjit opened her eyes to the fact that many non-Christians were selfless and dedicated. He had his faults, to be sure. As a young man, he was a womanizer. But there was no doubt as to his dedication and skill. *He has helped me so much with Christian discernment*, she thought, *but he doesn't even know it. And he'd probably reject the term.*

Ranjit enjoyed these times as well. *It seems like only yesterday that she came here, but there have been so many things we shared. She and Ram are the last links to my youth. I never thought a woman doctor could be as good as a man. She makes all of us better at what we do.*

She wondered what he was thinking. *Don't think, just be.* Ranjit said it so often that Sara was automatically listening to the sound of a cuckoo in the distance. They sat as if they were part of the landscape.

Out of the darkness, two women in green uniforms came through the plaza, trotting as they carried on their shoulders the two ends of a bamboo pole with a weight suspended between them. They wore caps with a red star above the visor. This was unusual. *It might be a pig but this is not the right time of day*, thought Ranjit. *And that is a man's job.* A small gleam of silvery metal from the middle of the pole revealed a large pressure cooker suspended there, with two twisted wires hanging from it, bouncing with each step. Within a few seconds, four more teams of women came through with similar poles and similar weights. Each wore a camouflage cap with a red star on the front; some wore a kerchief over their mouth and nose.

After seven years of civil war, Ranjit and Sara were no longer capable of surprise, but both of their mouths hung open for a minute before Ranjit said, "Kettle bombs. They are starting the attack." The cookware was stuffed with explosives and possibly with small nuts and bolts to make shrapnel. *So much easier to make than the pipe bombs the IRA used*, Ranjit thought.

"I have dreaded this for two months," said Sara. "God help us."

"I was wrong. Beni is the objective after all." Ranjit looked up to the hills, knowing that mortar teams waited there for a signal and that soon, there would be a storm of flying metal in the town. *I can't see them. But they have to be there.* Ranjit stood and tapped his pipe against the sole of his shoe, releasing a small shower of embers to extinguish the tobacco. Sara felt a wave of nausea. *This is going to be very bad, very soon.*

"Not only is Beni the objective, but look – they are gathering right here," she said. "This is the worst possible scenario. What if they have a shootout right at the hospital and it's too late to mobilize the staff if they are not here already? Oh Ranjit, I feel sick."

"Sara, this is not the time to be afraid. We just have to step up to the wicket," he replied.

"Hurry then. You go get the mass casualty supplies, and I will alert the staff, " she said.

Before they could do anything, three Maoist soldiers approached, with weapons drawn.

"You are the doctors?" asked the one in charge. "You will stay right here. Give us your mobile phones."

Sara and Ranjit now stood while the crooked path between the hospital buildings filled with Maoist soldiers. The soldiers lined up according to assigned groups. Each fighter wore a kerchief tied over his or her mouth and nose, dampened, to protect against tear gas. A few carried large red flags with the hammer and sickle painted in white. *This is big. And they are staging it right here on our property. Amazing that they still use banners,* Ranjit thought. *The Irish Republican Army was never that formal.* Then, *The IRA would never gather in such a large group.* He thought back to the days of his medical residency in Belfast and the vicious civil war that took place the whole time. *To be a Buddhist on the sidelines while the Catholics and Protestants fought was a luxury he did not have here with Buddhists on both sides.* He thought about the nights of the bombings in Belfast. *Not again. Not here. We can't escape this. It's right here.*

In the dark, he took inventory of the soldiers. Most of them were short and small, and from under their caps, a long braid streamed down their backs. *Women. And young boys.* Less than half were men. He tried to count or estimate. *More than the eye can see. Maybe a thousand.* He did not know whether this was all, or whether more waited. Many soldiers carried AK-47 automatic rifles, but the majority hefted the old Lee-Enfield rifles issued to the Indian Army by the Viceroy. *The same rifle used in The Troubles.*

A tall man approached them and dismissed the soldiers guarding them. He spoke and Ranjit took a closer look. Ranjit had seen this man before, at the Hotel Himshikhar with the Lions. He was with a trekking group that came through a few weeks ago.

"Namaste, Uncle." The man smiled showing a gap between his front teeth. "We meet again."

"Your troops have rifles that are older than I am," said Ranjit, "Aren't you Thul Pun? We met at the Lion's Club."

"That may have been my name in a past life, but for now I am Comrade Barood. We will not be bothering you for long. It is best to wait inside. Be advised, we do not want you to use your mobile phone. We will not harm you. Please tell the hospital staff. We may have a few wounded fighters later. You might want to help if that is the case."

Ranjit felt a tightening in his chest as he thought of Sushila. *I can't get word to her. She will know this is the attack. It's obvious. And the boy. He's not that much younger than these soldiers. She must be home in the Bajaar.*

But her home is right near the police barracks.

The soldiers sorted themselves into their groups, as if they were runners lining up for a footrace. Soon the signal was given, and they marched off. For five minutes, there was an eerie quiet, then a white flare went up and everything erupted all at once. Ranjit heard machine guns chattering in the town and mortars in the distance. Looking up to the hills, he saw flashes of fireworks as the mortars and machine guns fired on the targets below. Tracer bullets lit the sky overhead.

Another group of soldiers appeared, to organize into the second wave. This group chanted slogans while they lined up.

"Down with Monarchy and Feudalism!"

"Long Live People's War!"

"Political power grows from the barrel of a gun!"

"Long Live Marxism-Leninism-Maoism and Prachanda Path!"

Then, they, too, marched off. He heard large explosions in the distance. *The kettle bombs. Right near Sushila's house.*

Sushila lay in her mother's old bedroom, on the first floor of the house. At first, she thought she heard a strong lightning storm with distant thunder, and then came a thunderclap as if her house was struck. The whitewashed stone walls shook and a cloud of dust cascaded from the wooden ceiling. The first blasts shook the ground and shattered every pane of glass, blowing shards inside like sharp, hard rain. She rolled off the bed to the floor and shivered with the cold air, pulling the blankets down around her.

From the other room, Arjun cried "Mommy! Help!"

She knew that this was the attack they anticipated for so long and talked so much about, but for which the town would never really be prepared. *Arjun. Is he hurt? I will go to him.*

She heard shouting and movement in the street outside. She wanted to look out the window on the second floor in the direction of the old Shiva

Temple where the tree grew out of the roof, but she thought better of it. There were explosions outside, many sounds like a bang-whine-tap, and she realized that bullets were being fired – many bullets. *They are hitting my house. I am lucky for stone walls*, she thought.

The boy was in her old bedroom, also on the first floor. Each time she heard a bullet hit the house, she ducked. *I want Arjun right where I can see him.* She dashed across the floor, calling out to him. Ram Dai had warned her about mortar rounds and stray bullets.

Ram Dai said that the same walls that kept them safe from bullets would act to contain and magnify a blast if a mortar shell were to come through the roof. She looked Arjun over, and he was scared but not hurt. She hugged him.

"We will be brave like soldiers. And now we will build a make-believe fort," she told Arjun. "You will be the commanding general of this fort. First, pull the table near the wall for a roof. Now, we turn over the sofa, as well, and move everything else for walls. And now we climb in and sit on the cushions."

They listened to the real battle outside. Arjun looked at her. "It sounds like the growling of a very big dog," she told him. "Remember how you tamed the dog? We can tame the noise. The key is patience. We must wait."

She hugged her son and said, "You will be the man of the house, Bahadur. Remember that your father was a member of the Royal Gurkha Rifles, in service to Her Majesty, the Queen of England." She looked into his eyes and said, "I love you. I see your father's face when I look at you. Be brave."

Less than fifty meters away, Comrade Barood Pun directed his fighters at the police barracks. The attack went according to plan, at first. Then came the time to storm the barracks.

"Janayuddha Jindabaad!" Comrade Barood shouted. The fighters responded, and Comrade Barood repeated the call-and-response.

"A death is only a death and a victory is immortal!"

The attackers gathered the courage to follow their leader. Comrade Barood stood up. He puffed his chest, and made a gesture of defiance toward the police. He shouted, "Now! Stand and follow me!" He turned to begin the charge. He knew his fighters would follow him. He took two steps to the barracks before his personal battle ended. Two of his fighters dragged him to safety, unconscious. The fighters decided to stay where they were and fight a slower battle after Comrade Barood Pun was hit.

Soon, soldiers returned to the hospital. Some carried litters upon which wounded comrades lay. Others carried a doko, the packbasket of rural Nepal, and these too, held wounded soldiers, the boys and the women, small enough for one person to carry. *Some of the Maoist soldiers did not even weigh forty kilos*, thought Ranjit. *Well within the carrying of a doko.*

The night didi and the chowkidar retrieved both of the footlockers that held mass casualty supplies. The team set out the contents for use, and soon everything was lined up on a bench in neat rows. Sara surveyed the scene, hoping that maybe some employees would venture through the town. *Surely, they must know that this was the attack.* She saw only those few that were there all evening. *This was hardly an organized response. We are in grave danger. No amount of planning was enough to get us ready.*

If the Maoists brought their own medical team, it was not here, not so close to the battle. Sara evaluated the first casualties. *All of the eyes are swollen.* Next she saw tears streaming down the cheeks of the fighters. Everyone seemed wheezy and short of breath. *Tear gas. I wonder how many canisters the police fired into the street at the Bajaar.* Colorless and odorless, it was an invisible god of street fighting in this civil war. A person would not know it was there until the Tear Gas laid her hand upon them like Sitala the Goddess of Smallpox.

Sara knew that tear gas left a powdery residue. She stood back, knowing that she would be useless with the powder reacting on her hands. Each casualty would need to be washed with water to keep the toxic, powdery residue from spreading to the doctors.

"You!" she called to two of the litter bearers. "Go get water from over there and bring it here. Take those jugs there. Then make sure that you pour some on the face of every fighter. If you don't wash their face, we can't examine them."

She told two others to set up a place where every litter would stop, just for this. "Don't try to be fancy, just pour it on their face."

She watched. The soldier used the water to wet a cloth, then with careful motions he daubed the face of the first wounded fighter, gingerly.

"No. We'll be here all night if you do it that way. Watch me. Like this." Sara took the bottle and splashed out the entire contents in one gesture until the patient coughed and sputtered.

"Use one whole pitcher for each person. This is not the time to be neat or gentle. Do not be dainty." Sara stopped. *They think I have gone batty.* She laughed to herself. *Laughing? Yes, batty. That's me.*

Ram appeared and made a sweeping gesture.

"Sara Ma'am. And now - you get your wish. You are conducting the largest baptism ever held in Beni."

She curtsied and said, "Ram dai, when the time comes to baptize you I will be ready. But not tonight. Why don't I triage while you treat? You can thank me later. In the meantime, don't get this on your hands. Be a sweet boy and get to your station."

Bottles of intravenous solution were laid out with the tubing primed. After Sara triaged, she would send the patients to Ranjit or Ram for treatment. The main Theatre would remain locked overnight.

Sara's assignment was to divide the wounded into three groups. First, those who could never be saved. These would be laid on the ground around the corner, next to the ones who were already dead. The second group consisted of those ambulatory soldiers whose wounds would not interfere with their ability to leave. These cases required bandaging and minor sutures. In the middle were the wounded who might survive, but needed surgery or a longer stay. Ram and Ranjit would look after these. The goal was to stabilize now and organize definitive treatment for later. The night didi was to start an intravenous on each soldier in this category.

At midnight, two men bearing a litter bypassed the washing station, going straight to Sara, insistent about not waiting their turn. On the stretcher was the tall man with the space in his teeth, now covered in dust. Thul Pun, the commander, lay there unconscious. He was leading a heroic charge until a tear gas canister fired from about sixty feet away hit him in the head. His scalp was covered with blood, and the two men demanded that Sara see him immediately. Sara knelt to pour a liter of water over his head to clean it for further examination, the water mixing with the blood, running onto the ground below.

His pupils were equal and reactive to light. He did not respond to commands. Sara pinched his fingernails and he twitched, just a little bit. Same reaction on the other hand. His breathing was labored. Pulse was slow and bounding. She repositioned his head, used the bulb suction device from the Delivery Room, and then placed a padded tongue blade in his mouth to hold the airway open. His breathing improved. She found a large bruise on his scalp, and she motioned for one soldier to apply pressure. Sara used her fingers to examine his scalp for a bullet wound. There was none. For now, direct pressure was applied to stop the bleeding. A concussive injury due to blunt trauma. He was going to die.

"Help me position him on his side." The two stretcher bearers helped her and asked where they should go.

"Leave him here, it's as good as any place," she said.

"No. He is Captain; if he is out in open, it will be bad. We must hide him in case Army comes," said one.

"Do surgery. Fix his head now," demanded the other, grabbing Sara's arm.

"I told you, leave him right here. He will be under my personal care," she said as she shook her arm loose.

The first stretcher-bearer took a rifle that lay next to another patient. As he checked to see if it was loaded, he said, "You must hide him from the Army. He is special."

"We are neutral. The hospital is neutral. Look around – can't you see we have no place to hide?"

"We will break down the door to that building over there if you don't let us in."

Sara set her jaw. At that moment, another officer approached and said, "Take him elsewhere. Can't you see that our other comrades also need help? Stop telling this doctor how to work. She is Videshi. Hide him in a house somewhere. We will send for him when we leave. Go. Do it now."

They picked up the stretcher, carrying Comrade Barood back toward the houses of that part of town.

Ranjit and Ram worked to stop the bleeding for each wounded fighter. In some cases, this meant applying a tourniquet. In others, it meant suturing a wound without local anesthesia. Several fighters needed chest tubes. Some would be queued for surgery in the morning. Ranjit and Ram used magic markers to write reminders to themselves on the forehead of each patient. *I hope the staff gets here in the morning so we can finish this up*, Ranjit thought.

At two in the morning, a helicopter flew overhead, one of the Russian-built Mi-17s. It hovered directly over the Tundikhel but did not fire on the ground below. The helicopter was equipped with a powerful spotlight, and the pilot turned it on. There was immediate small arms fire from the ground, and the spotlight went dark. The helicopter dodged and weaved to avoid being shot down. Ranjit guessed that the PLA was in close quarters with the police, and the helicopter was not able to find a clear target. The rotor wash raised a cloud of dust over the parade ground, obscuring the stars, adding to the night. The helicopter gained altitude and headed to circle the ridges above, searching for prey, but the mortars became silent, not betraying their position.

The helicopter made another pass over the town and headed directly over the hospital, creating a momentary panic. Everyone ran for cover under the eaves of a building—the soldiers scattering for cover like kids playing hide-and-seek. Sara and Ranjit squeezed under the outpatient porch with

116

a dozen Maoists, hoping the pilot saw the Red Cross on the roof. The helicopter hovered for a moment and flew in a different direction.

An hour passed, and there was a change in the intensity of the firing. From the west, a fierce gun battle still raged, staccato bursts from the machine guns mixed with individual rifle shots exchanging fire. Directly to the south, quiet. The PLA attack was a success even though Comrade Barood was not there for the grand finale.

The retreat was about to begin, but first the PLA fighters gathered into their groups and chanted. Now they were defiant, even though they knew they were about to retreat like running animals. The banners were not obvious now, and the uniforms were not so neat, but they chanted.

"Down with Monarchy and Feudalism!"

"Long Live People's War!"

"Political power grows from the barrel of a gun!"

Each group gathered some of the wounded. The more severely wounded could only remain to become captives. Around the corner in silence lay a row of dead combatants, extending the length of the building. A grim detail of PLA searched each of these bodies for ammunition before they, too, left.

Sushila looked at her watch during the battle, but after each eternity of noise and shouting, it seemed that only five more minutes passed. At two in the morning, it became quiet. The police were out of ammunition and did not want to be burned alive in their barracks. They surrendered. The PLA fighters watched the police come out the front door, dusty and stained with the sweat of exertion and fear, some still wearing nightshirts, nobody fully dressed in uniform. There was no time to buckle the belts or lace the boots.

The police all knelt with their hands over their heads. Some coughed and choked from the tear gas. The Maoists circled them, weapons ready. The new commander told some of his men to bring the prisoners to the retreat route. At first, the police did not cooperate. The Maoists then shot three. The rest now fell into a line, wrists bound to a rope. The guards prodded them and made them trot off like goats going to market.

Sushila saw this from her window. She felt sick. The battle for the Royal Nepal Army post continued in the distance, but here, the Maoists completely controlled the police barracks. Now the PLA troops regrouped, some to join the siege of the Army barracks, some to retreat with the new hostages, and some remaining to set the police barracks on fire.

Most of them left, but a small party of Maoists went door-to-door, looking for a spot of white paint marking some of the doorframes. The advance team placed these marks after scouting which residences to target. Sushila noticed it a week or two before but not given it much thought. The Maoists were demanding entrance, shooting bullets into the wooden door of each house if the answer did not come soon enough. The paint guided them to each house where a boy of the right age would be found, to be conscripted into the PLA. It was now time to gather the "recruits." Sushila saw two soldiers drag a boy out of the house across the street. *This was new.*

Now a Maoist soldier broke into her door and entered in a crouch. He stood there squinting in the darkness, holding a military rifle, looking at her and then at the table. "Come out from there," he said, "you will be safe now."

Sushila stood and pushed Arjun behind her. Arjun knelt and held on to her legs. The soldier saw the boy, smiled, and reached out a hand.

"Come with me, now. Get your shoes on and come with me. Hurry."

He turned to Sushila and said, "Your boy will now join the glorious people's war against imperialism. Now he will come with us."

"No he won't. He stays with me."

"Yes he will. Every family must contribute one son." He turned to Arjun and repeated, "Get your shoes and a jacket."

"He's only seven years old! No!" Sushila screamed. *I will die without him*, she thought.

She lunged at the soldier like a tiger and tried to hit him with both fists, but he was bigger, faster, and quicker. He slapped her with one hand—a full palm to the face, sending her reeling. She staggered backward and fell like a sack of rice. The soldier jumped on Sushila as she lay smarting from the slap.

The boy stood, frozen and wide-eyed.

"Get your jacket and shoes, and do it now." He restrained Sushila as she struggled but he spoke in a cheery voice and smiled again at the boy. Arjun put his shoes on.

Then the soldier bent down and whispered into Sushila's ear, "So you wish to be a bhalu I see. Act like a bhalu and I will treat you like one. If you wish to ever see your boy again you will learn to act properly."

He tied Sushila's hands behind her back and bound her ankles. He knelt on her back and bent down, pushing her face into the dusty floor.

"This is to help you calm down. You will be the glorious mother of a proud comrade in the People's Liberation Army."

"No!"

He pushed her head against the floor, and snarled, "Show some dignity. We will take good care of him. I don't want to shoot you but I will."

He shifted his weight from her back and wrapped a shawl around her head to cover her eyes. He turned to the boy, smiled, and said, "Say goodbye to your mother. The next time you see her you will be a man, proud to fight for the people and justice and a new Nepal. Hurry now."

Arjun knelt. He tugged on the shawl and brushed the hair out of her eyes so she could see him. He whispered. "I love you, Mom. I won't be afraid. Don't cry."

The fighter grabbed the boy's arm. "We must go." He dragged the boy outside, and pushed Arjun into a group with other boys of the town, marching north out of Beni.

Dawn approached. More Army helicopters came, unloading soldiers to reinforce the town. The Army still controlled their barracks during the night, despite close combat in some of the buildings. Now at dawn, the Army could regroup. It was obvious that the PLA was leaving. Army patrols fanned out from the Bajaar to re-take the town and re-establish control.

Sara and the boys were still awake at dawn. The hospital courtyard was now deserted of people in uniform, although occasional stragglers came trotting up through the town. Soon, fifty people stood in the line, seeking treatment. Ranjit and Ram decided to unlock all the doors and open the Theatre for surgery. The first civilian patient of the morning was a little girl. Pieces of window glass from a bomb blast were embedded like spattered paint. Ranjit did his best to re-assure the parents as he worked, but tears streamed down the mother's face. With a clamp, he probed for pieces of glass in each small wound, fishing them out one by one when his fingers told him there was a hardness there that didn't belong. He knew he couldn't get all of the slivers, but at least the larger shards could be removed.

Another wave of patients began at eight and continued all morning as people from the town started to come out. Some were wheezy and short of breath due to the CS tear gas; others were bleeding from shrapnel or ricochet bullets. Most of the townspeople, though, stayed inside their houses. *Thank God for small things in a battle*, thought Sara.

Ranjit wondered what kind of a rear guard the Maoists deployed. He listened for sounds of firing in the direction of the retreat route, but it was quiet in that direction. *They planned an attack; they are not so good at planning the retreat.* The grounds around the hospital were trashed. Pools of blood. Articles of clothing. Mismatched pieces of weapons. Wrappings of a Cadbury bar. The chowkidar reported that every cistern in the hospital was drained of water. The toilets were filthy and overflowing. Some loose dogs from the town came by, lapping at the blood on the ground. Ranjit threw rocks at them and muttered, "Show some respect."

Sushila lay on the floor. *I am not helpless*, she said to herself. *I have the power to breathe. The first lesson of worshipping the Goddess.* There was nothing else to do right now, so she breathed in and out, mindful of each exhalation. She allowed herself to sense her whole body – the cold feel of the floor, the pressure on her knees, the texture of the material that bound her arms, her hands behind her back, the position of her legs. *I will survive this. And Arjun will come back.*

She discovered that she could move if she bent a certain way. She rolled and writhed like a worm to the door, then partway out, tumbling into the street. There, she breathed again, in and out and in, and prayed that somebody, anybody, would come. A neighbor ventured out an hour later and came to her, freeing her from the cords tied around her wrists. Sushila scrabbled to her feet, steadied herself, and surveyed the damage of the brief time the battle came into her house. The flat light of dawn came through the windows and the sounds of battle receded.

Arjun was gone. She didn't believe it at first and went from room to room in the house, calling his name. *Arjun is gone.* There was dust in her hair, and her lip was split and swollen. She didn't know what to do at first. Then the idea came. She must find Ranjit. *He would know.*

She headed up the street to the hospital. She walked like a ghost, conscious that she was moving, almost gliding, but not aware of effort, disconnected from feeling her legs move. Spent shell casings rolled under foot as she passed over them. Across the street, she saw the bodies of the three police, small pools of blood now congealing into a sticky mass.

Other women of the town were out walking in a daze. Sushila passed the public water tap, the ancient one that was sunken, with the stone spout that ran water into a trough-like pool. The pool was red with blood. Three Maoists lay in it at odd angles, half submerged. The Royal Nepal Army soldiers were now on the street, working their way in the same direction, paying no heed to the residents of the town. Every time the small patrol came across the uniformed body of a Maoist, they stopped to kick until it moved. One wounded Maoist moved slightly and the soldiers jumped to her side, beating her head with their rifle butts. Sushila kept moving.

March 21 – Shanti Nawajeevan

"Have compassion for all beings, rich and poor alike; each has their suffering. Some suffer too much, others too little."

– Buddha

Shanti Nawajeevan, the AIDS hospice that Sushila founded, was on the way to the hospital, so the route brought her there first. It was still too early for anybody to stir. Just down the street lay the bodies of two rebel soldiers. Between them lay an empty stretcher.

She entered the front door, now ajar with a broken latch. The night didi met her and motioned to follow into the room where the sickest HIV victims lay.

Behind the portable screen, the two beds at the far end were occupied. On the left, the patient was shrouded by the dark blue blanket. The night didi lifted the corner so Sushila could peer in and see. It was not a woman and not an AIDS victim. Here was a man, a Maoist. He lay on his side and there was a padded tongue blade sticking out of his mouth. She put on gloves to look at his face. The bulky bandage wrapped around his head showed rosettes of dried blood. His face was bruised and crusty with blood. He was unconscious. He snored with each breath and a pool of saliva collected on the pillow. She turned his head to get a better look and noticed that the wrinkles of the pillow made corresponding red lines in the swelling of his face. His lips and teeth were black with old blood.

"They came in the night and demanded we hide him here. I protested, but they dumped him in this bed and left. He is their commander. What shall we do?" said the night didi.

"The Army patrol is headed this way," said Sushila. *I wonder how long before they arrive.*

They will kill him as soon as they find him.

They will kill us for harboring him. Everything was going wrong. Today her fate was to die, if not by the Maoists, then by the Army. There were no police in the town as of today. She felt the panic welling up once again, trying to maintain composure.

Then, "Ke Garne." *How many times have I said Ke Garne? That is all I can do. I will live and see my son again, no matter what it takes.*

I will live. Arjun cannot die.

At that moment, the small army patrol appeared at the entryway, shouting and pounding on the door that lay ajar on its hinges. They acted wary, ready to use their weapons on a split-second decision.

"Don't shoot! Don't shoot! We are women!" shouted Sushila.

The didi stared at the gun barrels and then started to wail and wring her hands. "Don't kill us!" she echoed.

Sushila looked over at the woman on the right-hand side behind the screen, who lay there near death, and noticed the puddle of liquid stool waiting to be cleaned by an attendant who would not be coming right away. She reached under the covers and smeared some feces onto her left hand. It was warm and she grimaced with disgust.

Sushila approached the soldiers with hands outstretched, greeting them, talking fast and loud.

"What are you doing here? Can't you see that everyone is sick? This is a hospice for victims of human trafficking with AIDS. You must respect the privacy of these women, they are low caste, but they are children of God, they have a right to a clean place while they die of their terrible disease!" She was intentionally theatrical at first, but the emotion took over again and it became real, not an act.

She touched the sleeve of the first soldier with her dirty left hand, and he recoiled in disgust when he saw the feces on his uniform. Behind Sushila, the night didi wore a surgical mask and held up a canister of bloody sputum that she picked up from beside one woman's bed. "And some of the patients have TB and leprosy!"

"Look at yourself – you have cuts on your hands. Go unless you want to catch AIDS yourself."

The soldiers backed away while the one with the soiled sleeve wiped it on one of the drapes. "You. Stay away from us," using the verb tense assigned to speech with an untouchable person or servant. Then he was away and the others followed.

I can't believe it worked. They watched the soldiers go. Sushila looked at the didi, who started to cry.

Sushila took off the gloves and washed her hands.

"Now what?" asked the didi, "You know they will be back."

"We can't just dump him in the street, " Sushila replied.

Ranjit would know what to do, Sushila repeated to herself. She ran up to the hospital. She saw Sara but went straight to Ranjit. He was napping now, still wearing the same clothes from the night before, now stained with blood from some wounded fighter. He rubbed his eyes as she told him her predicament. She was urgent and hurried. "Ranjit you must come and help me. Ranjit-ji, please. Come now."

He trotted along behind her as she took the path to Shanti Nawajeevan at a measured pace. The same trash occupied this street. At first, things inside the hospice looked the same, forlorn women laying, waiting for food that was not going to come today. The same smell of carbolic. She brought him to the bed at the far end where she lifted the covers. Ranjit saw Thul Pun lying there. He was still unconscious, swollen eyes black and blue, and the tongue blade was still in his mouth. Ranjit checked the airway and noticed a gap in the front teeth. *Yes, that's him.*

"This is not just any Maoist. This is the commander of the Maoists, and he was here as a spy a month ago. If the Army sees this, they will think you harbored this Maoist. They expect the hospital to treat the wounded, but if anybody else is found helping Maoists, the retribution will be severe," said Ranjit.

"Exactly. Oh, my fate is bad today. What shall we do?" Then, "There is something even worse."

"What could be worse?" Ranjit replied.

"They took Arjun. They took my son."

"Who? The Army? The Police? The Maoists? Who?" Ranjit clenched his fists. Every muscle in his body tightened. *What will I do without that boy?*

"The PLA took him. They said he will become a soldier." She was on the verge of hysteria. *Only a couple of years ago we cut his hair for the first time, and now this.* She thought about Arjun learning to shoot a rifle and kill people. *That is not the teaching of Buddha.* He would follow a new path, without his mother, and become a different person from what she thought. *He was the last link to his father, and now that too would be gone.*

Ranjit asked, "Who knows of this?" He looked at his watch. "How long ago?"

"Nobody. And it happened four hours ago. I don't know what to do."

"Four hours. He is miles away by now. Stay here. Do not let anybody else know of this. You have done well to keep the Army away. Your Maoist is our only chance. I have an idea."

Ranjit found Sara making rounds on the gynae ward, quietly dictating doctor's orders to the didi. She ignored him at first.

He listened politely. She examined a woman with post-partum fever and spoke to the nurse about antibiotics. Sara moved to the next, recuperating after hysterectomy. Ranjit realized that she was behaving as if it were still a normal day in scenic, tranquil Beni.

"Dear Ranjit, how can I help you?" she asked, "I need to make rounds on my patients."

He wanted to ask if she saw the sad rubbish of a military casualty station that littered the grounds. "Sara Ma'am, there is a matter of urgency." Today he noticed how pale she was, moving very deliberately.

She replied in a British accent that was unexpectedly proper, "I have to finish rounds. One must carry on." Her lip quivered and she brushed her hair back nervously.

"We must meet with the Maoist. It is urgent."

Sara continued making rounds. "Arjun has been kidnapped."

Now Sara stopped, frozen for just a second before she turned and tried to focus. "I am afraid I met all the Maoists last night. They were dreadful." Her voice was far away, "I need to finish rounds. Mustn't abandon the patients."

Ranjit stood in front of her and put his hands on her shoulders. "Sara, listen to me. I was there too. We have a hundred bodies in the courtyard. I don't want Arjun to be the next. How can we get word to the Maoist?"

She stopped and faced him. Her eyes were red. "I heard you. I will send for him, but do you honestly think that any of these people care about one little boy? And what if the Maoist is dead? What if he is hiding? What if he is gone? Then what?"

"Then I will go out and look for Arjun myself. Sara, it is our only chance, and if we don't try, I think I will die of heartbreak. The battle is not over until everyone is accounted for."

"I will send word."

Sara sent a messenger to find the Maoist and resumed rounds, but now she jumped nervously when she heard the door open or shut and kept looking at it while she worked, wondering if the Maoist would appear. The sound of random gunshots in the distance made her flinch. An hour passed this way.

She drew a quick breath and froze when the Maoist walked into the gynae ward. His eyes were baggy. He wore a white shirt and a vest with many pockets like a hunter would wear. He smelled of cooking grease. She sent him to the chautara and summoned Ranjit.

"I will dispense with the usual formalities. We need to make a deal here. We have Comrade Barood in our possession. Or should we call him Thul

Pun? I know he was the commander of the assault troops last night," said Ranjit, expressionless, "Would you like to have him back?"

The Maoist looked at him, also devoid of emotion, for what seemed like a full minute.

"And what do you need from me in exchange for this generous gift?"

"I propose an exchange, one man for one man. The retreating Maoists took Arjun, the son of Sushila, when they left the town. You would call it 'recruited' by the PLA. I call it kidnapping. But I will not argue about such trivial details. We want him returned to us."

"That is not so easy. The RNA helicopters have arrived from Pokhara in force and have begun pursuit. They are using machine guns and rockets to strafe anybody they catch in the open. The boy may be dead already. The retreating army will not be reorganized for a week, until they get out of flight range from the helicopters."

The Maoist paused and added with disgust, "And this was a great Maoist victory."

Ranjit repeated, "A one-for-one trade. We do not expect him to materialize on command right this minute. We know this will not be easy. Your word is good with us." Ranjit would not have trusted the Maoist to hold a hundred rupees, but now he trusted him to hold Arjun. *Here is a man who would shoot me in a second if he thought I would turn him in*, thought Ranjit.

"How long can you hide Thul Pun?"

"An hour. Not more. The Army will be back. As time passes, you will be less likely to evacuate him from Beni."

"I will return and you will bring me to him. I will take custody of the commander. I promise you that Arjun will be returned to you unharmed, if he is still alive."

"Namaste."

March 21 – Shanti Nawajeevan, 11 am

The Maoist returned. At first, he was alone. Then Sushila noticed the small boy following ten meters behind him. *It's a miracle! Arjun is back,* she thought, and her heart leapt with joy. But it was not him. It was the Maoist's son, about Arjun's age, carrying a black plastic grocery bag. An oil-stained blue cloth spilled out of the top. The Maoist followed Ranjit and Sushila down the stonepaved alley to the hospice.

He hesitated when he saw the sign. "This is a place of disease."

"The Army thought so, too, and only peeked in. That is what saved Thul Pun. Shanti Nawajeevan is a hospice for former prostitutes who have returned from bondage in Mumbai to die with dignity from the AIDS they caught in the brothels of that city," said Sushila.

"These vile persons who engage in human trafficking will be brought to justice when the Maoists take power. The women of Nepal deserve dignity. I am raising my daughters to be citizens of the new Nepal." He spat out those words. "The pimps that treat women this way are not real men. We will teach these pimps to value the women of Nepal."

He solemnly took the bundle from the boy and asked for a smaller bag from the boy's pocket, then sent him outside to wait. The Maoist walked to the end of the ward, eyes straight ahead. He stopped at Thul Pun's bedside.

"What's this? I thought he was able to talk." He scowled at Sushila and Ranjit. "You liars."

The Maoist sat on one of the low stools and watched Thul Pun breathe for a moment. He said nothing. He held Thul Pun's hand and shook it, trying to wake him and calling his name. With dirty fingers, he pried at one of Thul Pun's swollen eyelids. Both were black-and-blue; he did not see the pupils of Thul Pun's eyes.

"Yes, I will evacuate Thul Pun." The Maoist bent down to set the blue cloth at the foot of the bed and slowly unfolded it as if he were spreading a new blanket there. In the center of the stained cloth was a 9 mm handgun. He emptied the smaller bag onto the cloth and out poured a dozen bullets, stubby brass casings with dark silvery tips like acorns. He chose six bullets for the gun and put the rest back in the bag. He checked the magazine and snapped the receiver to make sure the first round was in the chamber. He stood up and walked to the head of the bed. He put his hat back on his head.

He placed the muzzle on a spot just behind Thul Pun's ear. He looked away as he pulled the trigger. In the small space, the sound of the handgun seemed impossibly loud, smoke twirling out of the muzzle like a tobacco pipe. Thul Pun's body twitched as the blood pulsed out of the new wounds in his skull. The back part of his head was open like a dropped watermelon. Ranjit noticed spongy pale brain tissue mixed with the bright red blood. The gush of Thul Pun's blood created a waterfall, first onto the pillow, from there to the floor. Sushila flinched. Her ears were full of a loud ringing.

Within fifteen seconds, Thul Pun was dead. His chest twitched like hiccups, twice, then once again after a pause. But – dead.

The Maoist pointed the muzzle to the ceiling while he checked his handiwork. He lowered the weapon and waved it at Ranjit and Sushila. There was no expression in his face.

Now everything was eerily quiet by comparison. The muzzle seemed ten times larger now, a gaping hole from which her death would come next. *This will be the last thing I see*, she thought. She looked straight at him. The Maoist straightened his arm, now extended directly at Ranjit.

Ranjit took deep breaths. *There are five more bullets in that weapon*, he realized.

I watched him load the gun that will kill me.

And did nothing.

Ranjit pulled Sushila behind him. To Sushila it seemed as though Ranjit puffed his chest up to make a bigger target. She saw Ranjit bow his head, and clasp his arms in front of him, standing the same way a good Nepali would stand while singing the national anthem. *At least I told Arjun that I loved him, on the last day of my life*, she thought. *Arjun's father will not know his fate. Or even that he existed.*

After a pause, the Maoist put the gun down.

The Maoist spoke slowly and quietly. "You kept your part of the bargain. I received Thul Pun from you. Your son will be returned to you, unharmed, in a few days. I am a man of honor." With that, he slowly wrapped the handgun into the blue cloth and left, not looking back at the scene.

Sushila and Ranjit stood motionless. Sushila shivered and her teeth chattered. Finally, they moved. They hugged each other. Sushila knew very well that it was not part of the culture to touch other persons in public. As she hugged Ranjit, his tears fell onto her neck. Neither spoke.

The didi from Shanti Nawajeevan returned and put her arms around Sushila, to lead her away. Ranjit collected himself, knowing he needed to return to the hospital, knowing that a flood of patients still awaited there, probably each and every one was bleeding. *Even Belfast was not like this*, he thought. *Or maybe I was young then and did not really know. These bastards planned a glorious victory as if they were moving little brass tigers and goats around a bag-chaal game board. It was only a useless exercise in suffering and death.*

"You must go and rest. It's been – difficult," he said to Sushila as she left.

He couldn't bring himself to say the truth. *I love her. I want to cry. I want to hold her like when she was a baby. These things happen to other people, not to us. Not to me.*

Sushila picked her way through the streets back to her house. She heard more helicopters in the distance and watched some descend to the parade ground before they disappeared below the line of roofs in the Bajaar. These helicopters were ferrying bodies of RNA and police to Pokhara. Other helicopters flew passed the town. *These ones are looking for the PLA fighters. The ones who have Arjun. They will shoot from the air. At anything that moves.*

Here on the street, the soldiers dragged dead bodies to the edge of the road so they could be collected. Now, the bodies of the three PLA fighters from the water trough lay dripping closer to the road. A dog lapped the blood from one uniform before it was shooed away. She saw a queue of water pails at the tap, women getting the day's water, ignoring the bodies and the blood in the pool below the spigot. She heard a random explosion in the distance followed by screaming and shouting. A woman washed a pool of blood from the steps in front of the metal rolling screen that protected the storefront.

She could not get all the way to her house because this section of the street was now cordoned off. Empty metal boxes lay strewn about, evidence that a cache of munitions was nearby. *This is where the Maoists resupplied with ammunition.* Her neighbor from three houses up, the shopkeeper, lay dead. The man's wife knelt next to him, weeping as she held her baby. Two Army soldiers stood by, hefting their rifles and trying to look relaxed as if this was normal. At first Sushila thought they were guarding the woman, then she saw the other soldiers whose weapons were set aside while they formed a line to pass the rest of the boxes hand-to-hand from the shop to a pile in the street.

Sushila waited for permission before she could pass. A dozen other people watched.

"What happened?" she asked.

"This man was a sympathizer and he allowed them to store munitions for the battle at his shop. The PLA killed him themselves. They didn't want him to inform on local Maoists. One bullet behind the ear and he is no more."

A truck came down the street. Sushila saw a stack of bodies in the back. Two soldiers added to the pile as the truck made its way. The wife of the shopkeeper pleaded for the soldiers to allow her to cremate her husband as a Hindu and not throw him in a mass grave. They threw his body on the truck and went on their way.

That could have been me. And Ranjit. We were that close.

Or Arjun.

Sushila returned to her house. She stood at the door and could not go in at first. It was quiet. She finally stepped over the threshold. Looking around, nothing was in its proper place. Shards of window glass were everywhere. She turned the sofa back on its feet, knowing she might never put her life back on its feet. Not after this. She was too tired to cry. She called Arjun's name. There was no answer. She knew he was not there, but she couldn't get the idea out of her head that maybe he was just hiding and she could find him. Sushila called his name as she went from room to room.

There was not even an echo. She found Arjun's favorite quilt and threw it over her shoulders for warmth. She brushed off a spot on the sofa and sat down. *How can I feel safe in this house again? No door can be strong enough.*

She thought of Arjun's young body and the last time she held him. *He might be lying somewhere, calling for her. What if he is wounded and alone? Two soldiers would pick him up and throw him on a truck. Arjun would truly be no more.*

She wobbled to a standing position and found the door to the Puja room. She crouched through the low door, reminded of all the places on her body where pain and stiffness cried out to move slowly.

Breathe. Just breathe.

It hurts to breathe.

Pray to the Goddess.

Remnants of a burned out candle lay melted in front of Ishta Devi and the family gods. She knelt on the small rug. *Yesterday is gone. Tomorrow may never come – and today – is the worst day of my life. O Buddha, how to spend this day?*

Yesterday's puja supplies lay on the plate in front of her. She picked up a wilted flower and set it aside. She brushed the hair from her eyes. *This is where he touched my hair just before he left.* "Don't cry."

She cried. The tears ran until she tasted them. Enough to clean the palm of her hand when she wiped them away.

She looked at the Goddess. *Is this also the Goddess? Am I now One with the Goddess of Tears? What is the name of that Goddess, so I can make an offering? The tears of a mother must be the purest offering to any Goddess that anybody can make. Here. I offer them.*

And what shall I do now? Today I know that to be human is to suffer. I am not able to begin japaa.

He can't possibly be dead. I will do anything to get him back. *My fear is a dog I will not tame.* Again, she wept and asked for wisdom. *O Goddess of nurturing, today I have seen the power of destruction. O Kali, You who vanquished Kalaratri, help me overcome my fear. Give me the strength to go on.*

A tired feeling overwhelmed her. Her arms and legs felt heavy and she collapsed on the floor, unable to keep her eyes open. She awoke as evening came, a bit shivery with cold, now feeling the pain from every wound of the last day.

Arjun had to survive. There was no other alternative. Do not surrender.

Army Headquarters, Beni, Nepal – March 22, 2004

The days passed but there was no word from the Maoist. He had disappeared from the town of Beni, vanished in fact. *He lied to us,* thought Ranjit. Each day, panicky parents brought one or two more children of the town to the hospital, injured when they played with unexploded bombs. Each time, Ranjit's heart sank. *What if I walk into the room and find Arjun on the stretcher?*

The lack of news weighed upon Sushila. *There will be a happy re-union,* she thought. Then Arjun did not re-appear. *There is that other kind of reunion that ends the not-knowing, but is not a happy reunion.* Sushila pushed this idea out of her head and begged Ranjit to go to the Army and ask for news. He heard the panic in her voice. He walked across the town. The Army captain agreed to meet with him. Ranjit told the captain that Sushila's kidnapped son was with the retreating column.

The captain replied, "The retreating column is smaller than you think. They seem to have melted away into the countryside. The pilots report that they have not seen any groups of young boys among the retreating troops." He looked at Ranjit. "We aren't going to just let them get away, whether they have hostages or not. They have killed many of our men. Ke garne."

"Ke garne? You ask, 'What can be done?' " Ranjit was incredulous. "Plenty can be done. For one thing, you can find some way to get them back without shooting them from a helicopter. They are innocent victims. Twenty young boys of this town were kidnapped. They didn't just vanish into thin air."

"Well then, tell me where they went," said the commander. He addressed Ranjit in a disrespectful manner using the verbs reserved for a servant of the lowest caste. "This whole region is thick with sympathizers. I think half the attackers live right here in Myagdi District, not in Rukum. They take off their uniforms and today they are planting paddy, laughing at us. You treated the Maoists last week, maybe you know their plans better than us. Go to your Maoist friends."

Ranjit tried to remain calm. "Hajur. Why do I receive this disrespect from you? The hospital is neutral and you know it. This week we treated every RNA soldier that was brought to us. That is the whole point of why I came to you. I am asking you to find the boys."

"Yes, you and a crowd of other parents. The rest are waiting outside. Go see them. I will ask the pilots to look for an obvious group, but many of the PLA soldiers are women and boys, and our objective is to kill them. This is not easy. You are not the only person affected by this. If we find them, we will tell you. Now go."

Ranjit walked out and saw the parents, waiting in a group. *There are people here I have treated for twenty years. They expect me to be a leader*, he said to himself.

"I have asked the Army to help us, and they will," he told them. "The most important thing is to not lose hope."

Ranjit returned to the hospital. He found Sara in her office. "The army says they have not been seen from the air. But if they see the boys, they won't promise not to shoot. I thought the battle was over. I didn't think the battle could get worse, but it has. Arjun is in deep trouble."

"Ranjit, there must be a logical way to solve this. If they didn't see them from the air, maybe they are not in the retreating column. I think the PLA is hiding the boys somewhere."

"Of course. Sara, you are brilliant. I see it. They would never have expected twenty boys to hike over a ten thousand foot pass and back to the training camp in Rukum 200 kilometers away. That's got to be it."

Ranjit's mind was racing, and he continued, "Well then. Can't we ask the Maoist to get Arjun back? It ought to be easier than he said at first. He lied to us when he said he didn't know. If they are hiding them, surely the Maoist knows."

"Ranjit, he's disappeared since the battle and nobody can find him. You just said he already lied to you. Are you seriously thinking of threatening the Maoist? He's a desperate man, and he is armed. You told me what he did. What do we do about the other nineteen boys? Do we just go for Arjun and abandon the others? If we find out where Arjun is, don't we have a responsibility to all the other parents?"

"They won't simply let them all go," he said.

"I know. That's what I am saying."

"But we must talk to them anyway," he replied. "If only I could find who was hiding them, maybe I could bypass the Maoist."

"It's worth a try."

With that, Sara solemnly asked Bimla, her secretary, to come into the office. *Of course. Bimla was somebody Sara worked with every day. That was how she contacted them*. Until this moment, Ranjit did not know that Bimla was the wife of the Maoist - the conduit for all requests to him.

They shut the office door behind them.

"Bimla, I have only asked you to be a go-between when we set up meetings before, and never involved you in the actual difficult work. This time, I must ask. Do you know where they have taken the boys?"

Bimla hesitated, her gaze fixed, first on Sara, then Ranjit.

"He will kill me," she said, trembling.

"Bimla, I remember delivering your son, and I have watched him grow. Your young daughters are beautiful children. Every one of those boys has a mother, just like you. There are twenty mothers of this town who are on their knees tonight," said Ranjit.

"Sara Ma'am. Ranjit Sar. I beg you. He will kill me, and he will kill both of you."

"Bimla, the Army is looking for the boys, and if they start shooting, the boys may get killed anyway. I swear to you, if you help me, I will not tell anybody how I learned where they were," said Ranjit.

Bimla cried and Sara held her in her arms.

"Bimla, you must tell us. I will keep you here until you do." growled Ranjit through clenched teeth.

Sara shook her head at Ranjit, but the angry words were out. Finally Bimla spoke.

"They are hidden in the stone barn of a farm ten kilometers north of Beni, on the path to Tatopani. Surely, you must know it. It is near a chautara where a brook joins the river. The path to Tatopani goes over a bridge at that place."

"How do you know this?" asked Sara.

"I brought them dal-bhaat this morning. They plan to move the boys to a new location in the morning. Two adult hostages are also with them; both are wounded."

Ranjit looked at the floor as he said, "Bimla, you have done a great service. Nobody will know that you told us this."

Bimla was excused and returned to her desk. Ranjit turned to Sara and said, "I will go to Tatopani. Maybe if I offer to treat their hostages, they will release Arjun."

Hospital Guest House Dining Room – 2007

In war, truth is the first casualty.
       – Aeschylus, Greek tragic dramatist (525 BC - 456 BC)

Thoughts of the battle went through Ranjit's mind, and he could picture everything if he closed his eyes. Even now he felt a heavy feeling in his chest as he thought about the Maoist. *Waiting for Arjun was unbearable, even if it was only waiting for the body of Arjun. A week of waiting for the Maoist. Then it all happened at once. The Maoist. The police and the Army. Then the American CIA. They all lied. How can I talk of this?*

He looked at Matt. *I can only discuss this with people who were here with me. Does he not know that we are people with feelings, people with our own experiences of love and pain?*

"It was bad here."

"I read about the battle at Beni in *The New York Times*. It seemed so - small. It happened the same day the USA invaded Iraq. Everyone in the States was worried about whether Saddam Hussein would use poison gas. Bush was looking for weapons of mass destruction in Baghdad," said Matt.

To this Ranjit replied, "I got your letter. And here you are." *Yes, here was Matt. And he doesn't know anything.* Ranjit thought about Sushila. *I can't separate Sushila from the battle. I want to forget all of it. I take refuge in dharma.*

"It was not small to those of us here," replied Ranjit. "What did the USA news say about the casualties? Did they report the numbers? Did the USA news care about how many?"

"Eighteen police and three hundred PLA, if I recall correctly."

Ranjit continued. "We were here. The PLA report about government dead was more accurate. The PLA claimed more like 120 RNA and 26 policemen. Thirty three police men were taken prisoners by the PLA, including the Deputy Superintendent of Police. The PLA never list their own dead. Not ever. There was one report that said 1,800 people died, which would mean 1,500 PLA dead, but I don't think it was true. And of course, 50 civilians were killed, but neither the government nor the PLA counted them. In the pursuit, the RNA may have killed 500 more PLA fighters. There was a bottleneck over the high pass when they retreated."

And I treated every wounded child. And I was forced to look at every dead body it seems. And I was forced to think that a mother waited at home for every single one.

"Nobody really counted the civilians, and the deaths did not stop just because the battle was over. We kept finding unexploded ordnance for months afterwards. A number of children were killed. We all told them never to play in any field. The mothers of the town formed a group to identify the stray bombs. A water buffalo was killed when a mortar round detonated. The round landed in that field the night of the attack but did not explode. It lay there waiting for the next season of plowing. The man using the plow behind the water buffalo lost an arm. He nearly bled to death before they arrived here. "

"And everyone at the hospital was – okay?"

"What did I just tell you? Ask your President Bush, Matt. The American CIA trains the Nepali Army. The CIA was here in Beni the very next day. How will we ever be okay? This is the problem with Americans. You think you can just do these things in foreign countries and it doesn't affect anybody. You forget that we are actual people right here. Our lives go on, even when the foreigners go home."

And who is 'everyone,' Ranjit asked himself, Matt wants to know about one person, that is obvious. Ranjit thought about telling Matt everything. *If I start, where do I finish? This is not my place. What do I tell him about my grandson? I am still angry and to stir this up will only rekindle anger and bitterness in my heart. Let this go. Take refuge in the Goddess of lovingkindness and compassion.*

"Please. Never ask me about this again. The past is gone. The future may never come. All we have is what is here and now. We must make the best of each day as it comes to us." Ranjit said the ancient Buddhist prayer aloud. Today it was a warning. "Seek the wisdom of Buddha while you are here."

Matt wanted desperately to ask about Sushila. He thought back to the dire warnings from Sara and Ram. *Should I? There is more to it than I am being told,* he thought, *but Ranjit is right on the edge.*

I need to know. But I can't push it. It would make Ranjit crack.

He left. He knew that the conversation had not gone well.

2007 – Building Trust, One Patient at a Time

The only real failure in life is not to be true to the best one knows.
                                                        – Buddha

One day that week Ram called Matt to the Casualty room to treat a thirteen-year-old boy. The boy swallowed a chicken bone at lunch the day before. Alok already took the x-ray and it showed a 3-centimeter shard of bone stuck at the level of C5, just behind the voice box. There was no endoscopy at Beni, so Ram suggested the rigid scope. *I think I have used a rigid scope twice*, thought Matt, as *a first year resident, with somebody watching every move.* He needed a grasping tool. He pictured a tray of instruments in his mind and decided to bring an Allis clamp as a grasping tool. *I am a surgeon, I am clever*, he thought.

He met Ram and the boy in Theatre. The nurse showed him the two rigid esophagoscopes –one was too small and the other was too large. He played with them for a moment and concluded that at least the fiberoptic light source on the big one would work and it had a long grasper. Impulsively he set the instrument back on the tray and decided to use an adult straight laryngoscope blade to provide a view of the upper esophagus. *No. I don't need either rigid scope.* He congratulated himself on his wisdom.

Ram sedated and intubated the boy and said, "Aha," grabbing at something with the McGill forceps. He moved his head aside so Matt could look over his shoulder into the esophagus. Matt looked, hoping it would be easy to see, but it was evident that Ram had simply latched onto some mucosa, tearing it. Matt asked Ram to stop because too much blood would obscure the view. Matt then slid the big scope blade into the back of the boy's throat.

"I see it. I see it," he said under his breath. The shard wobbled in and out with each breath and bobbed with each pulsing heartbeat. Matt needed to grab it with perfect timing. *Like catching a mosquito out of the air.* At just the right moment, Matt grabbed it with the Allis clamp. Now he was a bulldog with a bull's nose between his teeth, and nothing was going to make him let go. He pulled it up into a better view just before it slipped out of the forceps, and the nurse handed him the long grasper. The bone was now out, a sheet of jagged bone 2.5 X 4 cm across, though only a couple of millimeters thick. Matt held it up like it was a championship trophy, and Ram expressed delight.

"Look at the size of this. It's so big it is a miracle that he swallowed it in the first place," said Matt.

"Yes. I wonder how big a hole it made," said Ram. "What is the likelihood of a fistula?"

"At the fifth cervical vertebrae he ought to be okay. It was high enough in the neck not to drain into the mediastinum. But the way it pulsated made me worry that it was close to a great vessel. We need to watch him. Just give him liquids for a few days. And antibiotics. Let's pray that it heals."

Outside the Theatre, Matt and Ram met the older brother and presented him with the bone shard. The brother thanked Matt in English, three times.

"Matt, you have participated in a rare event," said Ram.

"Not so rare. People thank me all the time," Matt replied.

"Here? In Myagdi district?"

"Well, no – in USA they did."

"Exactly. That is a difference between USA and here. In Nepal, nobody credits a good outcome to the skill of the surgeon. It's all judged according to their karma. Everything in life is tied to karma. Fate you would call it. If you use your skill to help them, then it is your own karma to help. Nothing they can do will influence it. So why bother thanking the surgeon when it is the surgeon's destiny to do what he did? You're helping your own karma, not theirs."

"But Ram, somebody told me they prayed for good karma to come their way."

"Of course. More good karma for yourself is always welcome. And it would be foolish to pray for bad karma when it already enters your life uninvited."

Even though it was a simple procedure, Matt now basked in the secret conceit of surgeons. Here was a "surgical problem." *It needed to be done*; there was no way to pretend the bone wasn't there in the boy's throat. But Matt was not really sure how he would actually come up with it until he got there. He needed to stick his finger in the cookie jar if he was going to get the cookie. Retrieving the bone produced the same feeling of getting out of the kitchen before his mother saw him trying to hide not just one, but two cookies.

"Matt Sar, you do have clever hands," said Ram.

Matt shrugged and said, "My dad used to go out of his way to enlist me in activities that would help eye-hand coordination. 'It will pay off eventually,' he always said. As for Karma? I have my own. There's nothing like the feeling that luck is on your side."

Karma works both ways. It is like having 'the force' be with you. Matt was secretly pleased at Ram's words. *Maybe this is how I will do it. Build trust one patient at a time.*

January 2007 – The Cautery Machine

I never said half the things attributed to me.

– attributed to Siddharta Gautama Buddha

Matt sent the didi to the Bajaar to buy a ham and she returned with a nice one, about five kilos. The butchers always rubbed the skin with bright orange-yellow turmeric. The skin on this one glowed with color. It was too big to fit in the fridge at the flat, so he brought it to dinner.

"I've been wondering all day what a single man would do with a ham that size," said Sara. "I thought maybe you were surprising us with a treat for dinner."

"Wondering? How did you know?"

"Matt, you may not know many people in this town, but the whole town knows you and who you are. And the didi was not sworn to secrecy," she replied, "As soon as she bought it, somebody else phoned me to ask what the ham was for. What are you going to do with it?"

"Fix the cautery machine."

"And how, dear boy, will a ham repair the machine?"

"Oh, I am the one who will fix the machine. I have been thinking about it, though, and when I do, I need to test it on something realistic. It would be unethical to try it out for the first time on a living breathing human being. A ham is the closest thing. I'll conduct the acid test on the ham before putting it into full service."

"I see. And when will you perform this feat?"

"I'm going there after dinner."

Ram listened eagerly. "Matt Sar, you have many talents. And when the cautery smell returns, we will have a proper Theater."

"Ram, did I ever tell you about the time in Boston we were using cautery and a medical student came to observe?"

"Boston? Is it near Texas? My daughter is in Houston."

"You have a daughter in USA?"

"Yes, someday I will tell you more. What about the medical student? Surely, he was not the only student in Boston."

"No, but he was the only one who came to the O.R. without eating breakfast. We were using the cautery quite liberally, since it cuts and stops bleeding at the same time. The room was hazy with the smoke and acrid pungent smell. The student wobbled for a bit then fainted."

"That does not surprise. Sometimes the most valuable lessons are those you did not set out to learn," said Ranjit.

Matt continued, "At the time, the senior surgeon said, 'it's just a vaso-vagal reaction. He'll wake up. For now, just step over him. There is an open wound on the table. Right here. Focus on the task at hand.' That is what we did. Eventually the student woke up and crawled to a corner where he sat in a daze until he felt better."

"Boston is a great center of learning. That surgeon was a tantric Buddha," said Ram in admiration, "The smell of cautery is the finest incense. It sharpens the mind."

After dinner, Matt stuffed the ham into his daypack. In the Casualty Room, he rummaged through the cabinet where they kept every key to every lock in the place. The Theatre key was clunky and old-fashioned, with a small wood block wired to it to prevent loss. Alok was evaluating a febrile child and they said hello. Matt swung the block idly as he walked to Theatre. The cautery machine waited. Ranjit would stop by later.

Matt turned on the light and something moved, a black blur skittering along the edge of the floor. It was a mouse, then the next one scurried more clearly out of the corner of his eye, hurrying for safety under the wooden bench whose counter held the stainless steel tins of sterile gauze. He looked for the machine. On the counter in front of him was a European unipolar cautery machine from a manufacturer he did not know, built in the 1970s. *A relic from the days when a car engine still relied on a carburetor.* He was armed with a screwdriver and pliers but there was no schematic of the wiring. *This should be easy enough to figure out.* The inside was dusty even though the machine was always under cover when not in use. *The dust gets everywhere.* He attached the foot pedal, then the wand, finally plugging in the Bovie Plate that served to ground the current. He left it unplugged for now until he was certain of the probability of successful repair.

It was easy to remove the cover and reveal the components, and he decided to leave this off until the very end. Matt peered in and blew the dust off, then traced each wire from the inside of the faceplate to the component it activated. *Just like working on my old Jeep. Or following the arteries from the aorta to an abdominal body organ.* A sense of triumph came over him when he found the rheostat. One wire was obviously loose, making intermittent contact. *Eureka.* He disconnected it, wiped it between his fingers and twisted the strands tightly. He was able to thread it through the connector and to crimp it tight with the pliers. He searched for any other loose wires. *None.* He did not have any solder, the heated liquid metal that would make the connection firm. He churned this over in his mind, promising himself that he would take this machine to the Bajaar and ask the goldsmiths to solder it with silver if that was what it would take. Matt thought that would be romantic and would make a great story, but there was also a television repair shop in Beni these days, and they would be more likely to help with the repair supplies he might need.

He told himself this whole adventure would make his dad laugh out loud someday, although his mother would cringe. *Barbara needs to learn how to relax. Look Ma, no hands.* Matt was feeling more heroic than usual.

Ranjit and Alok appeared at just the right time. Matt was proud to show them what he had found. They watched as he traced the wires and showed the loose fitting.

"Very impressive. Have you given it the acid test?" Ranjit asked.

"Watch this."

He placed the ham on a metal tray on the wooden table. He found the business end of the Bovie plate and slathered it with conductive gel before seating it under the ham. He made sure he was standing in a dry spot. Before he plugged the machine into the wall, Matt preset the output dial to the lowest position and stepped on the foot pedal a few times, listening for a click. Then with a flourish, he plugged it into the wall socket, reminding himself that this was 220 current, not 110 as in the USA.

"I feel like Thomas Edison," he said. "I'm back at the junior high science fair."

There was the machine. There was the ham. There was the audience. There was Matt, wearing a latex glove with the wand in his right hand as if he were Harry Potter. Matt put his left hand behind his back and imagined himself as an Olympic fencer.

"Touché," he said as he flourished it in the air.

He touched the wand to the skin of the ham. "Stand back," as he stepped on the foot pedal. Nothing happened. He stepped again, rocking this time. He was looking at his foot, not at the wand.

Now the machine hummed for a second just before it made a bright flash and the spark ignited. Matt felt an immediate shock in his arm, like somebody hammering his funny bone. A small puff of smoke and the smell of burning plastic. *He couldn't let go of the wand.*

Ranjit jumped to unplug the wall socket. Matt dropped the wand, using his left hand to stop the right from shaking. Matt bit his own tongue while receiving the current, and now the blood dripped out of his mouth as he shouted, "Dammit! Dammit! Dammit!"

Ranjit steadied Matt and helped him find a chair, then ordered Alok to run and get some ice to put on Matt's hand.

There was a hole in the latex glove on the middle finger. A small blackened area at the tip of that finger was surrounded by a burn and another on the knuckle. Matt's arm continued throbbing, but there was no other visible mark. He could not clench his hand with any degree of strength.

"I zorked myself good, said Matt, "Take a look."

Ranjit examined him and pronounced a diagnosis using his clinical voice. "This is a third degree electrical burn." He shook his head. "Superficially it is not much, but it is not easy to tell the degree of injury to underlying tissue."

Ranjit looked at the ham. "The ham is unscathed. The current blew a hole right through the glove. Whatever just happened, I think we can agree that the machine is truly unusable," said Ranjit. "Obviously still an electrical fault somewhere. Truly, very impressive."

"It certainly impressed me," said Matt through clenched teeth.

"It is a unipolar wand. Maybe it's also the Bovie Plate, and the insulator for the wand, as well as the regulator," said Ranjit, "Now I recall. When I used it last I also felt a small tingling to the hand. Not anywhere near the magnitude of what you just experienced."

That would have been a handy clue to know. Matt felt like blaming Ranjit for a moment but thought better of it. He surveyed the ham and decided to lighten up the mood. "That would be one lucky pig if it weren't already dead. Don't tell Ram about this, okay?"

Ranjit said, "My lips are sealed. But Ram is an observant fellow, for all his bluster. How can you hide such an injury? Ram will know that you were struck by a Buddhist lightning bolt. I can picture him now, telling you that you should have done *Ganesh puja* and *Agni puja* both, prior to this work. And then he will quote some piece of literature nobody else here has ever read."

"Even more important, Ranjit. Don't ever tell my mother, okay?" *I can just hear the words, 'Oh my God, my son is giving his poor mother apoplexy.'*

"I will observe the highest level of patient confidentiality, I assure you."

Ranjit held Matt's arm under the light to examine the hand again. The fingers were not swollen, yet. "Let's hope that this injury heals soon. How will a surgeon work with no right hand?"

Alok returned with a bag of ice, and they wrapped it around Matt's hand and forearm. Ranjit was right. They sat together as they took it in. *How would a surgeon work with no right hand?* Months of planning and now – this.

Ranjit gave him some paracetamol for the pain. The hand and arm were no longer throbbing the next day. The middle finger still hurt and was swollen. He would be unable to operate or assist until it healed. Matt waited outside the Gynae ward for Sara to arrive. She saw his hand in the bandage. Sara was forewarned by Alok and showed little emotion. She pursed her lips when he showed his finger. He could bend it, but there was no strength.

"Thank God, you were not electrocuted. Thank God, Ranjit was there. You probably know that we don't own a defibrillator, in case your heart stopped." She asked him to grip her hand with his and to wiggle the fingers. "Close your eyes and tell me if you can feel which finger I am touching."

She frowned.

"I think it's going to take a week or two before you're ready to go to Theatre again. Boys will be boys, and it seems as though a surgeon always needs to be holding some kind of tool or other."

"Sara, I come from a long line of surgeons, and my grandfather developed an instrument named after him."

"Did the tool he invented require electricity in order to function?" she asked sweetly. "That just proves my point. Normally, I don't allow Ranjit and Ram to conspire in these escapades, but I must admit that I myself had a hand in authorizing this. Never again. If by any chance the anesthesia machine breaks, or perhaps the hospital generator, or the Land Rover needs repair, please check with me before you try to fix it. The team from Samaritan's Purse is scheduled to come here in two more months. This would not have happened if we had waited for them. "

They decided on a new plan. Matt would be reassigned to medical service until his finger healed.

"There may be an unexpected blessing in this. The medical service is where we send all the communicable diseases. You will be in the front line trenches against the tropical illnesses. You will no doubt find some things you don't see in the States. After all, there is nothing wrong with your mind."

She continued, "Alok is MBBS and still has exams to take, so we need to recheck everything he does. That has been my role. If we re-assign you while you heal, you can still help the team by freeing me up to focus on paediatrics and gynae."

The nurse interrupted them, pushing the cart that held the patient's charts as if it were a baby carriage, ready to start rounds. Sara finished by saying, "In the meantime, if Ranjit asks, tell him I said, 'We are not amused.'"

2007 – After the Cautery Incident, Sara and Ranjit Meet

Believe nothing just because someone else believed it…
 – Gautama Buddha

"Ranjit dai, I am afraid we have failed Matt in this episode with the cautery machine," Sara began. "I think we need to take a more pro-active approach to preventing such things from happening."

Ranjit thought to himself *This woman never does anything without planning. Ever.* "Sara-Ma'am. Matt truly was doing well until the very time the spark flew from the machine. You know that I shared my misgivings when he contacted you. But if I thought he lacked judgment, I would have told you. He's done many surgeries now, and he has good judgment. Very sound. I thought if anybody could repair that machine, it was him. He has a good attitude and he works very hard. I think of all the videshis we have hosted, short- and long-term, he is among the best."

"I am not blaming anybody here. I personally told him to see if he could fix it," she said, "I am to blame."

"Do you recall that kuire who referred to the people as heathens? The one who would not treat anybody unless they washed the tika from their forehead? The one who told us that the idol-worshipping people here brought the wrath of God upon themselves?"

"Yes. Of course. That same man said that Asians don't feel pain. Ludicrous. And he insulted Ram to his face. Please allow me credit where it is due. That fool was cashiered from here within two weeks," she replied.

"Exactly. Matt Sar does not pretend he is the White Savior who is above the rest of us. Yes, he is Christian, but his heart has lovingkindness. He does not carry the baggage. This is a quality I value."

Sara smiled and said, "The way you are describing this reminds me of that other doctor, from the UK, the one with the secret plan. What was his name, do you recall?"

Ranjit thought for a moment and said, "Are you referring to the one who swore that he heard the actual voice of Jesus Christ, bestowing upon him a miraculous gift to convert the entire Kingdom of Nepal, 22 million people, to Christianity? That was hardly a secret plan, Sara. He shouted it from the mountaintop. It was clearly a manic episode, during which he insisted on a direct audience with the King of Nepal, during which he would cast Satan out of the King and convert His Royal Highness to Christianity. Then, in one fell swoop, the rest of the country would accept Jesus overnight. Buddhist problem solved. Pagan Hindus now singing Handel's 'Messiah.' That guy?"

"Yes, that's the fellow."

"It is odd that you recall him. Since the battle, I have been thinking that maybe we should have helped Doctor Lancaster get that direct audience with the king. Things could hardly be worse."

Sara blushed. Then she focused on something else. "Since the battle? I'm a bit surprised to hear you recall that there was a battle here. It's been three years and you hardly ever mention the battle. You have gone out of your way to stifle it. For that matter, you seem to be softening your attitude about Matt. How are you doing, yourself? Does this mean that that you will talk with Matt about –things?"

He turned a bit somber, and she wondered whether she pushed a little too far. "Sara, we are all wounded by that event. I honor you for being with me those days. Lately, I have been thinking that I never told Sushila that I loved her, and I was never honest with her about the circumstances of her birth. It's too late now. The battle was bad, but not the worst."

He was actually going to talk now. That was unexpected, she thought.

He continued, "It wasn't the battle, it was a week later. We waited a week and then we interrogated Bimla until she wept. I hated that. I want to say that it was not me who did it, but – it was. How could I be that cruel?"

Sara could see that he was shaking, visibly. She touched his hand.

He continued, "And from there I went to Sushila to reassure her that Arjun was alive and with the PLA and the other boys in Tatopani. I told her too much. I thought I could go to Tatopani and negotiate with the Maoists. Sushila was desperate with fear and I told her what I knew, to offer some hope. Never in my wildest imagination did I think that she would run to the Army post as soon as I left. John Smith was there and she trusted him because he was American. She came back and said that Mister Smith was so kind, and he promised her that nobody would be harmed. I knew immediately that the RNA and their CIA friends would get to Tatopani first with guns blazing. And it was just as obvious that the Maoists would seek revenge. Her absence haunts me. I am consumed with regret."

Sara looked at him as if he was a total stranger now. *Maybe I have been taking him for granted.* She was annoyed when Ram and Ranjit started to tease her, but now she saw that Ranjit desperately needed the laughter that Ram supplied. Ranjit needed to find some kind of joy.

"Ranjit, we prayed for you. God walked beside you. And Arjun was unharmed. We all cried when they were reunited. Why can't you focus on that instead?"

"Because there is never any joy to be found as long as others are suffering. I have given up on most material things these days, but a man needs grandchildren. Never have I understood the meaning of sanga as well as I did that day. I am old, but since that day, I feel guilty that I survived. Matt and Ram laughed at dinner about the student that fainted in surgery – I just no longer am able to shut things out. My Buddhist teachers used to call this 'monkey mind' – I can't turn it off and I feel ancient."

She thought for awhile. She thought about her argument with the soldiers the night of the battle. *What I went through pales in comparison.* "Oh, dear. Why did you not have the talk with Sushila to tell her you were her father?"

"Sara, maybe she knows. But it is not something we discuss. It is not our culture. Men don't discuss such things with women."

"But you are discussing these things with me."

"That is different."

"O good Lord, Ranjit, tell me how!"

He stammered for a bit. "You are a foreigner. It's just not our culture."

"Oh, bloody hell," she said in exasperation, "What does 'not our culture' possibly mean? How many times have I been told that? 'We don't talk with women.' 'We don't talk about death,' 'we don't talk about love.' 'It's not our culture.' We don't expect our daughters to have a mind of their own. We certainly don't discuss sex with them until they are already pregnant. We simply can't deal with a woman who is having her period, so it's easier to get them pregnant and keep them that way. 'It's not our culture?' From my view point it looks like it's not the culture to talk about anything that matters. If somebody older than you tells you to do something, you do it. If the crowd says to do something, you join in. We expect everyone to accept everything, even if women are treated like rubbish."

"Are you finished?" He crossed his arms and sat back.

"For now."

"Sara, you've come thousands of miles to lecture us about how to be like an imaginary family in a British fairy tale. I have been to UK. Every day I saw the housewives there, waiting for their men to come home from the pubs. Don't pretend to me that every woman in UK uses fine china and has lace curtains on their windows. I know better. The British beat their wives. Not everyone there has tea with the Queen. Maybe Nepal should send Buddhist missionaries to UK. Does the Christian Bible not say, 'Wives, submit to your husbands?' " asked Ranjit, "Where does that fit in?"

"Ranjit. Stop right there. Buddha said our wish to rise above is the only thing to separate us from the barnyard animals. If we don't aspire to greater things we might as well be contented swine. So please, please, don't make this into a Buddhist versus Christian issue," she replied. "I just think there is a cost to keeping secrets. You just told me Matt is making progress. When will you talk with Matt? Will you ever talk with him?"

Ranjit shrugged his shoulders. "It's not our culture."

"I think we owe it to him. There are things he needs to know. If you can't, there is a point where I will."

They glared at each other for a while, in silence.

A Surgeon with Bare Hands

Public health is the second casualty of war.
— Author Unknown, but attributed to the 1918 Spanish flu epidemic

The Medical Service at Beni consisted of a male ward, a female ward, and a small "critical ward" of two beds. The only advantage of the "critical ward" was that it was closer to the nurse's station. Today there was one patient, a man with Hepatitis A. He lay there with bright orange skin and a swollen belly. The whites of his eyes were bright yellow like bananas. He looked around, blinking, but did not speak.

Prakash was there. He and Matt joined Alok for morning rounds. The first two women were victims of chronic lung disease who were now coughing and producing sputum. It was easy to diagnose pneumonia in these ladies because the sputum was stringy like melted mozzarella cheese and smelled funny.

The third case was a thin, young woman coughing up wads of clotted bloody sputum, like cherry pie filling. She was newly diagnosed with active TB, transmittable until she received ten days of drug therapy. In the meantime, the hospital needed to prevent others from catching it. The nurses gave her a mask to cover her mouth and assigned her to a bed in the corner of the eleven-bed room. The drapes in that corner were closed to decrease airflow.

"The cornerstone of the team's TB isolation strategy is to not stand too close," said Matt. They moved to the next bed. A fourth young woman sat cross-legged on the mattress, tethered by a chest tube attached to a one-chamber drainage bag dangling where it was hooked to the side of the bed. On admission, her initial x-ray showed that one lung was completely collapsed - a fifty per cent pleural effusion due to TB.

"Matt Sar, we explained about the chest tube and how it would be placed into her thorax, but at first she refused to give us permission to place it, saying she was afraid of needles. I learned then never to allow the patient to see the trocar. When we examine her, you will see that she has a collection of Hindu tattoos. That is the paradox of this young woman."

They knelt to look at the drainage in the bag. The fluid in the bag was yellowish and opaque, like the broth of chicken soup, but not quite milky.

Matt said, "There must be enough TB bacilli in there to infect the entire Indian subcontinent."

"You would think so, but according to *Harrison's Internal Medicine*, the main component is casein, the same protein to be found in cheese. Simple gloving and handwashing is enough to prevent spread when we deal with this drainage," said Alok.

"Good. You are studying. I have to admit, I also need to learn. We need to develop a system of what to study so that we stay focused on predicting the problems and what the patient outcomes will be. We'll learn it together."

"Medical service is not an area of elegance and glamour," said Alok with a wry grin, "Most people come with one of three symptoms - cough, headache or diarrhea. We treat diarrhea every single day. Last year Doctor Fitzmaurice told me that we have developed the science of diarrhea to a high level here in Nepal. It's possible that we lead the world in this area of medical science." Alok winked at Matt.

They started the day with four diarrhea patients, discharged three and admitted four more. "We will send stool samples, but the key thing is rule out cholera and typhoid from among the routine cases of acute gastro enteritis," said Alok.

"And exactly how many cholera victims do we have here on any given day?"

"Do not be alarmed. Cholera is endemic in rural Nepal. We always have a small number of cases. In other parts of Nepal, they may get small epidemics, but not here," said Alok. "The stool takes on the characteristic appearance of rice water. It's so easy to diagnose. You don't need a lot of fancy tests. If I see one I will show you."

"You are well versed in this, I see," said Matt.

"That's not all. We also go to Shanti Nawajeevan, the hospice," said Alok, "It's only a hundred meters down the hill. I try to stop by there when I can."

"The place where Manju works?"

"Yes, it is hospice for women with Haitche Ivy. We usually have a dozen or so patients there. They do not last long."

"Haitche Ivy?"

"Haitche. Eye. Vee. You know – AIDS. We don't have Haitche Ivy drugs like in the West. Too much money. They mainly come here when they are in advanced stages anyway."

"In the West it is a disease of men more than women. How do they get it?"

"Some are married to truck drivers who have sex with prostitutes while away from home. Others are human trafficking victims. They come back from Mumbai when they are too sick to work."

Peach Soap

Believe nothing just because someone told you so…
— Gautama Buddha

A week or so later, Sara brought a patient who was having seizures. "We have a 42-year-old woman who complained of a headache in the village. She took oral antibiotics for four days instead of coming here to get intravenous antibiotics."

The patient arrived on a stretcher, unconscious, accompanied by Sara and three peons. They picked up the woman in their arms in a three-man lift and put her in the empty bed in the critical ward. Sara already placed a tube in her trachea to assist breathing, and it stuck out of the patient's mouth like a cigar. She was breathing spontaneously through the tube, but an ambu bag lay near her head.

"She has meningitis and arrived with seizures. She has been given ten milligrams of diazepam, and she is no longer seizing, but I am a little concerned about her airway," said Sara.

She continued, "This lady is critically ill. The only ventilation machine is the one in Theatre we use for anesthesia. If she stops breathing, you have two choices. Either use the bag-valve-mask, or allow her to die." They all listened to the lungs to confirm tube placement, and then Sara returned to Casualty.

Matt and Alok put on gloves to examine the woman. The first thing they noticed was her skin temperature. They would not need a thermometer to confirm that she was extremely febrile; she was simmering to the touch. Matt lifted the sheet to look at the woman's feet, beckoning Alok.

The woman's feet were cold and mottled purple below the knee, and covered with dark purplish-reddish spots as well. Dozens of reddish spots. They both froze for a second. A quick look at the woman's arms confirmed that these, too, were purple with spots on them.

"You check the pulse in her wrists while I check the pulse in her ankles," said Matt. All pulses were absent.

"Alok. Wash your hands. This is meningococcal meningitis."

They went to the sink and washed their hands for five minutes. Matt's hands reeked of peach soap, but he still felt as though they were crawling with germs.

Sara returned. They showed her the rash.

"You weren't kidding when you said this was life in the trenches," said Matt.

"Yes. It is a death sentence. Even if she survives, she will lose all four limbs. As for exposure, thank God we all are immunized," said Sara.

"No. Not me," said Matt, "I went to the travel clinic in Boston and the doc there said I wouldn't need this shot."

"Oh well, it's treatable in the early stages with penicillin," she said.

"Um, I'm allergic to penicillin."

"You followed universal precautions, didn't you?"

"In the USA that would mean assigning the patient to a private room with negative air flow; only approaching the patient while wearing gowns, gloves, and masks; and special handling of trash."

"I see. I am not minimizing the seriousness of this, but obviously, we are unable to implement the full regimen at the present time. It's the unpleasant reality of life in the trenches."

He giggled. *'Life in the trenches.' O my God now I know the trench we are talking about.* In his mind, he replayed an old *Three Stooges* short in which Curly, Larry and Moe inhaled laughing gas by accident before they marched into a World War One trench under artillery fire.

He chortled, then giggled more. He could picture Moe saying to Larry: *They're going to kill us!*

Larry holds his belly and replies with laughter, *that's a German artillery shell!*

"I fail to see the humour in this situation. What might be so amusing?" she asked.

"Sara, if this was a trench, I would expect incoming artillery rounds. Why am I letting it surprise me? I'm here on an infectious disease ward. I am exposed to a disease. The absurdity of it. Why worry? Just because it's fatal and people die? I chose this."

"Okay Matt. I think continued handwashing is in order. You might isolate this patient as well."

Matt collected himself. He and Alok developed a plan and explained it to the nursing staff. The didi took a rectal temperature, and reported 107 degrees Fahrenheit. They moved the Hepatitis patient out of the isolation room and moved this patient in.

"This is far more dangerous than plain old hepatitis," said Matt.

The antibiotics and anti-seizure medicine were discontinued. The endotracheal tube was left in place.

Later that afternoon, Alok brought Matt to the bedside.

"Matt Sar, she has stopped breathing. You need to declare death."

Matt looked for the heart monitor, almost as a reflex. *I can't confirm asystole*, he thought. He took a stethoscope and listened for heart sounds. There were none. Alok handed him a cotton ball.

"What is this for?"

"To check corneal reflex, Matt Sar. It is reliable. The last reflex to leave before death. If she does not blink, she is truly no more."

He tested the reflex and declared that the patient was dead.

At dinner Ram said, "One time we were visited by an actual infectious diseases expert, on a fellowship from a famous university in USA. We told him that there was a test. If he caught diarrhea within the first two weeks, he would fail the test."

"And?"

"He caught diarrhea within three days. Some things you cannot learn from a book. He was very humble for the remainder of his time with us."

"For me, I am mostly doing well so far, then," replied Matt. "Are you familiar with the term 'fecal veneer'?"

"Perhaps not by this name. I am sure you wish to share with us," said Ram.

"Humans transmit a thin layer of enteric bacteria to everything that they touch. In some places, the fecal veneer is obvious. In others, you can't see it with the naked eye, but it is still there. It is the signature of humanity's presence on the planet."

"This is an ancient concept in South Asia," said Ram, "It is not our culture to touch anybody. It is the original basis of caste rules. We invented public health long before those people in London took the handle off the Broad Street pump."

Matt could still feel a certain itchiness of his hands, as if they would never be clean again.

Sewing Class

Believe nothing just because it was written in ancient books...
— Gautama Buddha

"Matt Sar, there is good news. The incubation period is two to four days, but sometimes up to ten days. If we treat you at the very first sign of a stiff neck, you have a ninety percent chance of survival. And the hospital has some ceftriaxone in stock. They will keep it just for you."

"Alok, did you really look this up just for me?"

"Matt Sar, of course."

"That's very hospitable of you. I truly appreciate how you have planned for every eventuality."

The MBBS system of medical education in Nepal was based on the British model, and Alok was a bit younger than the average medical resident in the USA. One evening at dinner, Alok confided in Matt that his ambition was to be a surgeon. Matt thought back to the one appendectomy Alok assisted with, and his first reaction was to shudder. He thought about it some more and said to himself, *the guy needs to start somewhere.*

At dinner a few days later Matt unveiled a present for Alok. First was a piece of leather about a foot square, flattened out and stretched in a crude square frame. Along with it, a pair of latex gloves, a needle holder, a pair of surgical scissors, a small clamp, and some silk suture material that was attached to a curved needle.

"My dad is a surgeon. He taught me this when I was in elementary school, using the exact same materials. It will help your hands. " said Matt.

"I learned how to do this from my mother, as she repaired clothes," said Ranjit.

Matt gave Alok his first lesson after dinner. They sat side-by-side on a bench directly under the light. Matt made a four-inch incision in the leather and then took the clamp in one hand and the needle holder in the other. He brought the two edges together with the clamp then placed a suture to reconnect the sides of the incision. His hand still hurt, a reminder of his folly with the cautery machine.

He watched Alok try it. Alok fumbled through and was even slower than Matt. Matt resisted the urge to correct Alok. This would be a long-term project, like teaching somebody to play the guitar. He needed to start at the very basics, such as the proper way to hold the tool, how to do a forward and reverse, and how to tie a knot.

"You are a beginner. Every tool is a knife, a fork, or a spoon," said Matt, "That's the first lesson of surgical instruments."

The first assignment was a running suture, drawing the thread after each stitch. After mastering that, Alok would learn the mysteries of an instrument tie-off, how to double-wrap when making a knot, and how much traction to apply.

"From now on, a hundred stitches a day," said Matt.

"Matt Sar, take pity on me," said Alok.

"Work is your destiny. If you can't master this, you will never learn the one-handed tie or the two-handed tie. You must learn this so well that your hands do it while you are thinking of something else, such as how to save the patient. A surgeon is nothing without good hands."

From then on, Alok practiced every evening.

Amanita Phalloides

*There are people in the world so hungry, that God cannot appear to them
except in the form of bread.*

– Mahatma Gandhi

Matt decided to view his time on the Medical Service the same way he
would have approached a fellowship in internal medicine. He would
study each day and apply problem-solving skills using the least invasive
assessment skills possible. He would also analyze the patient population and
apply statistical methods to determine how to improve. The run-of-the-mill
problems of COPD, pneumonia, and meningitis were the bread-and-butter
of the job. *Easily covered by Harrison's.* Matt studied this as well as the
"Cheese and Onion" spiral-bound handbook.

"I have a small present for you," said Ranjit one day, "You will find that
the tropical diseases here add an extra element and this will help."

He gave Matt a worn copy of *The Oxford Handbook of Infectious Disease.*
Matt opened it and looked at the date of publication. 1975.

"Ranjit Dai, this was published the year I was born."

"Matt Sar, don't remind me how young you are. In the scheme of things,
that was yesterday. The diseases in the book have not changed since the
days of Gautama Buddha. This is the best we have."

Matt kept it handy near the Medical Ward. Soon it was full of
bookmarks. Each day at noon, Matt and Alok updated their database and
tried to find ways to improve the care.

"Accuracy in diagnosis is one thing, but we must also look at outcomes
to find ways to improve," Matt told Alok.

Ranjit looked over their efforts and said, "This is good. It will teach you
how to be humble. You will no longer lean on surgery like it was a crutch."

Monsoon progressed and the roads and pathways to Beni became studded
with small landslides and rockslides. In good weather, a truck or Jeep would
appear with three or four people hanging onto the outside, but now the rain
was too miserable to allow this. The flow of patients slowed to a trickle,
and so it was unusual when a family of six arrived all at once.

Here was a 23-year-old woman with four boys. The youngest was still breastfeeding and the others were two, three, and four years of age. The man with them was her father, about 50 years old, a thin man, wearing a topi.

Ranjit came with them and took Alok and Matt aside for a quick conference. "This family is going to die."

"They walked in here. How can this be?" Matt asked.

"They have ingested Amanita Phalloides, the death cap mushroom, and it is fatal. They will all develop liver failure and die within about five days."

Matt looked at the family. The three pre-school boys were healthy and vigorous up until now. They were a bit dehydrated and queasy-looking but an intravenous would relieve that problem.

"It seems overly dramatic to say they will die. How do you know it was Amanita and not something else?" asked Matt.

"They told us that her husband is in India, and he does not often send them any money. To stretch the food budget, they went foraging in the jungle and found plentiful mushrooms. We only have two varieties of poison mushroom. One causes immediate hallucinations, and the other is Amanita. These people are not hallucinating. If Ram were here, he would say, 'Elementary, my dear Watson.' The baby did not eat any mushrooms. He is breastfeeding. He will live. The others will develop liver failure and die. There is no cure. Even if they were in London or Boston, the outcome would be the same."

The boys were admitted to paediatrics, under Sara's care. The baby would bottle-feed for a few days, then a wet nurse would take over. Matt and Alok would care for the two adults.

Morning rounds were different from usual. Normally, every patient brought a relative to sleep under his or her bed at night and help them with such things as bathing and toileting. Today, a whole village moved to the Medical ward. There were forty, including children and women with babies at breast. A carpet of blankets covered the floor, as if this were a re-enactment of the Woodstock rock concert. All the people stood like schoolchildren when Matt, Alok and Prakash entered the room and gave a chorus of namaste.

"What's this?" Matt asked.

"It's the villagers way to say, 'We are here for you' to the victims," said Alok.

"They need to let us do our work," said Matt.

The team started rounds, and the visitors crowded around the first bed as if they were a church choir.

"This first patient is not from their village. Tell them to back off," said Matt, "Can't they give some privacy?"

Prakash gave an extended speech in Nepali, so long that it was obviously not a literal translation. There was no apparent effect on the crowd. The team moved to the next patient and the crowd followed in a haphazard procession from bed to bed.

They finally arrived at the woman's bedside, where Matt and the didi reviewed the patient's graphic chart as well as the amount of intake and output. Everyone watched as Matt examined the woman and her father. Each had vomited all night long. Matt looked at the floor. On each side of both beds, the nurses had placed large metal bowls.

"And what might be the purpose of those?" he asked.

"We instruct them to aim their vomit into the bowl, Matt Sar."

"Wouldn't it be more effective if the bowl were in their lap? I just don't see how they can aim with accuracy from that distance."

As if on cue, the woman vomited. It was no run-of-the-mill Western expulsion of gastric contents. She did it with such force that the stream came out like a garden hose. Matt and Alok stepped back. The stream landed squarely in one of the bowls. A murmur ran through the crowd.

"It's like somebody turned on a spigot," said Alok.

"Certainly not the usual. This is some kind of deep vomit, some kind of soul-vomit. And I never thought you could aim at such a time," said Matt.

Alok decided to address the mob scene himself, since the crowd ignored Prakash. The nurses could not do their work. After a little discussion, Alok announced that everyone needed to leave. The chowkidars came as the villagers gathered their belongings from the floor, grumbling as they packed the food and rolled up the rugs. Soon the crowd thinned to the usual level of population, only one or two visitors per patient. The busload was gone.

That night Matt told Sara about the mob scene.

"I fixed the problem," he said.

"No. You didn't fix anything. The villagers did not leave. They simply moved to the Paediatric ward where the three boys were admitted and set up camp there," she said.

The following morning both adults were unconscious at the time of rounds. The room was pungent with the peculiar smell of melanotic stool, because the father oozed large clots of partially-digested blood from his rectum. There was nothing new to add to the plan of care. *These two may be the sixtieth or seventieth deaths that have happened since I got here,* he thought. *I seem to have lost track.* He reminded himself that somehow he needed to value each passing more than he was. *That is a fact of life in any hospital, it's just a little more obvious here.* At midmorning, Matt and Alok took their lunch break and decided to go over to paediatrics to see the boys.

"Thank God you are here," Sara said as they entered. All three boys made grunting noises as they breathed, lips rimmed with frothy sputum. She and the didi were using a bag-valve-mask on the youngest.

"We have our hands full with this one, but the other two are drowning in secretions as well. Do something about their airways," she commanded. Matt rummaged through the airway box and found the correct airway sizes, then inserted a plastic airway device in each mouth of the two older boys. He used the suction machine to clear oral secretions from each boy in turn. Their breathing improved.

Matt took a closer look. None of the boys showed jaundice but each of their bellies was bloated with ascites like a term pregnancy. None was conscious.

The boys died later that day, first the smallest, then the middle, finally the oldest. After the last boy died, a group of men came to meet with the doctors.

"We are the leaders of the village. We need to take the boys home for cremation. Also, we do not have money to pay for the medical costs here, and we know that it is expensive. If it is inevitable that the woman and her father will both die, we want to take them all at once. We can get a truck and they will be transported together in the back."

This was a very practical approach, but Sara was adamant. Sara told the committee of village elders that they would not be asked to pay for the hospital costs. She pointed out the problems with moving everybody. They agreed and left.

Later she took Matt aside.

"To transport this way along bouncy mountain roads is not the way to die. Every woman deserves the simple dignity of dying in a bed with clean sheets and an electric light at hand. They wanted me to participate in a horrible abomination. I simply will not countenance the lack of respect for the poor mother of those boys. Imagine how she would feel if she woke up and saw her sons piled at her side."

The two adults died the next day. The bleeding from the man's rectum took on a tarry, sticky consistency. Now he vomited bright red blood until he died. The woman stopped breathing at noon. In both cases, Matt used a wisp of cotton to confirm the absence of a corneal reflex. The committee from the village collected the bodies later that day.

Sara was very practical about the episode. "The men told us they always found plentiful mushrooms from that same spot with no problems. I think whoever picked the good mushrooms last year simply pulled them out of the ground. They should have used a knife. The roots would have sent the same species the next year. The improper harvesting served to deplete the good mushrooms from that spot. There were no roots, nor any spores for this year's crop, but the ground there was shady, warm, and moist, a perfect site for some kind of mushroom, and the Amanita took over."

As an aside, she said, "Two years ago, we admitted an entire village of thirty people who all ate amanita and died. This event was not quite so dramatic."

"Sara, I have been here seven months, sharing who-knows-how-many meals swapping war stories. How is it that nobody told that story?"

"You bring fresh eyes, Matt. For us, something crazy may happen, and we all say, 'Oh my' at the time, but the next week some new crazy event happens that wipes the memory clean. And we go on to the next. La-di-da. I guess we just forgot about that other incident until now."

"Or maybe there is stuff that just gets pushed to the bottom," Matt said.

She studied him for a moment. "That, too. Matt, whatever happens, it is our job to get up the next day and do it again."

"I am well aware of that. Everything we do is designed to hold things at a distance. As a matter of fact I find myself wondering whether I am taking these deaths too cavalierly."

"Matt, it is a way to cope. As I say, even in Boston this family would have died. That actually makes it easier to rationalize. When the time comes that you need more coping, let me know."

A week later, the didi at the Guest House made a surprise dinner -"pijja." It came straight from the oven to the table. Pijja was one of the favorite menu items. It was very colorful with tomato sauce and cheese. At first everyone smiled when it was unveiled, then looked over at Matt who was horrified.

"I can't eat this. Look at those mushrooms."

Sure enough, the pijja topping included mushrooms. Sliced and sprinkled on top. Ram excused himself and disappeared into the kitchen, returning a moment later with an empty red can with a label that read "Chef Boyardee."

He set it down in front of Matt's place. Still, Matt used a fork to separate the mushrooms and set them aside. And the team enjoyed the rest of the meal.

Tantra

While Matt recuperated, Ranjit handled the surgical caseload. A couple of times Matt visited Theatre just to observe.

One morning, Matt joined Ranjit on the chautara. Ranjit sat next to five pipes neatly laid alongside his pipe-cleaning tools in two neat rows like surgical tools. He was intent on scraping each bowl in turn and now he held his favorite one, taking pains to avoid soiling his surgical scrubs and white lab coat with pipe ash. Matt's hand was better and he would rejoin Theatre soon.

"You have such strength in your hands, you could have been a sculptor," said Matt.

"I am. It's just that human tissue is my medium," replied Ranjit. "It's the tantric path to wisdom and knowledge. Only by direct experience can you see the folly of being."

"Tantric?" said Matt.

"Yes. You Americans are all alike." He pointed at the pipe brush, then opened his hand as if he were in Theater, expecting Matt to pass the next instrument. Matt smiled to himself as he slapped it into Ranjit's palm.

"You hear that word and you immediately think about sex," Ranjit said, "That is a misapplication of the concept. Taking the tantric path to knowledge implies departing from abstract study and immersing yourself in the facts of the practical world."

"I see. That's pretty important stuff for a surgeon," said Matt.

"Exactly. I think the original tantric Buddhists took notice of some very wise old people who never studied in their youth, but took part in a range of risk-taking adventures when they were younger, and finally became wise when they reflected upon their lives in old age. There is only one problem."

"Which is?"

"Risk-taking is a way to die young. It is dangerous and you may forfeit the opportunity to grow old. An early death is not a sure path to wisdom in old age," Ranjit said, running his finger around the inside of the pipe bowl, "and if you survive without reflecting, then you simply become an old degenerate."

"Which one applies to you?"

"Matt, the first rule of knowledge is to admit what you do not know."

Later that day Ranjit sent a messenger asking Matt to join him in Theatre. A newly delivered woman of the town was shocky due to a possible cervical tear, and a surgical repair was needed. If suturing did not stop the bleeding, she would need a laparotomy and possible hysterectomy. Fortunately, the bleeding stopped with just a couple of stitches, but the patient was now clinically anemic and needed blood. Two units were ordered.

"We started the blood bank since 2002, and it has been a lifesaver. We rely on families to donate. Always remember to ask. Even if your patient will not actually need the blood, we can use it for somebody else. It's not unusual for a postpartum woman to hemorrhage. There was one woman with a rare blood type, and none in the blood bank. We asked every hospital employee for a sample to see if anybody could donate. We could not find a single person with that blood type and the woman died of hemorrhage. Since then we keep a list of everyone's blood type."

"Ranjit, when I was here in 1996, I received a transfusion, I know I did. How was that possible before the blood bank?"

Ranjit could not conceal his surprise.

"I have wondered whether you would ever ask that question. Don't forget that I went to medical school at Patrice Lumumba University in Moscow and my residency was in Belfast, Northern Ireland. I know a few things about trauma."

"I am not asking about your credentials, I am asking about what exactly you did. How was it possible with no technician to perform a type and crossmatch?"

"Doctor Matt. You are a Western doctor in Asia. Have you never heard of Norman Bethune?"

"Enlighten me."

"Norman Bethune was a Canadian surgeon. He pioneered battlefield blood transfusions in the Spanish Civil War and then accompanied Mao Tse-Tung on the Long March. Naturally, the Soviets held him up as an example for us all. I used a technique he described. I did not often do it, but in your case, I was angry and frustrated. I took a gamble and it worked.

"You were in shock and near death. I took a blood sample and collected a sample from some willing donors. The blood test was simple. I mixed the two samples together. Hemolysis and hemagglutination due to blood mismatch can be seen with the naked eye. I held the test tube up to the light, and there was no clumping or plasma discoloration. That was good enough. Somewhere I saved a section of tubing with a needle at each end for just such an eventuality, and I found it for the occasion. One end went in the donor's arm, the other in your arm. We put the donor at a higher level than you, and the blood flowed. Very simple. To this day, I don't really know what your blood type is, or what the donor's type was. They were compatible, that was enough. A rose by any other name would smell as sweet."

"Oh, my God. You did this with me?"

Ranjit was thoughtful. "I believed you were dying at the time. I told you to be thankful that you were alive. Is this not a gift? I knew I was taking a risk, but there was nothing to lose. You were already dying."

Ranjit thought for a moment and added, "We have a range of blood types here. I later learned that there was only a fifteen per cent chance of success.

"Remember. I was young. Now, I love this town. I was born here and I will be lucky to die here. The Christian missionaries sent me to medical school in Moscow so I would return. But – it was a shock to be here after Belfast. In those days, I was hot-blooded. We possessed few supplies and not many trained staff. We were primitive by Western standards. We needed so much work to build this hospital into something. I remember thinking, 'I can't just accept the universal nature of death, no matter what I believe about Buddhism. If I can only save one person here, it will be worth it.' And you were the person."

"And how did you get the donor to agree?" Matt debated whether to say Sushila's name aloud. "Or was there more than one? Was there one donor or two?"

"Matt Sar, I can be very persuasive, you should know that. Let's move to topics that are more important. I need to think of this. We will talk no more of this for now."

Ranjit paused. "In the meantime, remember to ask the patient's relatives for a donation."

That evening, Sara made an announcement at dinner. Samaritan's Purse was a charitable group that refurbished surplus biomedical equipment in the USA and sent it to low income countries. She wrote them when Matt proved that the cautery machine was inoperable. The reply arrived that very afternoon with the Land Rover. Beni Hospital would get a new cautery machine.

In truth, it was not exactly new, but pre-owned. These days many hospitals in the USA were upgrading to surgical lasers. Cautery machines were surplus. The unit would arrive within a few days and somebody should go to Kathmandu to pick it up. This one was thoroughly checked out by the NGO. It would be serviceable and safe to use. It would come with spare parts and the manufacturer's manual.

172

The Picture on the Wall of Shanti Nawajeevan

A speech should be like a woman's skirt. Long enough to cover the subject, but short enough to create interest.

— Sir Winston Churchill

Matt went to the Christian Church for the first few months but then did not attend for a while. He always found something else to do on Saturday morning. Sara never gave up hope that he would attend, and she was persistent about asking.

"I'll meet you there Saturday morning. Will you be delivering the sermon?" he asked.

"No. I loathe public speaking. I will avoid it at all hazards. I would run out of things to say, since the congregation expects a ninety-minute sermon. I go there to worship and see my friends. The Nepalis have their own church and are in charge of all aspects. And of course, God speaks and understands Nepali just as well as he understands English."

"Ninety minutes for the sermon?"

"Yes. I follow along since I can speak fluent Nepali, but you may find it a challenge. Take this." She gave Matt an English-language Bible. "If you are bored, choose any passage you like, and meditate on it while the sermon takes place. Try not to fall asleep."

Sara wrote on a small piece of paper and gave it to Matt. "Be advised, they will ask you to introduce yourself. Here is what you need to say."

Matt read:

"Jah ma sih. Mero Name Matt ho. USA-ma boschun, ani hijo-aja Hospital-ma kam gareko-lagi. Beni mon par cha."

"Thank God it's not ninety minutes," he said.

"Precisely. 'Brevity is the soul of wit.' "

On his way to church, he passed by Shanti Nawajeevan, the hospice. Matt always intended to go there, but so far, he relied on Alok to make rounds and report back. Manju met him at the door.

"I don't often work Saturday morning," she said, "How is your hand? I heard that you tried to capture lightning in a bottle. Didn't your mother teach you not to play with matches?"

"Very funny. Let's keep my mother out of this. I'm going to church, I don't have much time, but I would appreciate a tour."

Manju showed him the hospice. On the ambulatory side, some of the mothers played with their children. On the acute side, there were a half –dozen women in the end stages and it was more somber. The final stop was the nurse's office. Next to the bookshelf was a faded photo, a dozen or so people smiling as they posed stiffly in front of the sign in the street. He peered at it more intensely. He recognized Ranjit, Sara and Ram along with three foreign doctors all in lab coats. Two foreigners wearing suits and neckties. And several women. One of which was Sushila. *Or was it?*

"What is this picture?"

"It's from the dedication of the hospice in 1999. Ram looks really thin in that photo, don't you think?"

"But – who is this woman?" he pointed to the one with the long braid.

"She was the first administrator. I never met her."

"What happened to her, do you know?"

"Funny you should ask. I think she died during the battle. I came here a year later, and she was gone. Nobody will talk about her. They just clam up if you try to ask. Ram was angry with me once and told me never to talk about it. It sounds like it must have been tragic."

"They told me she went to UK."

"Yes, she was in UK at one point. But she came back when her husband died. Then something happened. The civil war really sucks."

Matt felt a visceral reaction but struggled to maintain outward control. He hesitated momentarily. "Thank you. I need to go now."

Outside, he leaned against the wall. Matt felt like his gut was punched. *I fell in love with a Goddess last time I was here*, he thought. *Now I know what happened. That was the main reason for coming here, really.* Manju said it so matter-of-factly. "She died during the battle"- but Manju had never met her. He wanted to tell her to be more respectful – but Manju didn't know. *How could she?*

If I had stayed here, I could have taken her with me. She would have missed the battle and still be alive. With me.

At church, Matt didn't pay attention to many of the details. Prakash greeted him warmly and sat next to him. "I will help you find the hymns in the book."

It was all a blur. The service was crowded. Matt read from the little piece of paper when called upon. There was applause, and Prakash told him he did well. For ninety minutes, the service was nonstop music, one hymn after another. The audience swayed in unison and clapped to the beat.

The room was packed. Everyone clapped and sang in the high-pitched harmonies of south Asia. For one of the songs, everyone lifted their arms in praise as they reached the chorus, and the room became a forest of uplifted palms swaying back and forth—everyone except one person who was now praying an entirely different prayer.

O God, if it's true, I hope that she did not suffer, he prayed. Deep in his heart, he always worried. *So she was not safe in London during the battle. Her husband died. She was here. I hope she was with friends.* There were too many questions. In his mind, he listed all the reasons why everyone had conspired to keep this from him. *I am sure they all loved her the way I loved her. Their grief must be impossible.* He found himself saying the Confiteor, the Catholic prayer asking for forgiveness... *For what I have done and what I have failed to do.....*

Was I better off not knowing?

The music faded into the background. All present lifted hands in praise, swaying to the music. One by one, the men and women of the crowd created their own prayer, speaking in tongues, everyone all at once, in personal communion with God. The crowd was in a place of ecstasy. Tears came to his eyes, and he prayed aloud in English, for Sushila, for everyone who loved her, and everyone in Beni, all those around him, and the whole country.

The crowd came down from the crescendo. Matt dozed off during the sermon, head slumping forward for just a bit until he jerked upright and awake. Prakash nudged him a few times.

After the service, Prakash introduced people to Matt. First, the parishioners who worked at the hospital. Next, the guys in the praise band. Then the pastor spoke and invited Matt to dinner at his home. Through all this, Matt was not paying attention. He needed to be alone.

He walked to the Bajaar, to Sushila's house. He stood in front of the door. There was a padlock and faded paint. The step was dusty and the curtains were drawn behind dirty window glass. *I knew this was possible. I wasn't sure but now I know. Still, it's better to know. Now I see why everybody said to go slow. I need to respect the grief of those who were there with her.*

Homemade Raksi

Tact, sympathy, and understanding are expected of the physician, for the patient is no mere collection of symptoms, sign, disordered functions, damaged organs, and disturbed emotions. The patient is human, fearful, and hopeful, seeking relief, help, and reassurance.

— From Harrison's Principles of Internal Medicine

"I will admit this man to hospital, but I need a second opinion. Here is a 26-year-old who is a heavy drinker and looks like he is in Adult Respiratory Distress Syndrome," said Ram over the phone, "ARDS - I think he is going to die. Please come to Casualty and tell me what you think."

Ram is so courteous to ask, thought Matt. *He already knows the answer, but it's nice of him to include me.* Matt looked at the young man. He noticed stitches over a newly healed scar on the man's face. He took a closer look. *That's my own handiwork. I sutured him after a drunken brawl in town. The same guy. This man is a frequent flyer.* Matt did an abdominal exam while he questioned the father through the interpreter. Yes, the young man drank about a liter of raksi a day. The father tried to get his son to stop drinking but could not. Two other men sat with the father.

The young man was drenched in sweat. He breathing was labored despite an oxygen mask. The hospital did not have the capacity to do blood gas analysis, but the oxygen saturation was fifty per cent. He had all the signs of pancreatitis and ARDS.

Matt left the room to talk with Ram. "I have nothing to add. His illness is well advanced. He's about to die."

"How would you treat this man if he was a patient in Boston?"

"He needs intubation and a mechanical ventilator and probably a bicarb drip, but he would still be in a high-risk group, probably less than a twenty per cent chance of survival even with every high-tech tool we could use."

"None of these are available to us."

"Well, he's circling the drain right now, let's at least give him some morphine. And tell the father."

Ram entered the room just as two women arrived with three more men. *Everything in Nepal always gets a crowd of onlookers. Everything. There was no such thing as privacy in this country.* Not just that, but every one of the men was distraught. The two women were the wife and the mother. When the mother walked in, the father jumped up out of the chair. Until now, the older woman was quietly grim, but as soon as she made eye contact with her husband, she started to berate him. Now the husband's friends held his arms to keep him from punching her. The younger woman, the wife of the patient, went to the bed where her dying husband lay and began to wail. Matt saw this from a distance, and he asked the didi to go get all the chowkidars and all the other doctors to come right away. The situation was escalating and it was going to be bad.

The young man stopped breathing. Matt saw cape cyanosis and jugular venous distension. The man was unresponsive. Ram listened to his chest with a stethoscope, and with his eyes signaled to Matt that there was no heartbeat. He shook his head. Ram took a cotton ball from his pocket. He opened the patient's eye and touched the cotton to the cornea. There was no response. Ram told the father that his son had just died.

The father jumped up and grabbed Ram by the lapels of his lab coat, dragging him over to the head of the bed, demanding that he do something. One of the other men took the ambu bag that was on the small bedside table and tried to apply it to the face of the dead young man, shouting for help. The mother held the wife. They both wailed as the younger woman removed the bangles from her forearms and threw them on the floor. She stomped on them with a crunching noise as small bits of red glass went flying. One man started pounding Ram on the back, and soon two of the other men joined in, trying to pull Ram's lab coat down and immobilize his arms. One was trying to get Ram in a headlock. Everyone was screaming now. Ram was almost dancing with the father as they were locked in a strange embrace, and Ram shouted for help.

Ram was bigger than any of them, but he was outnumbered. For a moment, Matt watched as if it was a boxing match on TV.

This is not a drill.

Nobody will come.

Ram will get thrashed - or killed.

Matt abandoned any sense of dignity and composure and jumped in to the fray, trying to prevent the wiry village farmers from strangling his colleague. He grabbed the father from behind and tried to pull him away.

All the chowkidars, three of them, converged from other parts of the compound, along with Alok, Sara, Ranjit, the business office manager, a laundryman, and the Land Rover driver. A struggle ensued for several minutes, with Sara shouting, "Stop this!" over and over. Now the wife and mother both jumped on to the stretcher with the dead man and would not leave; one man started pulling equipment trays from the shelves and throwing them to the floor. The chowkidars brought nightsticks and started hitting the men on the shins, knocking them down. After awhile the two sides were separated. The father wept as he lay on the floor clutching his shin.

Ram steadied himself against a shelf, red-faced and sweating as he regained his breath. "Never say for whom the bell tolls, Matt Sar. And now you see an ugly side of medicine in Nepal."

"No kidding."

Somewhere along the way, two hands twisted the collar of Matt's scrub shirt around his throat, trying to strangle him until his eyes bugged out. Now he had a headache. His clothes chafed, and he was short of breath. Looking around, everyone looked like a rugby team resting during a time out. Even Sara took part in the jostling. She was at the sink, washing her face.

Matt heard protests from the corridor as the last men were escorted away.

"That was eleven against six. I am glad we outnumbered them. It is much easier," said Ranjit.

Sara looked at Matt. "This - has been - a problem. Last year there was an assault at a hospital in Kathmandu, and the doctor received a skull fracture. The doctors of Nepal called for a nationwide bandh on medical care for one day."

Then, "This could have been worse, a lot worse."

"And where are the police?" asked Matt.

Sara spoke up. "They are at their station in the parade ground. The police would never get here in time. They are not invested in helping us. Every doctor in Nepal worries about this, every day. The families think we ought to do miracles. They are ignorant about medicine. They have unrealistic expectations."

"Now you have seen it. This is ugly. You are part of the family now. We have no secrets from you any longer," said Ram, "This is why so few doctors want to work in the small hospitals. These people are ignorant, and they make it worse for everyone. Usually they leave me alone, but not this time."

"Jesus H. tap-dancing Christ. I didn't want to stand here and let them kill you," said Matt, "I wondered why the staff ran away during these emergencies, and now I know why." He was still collecting himself, and his hand throbbed. He did not recall gripping or punching anyone. He clenched it a few times.

Sara stood right next to him. As soon as he said the name of Jesus, he knew it was a mistake. She set her jaw and caught her breath, just for a moment. Then she resumed that aura of imperturbability. *Showing a bit of phlegm.*

He looked over at her. *The swear word bothers her more than the brawl.* He surveyed the room to see if anybody else was hurt.

And Ram is still quoting literature. Naturally. Of course.

"That was a farmer with no money who does not have electricity or TV in his house. They make their own raksi. I am surprised the boy didn't have a bleeding ulcer first," added Ranjit. "That father has listened to the promises of the Maoists. Only since yesterday is talk of peace, but hardly one day passes, and he is furious that the promises of advanced medical care did not come true overnight." He gestured at the body of the dead young man and said, "That was his first-born son. Now there may be nobody to conduct the rituals when he dies and his next rebirth may be worse than this life."

"And this is a Buddhist country?" said Matt, "This is a country of lovingkindness and compassion? Hah. I think the Americans would call this 'tough love.' "

"That is the paradox of Buddhism," said Ranjit, "As a young doctor I would see these violent things and wonder why they happened, knowing that it was not something that Buddhists should do. Then I realized we are not born Buddhist. All the focus on channeling anger and dealing with hardship did not emanate *from* these people…. It was a lesson *to* these people. We are a land of Buddhists because we need to hear the lessons of Buddha, not because we follow Buddha."

He wiped his forehead. "We are not Buddha."

Ram continued, "Imagine what this would have been like if there was never any Buddha to show a better way. Is it not better to aspire to be Buddha?"

Matt said, "I don't have an answer, Ram dai. We need to pick up the pieces here and get on with the task at hand." *So this is part of the deal,* he thought. *I'm going to need to think of this, like setting an alarm clock.* He decided that the next time he saw the chowkidars at the canteen he would take time to talk with them and pay for their samosas and chiya as a gesture of friendship.

Cyber Café

The day after the rugby scrum in the Casualty, Matt took a walk to the cyber café at the Bajaar. He had not checked email in a month. The café was in an old building near the big chautara. Next door was the store that sold TVs, and Matt wished he had recruited the TV guy to fix the cautery machine.

The boy at the counter gestured for Matt to sit at the computer closest to the door. There were three other computers, and small groups of teenage boys sat at each, looking over the shoulder of whoever it was that happened to be sitting at the keyboard, and jostling for the chair. *They don't even check their email alone here*, thought Matt.

The internet was working today. There were reminders from his bank and cheery messages from former colleagues of his residency program, now beginning their careers. Next came some business-like emails from his dad, taking care of financial details and his loans, and about the plans for Matt to join the group practice when he returned. He decided that somehow, he needed to talk with John about the important stuff. *There is no future after Nepal. There is only the here and now.*

Maureen, the red-haired nurse from San Francisco, sent a cheery email. Her trek was wonderful, and she gave toothbrushes to village children along the way. She hinted about his quest and wondered if he was keeping hope alive.

He thought, *that's the one who was so devoted to orderliness. It's obvious what she wants to know. How do I tell her that nothing here has been orderly?*

He deleted her email.

The next message was from Barbara, his mother. She was worried about his safety and reminded him to be careful of Maoists.

He needed to reply, but if he wrote about the accident with the cautery, or the meningococcal meningitis, or the bench-clearing brawl in Casualty, she would have an anxiety attack that not even his dad could pull her out of. *She might call the CIA and demand backup*, he chuckled, *and I'd probably meet John Smith again. Barbara could teach these people a thing or two about anger.*

He wrote:

Mom:

I'm just fine. I'm lying in a very comfortable ditch.

Matt.

She will know I am mocking her. That would be like taunting the tiger at the zoo. He deleted that one.

He wanted to write about Sushila. To find her was the original goal. The short conversation with Manju replayed in his head. *I am no closer to unraveling the mystery of what happened.*

The fact of finding out that she was dead.

But Barbara and John never knew she existed, how could they understand what she meant to him?

No, can't write that one.

He composed a bland little story about all the prayer, the Nepali Christian Church, and all the Bible study in Beni. He completed a full page and looked it over.

Then he stopped.

Barbara would see through it. There are limits to how much I can lie to my mother, after all.

The truth is so crazy that everyone else would think I was exaggerating and lying, he thought, *I'm caught in a trap. I need an alibi for my whereabouts over the last seven months. Who I was with and what I was doing. And Mom knows I haven't been in San Quentin after all.* He found the delete key and held his finger over it for a second as he re-read what he had just written. And deleted it all.

Then Matt started over from a blank page. *Write something. Anything.* He sent a short reply to say:

Dear Mom,

I'm sorry I haven't been in more regular contact, but I've been busy. I'm exercising a lot and the leg is just fine. The people have been great and the locals are very spiritual. I'm getting closer to God than I ever was. Mom, I love you so much and I think of you. Take care of Dad and write when you can.

Love, Matt

The Reason Why Surgeons Practice the Art of Surgery

No greater opportunity, responsibility, or obligation can fall to the lot of a human being than to become a physician. In the care of the suffering, (the doctor) needs technical skill, scientific knowledge, and human understanding…

— From *Harrison's Principles of Internal Medicine*

Alok was not doing as many sutures in the frame as Matt had assigned, and Matt was disappointed.

"What's gotten into you? You don't seem motivated to practice."

"I still want to be a surgeon, Matt Sar, but I am distracted."

"Alok, developing manual dexterity is like playing a musical instrument. Practice, practice, practice. You need to be able to do this at any time of the day or night, no matter what is distracting you. What is the problem?"

Alok was hesitant at first. "Matt Sar, no matter what I try to do, I can't get the thought of her out of my mind. She is so beautiful and wonderful."

Oh no. "Who?"

"I have trouble saying her name out loud, Matt Sar."

"Well then, I can't help you. Whisper the name in my ear."

"Okay then, Matt Sar. She is – Manju."

Now it was obvious. *No wonder he was so eager to make rounds at Shanti Nawajeevan.*

"Alok, you have contracted a sickness with no known cure."

"I thought so. What shall I do? Ever since we were together on a medical camp last year, I have loved Manju. Trying not to think of her only makes it worse. She is so – mysterious. She did further study in America, she lived in Singapore, and she is daughter of Gurkha."

Alok was on the verge of tears. "I don't have a chance."

It didn't hurt that she also had a nice figure and beautiful teeth, thought Matt. She was a year or two younger than Alok. *This has sprung into full blossom under my nose,* he thought. *Oh well, join the club.*

"But you must suture, it is not good for a surgeon to be pre-occupied with thoughts of sex all the time."

"Matt Sar, this is not about sex, this is about love and romance." said Alok.

"Okay, that was a poor word choice. Here is what you can do. She is a nurse, right? She knows about suturing. When you start thinking of her, dedicate each stitch as you go along. Pretend that she will inspect every one. Maybe that will help."

"Matt Sar, you are a genius."

"No, this is simply the way I learned. When I was a boy, I practiced just as you are doing, and my mother praised my work lavishly. She would hug me, reward me with milk and cookies, and predict a bright future."

"Matt Sar, your mother must be wonderful."

"Let's put it this way. My mother made me what I am today."

When I have a son, I wish that Manju would be just such a mother."

"Aren't you getting ahead of yourself? You have a long way to go before thinking about a family. Say, do you have any sisters? Perhaps they could visit and you could ask Manju to show them the town. You can ask them to sing your praises. It always helps. Most of the time a woman will be more eager to do something when there are other women around encouraging her. They can be your cheerleaders."

"Matt Sar, I have three sisters. I will send them email today. Are you sure it will work with Manju?"

"A woman's heart turns inside out when she meets a sensitive man who carries the heavy burden of saving humanity. Of course it will work. But for now - practice."

Manju often joined the team at dinner. Sara enjoyed having another woman at the table. It kept the boys civilized. Alok could not hide his interest from the all-seeing eyes of Ram or the others. He would steal glances at Manju, and if the bowl of chicken happened to rest in front of her setting, he was too shy to ask her to pass it his way.

"What to do about Alok?" Ram asked Ranjit, "We are depriving our precious MBBS student of an education. If he were in Kathmandu, he would hang out with a group of young men and Manju would be in a group of women. The groups would get to know each other the way that young Nepali men and women have done since the days of Siddhartha Gautama Buddha. But here he is isolated. We are his only sanga."

"Ram, I agree that Alok needs some direction away from thoughts of carnal pleasure. But I fear that you have left the realm of logic. Are you now reading love poetry? May I suggest that you stick to military history or *The Life of Gandhi?* And why not read a medical journal?"

"No, I have been meditating on the Bhagavad Gita as befits a proper Hindu. But you have given me an idea. In my wife's possessions, there was a book of love poems by Pablo Neruda. He is the Spanish Buddha of love. Do you think I should give this book to Alok? I will look for it in my library."

"Do not mock the Buddha. We need to find a better way to teach the young man to control his passions. He will do better on his exams if he studies *The Cheese and Onion.*"

From then on, the two older men changed their tone when they addressed Alok at dinner. They were careful to include Alok in the professional conversation, giving him openings to display his scholarship and compassion and his other fine qualities.

Alok sensed this and he was grateful. He thanked Saraswati, the Goddess of Learning, for his good fortune. He could not bring himself to talk with Ranjit or Ram about his feelings, but somehow fate delivered these two unlikely wingmen to help him. He now gained a sense of confidence regarding Manju.

Finally, a time came when Alok gathered his courage and invited Manju to dinner at the Hotel Himshikhar in the Bajaar. They would share momo along with spicy lollipops of chicken legs.

Manju met him at the hospital and they walked together. Like Alok, she was dedicated to her job. She was also in charge of a women's knitting group and a women's support group. She also took a Bollywood dance class.

Manju wore her brown and white kurtha suruwal. It was the best one she owned. It flowed as she walked, and she knew that somehow the fabric invited onlookers to watch the way she moved.

Alok made a conscious effort not to stare at Manju. He was nervous to see her sitting across from him and gazing into his eyes, smiling. He didn't know how to converse. He told her all about his three sisters and his mother. Alok wanted to hold Manju's hand on the walk back to the Guest House, but she pulled away.

At the Guest House, Alok sat on the bench by the suturing frame to show her his skill. He wanted to impress her. Manju looked at him in a new light. She knew plenty of surgeons but they were all older, and she had not really met a surgeon-in-training before. *He has never seen me knit,* she thought.

She said, "Anybody can do that."

"You try it, then." With a flourish, he moved aside.

He was still next to her and reached his arm around her waist to guide her hands. He was close enough to enjoy the scent of her hair. Manju pushed his hands away, and their eyes met.

Manju needed a second to collect herself. *Will I ever be able to relax?* Manju asked herself. *I like this guy. But - I am not ready.* Then, she started the same stitch Alok had just shown her. It was obvious that her manual dexterity was superior to his.

"You're good. You are putting me to shame."

"I have used knitting needles ever since I can remember," she said, not looking up.

"Manju, I am in awe of your hands."

She was not ready to reveal anything that was personal about herself. It still hurt to be Manju at times, but she was dealing with this new idea. She returned to suturing on the frame, faster this time.

"There is something you need to know about me," she said, waving the needle driver at him, with the needle still attached. "You and I may be able to take our relationship to a different place, someday. But, I am not ready to go there right now. Can you accept that?"

Alok said, "Manju, I want to have you in my life, and if this requires waiting until you are ready, I will do so."

*Maybe at last.....*she went back to the frame, examining her work, not giving Alok eye contact, trying to stay cool, but hanging on every single word, hiding this from him.

"If we are ever to become a couple and have a future together, I think we need to start off with mutual honor and respect," he continued, "It's okay to start with the idea of having a relationship, something that might develop someday."

Manju reached over to clasp Alok's head and bend it to her, then kissed Alok's forehead. She cradled his head in her hands and felt the way his hair curved over his ears, massaging his neck for a moment. They looked into each other's eyes.

"Here," she said, "I have done enough. You take over."

She watched and smiled while he worked with every bit of dexterity he could summon and described to her the different stitches. He showed her the one-handed knot—with each hand. She told him about the village knitting project and the way to knit a ski hat for sale in USA sports catalogs.

186

Madonna and Child

Matt and Ranjit sat out on the chautara after dal-bhaat one day, Ranjit smoking his pipe, expounding on the subject of malaria in the district. Beni was at a low altitude and malaria was a known risk, but there were only a few cases here. "We made major strides against it with DDT," he said, "Look overhead."

Matt was sullen. *I just don't know why I am sitting here. Is he jerking me around on purpose?*

Ranjit blew a stream of tobacco smoke skyward to accent the direction. "See the birds?" Matt squinted into the sky, through the leaves of the shade tree, barely making out a half dozen birds like the letter "W" in the sky, soaring.

"Matt, those large circling birds are lammergeyers. They are the carrion birds of Nepal. Surely, you must have seen them on National Geographic Channel. They make their nests at timberline."

He continued, "Many people here favor sky burial. They bring the body to the mountains and leave it for the scavenger birds. The lamas dismember it with a khukri so the birds will make quick work. Later the lamas go back to collect the bones. That is a fine way to recycle the remains of a person if you ask me. When we used the DDT, the bird population dropped. Now they have returned to their past levels. And the circle of life goes on. Sometimes I wonder if our main task here is to feed the lammergeyers. They fly overhead to remind us of something."

"What might that be?"

"For me, it is that I will not have this life forever. The next one waits for us."

Matt just gazed at the sky. *It's time we talked. I feel like I need to challenge Ranjit to a duel. I've had about as much secrecy as I can take.*

"The first Christian hospital in Nepal was founded by an expedition of birdwatchers from Britain. The birds of Nepal brought us the healing powers of Jesus," said Ranjit as he tried to blow a smoke ring.

What does it take to talk about something important? thought Matt.

Matt was just about to bring it up – the one thing they never talked about – when Ranjit said, "Look."

On the pathway, a young woman shambled along stiffly and painfully, her shoulders hunched. Her face was shaded by a cheap cotton shawl. She wore a lungi, a loose one-piece garment like a muumuu or housecoat, with no belt. Alongside her, two other women, also young, held the edges of the lungi in such a way as to create a tent inside which the woman walked.

A fourth woman walked behind holding a crying infant who looked to be less than a month old, not even able to hold its own head up and very small. The woman in the tent wore cheap sandals and placed her feet with great care like walking on stones. She stopped to look over at Matt and Ranjit.

Ranjit made the namaste gesture to the woman. She made eye contact with Matt and held it – for a bit longer than Matt expected.

She is beautiful, Matt thought, *Like Sushila in those long ago days. I think of Sushila, and this one appears*.....The resemblance was striking – long black hair, big brown eyes, a space between the front teeth, and that bronze complexion.

Ranjit said, "Enough idle talk. I can see that we need to work today." He banged his pipe against the sole of his shoe, showering sparks and grinding them to ash to extinguish the flame. Ranjit emptied his pipe so many times in that spot that Matt could see streaks of gray ash mixed into the red dirt. Matt and Ranjit followed the woman and her odd procession to Casualty.

In Casualty, the young woman shivered, teeth chattering. The didi cut away the garment, stiffened by dried blood, and it was obvious what was wrong. The woman was helped onto a stretcher.

The didi brought hoops to put over the stretcher and draped a sheet over the hoops. The bed looked like a Conestoga wagon, and the linen did not come in contact with the open wounds. Under the hoops, she lay on her belly. Matt went to the head of the stretcher to introduce himself. He saw her face again. Her name was Samjhana.

The first order of business was to examine the skin on Samjhana's back and arms and legs. At first, it appeared grimy with some kind of speckled dirt. Then Matt realized that no, this was eschar – the medical word for dead charred skin. And it covered her back, extending to the back of her neck, her legs and buttocks as well as looping around her belly. She smelled like burned hair and kerosene. Ranjit took the lead. He started an intravenous line and examined every surface of skin, turning her with the help of Matt and the didi. The didi asked the friends to tell the story as Ranjit listened. "They are saying this happened two days ago in the village about four kilometers away."

Ranjit tallied the extent of injury on a score sheet. "This is a sixty percent burn, mostly third degree, from kerosene." He ordered morphine.

Next was a conversation with the three friends. Samjhana was fifteen, as was her husband. The husband and his parents were unhappy with the dowry offered at the time of marriage a year ago, and a few months after the wedding, they asked her parents to buy him a new motorcycle, an expensive one. Samjhana's parents were unable to fulfill this demand, and this young woman was beaten and bruised by her new family. Then she became pregnant and things were better for a while, until a daughter was born.

Matt looked at the baby. "You are telling me that she would get punched and kicked and shouted at all day, then at night her tormenter used her for sex? That was her life?"

Ranjit stared at him for a moment. "Yes. Having a daughter made it worse. And the dowry. It is not legal for money to change hands but the practice continues. This is a bride-burning. I am ashamed of Nepal when this happens."

Bride-burning. The diagnosis burned in Matt's mind. *So frequent that they have a name for it. This is life in hell,* he thought.

Ranjit said, "Look at the pattern of those burns. This was not an accident with a cooking fire or boiling oil. She turned her back to protect herself when the husband threw the kerosene on her. There is a Hindu legend about a goddess who burned herself this way to achieve a higher rebirth. Never let anybody use Hindu beliefs to justify this. Hinduism is a beautiful way to lead a life. To burn a woman this way is not Hinduism, it is ignorance, poverty, and the greed of people who know nothing."

Samjhana seemed a little more relaxed due to the morphine. Now they could assess the need to relieve pressure on swollen tissue. The areas of burned skin were now shrunk and tightened while at the same time the underlying tissue was swelling due to the injury. The injury constricted her movement and breathing. Ranjit performed a series of escharotomy incisions to relieve the pressure. Ranjit smiled at her and spoke soft words of reassurance, but he set his jaw and shook his head when she couldn't see. Her breathing improved.

"Your baby is just fine. We will take good care of her until you recover," he said. He looked over at Matt with a blank expression.

The reassurance is all an act, thought Matt.

Matt leaned close to Samjhana. "Tell me the baby's name?"

She whispered, "Apsara."

He was looking at Ranjit as he replied, "That is a beautiful name. She is a beautiful baby." He did not know what else to say.

At the nurse's station Matt asked, "So will you debride the wounds? Or what about skin grafts?"

Ranjit shook his head. "Futile. We have a grafting tool, and we often conduct grafting for burn victims here, but the percentage exceeds sixty percent. Too extensive. For every square inch of burn, we need a square inch of donor site. From a practical point of view, there are not enough sites on her body from which to obtain enough donor skin. In USA, her hospitalization would cost a million dollars. Here it is futile. No pigskin, no synthetic skin. She will die of sepsis. We will give her pain medicine, but not antibiotics. We allow her to die of sepsis. This is the accepted protocol throughout Nepal. Futile."

"But you used the phrase 'until you recover,' " said Matt.

"I always offer the path of hope, Matt. Physical pain is one thing, suffering is another. Why does she need to know she will die? About Apsara, she seems healthy, but if we don't find a wet nurse, she may also die. The water quality here is not good, and this baby will inevitably acquire diarrheal illness if she is bottle-fed."

The next morning before rounds, Matt saw the hoops on a bed in the corner of Gynae Ward. On the nearby windowsill was a small dish of clear oily fluid with a faint smell of gasoline. Matt picked it up to discard it, but the didi explained that this was insecticide to keep the flies away. He called Samjhana by name and received a whimpering reply.

Next, Matt lifted a corner of the blanket and peeked under the hoops. She was still on her stomach and looked up at him with puffy eyes. Her hair was stringy with sweat. She was slathered in Silvadene, the white creamy paste used to prevent infection. He did not know what to say, he just took her hand and held it for a second. There was a cup of water nearby with a straw, and he held it for her as she sipped it. He touched her forehead. She was burning with fever.

He repeated to himself a prayer from childhood… *Hail Mary, full of grace, the Lord is with thee. Blessed be thou among women, and blessed be the fruit of thy womb…*

Matt turned away to complete the prayer. *Oh God, I don't know what happened to Sushila, but if she suffered somehow, like this woman, I wish you held her in the palm of Your hand and made it okay.*

He found the didi. He explained that Samjhana needed to get her morphine for pain every two hours around-the-clock, as opposed to waiting until she asked for it. He wrote the order in the book.

Later Matt went to Sara's office. He came upon Sara and Bimla, sharing tea and laughing at some private joke. Bimla was obviously pregnant. One cheek was bruised, and she turned her face away from that side when speaking to him. *And Bimla too? Surely not Bimla. Was she also a victim?*

Bimla returned to her desk, leaving Matt and Sara alone.

"Is Bimla..?"

"Yes, and she will be having her baby here. This is her fourth. She has a boy and two girls. She asked me for an elective Caesarean, but I told her we couldn't do it unless there was a medical reason. She has delivered vaginally three times. A proven performer."

"She has a facial bruise."

"Yes. There are issues of domestic violence here. I think you have seen it firsthand," said Sara, "Please sit. There is more tea."

"Thank you. I'll get to the point. I came by because I have been wondering what will happen to the infant of Samjhana."

"She is already with a wet-nurse. She will do fine."

"Is the wet-nurse from Emmaus Church?"

"No. Why? Does it matter?"

"Just –wondering. Ranjit was worried."

"Ranjit is a pessimist sometimes, and I think he is depressed. He should know better. Have you not read the life story of Siddhartha Buddha?"

"Not really."

"Siddhartha's mother died seven days after his birth, and he was raised by Mahapajapati, a wet-nurse, his mother's sister. She achieved a favorable rebirth because of it. Every woman in Beni learns the story of Mahapajapati from childhood. To breastfeed a baby under these circumstances is a way to acquire much good karma. It is also helpful that I know every lactating woman in this town."

"That's a relief. What about the fact that a crime was committed?"

She replied, "Our Nepali administrator reported this incident to the police. He actually used the word 'murder' when he told them, but I do not think they will investigate, let alone prosecute. The police will not come here to collect a statement before she dies. It is not murder unless she is dead. Her death is inevitable, but that does not register with the police. It is a shame that this woman's family is not around. Her husband may very well get away with this. That is a crime on top of the original crime."

"Oh, no."

"You sound discouraged."

"How do you cope with this? Doesn't it make you lose faith in God? Do you ever ask God why this happens?" he asked.

"Oh, dear."

She studied him for a minute. "I thought maybe you were depressed because it was taking so long to get your hand back in working order. It's been a month – but that's not it, is it?"

She poured more tea.

"Matt, somebody once told me, 'We are not here to confirm our faith in God, but to explore our faith.' Maybe that will help you."

"I don't get it."

"You are at a very interesting crossroads in your medical practice, Matt. Let me lay out a challenge for you, in non-Biblical terms."

"I am listening."

"People choose medicine or nursing because they have heard that it pays well, it's a profession, and there is prestige. Or maybe because they choose to follow their father, as in your case."

"Yes, that's true, and in my case it was both my father and grandfather. There was a never a time when I was not expected to be a doctor."

"Exactly. The point is they don't have a clue what they are actually getting into. How can you possibly know when you are choosing at the age of fifteen?"

"My dad used to cook up crazy projects for the sole purpose of developing hand dexterity. My mom taught me sewing at the age of eight."

"Yes, and I have noticed that most such people start off treating everything like it is just an intellectual game as in school. Some people go through their entire career and treat it like it's just a well-paying job."

"Well, frankly, I have been thinking that they couldn't pay me a million dollars to do burn care. And I can't get her suffering face out of my mind."

"Matt, you dear boy," Sara looked at him and put her hand on his shoulder, "There will come a time when you look at all the angles, all the clinical data, all the options, and you will say that exact thing to yourself. Then you will go in to the room, meet the person suffering in the bed, and you will make the conscious decision to serve that person anyway. Not for yourself. Not for any amount of money. For God. That is when you know you have finally put away the childish things. Maybe that day has finally come for you."

"You have blown me away." He was on the verge of tears. *I know I need to cry. I should allow myself to just be sad and get it over with. .I still can't quite do it.*

"When you see the face of a suffering patient, remember that you are looking at the face of God. Meditate on that simple fact and use it as a jumping off place for prayer, Matt. There is more to surgery than using a scalpel. Medical care has to be guided by love. You will be a better surgeon for it. In the meantime, God has his own time frame. Resist the urge to judge God. It is our task to do what we can and not wallow in a slough of despond. I will put you on my prayer list, Matt, and I think we need to chat about this more often."

The next morning Matt again stopped by the Gynae Ward. He looked in the corner for Samjhana's bed. He smelled bleach, lots of bleach. The bed was empty now. The bare hoops were piled next to it. After the bed aired out, the small pile of neatly folded blue sheets would be spread out for the next occupant. Matt looked in the census book. Samjhana died of burn sepsis at eleven-thirty. Samjhana was fifteen years-old at the time of death, and now she always would be.

The Arrival of the Cautery Machine

Matt's return to surgery was low key. Ranjit and Ram welcomed him warmly and they did two gallbladder cases together. Ranjit kept an eye on the clock. *He seems happy to have me back*, Matt thought. *Things are looking up*.

"Matt Sar, today at noon I take the Land Rover to the Pokhara airport. Now that your hand is better, I am taking time to go to Kathmandu. When I come back, I will have a present for you."

"I don't blame you for taking time off. Thank you for covering the schedule. And what's the present? Don't tell me – it's the cautery machine."

Ranjit laughed, "The very thing you have dreamed of, Matt." He and Ram exchanged knowing glances.

"Life is reduced to its essence when all you want is a working cautery machine," said Matt.

After surgery, Matt and Ram joined the sendoff at the Land Rover. Ranjit appeared at the last minute, smiling and happy. Sara and Ram gave Ranjit a tika and two kata scarves. He accepted them with a deep bow. Ranjit waved out the window as the Land Rover began the trip to Pokhara.

"You act like he is going away for a month, not three days," said Matt.

"Let's sit under the tree, Matt," said Sara. "Ranjit asked me to talk with you after he left." She sat with Matt on the stone of the chautara where Ranjit usually enjoyed his pipe.

"Okay, tell me. You obviously have news. I can't figure out whether it is good news or bad news." he said.

"I won't beat around the bush, Matt. He's bringing back more than just the cautery machine. A couple of days ago, I received an email from the U.K. You might as well see it."

She gave it to him. It was a flight schedule, starting at Heathrow and ending with Kathmandu as the final destination.

The passenger's name was Sushila Gurung.

Matt's hand trembled. "How can this be? I thought – "

"I gather that you supposed she was dead, isn't that so?"

He stared at the name on the paper. He was frozen.

"Yes… I just don't know what to say. This is a shock to me."

"If you don't want to see her we can call Ranjit…" she smiled.

He laughed out loud. "That's not it. Of course I want to see her. Bring her here today. But – this is like magic… what happened? I have to tell you, honest to God I did think she was dead."

"Oh, dear. I don't know where to start. When you and I talked about that burn victim, I was worried. Then Manju came to me. She told me about your stop at the hospice."

"Oh? Well – that was not a happy day, but give me credit. I was working things through."

"Matt, you are such a typical surgeon at times. You never ask for help. There is a limit to how much you can stuff your feelings. It was getting obvious."

Really?

"Manju knew she'd upset you, but she couldn't put her finger on what it was that she said or did. So she came to me. And we put two-and-two together."

"It was time to end the charade, and I sent word to London. I wasn't expecting her until next week, Matt. I don't think Ranjit knew for sure that she was coming. Believe me, it hasn't been easy to keep this secret. I participated as a favor to Ranjit and Sushila. There never was a right time to talk about this."

"She wanted it that way?"

"Yes. She begged us to never say anything."

"Sara. I am here. I am listening. I need to get over this surprise. Why not tell the story from the beginning?"

"Out of respect, I think she wishes to tell you some of the details in person. Let me just say that she has been studying in the U.K. and now her university is on Holiday. She has not been back to Beni since she left after the battle. The battle was particularly difficult for her. She and Ranjit witnessed a war crime."

"Was she wounded? Manju led me to believe she was dead."

"She was beaten but survived the ordeal with only minor injuries. Please don't blame Manju. We never told Manju anything. She is a bright girl but she guessed incorrectly. Manju meant no harm. No, Sushila is in the pink of good health. Right after the battle, we learned that there might have been a price on her head. She needed to disappear. And we helped her do it."

"That explains the news blackout."

"Yes. We thought there would be retaliation."

"Okay – but I need one more answer. Manju also told me that her husband was dead. Is that – still true?"

Sara chose her words carefully. "She is not presently married. Again, I think she wants to talk with you herself. You will simply need to wait. When she comes back, would you please allow her a bit of time to settle in? We all thought it best if she spoke to you herself. I know that she has a lot to talk about with you."

"I certainly need to take time to process this." *She's not married.* He repeated this to himself. Over and over. He wasn't listening so well once Sara gave him this fact.

"Matt, dear boy. I will allow you the time for this. But you may want to ask yourself one question. You've thrown yourself into the work of surgery. It takes a degree of strength to insulate yourself from the emotions of your patients. Have you worked so hard to hide the emotions, that you can't express your own when you have them?"

Boys don't cry. I can't bring myself to cry in front of a woman.

"I'm working on it. It's just not something I do when I confront a problem."

"There is a time for everything, Matt. The Catholic Bible still includes Ecclesiastes."

She took her leave and returned to clinic rounds.

Matt looked up at the tree branches. He thought about what she said. Finally he laughed, for the first time in a while. That day he noticed that everything around him pulsated with a new brightness and color. He stopped to listen to the birds and enjoyed the chorus. He imagined their plumage and smiled to himself.

The surgery schedule continued while Ranjit was gone. Matt did a Caesarean delivery with Ram providing the anesthesia. Alok assisted, tying off the bleeders and listening to Matt talk about cautery. Matt wrote in the post-op note that the delivery was "unremarkable" and smiled as he reflected upon this simple word. Usually the post-op note listed the problems and concerns during surgery, but this time there were none. *To reach the "unremarkable" plateau takes a lot of work. It is an accomplishment.* Matt could now lead this procedure, with Alok as the sidekick.

Surgery is therapy for the surgeon, thought Matt, the day the Land Rover was due back. He was grateful to spend the morning in Theater, knowing that it would keep his mind occupied. Matt kept an eye on the clock as he worked. He finished the case and went looking for Sushila.

2007 – Elisar

He found her in the dining room of the Guest House, making tea. "Namaste, Matt Sar," she bowed, using the old honorific nickname. She seemed so calm.

"Namaste Sushila Ma'am," a return bow, "You have a British accent."

"Yes. Do you like it? It seems to have come rather naturally. You were always so attentive to the nuances of pronunciation. It is something I remember about you." She smiled and chuckled to herself.

She looked graceful beneath a red sari and maintained a youthful figure. In the intervening years, she matured into womanhood. Long black tresses flowed into a thick braid with a red tassel that gave the illusion of reaching to her waist. She wore a gold ring on the index finger of her right hand and a small nose piercing. He caught the unmistakable scent of Elisar. She smiled but he could not see a hint as to her thoughts. Her eyes were as beautiful as ever, and she gazed at him without blinking or turning away.

"I have always thought of you whenever I catch the scent of Elisar," he said. "I still have your handkerchief."

"I have always thought of you when I wear it," she replied. "That was long ago."

It was awkward, but just then the teakettle whistled, making him jump. "Sushila Ma'am … Kali…." He approached her, wanting to take her in his arms, but she danced away from him to take the kettle off the burner, and laughed a little bit.

"There is time to talk, Matt Sar. Ranjit has not scheduled a helicopter evacuation, not for the next week or two. And I think I am pronouncing my 'w' sound quite well."

"Ooh. That hurts."

"I can laugh about it now, and so should you. Come. A cup of tea solves everything."

Together they filled the teapot with hot water, going through the calming ritual of British-style tea, two delicate cups with saucers and a slice of lemon with a cube of the refined sugar that Sara kept here. Matt and Sushila stood, a respectful distance between them. She played with her tea bag, wrapping the string this way and that around the spoon to squeeze out the last bit of liquid.

"When I was a school girl, my mother would bring me here for tea with Sara, using this very set of china."

He took a longer look at her. He wanted to talk about the time she walked with him to the temple at the river junction, the spring in her step and the way her skin shone as she looked at him. The way her eyes sparkled as she took his hand…"Kali - Sushila - I thought you were dead."

She looked into her purse and unfolded a small piece of paper she found from an envelope. "Here."

Matt held it in his hands and read:

Kali –

I didn't have time to say goodbye, but I love you. Come to USA. Doctor Ranjit knows how to contact me.

Love, Matt

"That was eleven years ago. And you kept this."

She said, "There is nothing to say. And everything. I suppose I should tell you that I am a widow and I returned from U.K. to work at the women's hospice when it started."

"I knew about the marriage," he said. "When I tried to write to you, Ranjit told me of your marriage and told me to never write again. He said that it would be best that way. You kept this note all these years."

"Matt Sar, Ranjit was meddlesome, wasn't he? I kept the note as a reminder. My life was once filled with hope, even during times when there was nobody to share that hope."

"Was your husband kind to you? I always pictured that maybe you would be happy in your life, I really did."

The teacup rattled against the saucer in her hand. She quickly steadied it. "Now is not the time to talk about Captain Gurung. He has been dead for five years. My son Arjun does not even remember his face or the sound of his voice."

"Did you just say you have children? I didn't know."

"Just one. Arjun was born in 1997. Exactly forty weeks after you left Beni. I suppose I should call him – 'our son.' "

She scanned his face. Their eyes locked. Neither looked away. An eternity passed. Matt knew he needed to say something but he couldn't seem to think of anything. Finally he croaked out the words.

"We have a son? I have a son? With you?"

"Yes, Matt. I seem to recall removing our clothes, piece by piece, and popping a few buttons here and there along our way to Nirvana. Not only that, but we were quite eager….."

"Is he here? I want to see him!"

"No, he's still in UK."

"All this time… I had no idea!"

"Over the years I used to ponder that very question. We didn't keep you in the loop. So I don't blame you. But – there is some basic biology that would seem obvious. The practical application seems to have eluded you in those days. I daresay it's a shocking commentary on the Dartmouth pre-med curriculum."

How could she be laughing? He closed his eyes and pictured the afternoon years ago. They were both so innocent, two young lovers, unsure of themselves, overcome with passion and discovering the physical delights of another person's body.

And everything else flashed all at once. Despite completing medical school and a residency, his life was carefree compared to hers. *I did this. And never really considered it. And moralized about every other guy who ever walked away. But that is something that I did. I'm not any better than anybody else.*

That was me. Please, God, forgive me. I didn't know. I know now.

He opened his eyes again. She was still there, and the eyes of young Sushila still scanned his face with a twinkle.

He felt frozen in space. He reached out his hand and said, "You've had more time to think about this than I have. Right now, I feel terrible. You are laughing at me when I am thinking of ways for you to forgive me."

"Matt. Take your time. Breathe in, breathe out. I knew you would be a bit overwhelmed by this."

"A son. You're going to have to tell me everything. Pictures, too. Does he – does he look like me?"

She pulled a photo out of her purse, holding it at arm's length to compare. She squinted and said, "Yes, Matt. He has a dimple like yours. Definitely tends toward your complexion. Darker than you – lighter than me. And he's very clever with his hands."

"Forgive me if I just don't know what to say." Matt looked at the photo. "I guess I have something new to learn."

"I'm here for you while we sort it out. If it's one thing I have learned, one or the other of us needs to stay focused. If emotion overtakes both of us at the same time, we will be swept away. Like last time. Everyone around here tells me that you are a highly moral person. Don't be hard on yourself. Events conspired to push you away and keep you on the opposite side of the planet. This was our karma. Today I am not here to forgive you, and you don't have to pity yourself, or me for that matter. I am with you for one purpose, and one only."

She put the teacup down and leaned forward. The scent of her perfume was overwhelming as she lightly touched her lips to his. He started to reach for her but she stopped him. The kiss, just the slightest of touch like a butterfly, was over.

"Matt Sar," she whispered in a husky voice, "I think we spent ten years making each other into an idealized version of what we remember. I know I did. We shared something once. And I want it back. I am here to see if it is possible. And to invite you to participate. I will leave now. I will give you time to decide how you wish to proceed. I think you need to talk with Ranjit. He may have more to tell you. Then we will talk again."

She left. Matt looked at the photo of his son for a long time.

Advice from Village Elders

And now this takes it to another level. I thought I was in love. I can only guess about the sacrifices she made in life for her son. For – our son. For me. And she could have died each of those times. And she did it for love. I didn't have a clue as to how love showed up in my life until right now.

It was plain that he still loved Kali. He experienced the old feeling of desire and wish for togetherness. *We have a son and his name is Arjun.*

He found Ranjit at the chautara.

"I know why you are here. Obviously, Sushila is back. This is the gift I brought from Kathmandu." Ranjit laughed.

"Why are you laughing?" demanded Matt.

"I'll bet you haven't even touched the cautery machine."

"Sara told me that the information blackout was Sushila's idea, not yours. So I won't blame you for it, but I just want you to know that it nearly drove me crazy. Was there ever a plan to end it? What did you expect would come of it?"

"Oh, I expected that sooner or later she would come here. Or maybe she would not come. Or maybe make some other choice. You are asking me to predict what a woman will do. I am notoriously unable to read the mind of any woman," said Ranjit, "especially this one."

"Sit down," said Ranjit, "You look angry and confused. I am happy to talk. Matt, did she tell you about her son? Or the kidnapping? And the price on her head?"

"She told me only that I – we - have a son.. I had no idea. And what about a kidnapping?"

"It is finally time to tell you what happened here. There was a battle. The journalists summarized it and the world moved on."

"That much I knew."

"The boy was conscripted as a child soldier, and we got him back. The Army summoned us when they returned from the rescue. Sushila was too agitated to go, so I went in her place. I walked to the staging area in the parade ground with thirty other citizens of this town, families whose babies I delivered. We held hands in fright. That was my sanga, and as we walked together I realized that I was walking kora with them, aware of every step

I took and every breath I made. We Buddhists are taught to heighten our awareness. The day of the rescue, I saw everything in clarity. We did not walk like people but like Hungry Ghosts. First came news that the rescue was over. There was joy. The next thing we were told was that two boys died."

"Oh, no."

"Oh, yes. Arjun was alive, but for a week I feared that he was dead. What was I going to say to Sushila? All the people there turned to me like I was the leader, and I told them not to give up hope. But I looked at the other parents and there was no difference between us. Wishing for Arjun to be alive meant wishing for somebody else's son to be dead. The boy I was looking for did not deserve to live any more than their boy deserved to die. The waiting haunted me. And most of all, the walk back after the surviving boys were delivered by the helicopters. In my joy of finding Arjun and bringing him to Sushila, I was forced to look at other parents who were crushed."

"Oh, my God."

"And even that is not the end. Arjun was the only boy who spoke English, and all the people saw the American CIA man speak with him. Would the PLA learn who betrayed them? Would the Maoist seek revenge? One of the dead boys was the son of one of the Maoists from Tatopani. If Sushila was blamed as the informant, would she get a bullet behind the ear? There was a rumor that they would pay a bounty to the person who killed her. We sent her away. We all decided to hide it, to lie about it, and for this, I make no excuse. It was safer to leave no tracks, and I still feel that way. But I see now that we couldn't lie to you forever."

"Where is Arjun now?"

"Arjun is in school in the U.K. He is a bright little boy, very resilient like his mother. We've always been amazed by how he bounced back. He and Sushila live in a flat owned by Sara's sister. She treats them as family."

"Thank God."

"Matt, I was angry with you for what you did to Sushila. I was angry with Sushila for her carelessness. I was angry with her husband even though he married her as a favor to me. Then I was angry with the Maoists, the PLA, and the Army. Finally, I was angry with Sara for allowing you to come back. I was angry with myself for the way I treated all the women in my own life, including both my wife and Sushila's mother. And most of all, I was angry with you for just leading your life as if nothing ever happened."

Ranjit wiped tears from his eyes.

"I knew that I needed to get the anger out of my life. I am a Buddhist. We study this. But even for me, no amount of study was going to fix the anger in my heart. I wanted to unlock my heart, but I couldn't find the key.

"But then I decided to unburden myself of the expectations of how I was supposed to be, and just be the person I am. I don't have to be strong, I don't have to be the leader, I don't have to be the role model. I don't have to fit somebody's expectations, I don't even have to fit my own expectations. All I needed to do was to talk. I could read this in books a million times over and not actually get it. Going to Kathmandu to bring back Sushila I realized that I will not live forever and I could not put this off until I was ninety-nine. I finally told Sushila that she is my daughter, I finally told her I loved her, I finally opened my heart."

"Wait a minute. Your daughter? This means….."

"Yes Matt, I also realized that the Buddha has a deep sense of humor. It means that you and I are related. I am the grandfather of your son."

Ranjit snorted with laughter and cried at the same time.

"In any case, the past is gone. I have now cast off my fetters. Finally, I am cured of monkey mind. I am at peace with my life. That is a gift beyond price. For a person who has been consumed with anger, to find the place of forgiveness is the only way."

"Ranjit, this still leaves a few questions unanswered. If this was such a problem, why did you prevent me from contacting Sushila after I left?"

"Matt, I am not proud of all my actions toward you. How does it help you if we dredge them up now? In those days, I was not in favor of love marriage. I did not know anything of your character. I did not want to yoke Sushila to some disreputable American who could be so easily overcome with lust. It is not our culture."

He looked Matt in the eye. "I suppose I know you a little better these days. Do you love this woman?"

What? Are you joking? Matt thought. Then, *He's serious. He actually thinks he has the final say.*

"Hell, yes."

"What do you want to do?"

"Ranjit, I came back here to find her. I want to have the life I dreamed about when I was with her in those days."

"Do you have honorable intentions this time? Would you marry her?"

He blanched. "Yes. If she'll have me."

"Then there is a clear path to follow. We will talk of this tomorrow. You need to finish rounds today, and you are on call. Go now, while I think of what will happen next."

"One last thing – why is it safe for Sushila to be here now?"

"That is a calculated risk she decided to take. The local Maoists don't know she is here. The Civil War is over. Maybe the Young Communist League will leave her alone."

Matt made clinic rounds that day, but his heart was not in it. He finished and took a long walk. There were no calls from Casualty to disrupt his time to think. Matt decided to eat dinner in town. He knew they would miss him at the Guest House and probably spend the whole meal talking about him. *Let them. I need time*, he concluded.

He seemed drawn to the river and found a shady spot right near the sand bar where he could think. He thought back to Sara's counseling when the girl with the burns was admitted. "You're not here to validate your faith," Sara had said, 'you're here to explore your faith." *And God brought me right here to show me that I didn't know what love was. Even the lowest-caste Nepali man who would have cared for his children and been faithful to his wife, and loved her, and been with her during times when she needed help is better than me*, he thought. He listened to the river as it flowed over the rocks on its way to the Ganges and the Great Sea. He threw pebbles into the water and thought about the path of his life until now.

Raksi

The next day Ranjit and Matt met at the Chautara prior to rounds. The leaves of the sal tree rustled in the wind above their heads. "I have spoken to Sushila. You know how these women are. They are prisoners of their emotions at times."

"It's okay. I knew that it would not be easy seeing each other for the first time," Matt said. *Prisoner of emotion? She was in control from what I saw. It's me who was on the rollercoaster.*

"She asked me to convey a message. If she is to see you, it is not to be some secret thing of which to be ashamed. She is open to the idea of marriage. But she no longer believes in love marriage. She will only marry you if it is an arranged marriage."

"What does that mean? Does she not love me?"

"That is not for me to say. Loving a woman is not the same as love marriage; and love marriage is separate from an arranged marriage. In an arranged marriage, the man and the woman are chosen by the parents. They are compatible first, and then as they spend time, the man and the woman grow to love each other. Sushila's mother is dead. As her father, it is up to me to arrange her marriage. But such things are not arranged directly with the groom. The parents act as go-betweens. Where are your parents?"

"They are in Boston, USA."

"That is difficult. I have asked Sara to help me negotiate with your parents as to an arranged marriage. Do not contact Sushila again yet. You must obtain your parent's permission and ask them to authorize a trusted agent to negotiate on their behalf. Your agent will do the talking for you."

"I guess I have work to do."

"Yes. If you think about it, there is only one possible agent for you."

"I know." Matt left.

Matt found Ram and asked him to serve as his agent in this matter. Ram listened carefully, and then burst into laughter. He took off his glasses to wipe them and laughed. He held his belly and laughed until the veins on his neck popped up like snakes, then sat down and giggled so hard that he could not complete a sentence.

"What's so funny?"

"Well, first off, you have come under the sway of a Nepali woman. There is an old saying every woman learns: 'When in public, be a Vaishnava. When among friends, be a Shaiva. But in private, always be a Shakta.' When the vision of Shakti occupies your mind, you do not have a strong bargaining position."

"Very funny."

"It's even better, Matt. You don't know what you have just asked. If I agree to help you, I will be honor bound to see that you get married, one way or another." He laughed some more. "I can see the alternatives laid out before us like a clinical algorithm. You make me feel young again."

"Ram, what is the bottom line of all this gibberish?"

"Sara and Ranjit are tough negotiators. Have you considered kidnap marriage? It is still legal in Nepal. We can do it if negotiations fail. I know it's old fashioned, but for a moment there, I enjoyed a vision of the two of us sweeping into Sushila's house at night to kidnap her for matrimonial purposes. I would hold the ladder and you will climb up. I would do this for you, Matt Sar." He started to laugh again.

"I hardly think it will be necessary. First of all, she lives on the ground floor."

"Ah, but it is also my duty to look about the town for alternative women, in case this one is unsuitable for you. You will get married one way or the other."

"Ram, please. This one and this one only."

"That's right, I am getting carried away." Ram wiped tears from his eyes and collected himself. He made a low bow and said, "Matt Sar, we are now brothers. I am honored that you would assign such a task to me. I will speak to your parents and this will be done. And if it comes to a kidnap marriage, I will drive the getaway car if called upon."

The two of them walked to the storefront in the Bajaar where a phone was available for international calls. Matt had not actually spoken to his parents while in Nepal, thinking it was better to rely on letters or the occasional email. Since the beginning, he knew he could not explain what happened in the hospital every day; nobody back home could grasp the day-to-day life in Nepal.

The call cost three US dollars per minute. Matt and Ram squeezed into the phone booth, it was so tight that Matt felt Ram's belly and he could inspect the turmeric in Ram's mustache. The call went through after several tries. Ram smiled as they shared the handset.

"Matt, its three o'clock in the morning here. Are you okay?" his father asked.

"Oh yes, I'm fine. Couldn't be better. How is Mom?"

"She's fine. Shall I wake her?"

"No, this is sort of a man-to-man thing. You know how she hates surprises. I have a huge favor to ask."

"Go ahead."

"I'm getting married and I need you to authorize a proxy to fill in for you in negotiating with the bride's family. It's an arranged marriage. Very formal. They need your consent."

There was a long pause.

"Dad? Are you still there?"

"Matt, it's not like you to do something this –sudden," John said. "Are you sure you are okay? You haven't joined a cult or something have you?"

"It's not exactly sudden, Dad. And no, Dad, I'm still a Catholic if that's what you're driving at. And yes, this is a carefully considered decision. I'm fine. Just fine."

Matt told him a few of the details, but the part about Arjun could wait for later. Matt tried to imagine the conversation that would happen back in Boston over breakfast. He was happy to be here in Nepal. *I don't know how to tell Mom that she is a grandmother. We'll have to give her time to process this one.*

"Matt, your proxy is authorized to act on my behalf. Send an email with more of the details and send us her photograph. Let me think awhile before I break this news to your mother. I'm proud of you, and we are still holding a place for you at the group practice. We're all proud of you here, son."

"Please tell Mom it's all going to be just fine. Kali will be a fine daughter-in-law. Tell Mom I haven't laid in a ditch even once so far on this trip. Not even for fun. And no, I still have yet to call for the universal implement. I will let you know if I do."

"It's settled then," crowed Ram as he clapped Matt on the back, "Someday I will meet your father and maybe we will work together," said Ram as they left. On the walk back to the hospital, Ram put his arm over Matt's shoulder and babbled like a schoolgirl.

"You are a man, Matt. So be a man. Don't allow the woman to be the man of the house. A man and a woman have different jobs and you must allow her to be a woman. That is the way."

Matt felt the arm on his shoulder and said, "I suppose next you will tell me neither a borrower nor a lender be."

"My brother, do you think I have never read Shakespeare?" asked Ram. "I know Hamlet well. Polonius was a Buddha of UK, and he knew that every important moment was to be marked with advice. Do you think I was never young? Do you think I was always fat?"

He turned pensive. They stopped walking, but Ram still held his arm over Matt's shoulder, gesturing freely with his other arm. "Polonius gave great advice that all should heed, but he left the veil of mystery over the subject of relations with women. I am giving you advice you may not hear anywhere else."

"You have missed your calling. You should have been a pashmina salesman. I can picture you saying, 'for you a special price,'" said Matt.

"Matt Sar, for this one time only I am trying to be serious and you disrespect me. Do not mock Buddha," Ram said. "Matt, my own wife died of uterine cancer, in Kathmandu. Do not begrudge me a moment of joy as I send another young man on the path to fulfillment. This is the paradox, my brother. You must be a man, and she must be a woman, but only when you have a woman every day, bringing the soft things to your life, can you revel in manhood. That is the eternal mystery of Shiva and Shakti."

He continued, "My children are in three different continents. I may never see them again in this life, but lately memories have awakened and I can picture my wife as she came to me—like Sushila now comes to you. In this life, my wife is no more. She is not now in my waking daytime, but she is still there for me in dreams. For years, she stood by my side and made me complete. Buddha says to pierce the veil of dreams that holds you to this earth, but I tell you, as a Hindu, to enjoy those dreams while they appear in the light of day. Allow her to complete you, not compete with you, that is what I am saying."

The rest of the walk was quiet. Ram never spoke of his family life, and for all his bluster, Matt tried to recall a time he may have ever heard Ram reveal anything about his personal life. Matt wanted to ask about Ram's children, but it was time to walk without speaking.

The day passed with a sense of predictability to the clinical work. The medical ward discharged some patients now cured of diarrhea and admitted more to take their place. A baby was born, and the clinics were booked full. Today there were no road traffic accidents or emergencies. It was as if the universe conspired to clear the agenda, a small miracle of unrelated non-events that added up to an uneventful day. Matt knew that the evening dinner around the Guest House table would be a departure from the daily routine and now he wondered what would happen.

Ranjit was dressed formally, with a daura, a suruwal, a topi and a woolen suit jacket, as if he were a government official. Matt never saw Ranjit in the formal Nepali outfit before. Ram's neck was too thick to button the top button of his shirt, and he wore a vest of dakka cloth with a matching topi. Sara wore her best kurtha for this meal.

Sara began, "Matt, I know you are a Christian, and Sushila is Buddhist. I am here mainly because this will repair a sin that happened in 1996, and I have loved Sushila since she was a little girl. And also to maintain the least little remnant of decorum and not allow the boys to muck this up. I have prayed for your success and happiness. "

Ranjit piped in, "From the basis of caste, there is no impediment to this matrimonial proceeding."

Ram said, "So it is settled then. We will have Janai Supari soon."

Ranjit said, "Not so fast. This bride is well educated and a professional woman. She is a proud woman who brings equality and many fine attributes to this new family. As her father, I request some token of sincerity."

He looked over at Sara. She frowned but said nothing.

He continued, "To preserve family honor, we must insist upon a payment. I think it should be a new motorbike. For this consideration, she will have my blessing."

Ram slammed his hand on the table. "She is a widow. And this is a thinly-veiled request for a dowry. There is no deal."

"That is as may be. But she comes with a son, and so she is a proven mother. She will bear many fine sons," said Ranjit.

Now Sara was rolling her eyes.

"It doesn't have to be a new motorbike," Ranjit blurted.

Ram relented and everyone laughed. It was agreed that Matt would visit an astrologer to determine compatibility and set the date of the wedding, and that Janai Supari, the puja of betrothal, would take place the next day. Ranjit produced a small glass peanut-butter jar filled with a clear liquid and poured a shot for everyone at the table. Matt did not expect Sara to join them, but she did.

"This raksi was given to me four years ago by a grateful patient, the best distiller in the district who is now deceased. It is about one hundred and ninety proof. Let us drink to the success of the two families who arranged this marriage," said Ranjit.

They all watched expectantly as Matt raised the raksi to his lips. Just the slightest sip burned like fire. Matt coughed for five minutes while Ram patted his back. Then he asked, "Ranjit-ji. Nobody here has ever seen you drive. Why did you insist on getting a motorbike?"

"Oh, it is not for me. Alok is courting a Nepali woman, and she is playing hard to get. He can take her to see sleeping Lord Bishnu at Galeshwor Temple and all the other auspicious places in the Myagdi Valley, but only if he has his own motorbike. It will improve his prospects. A motorbike is essential in courtship these days. The young Nepalis don't walk anymore it seems."

"I would say get him a red one," added Ram.

Matt finished his raksi after fifteen minutes of sipping. The meeting was over, and Matt thanked Ram for such fine representation. He slept like a log that night, and if he dreamed at all, it was a happy dream in which a Goddess came to earth and brought flowers and songbirds and butterflies into his life.

A Fine Day in Beni

If you are too busy to laugh, then you are too busy.
– Chinese Proverb

Ram accompanied Matt to the Bajaar to choose a golden ring. "I go to keep the merchants from driving a difficult bargain. If the merchant sees only a videshi, the price is doubled immediately. We also need yogurt, sel roti, and sweet candy."

At the monastery, Ram and Matt sat with the Buddhist lama while he made the astrology reading. The birth dates were declared compatible according to the Bikram Sambat calendar. The best date for the wedding would be in six months on the full moon of harvest.

That afternoon, Matt, Ram and Alok met at the hospital chautara. Alok would stay behind to be on call for the hospital. He placed a garland of marigolds around Matt's neck. Ram introduced the dol drummer and flutist. The music started and they walked through the town. The neighbors gathered on the street, and Ram gave candy to the children as they passed. It was to be the first time Matt stood in Sushila's house since that fateful afternoon in 1996. The door was flanked by two brand new brass water jugs, with red ribbons on them. Ram pounded on the door. After a moment, Ranjit and Sara opened it.

He stepped over the threshold to see Sushila, his betrothed, in a red sari with silver embroidery, standing with the lama. Everyone wiped away tears. Sushila wore just a small dab of Elisar and the brightest possible red lipstick. She gave him a long *Namaste*.

Janai surya, the betrothal ceremony, consisted of applying a large red tika to the foreheads of the happy couple using rice, red color and yogurt; then sharing a sel roti; then exchanging rings. There was a solemn moment as Matt and Sushila stood in front of her mother's photo and lit some incense. They meditated on the blessings of those elders that were no more. Finally, Matt and Sushila stood together as everyone else formed a tight clump around them. The lama circled the group, chanting and wrapping a red string as he walked. The families were now bound together, and after a decent interval, each person present was given a segment of the string to be tied on their wrist as a reminder.

Summer 2007 – Boudhanath Mandir

It is not so important whether you walk on water or walk in space. The true miracle is to walk on earth.

– Thich Nhat Hanh

The next two weeks passed in a blur. Each day, Matt started with hospital rounds, then joined his father-in-law in Theater. In the evenings, they joined the others for dinner and sometimes ate at places in the Bajaar.

"You need to meet my sisters," said Sushila.

"You have sisters?"

"Well, no, not in the strict sense. They are friends from school and hospice days. It would not surprise me to find some half-sisters, though. Ranjit was a bit of a runabout in younger days."

Matt saw her in a new light, and he realized that he was hardly the only one who loved her. It seemed like there were dozens of friends in the town due to her work at the hospice, and now Matt met all of them. Sara and Bimla took a day to shop in the Bajaar with Sushila and joined her for an evening with Sushila's friends where Bimla applied fanciful mehendi designs to her arms, hands and feet.

"I've seen it. Why do they do it?" Matt asked.

"It's girls' night out. Like going to the hairdresser in UK or USA. They say the designs ward off snakes and evil spirits. Bimla is quite an artist. Oh, and I still fast on Mondays. These days I am praying for your health," she said.

"Oh God, that reminds me of the time you fainted…."

"Yes. That was quite a scene. I recall being amazed by you and worried that day."

"You mean – you knew? You could tell?"

"Of course I knew. It was bloody obvious, Matt. I was curious and worried at the same time. I had no idea. Not a clue. I was young and innocent."

"At the time I was totally embarrassed."

"I never thought through the details prior to that time, Matt. That evening I doubled my prayers to the Goddess."

"You mean….." he asked.

"That is exactly what I mean. I did not have an inkling as to the actual size before that."

"Ma'am." He bowed and made a namaste. "Once in the life of every man, he should hear a woman tell him that, before he dies. You have made my day. I am able to show more restraint in these days."

"Good. This is not a society to condone public displays of affection. We'll see." She laughed, that same musical laugh of a songbird. "I still pray."

Sushila cooked dinner for Matt and Ram at her place. After the meal, Matt listened to them reminisce about her mother.

"You should have seen her when she came to UK for Arjun's birth," said Sushila, "I was so happy to have her there. I didn't know at the time that I would never see her again."

"She was so proud of you when she came back after those months. Your mother loved you. Ranjit visited her during her illness and took care of her," said Ram. "And when the time came, we both shaved our heads, down by the river at the cremation."

"I'm sure your support meant a lot to her and to Ranjit."

"Ranjit has always been a brother to me," Ram said.

"It's funny how he and I could share so much, yet never talk about it," she said, "The whole time I was in charge of Shanti Nawajeevan, I don't think we ever discussed it once, even though he played with Arjun."

"He was overwhelmed with guilt at the way he forced you into that marriage. He's not the same as he was. He has learned."

The spell was broken one day in the Bajaar. Ranjit and Sushila were spending time together when he became aware of somebody in the crowd. It was a man, staying fifty meters behind as they went from place to place. At first, he thought it was coincidence, then Ranjit noticed how the man busied himself quickly if Ranjit seemed to look back at him.

"Don't look, but – do you know that guy over there?"

Sushila looked, then turned her head quickly and said, "We must go, now."

Ranjit became pale, and they walked quickly back to the hospital.

"That was him, wasn't it?" asked Ranjit.

"Yes. I was afraid this might happen. That was definitely him," she said. "That is one of the Maoists from Tatopani. The exact one who kidnapped Arjun during the battle.

216

"I was afraid of this," he said. "Our other Maoist friend has kept a low profile lately, but surely he too will learn of this. Sushila, you have allowed me to gain serenity and I thank you for coming back. But maybe it is time to go to Kathmandu for a bit."

"It's never going to leave me," she said.

They told Matt, who said, "I need to go to Kathmandu for a visa extension. I'll take her out of town for a few days. Let's regroup while Sara gets some information. Maybe this was some sort of fluke."

Sushila stayed with Sara overnight. At dawn, she met Matt at the Land Rover. They held hands on the trip and talked about her time with the people of the hospital.

"It's like night and day now that the secrecy is gone. I'm discovering a new side to everyone," he said, "and to you."

"I wanted you to meet my sanga. In Nepal, we have a saying, that a man and a woman don't simply marry each other. It's two families that join. Everyone is entitled to call it 'our wedding.' " she replied.

"I had no idea about you and Ranjit."

"He risked his life for me during the battle. I don't think I ever thanked him. At the time it was over very quickly, but it took years for my mind to process what it took for him to do that. I needed to thank him. In person. To be at peace with myself."

"What happened during the battle, anyway?"

"Matt, someday I will tell more of that story but I need to be in a safe place. It was bad, okay? Can you accept that? For now?"

She turned away and gazed out the window.

"Here I am, saying 'we need to talk, talk is good' – and I still have trouble myself." Her voice trailed off.

He took her hand.

Matt reserved a room at the Patan Hostel and Sushila would stay with Manju's mother.

"This won't be so bad. I wanted to maintain formalities while we were in Beni, but we needed to see other," she said when they arrived.

"I have an ATM card in UK, but maybe you can show me how a Nepali ATM machine works," she said.

The first ATM was in a small alcove near Kalanki. They squeezed into the booth and faced the machine. He needed to reach around her to retrieve cash. *Elisar again.*

"Kali, the scent of you has not changed. You bring me to my youth. You smell so nice."

She turned to him and he kissed her. It was a tentative kiss at first, just grazing their lips against each other. She whispered, "Matt, I have been to the family planning clinic. I have learned some things since we were together."

She kissed him again, just a tease. They held each other for a long time, touching each other's hair. The next customer knocked on the door, and they quickly broke contact.

After getting Matt's visa renewal, Sushila turned to him saying, "And now I am in charge. We will not have a plan. For today it is okay to be a simple tourist."

The temple at Boudha is visible from ten kilometers away on the rim of the Valley, but from ten meters away, the neighborhood gives no clue as to what lays behind the buildings that front the street. Matt did not know they were near until they approached the alleyway. There it loomed, the largest temple of its kind in the world, spiritual center of two hundred fifty thousand expatriate Tibetans in Kathmandu.

They stepped off a dirty commercial street of Kathmandu and crossed over an invisible boundary into another world. Matt gazed at the large solid dome, a perfect hemisphere a hundred meters across, white like half a boiled egg but ten stories high, sitting on a raised platform with many angles. Today it was achingly white in the sunlight, the golden spire anchored by a hundred streams of bright prayer flags fluttering in the breeze, all-seeing eyes painted there.

The temple was ringed by a circular plaza where the monasteries mingled with shops and restaurants. Every Tibetan artifact ever seen was laid out for sale to the tour groups. A recording of "Om Mane Padme Hum" played in the background.

"Time to walk. This is not like a cathedral in London where you go inside. Later we can explore the monasteries around the perimeter." Sushila took his hand, and they set out on the path of flat stones that circled the dome. They joined a crowd with many women in traditional Tibetan costume, maybe an old person in the company of younger relatives, tourists with backpacks, young single ones, or else tour groups from Italy or other parts of Europe. It seemed out of place to see Italian women with short skirts and revealing skintight tank tops alongside Tibetan women in wool. Monks in saffron robes with spinning prayer wheels walked alongside regular people on their way to work.

"I have wanted to walk kora, the pilgrim's path, here at this temple, with my family. I am honored that you are with me," said Sushila, "and someday Arjun will also join us here."

Sushila and Matt held hands as they walked. At first they were quiet.

"Beni feels so far away," said Matt.

"Yes. It is good to be reminded that for most people life is not about suffering all the time," said Sushila, "To walk is to meditate. To walk is to feel your legs move. We all walk kora in life, every day. The goal is to walk and think only of walking. And breathe. You can always control your breath. In. Then out."

"Kali, I don't know how to regain the time we lost."

"Neither do I. I know I am not the same person you tutored in English in 1996."

"Yes. That's the part I love. Obviously, you can now speak fluent English, but the changes I see in you go beyond that simple fact. Look at these people. Nobody here is walking by themselves. I look at them and I realize that I have dedicated my life to surgery, and yet I have been unfulfilled and lonely. I always wanted a partner, an actual partner, in this whole thing. I need somebody to keep me grounded. I don't want to turn out like my dad, a great surgeon but who has no life when he is not wearing scrubs. I look at the challenges you have faced, the obstacles you overcame, and I am in awe. Other women may have given up, but you did not."

"Matt, thank you for seeing this. It's always nice to hear somebody say this out loud. We all need this. That is what a partner brings. But look at what I went through to get to this point of maturity. Let's make a deal: I will be your partner if you will be mine. "

"It is a gift that you are not consumed by anger. Kali, I think I took you for granted as a person. I now see things differently."

"And for me, the same. It seems so comical now."

"How so?"

"My life has a pattern, just like this kora around Boudhanath. It repeats itself. I am tied to Beni, but every time I return to Beni, something happens that pushes me away."

"It was a gift that you returned this time. Weren't you afraid of what you would find?"

"Yes, but not even the Maoists could keep me from going there. It's not what you may think. I came back for more than just you."

"What?"

"I have learned a lot since you knew me, Matt. I learned that you can be face-to-face putting a tika on somebody's forehead and still not say anything that matters. The ritual doesn't matter unless the feeling is there too. My mother and I shared a wonderful time in the UK when Arjun was born. We were able to reconcile. I had no idea that she would pass after she returned to Nepal."

"I heard you talking with Ram about her."

"Yes. That is another thing. I knew I needed to clear the air with Ranjit. I needed to thank him. There was one specific thing he did. We never spoke of it until this trip."

"What was that?"

"A bad man was going to kill me with a gun. Ranjit jumped in front of me."

"Oh, Kali." He reached for her hand, searching her face. "That's not a small thing. I can see how that would be difficult to discuss unless you are ready."

"It's okay, Matt. I'm really okay. Here we are, walking Kora. I finally thanked Ranjit. I said 'thank you, father.' "

Now she stopped and the tears flowed for the first time since forever. "Why was this so hard… why did it take so long?" and she reached out for Matt. They held each other, not seeing anybody else around them.

After a moment, she collected herself. "He and I are better now. Ranjit can be a cantankerous old man, but he is also on my path."

"He's just glowed since you came back."

"He's like his old self, the way I remember him from when I was a girl. He needed to let go and allow himself to be free. This alone was worth the trip. And being with you."

"Kali – we can create our own future, from here."

"Matt Sar, I want to. Do you realize that we both should have died in Beni? It is something we have in common. We both escaped. How does a person get out of such a cycle? I look back and I realize that my destiny was to follow a set of rules as to how a woman should act. I thought I could choose which rules applied to my life and which did not. What I did not know was that others would apply the rules even if I threw them away."

"And now?"

"I am a survivor. I need to take the steps that suit my situation, and if that means I fight the rules, then I will do so. I will not simply accept my fate. We are a new Nepal. The new government will be better than the King. But I don't trust Nepal anymore. Everything needs to change."

They took the stairs to the next level, the apron of the dome. Kali looked down on the first path. She said, "I took a math course in UK and thought of Boudha when I learned 'pi-r-squared.' This stupa is a giant mandala. The upper level shares the axis of the larger circle, and the math illustrates the concept of rebirth. It doesn't take as long to travel the rim of the upper level, but it's a circle just the same. Just like in rebirth. You can look down from here and see the pattern of everyone on his or her own path, becoming conscious of more than just yourself. We are destined to repeat, maybe with strangers who will be our new companions."

She looked at him again. "Matt Sar, you and I have been given the chance to share the path once again. Karma has bound us together in some way. Matt Sar, someday you and I will take Arjun here."

They talked about the boy. She told him the story of Arjun and the dog. "He's used to being the man of the house. And he is a charmer like his father."

To get away from the bright sun they stepped off the pathway, drawn to a monastery from which chanting could be heard. Now barefoot, they tiptoed in. The centerpiece of the main hall was a thirty-foot-tall golden statue of Buddha. At the foot of the altar was a collection of offerings – bags of rice, rows of gleaming silver cups with water in them, specially decorated cookies in the shape of a bo tree leaf. Matt's eyes adjusted to the dim light. Benches lined the center aisle, facing each other. A hundred monks wearing yellow shirts and saffron robes chanted in low tones, and an orchestra of a dozen monks played nearest the door. Older monks in the front row occasionally turned their heads to scowl at the younger ones behind them if the boys made mischief. The monks recited a long prayer ceremony, now chanting, now music, then chanting again.

The sound of the orchestra was like the sound of an ocean, not really a melody that Matt could hum along with, more a collective sigh, washing back and forth like waves at the edge of a great sea. The chanting continued for two hours, with only short breaks as the monks ate their bread with butter tea. Matt and Sushila dozed off a few times, in a trancelike state, carried by the sounds, floating somewhere — near the shore. Not even the large horns could wake them from their trance, it seemed.

The chanting ended. For a moment, Matt could not recall if it was morning or afternoon. He knew he was with somebody he loved. They stepped outside into a slight rain, and now the pilgrims walking the path carried umbrellas, a moving forest of canopies, as they circled the dome.

The taxi home took them on the Ring Road, crossing the bridge near Pashupattinath, the temple for cremation. Through the taxi window, they saw the spires of the temple and plumes of smoke. Perhaps they would return another time. Now, Sushila held Matt's hand, intertwining the fingers and thinking about gratitude for the people in her life.

Machhendranath

The taxi stopped in Patan. The driver could go no further because of the crowd. "O my God, I forgot, it's Monday. This is the day of Machhendranath," said Sushila.

"Wait a minute, is this the festival with the wagons?"

"Yes, they pull two large wooden wagons through the town to display the shirt of God. Every year they do this. Each has a tower on it."

"This kind of crowd makes me nervous," said Matt, "Is it going to be okay?"

"Matt Sar, it is silly to ask any such kind of question. If you want to be okay, stay home and lock the door. Even then you may die. If you want to understand Nepal, you need to see this, be a part of this. It is a jatra, a procession."

They paid the taxi driver and joined the crowd. The street was packed with people, and they held hands as they pushed their way through. Here they came upon a fantastical sight. In the street were two large carts, ten feet tall, with wooden wheels taller than a man and a huge wooden tongue attached to pull it with ropes. Each carried a sort of Christmas-tree structure on it, with green pine boughs woven into a bamboo tower. The taller tower was about sixty-feet high, and for now, there were ropes tied to it, acting as stays to prevent it from being blown over by a strong wind. The other one was shorter but equally top-heavy. A crowd of men filled the narrow street and every alleyway; the women stood on the stairs of a nearby temple. Every window of every building was filled with people leaning out to watch.

"Have you ever seen anything like this?"

"No. This crowd is big enough to fill a football stadium in USA. We never do this in the USA. I remember being twelve years old. At the Church of the Immaculate Conception of Mary the Mother of Jesus, the nuns gathered all the Catholics in town. Men from the Knights of Columbus showed up in their medieval costumes with swords and plumed admiral's hats. The Italian-American Veterans sent a team to carry the Virgin Mary's statue through the city. A hundred children who recently took their first communion showed up in their snow-white clothes. Two hundred boys and girls from the Drum and Bugle Corps provided music. It all ended with a Mass in which we sang every song praising the Virgin Mary that was ever written. My mom watched from the balcony and I sat with the Boy Scouts. There were maybe five hundred people all told. Not like this. This is thousands."

"That is sweet," she replied, "It was a jatra. I was raised Buddhist. Every year in May, we have Buddha Jayantri, a procession for Buddha's birthday. The Christians that come to Nepal are always too serious to do a jatra for Jesus. Oh, the Christians pray and sing but the ones who came to Nepal never showed any joy. You teach me new things about Christians."

Matt gazed at the crowd. "Look at how everyone is involved here. The Nepalis think Americans are religious because the ones they meet are Christian missionaries. The truth is, the Hindu festivals are much bigger than anything we do in the States. We just don't do this kind of pageantry anymore. Well, maybe at a Red Sox game. But this crowd—this crowd would fill Fenway Park and then some."

Thick ropes were tied to the wooden tongue of each chariot and two hundred men in matching white t-shirts awaited there. On each was emblazoned "Machhendranath 2064." A ceremonial drill team wearing black Gurkha uniforms with white belts from the 1840s lined up with muzzle-loading muskets and shields made of rhinoceros hide; in the background were several hundred Army soldiers. A band of Newari musicians serenaded the crowd, and some of the horns curved over the heads of the players like a deranged hula-hoop held vertically. Three dozen *dol* drummers pounded away, adding percussion to the scene. Overhead, the electrical wires that usually crisscrossed the street were missing. The wires lay limp, methodically taken down in preparation for the pulling of the chariot.

Matt surveyed the route where the lines were down. The chariots would need to go down a slight hill and around a corner. They debated where to stand. Matt chose a step underneath a porch at first, fifty meters along the route of the chariot. In an excited voice, a man told Sushila to move. "He says that if the tower falls onto the porch, it will kill everyone standing underneath. That is why nobody stands here."

The Gurkha team fired a ceremonial volley into the sky, and a surge of excitement rippled through the crowd. Every one sang the Nepal National Anthem, thousands of voices not exactly in unison. The drums throbbed as one, and the men at the ropes joined the beat. They were not actually pulling at first, just dancing in place to establish the rhythm of the effort yet to come. The whole crowd was on tiptoe as the stays were cast off. A team of ten men held one stay that steadied the tower, now swaying precariously.

"I read that last year it did topple and killed six people from the crowd," said Sushila, "Whatever happens, don't let go of my hand."

Oh, no, thought Matt. *This is a mob scene, and I'm in it. I might die.* He looked around and realized that they would be swept along, like jumping into a river at flood stage. *I just don't know where the rapids are or where this will take me…* He decided to stand there and let it pass. He wanted to hug the brick wall behind him. *Why did I do this…* He gritted his teeth. *O God, if a ditch of the proper depth were to appear, I would hop in and be grateful. And to hell with what Barbara would say. Sometimes laying in a ditch is just the right thing, Mom.*

Matt turned to Sushila to say this aloud, just as a Hindu priest standing on the chariot waved a flag to signal the actual start. *Here it goes.* The crowd scrambled–an immediate, chaotic frenzy of motion. Everyone moved in a human torrent. All the people nearby stretched out their arms and could not be avoided. Matt and Sushila now swam in a throbbing river.

"Don't let go." Matt cried. They lost sight of each other even though they were still gripping tightly, swept downstream with the crowd, only the grasp of straining muscles holding them together. The stampede of people was simultaneously frightening and exhilarating. The tower swayed above, the music blared, the drums throbbed, incense blew over in a cloud, and everybody was shouting.

The chariot lurched at the corner and stopped. On every roof, teams of men carried additional ropes, big and thick enough to anchor a cruise ship. Somebody sent them there in advance, he realized. The signal went out and one team dropped their rope from the roof, cascading it to the ground. A young man tied the end around his waist and climbed the green tower on the chariot. Two others also climbed, nobody wearing a safety harness, scrambling up like rock climbers, impossibly high until they were ten feet from the top, thousands of eyes focused on their climb and Matt wondered whether the crowd would cheer if one of them were to plunge to their death. *Nobody below would be able to move out of the way.*

The men passed the rope among them until it lassoed around the waist of the tower, securing it with two giant half hitches. The crowd cheered when the new signal was given and it lurched into motion again. The men stayed on the tower for the ride, but it would not have surprised Matt if they all of a sudden morphed into a tightrope-walking team and escaped using the hawser. *They are like circus acrobats. If they were to fall, it would result in certain death,* thought Matt. He couldn't bear to watch, but he was locked into putting a face to the people who were taking such a risk. He looked over at Sushila. He tried to get her to look at him, but she would not avert her eyes. Her mouth was hanging open. Matt looked around. Everyone else showed the same expression. *Like waiting for rapture.* Burning incense billowed over everything.

The drums started again, and the pulling team once again established the rhythm like a dance troupe before they finally pulled. The chariot did not careen around the corner; it bounced up and down in place, facing a new direction when it clattered to a halt. The crowd cheered, and a new team on a new roof brought a new rope to tie around the tower. The old rope was removed, hurriedly coiled, and brought to a house further down the street to be ready when the chariot lurched to a new location.

After making the corner, Matt and Sushila decided to slip away, and fought their way through the crowd, finally reaching a spot with breathing room fifty meters away.

"I thought we were going to die," said Sushila, "You seemed so brave."

"Hah. I was petrified. Did you know what this was going to be like?"

"Yes and no. I remember hearing about it but no, I grew up in Beni. We never traveled this time of year." They walked in the direction of the Guest House. As they did, they talked about the way that religious fervor manifested itself in Nepal.

"It's a sort of surrender to the will of the group, like this whole crowd is in the same trance," said Matt, "The men climbing the tower seem to truly believe that nothing will happen to them. It's like a football crowd in the States, everyone can see what needs to be done next to stabilize the tower, cheering on the team that is actually doing it."

"Matt Sar, that is the heart of Nepal. Not just the tower. Look at the way that everyone works together to get something done."

"I see it, but I don't see the point, exactly. Moving a juggernaut around?"

"The task does not need to make any particular sense, Matt. When I came back from U.K. to Kathmandu, I used to think, O my God, nothing works in this city. There is loadshedding, there is trash everywhere, you can't drink the water, there are beggars with leprosy in the streets, and nobody follows any traffic rules."

She ticked these off on her fingers like a laundry list, and Matt laughed. It was all too true.

She continued, "But it's all different now. They apply it to everything. I find myself saying that somehow, it all seems to work. Here we are with four million people in the valley, and we don't have enough parking spaces to fit every vehicle if every driver decided to park at the same time. It's a miracle that it works at all. We do Machhendranath festival. Why? Because we have done it for seven hundred years. Why? 'Because,' that's why.' It doesn't make sense, but nothing else makes any sense either, so we might as well pull a chariot through the streets one more time. Seven hundred and one."

"And if it kills somebody, well….."

They arrived at the Jawalekhel bus park just a kilometer away from the place where Matt was staying. Here Sushila would find a taxi back home. Matt held her hand, looking longingly. "Sushila, I …. We could… Are you sure you have to go?"

She returned his gaze and moved her lips as if she was kissing him from a distance, just subtly so nobody around them would notice. Hundreds of people stood nearby, but for this moment, it was as if everyone else had disappeared.

Then she turned to go. "I will come early tomorrow at seven to pick you up for a ride. We will have a special trip tomorrow."

He watched the taxi until it was swallowed up by the traffic.

The Sacrament of the Goddess

This is soft warm addiction… and it keeps on rising
I wish you could wake me like never. My heart has now known madness
My world has lighted up Like a new bride I've become yours, my love
— Translation of lyrics of "Saiyyan" by Kailash Kher

He waited for her at the front gate to the Patan Guest House. *Today I will take you to a special place in the Valley*, she said over the phone. Kali's smile lit up the sky. He was in awe to rediscover a connection after these years. He could share everything with this woman. He could put aside being a surgeon and just be a man in love. He asked where they were going, but she only said it was a temple in the countryside. She laughed, a musical laugh like a songbird, and she refused to say more.

Today would be the first time to wear his hiking pants since arriving in Nepal. They were baggy on him now, and he wondered how much weight he'd lost in Beni, eating lentils and rice. It seemed as though his buttocks disappeared, and the belt was four inches tighter.

She appeared in blue jeans, a leather jacket with padded elbows like a motocross racer in the USA, and a red kerchief over her face. At first, he did not recognize her because of the outfit, and he still wondered how it was that she drove her own motorcycle. She was indistinguishable from every biker, male or female, in Kathmandu. The only clue to suggest her femininity was the front and back panels of a kurtha like an apron that extended to the knee below the leather jacket. *I wonder if she is fearless like the other bikers here*, he thought. She handed him a helmet, as she set hers carefully over the ponytail. The old wound to his thigh hurt momentarily as he threw the leg to straddle the bike, then it was awkward as he put both hands around Sushila's waist. He smelled the perfume in her hair as it flowed out from the back of the helmet. She looked back over her shoulder and laughed. He took some deep breaths, and then pulled down his visor.

Sushila snuggled her torso as she drove through the town. "I will take you to my favorite place in the valley. My mother brought me here as a girl. Here I came to offer puja to the Goddess when I returned to Nepal as a widow. Here I was healed by the Goddess."

They passed Chaubahil and followed the paved road east. Soon it made switchbacks while it followed a mountain stream. They passed through a sleepy Newari town, which receded in the distance, then disappeared around a bend as the rough road continued for ten more minutes. They looked back down on the small village as they climbed, no more than a few houses really, like an island in a sea of rice paddies, water trickling through each. "This stream never goes dry, even in the driest of winters," said Sushila. "In time of drought, the ancient kings used to come here to offer Puja that waters may flow throughout Nepal."

The temple nested on the side of a steep hill set among dark trees. From the village they picked out the brass cupolas of the temple and colored prayer flags, small and almost hidden. It seemed so far away and he wondered if his leg would bother him today. The motorcycle navigated most of the way and the final stone steps to the temple were not steep. There was a small store at the side of the road, and Sushila stopped to buy cooked rice, mangoes, marigolds and bananas with which to offer puja. She paid the shopkeeper a hundred rupees and arranged the food on a copper plate she pulled out of her backpack, covering it with a cloth as they walked.

Here the stream flowed over rocks down a steep hill and two hundred steps followed alongside. They stopped by a place marked by a large flat stone with fresh blood on it. "The Goddess of this temple is the same Goddess we worship in Beni. She is Buddhist. But the local Hindus also worship here. The Buddhists will not allow blood sacrifice in her presence, as she protects every living thing, and so this is the place where the Hindus make offerings of animals." He looked at the spot as he walked slowly up the steps. His leg was stronger than he thought. Above, he heard the screeching of animals crashing through the branches. He could not assign the sound to any animal that he knew. Sushila smiled at him and said nothing.

From the distance came the sound of a half-dozen women singing a Buddhist hymn. The music grew louder as the women descended and their paths crossed. The women formed a small circle around Matt and Kali. Every woman in this group held a newborn baby to their bosom in a sling.

"They all have such a glow about them," said Matt, "Is that how you were?"

She smiled and replied, "They are returning home after a special puja for mothers of the town. The Goddess of this temple favors women."

From above, bells tinkled and pealed, louder now as they climbed nearly to the top of the stairs, random, high-pitched tones from the small bells, the bigger the bell the lower the tone, and finally one very large bell. The temple was not a single structure, rather a small complex of brick buildings with pagoda-like multi-storied roofs. They saw the spring, the stream's origin, enclosed by a small pool. He copied Sushila as she washed her face and hands at the nearby tap; the water was ice cold on his face.

The main temple was a square structure with a brass door in the front, a heavy padlock and chain wrapped on the handle.

"What is the intent of these images? I see the sun and moon, but – the rest? Are they some kind of spell?"

"No. Here is a conch; there is a fish; and next to it an umbrella. Nothing magical. There are eight, and each one symbolizes a Buddhist teaching."

"And the dog? I have always wondered why there is a carving of a vicious dog above the door of these places," said Matt.

"It's not a dog, it's Bhairav. He manifests raw emotion and fear. Bhairav is there to remind us that none of us will learn the lesson of the Goddess within until we have set all emotions aside."

"What are these other carvings for, then? Who carved those?" He pointed at the struts that supported the overhanging eaves of the pagoda. On each strut, a wooden carving depicted a different way to perform intercourse. "Certainly not the people who live here now – they are too straitlaced to show that much imagination."

"They are ancient. You act like you invented sex, Matt." She laughed at him and playfully poked his arm. Pigeons nested above each strut, cooing and leaving a white trail on the stone below. "Come with me."

A large troupe of monkeys was nearby, maybe a hundred, making noise. "Never make eye contact with a monkey," she told him, "If one stops and stares, cover your eyes and walk away. These creatures will attack if you threaten them."

Sushila showed him the small shrine dedicated to Saraswati, patron Goddess of Learned Women. Loose grains of rice lay around the icon, smeared with red paste. He watched as she touched her forehead, then the lintel of the door, then the shoulders of Saraswati, then the lintel again, then took a flower petal from the icon and put it on the top of her head. She motioned for him to follow.

"We will visit the Upper Goddess first. At the time of the winter festival, the Hindus have a custom to parade the Goddess through the village on a palanquin, but the Buddhists believe that blood should not be spilled in front of the Goddess, and they will not allow her to leave her Mandir. The Hindus solved this problem by making an exact copy of the Goddess for themselves. We will first visit the one for the Buddhists."

An attendant added fuel to the fireplace. Despite a chimney, an innovation in Nepal, the room was filled with smoke and the ceiling and walls were smudged with black soot. Matt's eyes watered as he adjusted to the darkness.

Sushila set the plate down in front of the window with a steel grate. A temple monkey soon crashed on the outside, rattling the bars and screeching, trying to get to the food. "These are the temple guards. One time some European thieves came in the night to steal this Goddess. The monkeys awoke the villagers and saved the Goddess. This is the best alarm system."

"You must remain respectful in the presence of the Goddess. Come." She took off her shoes and tiptoed up the steps. The icon was there at the far end of the room, serene, flanked by two smaller escorts. A table of butter-candles flickered and danced. Sushila told him they would have fifteen minutes alone with the Goddess.

A stone tablet was set in the floor just ahead of the Goddess. Carved into the tablet was a stylized lotus, smeared thickly with red ochre paste. Sushila knelt to put her arms down; on all fours, she touched her forehead to the stone. She lifted her head again. Now there was a large red ochre smudge on her forehead. Matt followed her example.

The statue of the Goddess smiled the way a mother would smile watching her children at play, serene and watchful. She sat on a large lotus with one foot off the edge, ready to get up and help somebody. First Matt inspected the red dress and the necklaces.

"Why is she wearing red?"

"Because she is a woman and wants to look nice."

Sushila approached the Goddess and once again touched the lintel of the enclosure, then her own forehead, then back to the lintel. She took a flower petal and put it over her head, then reached into the Goddess's outstretched hand to take some ochre. She beckoned Matt closer and gave him a tika. She waited expectantly and he did the same for her, which made her smile. She closed her eyes as he applied the tika.

She knelt, and he followed.

They sat in silence for ten minutes and a feeling of calm came over him in an odd contrast to the previous day in Patan when the mob moved the chariot through the streets.

"Kali, so long ago when we were together, you told me what the Goddess meant to you," he said, "and today I finally understand the Goddess."

She smiled.

"I was drawn to you when we were younger," he said, "but today I know that I was foolish and did not really know anything. Today I know I have learned new things about the Goddess. "

"Ah," she said. "I am expert in Buddhism. You need to make sure this is the right Goddess. Tell me the manifestations of this Goddess and I will help you identify the name so you can call her forward."

"This Goddess is a giver of life," he said, "She nurtures and protects all around her. She never asks for anything for herself. She is invisible, but a person who carries her spirit can endure the pain of childbirth and being a widow and saving her son from being stolen. A Goddess can do those things."

"Yes, that's the one. The same Goddess I have prayed to since I was a child," she said.

"I did not realize that a Goddess would reveal herself to men as well as women." Matt said.

"Yes, Matt. It takes a while for a man to recognize the worth of what the Goddess brings." she said in a low voice.

"And another thing I noticed about this Goddess," he said, "When she weeps, the whole earth reaches out to console her."

He said, "Kali, I have learned to value the people in my own life who are givers and never ask for anything in return. In Nepal I have watched other women suffer and yet offer themselves to others so that life can go on. I came back not knowing whether you were alive or dead, and I prayed that the Christian God would hold your spirit in the palm of His hand. I saw how women here took suffering and pain but were strong and never gave up. I know now that this was because of love, the kind that just never stops and never asks why but just keeps giving."

Kali thought back to her time in the puja room of her mother, praying for a man to be in her life who would treat her with kindness. She thought of all the Fridays she fasted and prayed. She could also feel the old aching in her heart to feel one with her lover, and at that moment, she offered her own body for the Goddess to inhabit. *I want to be a person worthy of the Goddess.*

"It's time to go," she said. They lit a small candle and left the meditation hall without turning their back to the icon, then went down the stairs to find the shoes.

A smaller courtyard to one side of the lower temple led to a door in the solid rock. This was a meditation cave dimly lit from a small window in the back. A small group of children joined them inside the cave, taking turns climbing out the window. Sushila said, "It is said that if a person is holy enough, they can escape this cave even though the door is locked."

"That must mean that only children are truly holy. An adult cannot possibly fit through there. I think every culture has a special place for the innocence of children."

"That may be true, but I will show you how to have a proper rebirth. It can be done."

She then gave him her backpack and the tray. The children started squealing with delight as Sushila put one arm through the window. "The trick is to put one arm through first and to twist the shoulders a certain way," she said. Matt waited outside the small window to see if Sushila could truly get through the opening.

The children all came out of the cave to see the show. They held hands, started dancing in a circle, and chanted "Chul-buli. Chul-buli. Chul-buli." as Sushila started through.

"What does 'Chulbuli' mean?" he asked.

"They think I am being silly like a teenager. There is Hindi cartoon character by that name. She always gets into mischief but wiggles out," she said, laughing.

"I may have to get some ghee to help you squeeze through," said Matt.

Her bosom came through the window, first one side, then the other. "You are enjoying, Matt Sar?" Matt blushed. The children danced around and laughed.

Finally, she was through the window and stood there straightening out her clothes. The children were shooed away. "If only rebirth were so simple," she told him.

The bells of the lower temple pealed a summons. Matt and Sushila joined the townspeople coming up the steps, carrying trays of cooked rice, bananas and mangoes. The temple monkeys saw the villagers approach and got more excited. This was the screeching Matt heard earlier. Monkeys clambered up the temple, skittered along the roof, and at the last possible minute, saved themselves from injury as they tumbled down the other side. One large male limped with a fierce erection. This one bounded after a smaller female across the roof. The female screeched especially loud as he entered her the way a dog would. A few thrusts and they both howled before resuming the clattering chase over the roof. Matt was embarrassed by this spectacle, and looked to see if anybody else noticed.

Soon Matt and Sushila joined the line to offer puja to the Lower Goddess. When it was their turn, he stooped to get a view of the dark chamber in which the priest stood behind a metal grill. Again, two companions flanked the main icon, again a red dress, this time the necklaces were made of gold coins. Tibetan incense burned nearby creating a juniper cloud over everything. Sushila presented her tray and a hundred rupees to the temple priest, and they both got a tika again. Sushila spoke in low tones to the temple priest as Matt turned to go. Sushila took his hand and pulled him back up the steps. "There is more. We are not done." He stepped back up, enjoying the warmth of her hand, reluctant to release her grasp.

She told him, "Remember those women going down when we came up? They were here last night for a special puja. They all presented their babies to the Goddess. They chanted and meditated all night. He says that today, the town shares their joy with a very special and unusual puja." The priest held a leaf-shaped silver dish with intricate relief work on it and beckoned them to approach.

"He is offering for us to share the sacrament of the Goddess."

She spoke in a conspiratorial tone and she was a bit breathless.

"Would you like to taste the sacrament?" she asked. Her neck seemed flushed.

The Sacrament of the Goddess. He was overwhelmingly curious. His first impulse was to say, *I'm a Catholic*, and reject it. Then, the scientist in him took over. *God will forgive me if I try this. One quick sip will not send me to Hell forever. This is one more crazy thing in a long string of crazy things. Why not?* To accept a moment of hospitality would not doom him to hell forever. And so, he cupped his hands as if receiving communion while the priest dripped about a tablespoon of white fluid into his palm. He slurped it up.

It was milk, a sort of translucent gray milk, thin but with streaks of yellow cream, sweet and with a lingering taste. Sushila again took his hand and led him to the bench where the shoes were. He licked his lips and thought about the taste. *Not cow's milk. Not goat milk.*

Could it be? Sushila waited for him to show any flash of recognition, and she laughed, that musical laugh like an oriole, when he started to speak.

"Yes, I can read your mind, Matt Sar. The Sacrament of the Goddess is collected for the temple only when young mothers share it. The sacrament is a blessing of this town. The stream from the temple nurtures the rice and feeds the town. The town feed its babies. To have healthy well-fed babies is the task given to every woman by the Goddess. That is the Sacrament of the Goddess."

They descended the steps, and she held his hand. She stopped at the sacrifice stone and looked around. Next she led him down a small path that led off to the side, one he did not notice before, only wide enough for one at a time. He followed her, watching the way her hips moved. She looked back at him over her shoulder and smiled.

They arrived at a clearing where a thick bed of moss smelled like pine. She removed her backpack and took out the leather jacket, carefully spreading it on the ground with the silky inside facing up. She took his day pack from his shoulder and stood directly in front of him. She leaned forward and touched her forehead to his.

"Can you sense my third eye?" she asked. "Do you remember how?"

"I think it was you who was the teacher that day, not me," he replied.

They kissed slowly at first. Just tasting the lips, just feeling the way their mouths touched. Then pulling away to breathe, and another try, searching out the sensual joy of a man and a woman. She put both her arms around him, feeling his broad shoulders. He felt the warmth of her breasts and reached for her kurtha, starting to pull it over her head, tentatively at first, exposing the black silk undergarment that now held her ample breasts. She was no longer the young girl he knew from long ago, but a mature woman, and her curves accentuated her femininity in a way that he did not recall from eleven years ago. His pulse quickened.

"The Goddess protects us and wants us to be together."

"This is not the place," he said. "If the people of the town find us here, I will be thrashed. Maybe both of us will be thrashed. You and I both know this."

"You are right. We will go back to the Patan Guest House. I have waited for this; I can wait a bit longer," she said. They collected their belongings, now holding hands as they walked back to the motorcycle. The forty-five minute ride back to the Patan Guest House seemed over in five minutes. Brilliant green rice paddies stretched on either side of the road, but Matt didn't notice. He held his hands on her waist, sometimes shifting to her hips going around a corner. The engine noise prevented them from talking. He considered the supple way her body moved and put his arms around her waist with more confidence. He wondered if she would push him away, but instead, she relaxed and snuggled a bit, giving him the idea that she would accept more familiarity. He felt an inner element of desire that drew him to her, one that went beyond the carnal passion they shared so long ago, a new element that came to the front of his mind.

They parked the motorcycle at the Patan Guest House. She took off her helmet, shaking her head. The braid still held her hair, thick as her wrist. She climbed the stairs first, and he watched her hips move with each step, feeling his own heat, thinking *this is the Goddess, right here. For me.*

Nobody else was there. After a moment she turned her back to him, asking him to undo the braid. He took the silky hair, felt it in his hands, and quietly reached down to kiss the back of her neck. She turned to him then. They embraced and sank onto the coverlet.

O Kali, she began – *guide me* – and then she realized.

Kali has never left me. Kali has guided me all along. Kali wants me to have this pleasure.

She reached to encircle him but he gently took her hands away and stroked her face. He touched her body, feeling the curves of her back. They surrendered to the pleasure of undressing, finding delight as each item of clothing revealed what was hidden to the world when it fell to the floor.

She loosened his belt, he too felt the freedom from clothes. They kissed again, this time with passion and a force that surprised them both. Kali's skin was glistening and her chest became flushed as he nibbled her neck.

She held him, guiding his hand to her most intimate place, warm and inviting, feeling herself open up like a lotus flower bursting into bloom.

Now Matt could feel a small firm bean ripening to serve as a wellspring of pleasure when she met her lover. Like the stream at the temple, the bean sent energy flowing outward into her body, demanding to be touched, ready to send its own lightning bolt into the universe, and she helped Matt find it to call forth the power it held.

Matt was no longer the young innocent, no longer the prisoner of quick passion, now able to control himself. He was gentle with just the barest caress at first, then matched her intensity. He caressed her body, loving every secret place, exclaiming over the curves and muscles, stroking her arms, gently awakening every nerve ending, like the turning on of twinkling lights in a city at dusk.

"Take me," she whispered.

"The Goddess has finally brought us back together. Allow yourself to feel the pleasure of life," he said between kisses, "Do not hurry this Goddess when she is with you."

"Take me," she said, "Now!"

He laughed and moved his lips to kiss her neck.

He held her hips, now straining with her desire as he moved to kiss her bellybutton, and slowly moved downward. He knew that the simple warmth of his breath on the center of her pleasure was enough at first. She swelled with pleasure at the first touch of his tongue. She was on the verge now, moving her hips to the music of the universe, swollen like the bud of a lotus ready to burst into bloom, wet as with rain upon a bed of flowers. With her strength, she pushed him away and made him lie on his back.

She reached down to him, guiding him. Matt paused with Kali, each holding their breath as they felt the special warmth of the approaching final closeness. First, he found the way, then she slowly eased herself on him, breathing heavier and heavier as their bodies joined. The heat and pleasure of entry stunned them both for a second.

They paused for a moment, and then Matt drew her face closer, whispering "Kali.... This moment is sacred to me...."

She managed to whisper, "I will love you - with all the power - of the force - that created - this universe."

The sensations overtook them in rhythmic waves. The softness of her breasts moving above him, contrasted with his own hardness; his hands guiding her hips in motion; the aroma of Elisar in her hair as it brushed his chest with each thrust; the sight of her eyes and skin, soft moaning as each motion matched that of a partner determined to share; the taste of her lips and skin. Matt and Kali moved and breathed together as one person.

Kali felt the climax as he did. This moment flew into their lives with a feeling of total blissful unity, the illusion of floating together with no body, just as beings of light and energy in the brightest of blue skies that ever existed on earth.

And it was over. They lay together, glistening with energy and exertion. He gently touched her face, knowing then that the true sacrament of any goddess was the love that she shared. The sacrament of any woman when bestowed as a gift.

She was lost in her thoughts of joy. She wanted to experience this again, ever since that first time in Beni when she was nineteen. She smiled and would not talk, but listened carefully for the sound of his heart beating as she laid her head on his chest. Finally, she said, "This was how it was meant to be and what should have happened. This is karma. We endured the hard parts of our lives, now we are able to say that the good parts are truly good. I have wanted this all these years."

"And me also. We won't be apart again. Kali, it is the love and willingness to sacrifice for another person which makes the Goddess be alive within you."

She lay her head on his chest and listened to his heart beat. *When I get back to Beni, I will make my last offering to Santoshi Mata,* she thought. *And cook the ceremonial meal to feed the neighborhood boys. Maybe I will still fast every Friday though.*

It seemed as though they dozed off, but soon she woke with a start, looking at the clock, and began to fumble for her clothes to get dressed. He wanted to kiss her again, wanted to caress her, wanted to take her slowly, methodically, but she brushed him off, saying that she promised Manju's mother to return by five, and now she would be late.

"Manju's mother knows I am a widow and already thinks I am out of control. And maybe she is right. Also, it is our culture to be very discreet about these things. This idea of you and me – even though you are my betrothed, we must give it time to become ripe and full in the course of our lives. We need to reveal it slowly. For now – this is best." With that, she was gone. He heard the motorcycle engine as he lay there, feeling physically spent.

Hunger finally caused him to move. The Bakery Café was only a few blocks away. He was alone at the table, using pictures on the menu to give signals to the waiter. He ordered a lemon soda, salty style, and majli dosa, one of his favorites. The roti was crispy and the filling was deliciously spicy. He ate in silence, looking at the couples and wondering if any of them were in love as he now was. He wondered whether any of the legends Sushila told him were true. He wondered where his life would go now. He loved Nepal.

He leafed through *Escape from Kathmandu* in the Guest House Library and thought to himself, there is no book yet written that will hold my story. He saw her face on every page. *It is easier for a Westerner to accidentally climb Mount Everest than to court a Nepali woman.* And I have found a wonderful person to share my life.

The next day the long return trip back to Beni began with a taxi to the airport. Sushila was there at the in-country terminal. She smiled when she saw him and stood so close that he could smell her perfume. He wanted to kiss, but she backed away with a smile. *Not here…it is not our culture…. Maybe later….*

July 2007 – Beni, Nepal, D.I.C.

Back in Beni, it was time for Bimla to deliver her baby. She was the wife of the Maoist, but she was a contrast to her husband's personality – bubbly and smiling. For Ranjit, seeing Bimla reminded him of the risk she took after the battle, and he was uncomfortable being too near. Ranjit felt feelings of guilt over the way he interrogated her that time in Sara's office. He took note of her outlook on life. "Somebody seems to have forgotten to tell Bimla she is not supposed to be happy," he told Sara.

Bimla wanted a Caesarean delivery and told Sara of her wish. She was disappointed that it was not possible but resigned herself to the idea of the impending labor. Late in the pregnancy, Bimla woke from a bad dream about the delivery. She repeated her wish to Sara.

"This we cannot do. There is no reason for a Caesarean in your case. You will do just fine. It's too expensive and there are risks." The next day, Bimla told all her friends what Sara said.

Bimla's labor started at 11 p.m. and she came to the hospital with two of her best friends. The baby boy came at midnight, but the amniotic fluid was stained with meconium. The boy was a bit flaccid at first, so Sara and the didi used the meconium aspirator to clear the infant's airway. While they were doing this, the mother passed the placenta, followed by a gush of bright blood as she hemorrhaged. Sara massaged the fundus, causing it to contract, but it did not stay contracted and there was a lot of flow. Bimla became shocky, and Sara called Ranjit and Ram. They gave the mother some intramuscular pitocin, Ranjit used a gloved hand to check for retained fragments of placenta, then used a fisted hand in the birth canal to prevent prolapse during vigorous suprapubic massage. She still hemorrhaged. Ranjit called Matt, because the need for surgery was more evident. Only surgery would save the woman's life.

The newborn boy was not able to achieve a pink complexion, showed signs of distress, and died.

Bimla was ready for surgery in a very short time. Matt looked at her lying on the operating table and said, "Do I know this person?"

"It's Bimla," said Ram, "this is Sara's secretary."

Bimla. Sushila's friend. This woman laughed and played with my son as if he were her own. Matt took a deep breath. *Focus on the task at hand.*

Matt led the hysterectomy using the cautery tool. Matt and Ranjit removed the uterus. To the naked eye it was bruised and purple, where it should have been bright red and meaty. The diagnosis was made. Disseminated Intravascular Coagulation. Unforeseen and unusual. One in ten thousand. Ranjit held the uterus in his hands for a moment before he dumped it in a bucket and re-focused on the surgery. Matt looked up to see Ranjit stagger just a bit and become pale. Blood oozed from everywhere in the open surgical wound, it seemed.

Ranjit needed to explore the source of the bleeding, and the scrub nurse suctioned as fast as she could. Matt cauterized as they went along. Ranjit used surgical towels to sop up blood, leaving the tails out and throwing the saturated ones onto the sheet on the floor or into the bucket, but now he looked into the wound and paused, with bare hands. Ranjit held his hands in the gesture of prayer for a moment, but Matt knew that it was to keep the sterile gloves from being contaminated.

Matt waited for Ranjit to ask the tech for the next instrument, but Ranjit reached directly onto the Mayo stand, something Matt never saw him do before. Ranjit picked up one particular instrument. Matt recognized what Ranjit was looking for, and why he chose that tool. *The Universal Implement. Does he know? Or did he just figure it out on his own? I'll be damned. There are three on the mayo stand.* He did not have time to ask Ranjit about it. He needed to focus on the task at hand.

So far, Matt was focused on achieving hemostasis and the probable outcome did not register with him. Now he realized. *She is going to die.* Matt needed to stay two moves ahead as in a chess game. *We do have dopamine, she'll go on a dopamine drip. An infusion pump would be handy but we'll use a burette instead. We will need ten units of blood. That we do not have. And a central line. That we do not have. And fresh frozen plasma. That we also do not have. And an intensivist. That would be me. God knows what else we need.*

We do have prayer. We can start on that right now.

They closed and wheeled Bimla back to the delivery room and left her on the stretcher. Now they would try to stabilize her, but Matt knew it was going to be like a roller coaster. First, a challenge would arise, then a small victory would be attained after which the team hoped the condition of the patient would improve. Then a new problem would crop up, repeating the cycle. Over and over. Matt was not a stranger to this. When events happened this way in Boston, it was a continual crisis. *We don't have the resources to sustain this. Even if she gets through the night, we are all dog-tired and there is nobody to take over.*

At four in the morning, the blood bank tech brought the last unit of blood and gave it to Ram. Ram announced that the blood pressure was sixty by forty despite the dopamine, and the oxygen saturation was fifty percent. Ram connected it to the intravenous. The team watched. It wasn't dripping fast enough.

"We need to run it in the vein as fast as it is running out elsewhere," said Ranjit as he took the bag off the hanger and held it in both hands. Ranjit squeezed until the drips merged into a steady stream. Matt looked at the way the plastic tightened in Ranjit's hands.

"If that bursts, we will all be covered in blood."

"That is about how the night has gone," Ram said, "I'd say we have an hour remaining. If you have any ideas, share them now."

Matt looked at the bruising on Bimla's arms and legs. The surgical incision continued to ooze blood and the perineal pack was saturated.

Turn it on. Compartmentalize.

"She is obtunded. This is most likely due to anesthesia and morphine, but we can't rule out an intracerebral bleed. There is pink frothy stuff in her endotracheal tube. Her extremities are shut down and cold. The last hemoglobin is four. We have not fixed the coagulopathy."

Everyone nodded as Matt recited this.

"The D.I.C. will not go away unless we find the cause. We're maxed on dopamine. I think her lungs are shot. And there is no urine in the urine bag. We have multisystem failure and we are flying blind. So - I have nothing to add to the plan here," Matt said. *There. I pronounced it, just like at MGH. And if I was at MGH they would all agree. Just like here.*

Sara took Bimla's hand in both of hers. Matt could not see the expression on her face.

"Lord, bring your light to this dark place," she said. Her voice cracked.

"I could lie down beside this woman and donate my own blood, and it would not be enough," said Ranjit grimly, "Damn this to hell."

He stared straight at Matt as he said this. Matt looked over to see that Ranjit was crying as he squeezed the bag. A surge of insight swirled in Matt's consciousness. *It was Ranjit himself. Ranjit's blood, for me. Of course. He was the other donor. Ranjit and Sushila share the same blood type.*

Ranjit is taking this hard. He wants to win this one, just like the time it was me on the stretcher. And there I go, but for the grace of God.

At dawn, Ram rechecked the blood pressure, which was forty by zero. Shortly after that, Bimla stopped breathing altogether and the mottling on her arms and legs became more pronounced.

"It's the end," said Sara. She stepped back.

Ranjit quickly stepped to the side of the stretcher and lowered the side rail.

"CPR. We should do CPR," he said. Ranjit quickly stepped to Bimla's side and palpated the sternum to find the landmark for chest compressions.

"Help me. Let's go," Ranjit said.

At first, nobody else moved and they all just stared as Ranjit placed his hands on Bimla's chest. Matt said, "No…. it is futile…no….please…. it's bad enough already…. Please, no… don't…."

Ram stepped up and took Ranjit's hands away, pressing them between his own. Ram murmured softly to Ranjit, "It is finished. You did what you could. Nothing else to do. You did everything. There was nothing else. This is not the way to let her go…"

Sara returned to the side of the stretcher opposite from Ranjit, took the hands of Bimla in her own, looked at Bimla's face and then at Ranjit.

"Bimla is no more," she said.

The delivery nurse put her arms on the shoulders of one of Bimla's friends.

The sudden silence in the room after a death always brought a ringing to Matt's ears. He heard it now. Matt crossed his arms, slumped against the wall, and surveyed the tableau. *Bimla's death was not an orderly one*, he thought, *Bimla never woke up after surgery, never knew whether her boy lived or died, never said goodbye*. For some reason he thought back to the red-haired hospice nurse he met on the plane. Tonight, he could not remember her name, but he recalled the way she described death in USA, and hospice, as if it were some sort of welcome release, a spiritual calling. Death with hospice could include angels descending from the sky, a benevolent God smiling and a welcoming committee of all previous loved ones greeting their new companion at the threshold to Heaven. *Damn, I could use a dose of God right about now. I can't even seem to muster a prayer*, he thought. *There is blood on the floor. Hell exists. I just spent an eternity there.*

Here in Nepal, there were a thousand ways to die in addition to the usual ways he already knew about, and none of them was orderly or dignified. There was no redeeming social value to end-of-life care here, no reward for a job well done except the knowledge that you were going to get up and fight the same battle tomorrow. Not even at the AIDS hospice where they ought to have anti-AIDS drugs but didn't. Manju tried to create dignity there, but she was in a trench on the front lines.

None of this meant that life was cheap here. Everybody knew about death; the process was there for all to see from a young age. It was not hidden. People here gritted their teeth and never gave up. Even to simply focus on the easing of suffering was not enough, the odds were stacked against the people here from day one, as if it were a curse from some unseen god. *No, Bimla's death was not an orderly death.*

Her two friends left to bring the news to Bimla's husband. Matt wondered how he would take it and whether the Maoist would do the full Hindu ritual of cremation. From a practical point of view, something would have to be done with the body and there was no cemetery here. In a while, the Maoist would return with a stretcher made of bamboo poles painted white, a cloth shroud, and maybe some garlands of marigolds. The river was nearby. The only real question was to gather the supplies and choose a spot along the bank.

The word of Bimla's death spread through the town. Women soon started to arrive for their only look at the body, which lay motionless in the labor room. The housekeeping staff sopped up the blood from the floor. The didi wrapped the baby and laid it on the mother's chest. Mother and child would be cremated together. The didi then composed the body by putting a sheet over Bimla's legs and torso. Bimla's pale face and hands were exposed, her long braid arranged to flow over her chest. It was not the custom for women to attend cremations in Beni.

The women wore saris of every shade of red, pink, purple, orange, and maroon. Even here, viewing a body, the clothes were impossibly bright.

There were two beds in this space, and another woman labored there, in the adjacent bed, with the drape pulled between; but no matter – the crowd of women came to pay their respects to Bimla. Each held their shawl across their face as they looked at the sight of their friend who was no more. Too many to fit in the delivery room. Soon a line formed, and then the crowd extended out the door and beyond the hedge. It seemed as though every woman in town was there. Some carried babies on their backs using the pashmina shawl as a sling. Others held the hands of young girls, the daughters of the town, as they waited to see the body.

Matt wondered when the Maoist would come. The crowd of women grew while the morning progressed. The women who viewed the body did not leave. They filled the entire area between the buildings. Sara came out to join Matt.

"This will be a spectacle I am afraid. I have ordered all the buildings to be locked. There will be no OPD clinic today."

"Are you afraid of a bandh?"

"I wouldn't call it that. I am not sure where this will go, but it pays to be cautious."

Soon an excited murmur came over the crowd and the women moved back to create an aisle. The Maoist was there with three children, two girls and a boy. The son was the oldest and he walked behind. Like his father, he held the hand of one of the younger girls. It was obvious that the two younger girls were groomed and wore their nicest clothes as if going to a wedding. The Maoist was wearing a topi this time, not his usual hat, and the top button of his shirt was fastened. He tried to improve his rumpled appearance for this, though he still sported the wispy beard. At the sight of the family, a great wailing went up from the crowd.

A few meters behind were fifty men. These men would carry the woman through the town. They waited at the edge of the crowd.

Soon the Maoist emerged. His eyes were puffy and he sniffled a bit but he did not weep now. Some women of the town, the friends of his wife, went in to wrap their friend in a white shroud. Loops of red string were tied around her neck, torso, and knees. A saffron-and-orange cloth was draped on top, then over it, a garland of marigolds. The women took the hands of Bimla's daughters, to bring them home where they would wait for their father.

Three men did a side-lift like a drill team, lifting Bimla from the stretcher, turning then lowering her to the white bamboo stretcher. Four other men hoisted the funeral stretcher to their shoulders. Two men blew on conch shells as the procession started. The women wailed. The men fell in behind the litter bearers, but the women did not follow, instead dispersing. On either side of the street, people lined the route to the riverbank.

The crowd flowed down the hill to the parade ground, stopping at the temple to wash the body and discreetly remove the clothes from the woman who was no more. These would be thrown into the river. Then they brought the body behind the temple, to the sandbar that jutted out into the very place where the rivers met. Here the third river joined the KaliGandaki and the Myaggi as they rushed toward the Ganges, the sacred river into which all Hindu remains would disappear, becoming one with the universe. It was an auspicious place for a cremation, and now a pyre waited, along with the temple priest.

Three men lifted the body from the litter and carried it around the pyre three times, then laid it there. The priest steadied the Maoist's hand as he, too, circled the pyre three times, flaming torch in hand. The shroud was peeled back and the Maoist gazed on Bimla's face for the last time just as he touched the flame to the oil in her mouth. The torch fell from his hand and he backed away as the priest fanned the flames. The flame started slowly at first and then blazed up as the priest added more ghee. The larger logs caught fire. Sheaves of wet straw were placed atop the torso to promote an even cremation, white smoke and steam, mixing together as they wafted skyward. The Maoist sat by the pyre and cried as the smoke carried the body of his wife to the sky. He was already bald on the top but now sat still as a barber shaved the rest of his head. The first-born son was there, and the Maoist stayed alongside while the barber shaved the head of the boy, leaving a small topknot, the topi, intact. The boy cried, "Aama," and held his father as he wept. A murmur ran through the crowd.

That day, after the cremation, things were quiet at first. Less than ten people came to the clinic. Patients were discharged and the hospital seemed quiet and empty. Finally at noon, a solemn man came to see Sara. He introduced himself as a friend of the family of the deceased woman.

He started by saying, "I am a serious man, and we have serious things to discuss." He did not wish to go inside. Instead, he sat with Sara on the chautara and they talked. He was the Maoist political officer from Tatopani, an intermediary, presenting demands for justice.

"I will come straight to the point. This family has lost a mother and a wife who was also a productive worker outside the home."

"Yes. She was a dear friend to me and a fine employee. We were so sorry that we could not save her despite our best efforts."

"We believe the hospital should compensate the family for the loss. We believe that two million rupees is a fair amount of money for that purpose," he said.

Sara gasped. "It was not the fault of the doctors that Bimla died. She developed a rare condition known as Disseminated Intravascular Coagulation, and nobody could have predicted that it would have happened. Even in the finest medical centers in the world, she would have been critically ill. Please accept our condolences for the loss of this beautiful and loving person."

"Is that all you have to say?"

"This hospital is run as a charity, and we do not have that kind of money. We need time to determine what our response will be."

The man stood up to leave, giving a namaste. Just at that moment, Sushila entered the courtyard from the other side. They made eye contact and both froze with a flash of recognition. Sushila quickly turned around to leave.

The Maoist from Tatopani turned to Sara and said, "You will hear from us again and very soon."

The man stalked off.

Sara found Sushila and took her aside. "What was that little scene?"

"That was him. Again. The one from the battle. He is the exact one who took Arjun from my house. The one who was following me last week. Maybe he'd thought I left, but now he truly knows I am back. He recognized me. I am certain. He is a very bad man."

"Stay here. I think you need to have people around you," said Sara.

Two hours later, Sara heard a crowd approach the hospital. She looked out the window. *So it has come to this.* She felt a hard knot in her stomach. *I need to warn the others. But they probably all know.*

Alok and Manju were walking back from Shanti Nawajeevan when the crowd swelled up around the corner. Here was a large crowd of men dressed in work clothes. Many carried lathis. Alok recognized immediately that the crowd was ready to "thrash" somebody - the polite term for administering a thorough beating with these. The crowd started a rally in the yard of the hospital. *There is nobody to stop them. The crowd is growing.*

Manju asked what was happening, and he didn't want to alarm her, but she could sense tightness in his voice.

"It's because of a death that happened last night. Let's go find Sara."

Sara was conferring with Ranjit. "Alok, we are thinking we need to activate the evacuation plan. There is a team of men in front of the garage gate. They will not allow the Land Rover to leave."

Alok nodded his head and looked out the window.

"We will have an early dinner and make a plan," she told him.

It was an ironclad rule for dinner at the Guest House to start promptly at six, but today the didis prepared it at four and left the grounds. Matt looked out the window to see other hospital staff quietly walking away. *They know something. It does not require a genius to see what is happening here.* He took his usual seat at the table. The whole medical staff was there, joined by Manju and Sushila. The dishes were fried chicken, mashed potatoes and boiled greens. Everyone sat quietly while Sara bowed her head to say a silent grace before she ate.

"We all know why we are here. I want to thank everyone for their help last night and into today," said Ranjit with a sigh. "Of all days, this has been the most trying."

Today Ranjit ate with his head down and was quiet. There was none of the good-natured banter with Ram, no teasing Alok about youth, nothing. *Last night he asked for the Universal Implement*, thought Matt. *Ranjit truly has proved he is a guru.* For the first time Matt considered the idea that Ranjit was old. He wondered exactly as to the age. *Maybe Ranjit was thirty the day he was born*, thought Matt.

He's a boddhisattva, a person who chose to stay behind and help others when he could have gone to nirvana by now. I should have called him that all along I suppose but it's too late now. He would tell me never to mock Buddha. Ranjit was an indestructible force of nature. He might never grow old until all of a sudden he was no more. The best Matt could estimate was that Ranjit was about sixty.

"I was delayed by two weeks on a short visit to Kathmandu in April 2004 when the Maoists started fifteen days of riots," said Ram, "Do not doubt that they can assemble a crowd and whip it into a frenzy. And the Maoists have already blocked every road, you can count on that. They know how to conduct a bandh."

"I have always felt love from the people of this town, until today," said Ranjit, "I know that the whole team did as well as they could. We did nothing wrong." At this, he was on the verge of tears. He looked pale. Matt saw beads of sweat on Ranjit's forehead.

"We all know what happened when the Maoists gathered a crowd at Tamgas," said Sara, "Until today I never thought we might get the same treatment."

"Not me. I don't know. What happened there?" said Manju.

"At Tamgas the Maoists goaded a mob until a hundred men with lathis stormed the wall of the hospital. They broke all the windows, all the equipment and furniture, and thrashed the workers, including two doctors of the town. They set it on fire when they left." She paused. "That hospital remains closed. There are now a hundred and fifty thousand people who have no hospital unless they go all the way from Tamgas to Pokhara, seventy kilometers. Most of them already needed to walk as much as fifty kilometers even before then. It's misery. "

"This is what happens when a medically unsophisticated population is manipulated into thinking that the Maoists can bring twentieth-century medical care to rural Nepal overnight. The Maoists need to create an enemy to blame. They have worked to create anger for eleven years, they do not know how to run a hospital," said Ram. "You around the table here are my brothers and sisters. I have been here twenty years and I now contemplate the idea that if a mob attacks, I will not get away. This is four hundred against six. I am too fat to outrun them."

Sushila sat quietly as she processed this information. Here were the people from the long-ago days at Beni. She looked up to them, and they were still the most dedicated and hardworking doctors she ever met. Now, she saw a side of them, a human side, in which everyone confronted fear. *O Goddess, make us mindful of our fear and help us see the clear truth.*

Sushila thought back to the beginning of her life in Beni. There was always a darker side, beginning with a sheltered upbringing from the world in which it was assumed she would always depend on a man and didn't need to think for herself. Then being forced to learn. She pictured the faces of women in the AIDS hostel who never received a fair chance in Nepali society, and then her own crisis during the battle. *"Act like a bhalu and I will treat you like one," the soldier said, and now he was back.* She herself was not the same innocent and naïve girl that came back from high school and fell in love with a videshi. *That person is far away from here. I wonder how old I am now. It's not measured in years any more. I am a survivor, but every time I have tried to be a simple woman, an obstacle appears.*

"Won't the Police or the Army come to help us? Send soldiers?" Manju asked.

There were knowing glances around the table, and everyone clenched their teeth.

"We do not have a good track record to expect the Army to mediate the Maoists," replied Ram.

Matt looked around the table. "We have to find a way to overcome this. I've been through too much to let it end this way." There was silence, except for Manju, sniffling back some tears. Matt watched as Alok took Manju's hand in both of his.

Matt thought *there would be no rescue.* This weighed on him, and he looked at Sushila. *I do not think I will get an orderly death, here. For me it's overdue. I did not think it would come this way, for me. Since she came back, this was the happiest I ever was in my whole life. Now, I will die defending Sushila, if I have to.*

"There really is a point where we have to accept what comes," Sara softly, "I want you all to know that I have always prayed for this hospital and for the people of Nepal."

"Prayer. If prayer will work, I wish to join you," said Ram. "I know that I have teased you about this since the day I arrived from Delhi. I have come to know that the Christian God looks favorably on martyrs, and if we are all to become a sacrifice to the Christian God, we ought to prepare ourselves."

Sara looked at her friend as she said, "Ram, people can do good works without naming the Christian God by name. Jesus, our Lord, never asked one person to proclaim their faith, He simply healed them. He asked nothing in return and went on His way. If you wish to join hands, now is a good time."

Everyone joined hands as Sara bowed her head. She began the prayer slowly, British accent in cadence shining through each word, letting each line hang there in the air until it floated away of its own accord before the next replaced it.

"The Lord is my shepherd; I shall not want. He maketh me to lie down in green pastures: he leadeth me beside the still waters.

"He restoreth my soul: he leadeth me in the paths of righteousness for his name's sake.

"Yea, though I walk through the valley of the shadow of death, I will fear no evil: for thou art with me; thy rod and thy staff they comfort me."

She looked up. Every head at the table was bowed. All hands were joined.

"Thou preparest a table before me in the presence of mine enemies: thou anointest my head with oil; my cup runneth over. Surely goodness and mercy shall follow me all the days of my life: and I will dwell in the house of the Lord forever."

Now she blinked her eyes and said, "That was the last prayer I shared with my parents before I ended my last homestay visit and returned here on my mission to Nepal. I never saw my father alive again."

Her voice cracked, "They have been here in spirit every step of this journey. You have all seen their picture on the wall in my office. I always honor their memory when I say that prayer."

Silence around the table. In the distance, the sound of four hundred people shouting and chanting. Angry sounds, gathering in intensity.

How many Christians have gone to their death with that psalm, Matt wondered. He thought back to early days in Catholic catechism class. He realized that he hadn't prayed lately, certainly hadn't been to a Catholic Mass since coming to Nepal. What would be the Catholic prayer? *"Holy Mary, mother of God, pray for us sinners, now and at the hour of our death, amen."* In his mind's eye, Matt was twelve again, dressed in his Boy Scout uniform on a spring day in May, sitting in the pew at The Church of the Immaculate Conception, singing "Ave Maria" to the Blessed Virgin, praying the rosary in a singsong voice, and waving to his mother smiling in the balcony. *If the Monsignor could see me now. This prayer rehearsed a thousand times without even thinking of what it meant. I don't think I will ever be able to say it again without mentally coming back to this table and these friends.*

If I survive.

There was a period of silence as everyone collected themselves again.

"Well, we've had a good cry, I think," said Sara. "The question remains: What shall we do?"

"We can get by with a skeleton crew until this resolves," said Ranjit, "Sushila needs to go. We were always worried that the Maoists would target her since the battle. We don't know if that is a factor now. Matt, it is logical for you to accompany her. Those others, who do not need to be here, can go."

"Yes, they can leave in the morning," said Ram, "I only see one small hole in the plan. How do we get from this point in time to that one?"

"I am afraid it is getting out of hand outside," said Sara, "I will talk to the people." She looked from one to another and said, "I want to thank everyone for the kindness you have shown me along the way."

Sara pushed away from the table. She straightened her skirt, preened her hair for a bit, and folded her napkin, laying it neatly at her place setting. She walked to the door. She studied it for a moment with her hands clasped in front of her. Finally, she lifted the latch and stepped outside.

"What did she just do?" asked Manju.

"She just led us in the Twenty-Third Psalm," said Matt.

Once again, Matt looked across the table to Ranjit, pale and sweating. This time there was just a hint of cyanosis around Ranjit's lips. Matt took Ranjit's hand and looked at the palm. He decided to check Ranjit's pulse. The hand was cold and clammy.

Just as the door shut behind Sara, Ranjit swayed in his seat and collapsed to the floor.

Standing on the Soapbox and Saying Goodbye

Those who are free of resentful thoughts surely find peace.
– Buddha

Sara now stood at the edge of a crowd in the cool night air. Soft lights glowed from the windows of adjacent buildings, and Sara knew that about a dozen patients remained in the beds, recuperating. First, she saw dark shapes holding the torches, casting a flickering yellow glow, wispy black kerosene smoke billowing into the sky. Her eyes adjusted and now she saw the rough-hewn faces of the Nepali men. She always found them to be handsome in a rugged way, like farmers and day laborers who wanted a better life, especially if they smiled. Nobody was smiling. *The torches are so lovely. The faces are handsome. If this was a festival it would be beautiful,* she thought. *This is like a postcard the tourists would buy at Pilgrim's Bookstore in Thamel.* The courtyard was packed with men, maybe four hundred. Many wore kerchiefs over their faces as they milled about.

She wished there was a wall around the hospital, but then maybe even a wall would not stop such a mob. People of Nepal were capable of swarming, forming a river of unstoppable humanity, a thousand people thinking as one, and creating a new reality just by the force of sheer willpower. She looked for the center of agitation. She knew the old rule about crowd events in Nepal. *If it was a religious event, those with the most fervor would be at the center of the crowd, and to take in the flavor of the event, you wished to get closest to that group; but if it was a political event or a bandh, locate the group with the most fervor and get as far away from them as you possibly can.*

Her next thought was, *Chin up. Walking past quickly with my head down is not an option this time.*

At the center of the crowd was the Maoist leader from Tatopani. He stood on some sort of wooden box and she wondered where it came from since it didn't belong to the hospital. *They have thought of everything.* This Maoist shouted and exhorted the men with angry words of revenge and cold justice. A hush went through the crowd as she appeared, and his voice trailed off as she came toward him. She shouted.

"Hajur!" She waited to get his attention. "May I speak? I have something to share!"

She consciously chose to use the honorific term for a superior in her speech. She was now going to speak in her best Nepali. Sara asked to step up on the box and to address the crowd. The Tatopani Maoist stepped off the makeshift stage and helped her to the spot from which she surveyed the crowd. She looked for any of the Christian Nepalis from the small church, the one named the Emmaus Church of Beni, but recognized none of those who worshipped there with her every Saturday. *Not a one. I hope they are praying for me.*

She spoke in Nepali, as loud as she could. Nobody ever heard Sara shout before, and the sound of her own voice was a surprise even to her.

"We are all here in sadness over the death of a woman, a woman who did not deserve to die. It was not a question of karma, it was not a question of whether the doctors did the right thing or not. For we are all going to die.

"I have been here thirty years, I have delivered babies, I have given you surgery, I have treated your children and wives, and I have treated you. I have been there for you in suffering and stood with you." She looked out into the crowd and called a man by name.

"Mahesh, I remember when you came here with typhoid, and we treated you. Do we deserve harm now because we were here those days?" then, "Dinesh! Your son fell from a tree, and we fixed his elbow! Where was the justice? Did you kill the tree because your son fell from it?" At this, the man whom she called by name, nodded as others looked on.

"I was here when we treated the People's Liberation Army on the night of the battle. You know it's true! Hear me out!"

"My brothers! My uncles! Please sit and I will tell you the truth!"

There was a pause, and one by one, the men sat or squatted to hear her speak. This marked a change in the demeanor of the crowd. The Maoist from Tatopani was now off to one side, standing there and frowning. To hear a woman addressing a crowd at night, during a torchlight event, was new for these men.

"This hospital was started by foreigners and is paid for by foreigners, but you know that it is mostly run by Nepalis now. I am the last Christian missionary here. If you trash it, the government in Kathmandu will not be able to replace anything, not one pane of glass. And you will go back to the time before there was one. We have never turned away anyone seeking treatment here."

She continued, "This is not a time to allow anger to destroy your soul. It will not bring this woman back. She is no more. It will not prevent death from reaching us here in Beni. Death will come to all of us eventually. But it will prevent us from leading a life of joy and happiness as we suffer from burdens that could be lifted if there was peace.

"Hear my message. I want this hospital to stay here and serve the people. If you ask your wives and ask your children, they will tell you that it is what they also want.

"The Christian God once said, 'let he who is innocent cast the first stone.' And so, I ask you whether there is any among you who would still be alive if there was never any help from the people here, or from their friends. Buddha says to rely on the word of your sanga. Look among the sanga and you will find the wisdom of not allowing anger to rule your soul. Look among your sanga and see that we can only improve things by building up, and not by tearing down. Take refuge in the Buddha. Let that person, who has never been sick, who has never held a sick child and prayed for healing, stand up and lead the destruction of something that was built by an international sanga of those who work with compassion and lovingkindness."

She was now breathing heavily and her face was red. "I am here. If you need to have bloodshed in order to right this wrong, I pray to Jesus, the Son of God that you will spare the hospital and spare those who work at this place. I am ready. In the Bible, the Christian Holy Book, it is written that nobody may see the face of God and live. I pray to God that today I will see His holy face. I pray that I will reach out my hand and touch the face of Jesus, the Son of the Christian God who sent me here." She let these words sink in.

Her voice rose into a crescendo for the final words of her plea, and she shouted, "If you need to kill somebody, kill me. I offer myself to you in place of the senseless violence that is planned. Take me now!"

Her words rang out with force and finality. She stood there, defiantly at first, holding back the great emotion, surprised herself at what she just said, half expecting to feel the first stone as it was cast, bracing herself for the shock that surely was about to come. *Jesus, look upon me with mercy, for I am a sinner. I am afraid of the dark. Show me your Light, Lord.* That would be the beginning of it. Standing on the box, an easy target, she surveyed the effect of her speech on the crowd. There was tense silence.

The nearest man with a torch was still standing, and he stepped forward. He walked slowly to her, about three steps, all eyes upon him. He placed his torch on the ground in front of her. It dimmed slightly as it lay in the gravel. Then he bowed, gave the Namaste gesture, turned his back and walked away. A second man with a fist-sized rock in his hand, a small paving stone from the walkway, stood up. He slowly walked forward, all eyes upon him, and placed the rock near the torch. Next, another man with a torch added to the pile. Then a fourth and fifth. The mob was now returned to a crowd, and the trickle of those leaving turned into a stream. The nameless crowd was once again a group of individual men. The spell of anger and hate was broken.

She watched the crowd disperse. She stood there, incredulous in the torchlight. The Maoist from Tatopani approached and said, "didi" before he, too, left.

The pile of burning torches continued for a while. Finally Sara left.

Inside, the others gathered around Ranjit, now on the floor. Matt felt for a carotid pulse, and it was there, slow and steady, but it was about forty beats per minute. Alok produced a blood pressure cuff and stethoscope, and the measurement was sixty by forty. Ranjit was experiencing profound bradycardia. *A heart attack. Probably the inferior wall. Damn that tobacco pipe,* thought Matt.

"He needs oxygen, a heart monitor, and atropine. Probably morphine and aspirin," said Matt.

"He will not swallow aspirin unless he can wake up first," said Ram.

"Good point. But when he does we'll crush it and put it in his mouth."

They dragged Ranjit out the door while Sara was speaking, but she did not notice, and the crowd was also watching the woman on the box, not the small desperate knot of doctors dragging a person. It was a short trip down the walkway then a small commotion as they lifted him onto a stretcher in the Casualty Ward. Alok started the intravenous. Matt asked the didi for the atropine, half expecting an abboject as used in the USA, stopping to file the groove on the thick brown glass vial, then snapping it to transfer the drug to a syringe by hand, shaking with the fear that he may not be moving fast enough. *His heart will stop any minute.* The old ways of dealing with a medical emergency were coming back, and Matt was happy in a way – happy to think about patient care and not the impending riot that was gathering steam all day. He realized that Ram and Alok, too, were engaged with Ranjit the patient, putting aside their feelings for Ranjit the man.

"Let's get a monitor on him."

"We have no monitors. We can take an oximetry reading. That is all. And a twelve-lead e.c.g."

After the atropine, Ranjit was now conscious again with a blood pressure of ninety by sixty. He watched as the twelve-lead e.c.g. test was run, a long strip of graph paper spooling to the floor, and then looked quizzically as Matt and Ram interpreted the paper strip like a ticker tape.

It showed a massive anterior wall infarct extending into the septum and an unstable heart block. *Tombstone T waves*, thought Matt. Ranjit needed to pause for breath as he spoke. "I can feel my lungs filling with fluid as I breathe," said Ranjit. "For twenty years Sara warned me about the pipe, - please tell her that I always knew - she was right. Where is she?"

Matt, Ram, Alok, Manju and Sushila were around the stretcher. Finally Ram spoke up, "Sara is talking with the Maoists."

"Thank you, I seem to have forgotten."

Ram reminded Matt, "We have no pacemaker. We have no streptokinase or TPA here. Last week I was meaning to tell Sara that the pharmacy stock of heparin is depleted. The effect of the atropine will not last forever."

Ranjit said, "I heard everything you just said. Take the suction cups from this twelve-lead e.c.g. monitor from my chest. I do not think it will cure me. We have taught you better ways to deal with death than to use machines," Ranjit was still drenched with sweat. "I do not object to morphine."

After the morphine, his breathing was a bit better. He was now propped up on the stretcher. "I will say my last wishes. Ram, where are you?"

Ram stepped up and Ranjit said, "Brother, do not cremate me. I want a sky burial. Arrange it with the lamas. Some day we will laugh together on the other side. I was proud to have you as a companion on the kora that was this life." Ram pressed Ranjit's right hand to his forehead.

"Alok, to you I leave every book I ever owned. You are a fine doctor. Be sure to wear a helmet on that motorbike. Don't forget to change the oil."

"Manju. Only when you know the value of suffering can you truly be compassionate to others. It is time for you to fill your life with love."

"Sushila. Thank you for being in my life, Chunumunu. I am so glad you are here for me.   I loved your mother, and you are the child she gave me. My wife at the time forbade me to acknowledge you. I am sorry for the turmoil this brought you. I wept when your mother died. I was always meaning to talk with you about this someday. Please forgive me for keeping these things from you. Now we can leave that past behind. In the time since the Goddess sent you back to me, I have tasted joy. Have peace in your heart. I love you."

She kissed his hand and said, "Father, the love in your heart was never a secret to me. My mother told me all this when I was eight. It was such a relief to say this aloud on the ride back from Kathmandu. I too wanted to speak, but it was not our culture. There is so much to say. Thank you for everything. I love you. I forgive you for everything. Do you forgive me? " Her voice trailed off.

"There is nothing to forgive, Chunumunu. You have always made me proud. I loved you when I first saw you in your mother's arms. And you are a wonderful mother."

"Matt Sar. You are the father of my grandson. Raise him to be a surgeon like both his grandfathers. Hug him and talk to him for me. For many years, I wished that my blood did not run through your veins. Between us, Sushila and I saved your life. I now know that you love my daughter. You helped me to release my anger. That was the greatest gift a Buddhist can receive. If you owed me a debt, I consider it to be paid in full."

Ranjit rested for a moment as the morphine made his mind coast downhill.

Sara entered and closed the door behind her. For a moment, she leaned against it, as if shutting it against a gale force wind, then she turned to face the group. The others all wanted to ask a hundred questions at once. They knew that some sort of miracle happened outside while they were all in the Casualty, but the telling of that tale would have to wait.

"Oh, Ranjit." Sara looked at him with the eyes of a physician, surveying the medical details of the scene. *IV, oxygen, shortness of breath, 12-lead e.c.g. on counter.* She put her arms on her hips and gasped. "I told you to throw that tobacco pipe away."

Everyone laughed. Finally, a laugh of joy, of knowing that it was a person in front of them, not simply a patient—a laugh of knowing that a miracle saved their lives. A laugh of knowing that life would go on, despite what was to come to Ranjit.

"Sara, you have taught me about the Christian God, the God of Love. In you, I see the reflection of that same God. I shall now know what exists beyond the Great Sea. You and I have taken different paths to God, but may we meet again at the place where all such paths converge."

He rested, and then said, "Turn me on my left side."

He mumbled as they helped him. His eyelids were heavy. They all cocked their ears as he spoke.

"I am of the nature to die. There is no way to escape death. All that is dear to me and everyone I love are of the nature to change. There is no way to escape being separated from them. My actions are my only true belongings. I cannot escape the consequences of my actions. My actions are the ground on which I stand. I will take refuge in the Buddha."

His voice stopped. There was silence in the room and Matt could hear a faint ringing in his ears. Every one stood still.

Sara pulled a cotton ball out of her pocket, twirling a wisp with her fingers. She looked at it for a second and put it away. Then Sara reached over and gently closed his eyes.

Closing a Door

There was a ritual of departure whenever a videshi left the small community of missionaries at Beni. Usually there were three days of goodbyes, slowly loosening the bonds that tied a person to the daily work, starting a mental transition back to a new role in the world. At Emmaus Christian Church hymns of triumph would be sung, the congregation would be joyful, and all flags would fly.

Given the circumstances, Matt's departure was compressed into one night of packing. The simplest thing Matt could do was to leave everything behind, though to be sure he did not arrive with much in the first place. In the end, he fit his belongings into a daypack. He woke at 0430, listening to the cuckoo and that other night bird he could never identify. He locked the door to his flat as he left and walked down the silent corridors of the hospital one last time. He carefully placed his key on the rack in Casualty near the Theatre key and left. He always loved the way the town stirred into action at this hour, women hurrying past with small covered plates for daily puja, and he wanted to remember it in the promise of a new day.

The Land Rover waited outside Sushila's door, and the driver leaned against the fender, still the essence of cool, smoking a cigarette while Sushila's things were brought out, then stopping his cigarette long enough to place the bags in the boot. She, too, would travel light.

Instead of getting on the main road, the Land Rover crossed the parade ground and stopped near the riverbank behind the temple. Sushila led Matt by the hand to the very end of the sandbar. In the gathering dawn, a small funeral pyre waited for a spark. Ram, Manju and Alok waited there.

"Ranjit wanted his body to be fed to the carrion birds," said Matt.

"And that is exactly what we will do for him," said Ram, "This is indeed a pyre, but we will not burn his remains here this morning."

"Thank you, I have grieved enough to last ten lifetimes. How did it get here?" asked Matt.

"We built it," said Manju, "Alok and I will stay."

"Who is it for, then?"

"It is a pyre for Sushila."

Sushila took Matt's hand and said, "I asked them to build this pyre for me, but as you see I have not died. In Buddhism we send the spirits to the sky, even the bad spirits. We will light this pyre to begin my new life, and all the bad things from the past will be truly sent away. Perhaps someday Nepal will be a place where a woman can have respect and love, and not live in fear. I will leave with you, Matt."

"Thank you for teaching me to suture," said Alok, "Someday I find you and you teach me cautery."

"There are better teachers for that subject, Alok."

"Then maybe you teach me how to earn love of Nepali woman."

"That is an easy one. All it takes is every bit of skill and strength and courage that you can find within yourself. And ten years of daily meditation about the Sacrament of the Goddess."

Ram said, "Matt, my brother, it grieves me to lose both Ranjit and you within the space of a single day. Doctor Fitzmaurice will be here tomorrow. We will go on."

From his pocket, Ram took Ranjit's old lighter and a sheaf of dried grass and handed them to Matt. In her hand, Sushila held a small piece of paper, a note from her lover that she held near her heart for many years. At one point, this little piece of paper was a deep sorrow, then it served as a bitter reminder of things that were lost, then it became her only hope of a better life. Now it was a promise that had come true. She placed the small piece of paper at the top of the pyre.

"Come, Matt. Light this pyre as a symbol of leaving the bad karma behind."

He looked at her face and hesitated. He looked up at the canyon walls. Here on the sandbar, it was eerily quiet except for the tinkle of water over the rocks. A large bird made lazy soaring circles way up in the sky, almost invisible due to the angle of the sun. *God forgive me*, he thought. Then he touched Ranjit's lighter to the small sheaf of dried grass and threw it on the pyre. He was surprised at the flash when it caught fire. *It wouldn't be long,* he thought. *I will move on, but I will never forget this place.*

They stood and watched for awhile, talking quietly the way that people do when they have shared deep experiences, acknowledging bonds of love that would never be broken, then each becoming lost in their own thoughts. The pyre was down to nearly ground level, but a column of smoke still wafted to the sky.

Now the final farewell as Sushila and Matt climbed in the Land Rover. The driver stubbed out his cigarette, slid behind the wheel, and slowly began the drive to Pokhara. Matt and Kali talked of their son. They talked about living in London while she completed her studies. First, Matt would bring her to Boston to meet his parents and break the news. Soon Kali fell asleep on his shoulder.

He adjusted the blanket so she would be warm. *I can always control my breath,* he said to himself. *Breathe in. Breathe out. I am going to practice until I get it.*

Acknowledgments

The author thanks everyone who provided inspiration and encouragement along the way.

Consultants: Elizabeth Getman shared literary advice with me as only a sister can. Julie DeCarvalho and Amy Niemczura remained the best daughters a dad could ask for. The world awaits the publication of "A Princess Incognito."

Cultural: Alok Rajourias, Shweta Shakya, Indu Karki, and Roji Gurung checked out cultural references for me. Any remaining inaccuracies in portraying Nepali culture are mine alone.

Editor: Anna Cruz of WordWright Associates edited this work. I recommend her to other writers. (http://wordrightassociates.wordpress.com/). Joyce Mletschnig was the final copy editor.

Legal Department: David Hayakawa, Wade Zukeran, Kris Henselman, John Barter and Alan Pransky were a lifeline of sanity.

Beta Readers: The sanga includes: Justin Acklin, John Barter, Betty Bullert, Ellen Bridge, Patricia Brooks, Clive Cowell, Julie DeCarvalho, Jasmine Cronin-Georgiadi, Betsy Getman, Lonnie Harris, LorettaJo Kapinos, Indu Karki, Emily Kessel, Binu Koirala, Emily Militoni, Joyce Mletschnig, Brigid Mulloy, Amy Niemczura, Stanley Niemczura, Stephanie Jae Park, Seth Rothberg, Kelci Schedler, Gaynor Sheahan, Hami Suzuki, and Isabel Whiston. Thank you for walking with me on this journey.

Special thanks to my old friend Ellen Bridge. That which doesn't kill us, makes us stronger. You made me howl with delight and inspired me to live up to my potential. Only a direct hit with a silver bullet will make me go away.

Colleagues: John Casken, Patricia Brooks, and Lynn Dubbs provided excellent advice along the way. I rode a wave of aloha from the faculty and students while editing and revising.

Joe Niemczura

Coffee: This book took shape at the Starbucks in Manoa, Hawaii. Thank you to Jason and the whole crew.

Beni: I do not pretend to capture every detail of the battle of Beni, but my quest for information about the town was eased by Mahendra Shrestha, a professional photographer and trekking guide from Pokhara. The reader can find links to his excellent work at http://mahendra-shrestha.deuxbleus.nl

Material Support: Mary Boland and Clementina Ceria-Ulep were generous in their support of this project. Thank you.

Glossary of Terms

Author's Note: In low income countries the health care team includes highly educated professionals from many countries. A pidgin language often develops, drawing on the diverse backgrounds. Consequently the daily speech provides a unique flavor to any such setting. A goal of this book is to convey the feeling of daily interaction. The author needed to convey the flavor and balance it with accessibility and readability.

The point at which an English word is substituted is arbitrary; for example everyone in Nepal knows what a Tundikhel is but the author opted to substitute "parade ground" for this even though few parades are likely to be held there. The author begs the reader's indulgence as to where the comfort zone may lie.

Place names are not included here.

Biblical references are best found in the Bible of the reader's choice.

Likewise, **detailed descriptions of medical procedures** which illustrate subtle differences between standards of practice in Nepal vs. the USA or UK, needed to be considered. Every effort has been made to convey the medical procedures in terms used by an educated reader; the author tried to simplify these descriptions but retain the interest of a sophisticated medical audience.

The Civil War – readers wishing to learn more of the Nepal Civil War are invited to find the book's blog page"

www.sacramentofthegoddess.wordpress.com

An illustrated and hyperlinked version of this glossary is also to be found there.

DISCLAIMER: Descriptions of medical diagnoses or procedures are depicted for narrative purposes only and should not be construed as medical advice. Do not attempt these at home. The reader is advised to consult a licensed physician for treatment of any illness depicted in this book. As soon as possible.

Glossary of Terms — 2

Bahadur – literally "brave" – used as a sort of nickname by members of the chhetri (warrior) caste. Abbreviated "bdr."

Bahini – "younger sister."

Bandh – a strike in which motorized traffic is halted and stores are closed. Enforced by gangs of men with lathis who threaten to thrash any violators. A bandh can be local, regional or national.

Bag chaal – "tigers and goats" a board game in the sense of chess or checkers.

Bhai – younger brother.

Bhalu – literally, a bear; slang term for a prostitute. *Offensive term.*

Bhagavad Gita- a holy book used in Hindu religion.

Bhairava – a manifestation of Shiva. With sharp teeth, he guards every temple door. Bhairava exemplifies fear and the passage of time. Knowledge cannot be gained unless fear is overcome.

Bijju – literally, the seed stalk of rice at the time of transplanting into the paddy. Figuratively, a slang term for man's semen. *This term is considered to be highly offensive.*

Bo tree – *ficus religiosa* the tree under which Buddha meditated and achieved enlightenment. Distinctive leaves of this tree are symbolic of Buddha.

Bodhicitta- a way of being which promotes better development of positive karma

Bodhisattva – a person of advanced development who postpones personal entry into Nirvana to help his fellow sentient beings achieve better karma.

Buddha – an old person, a wise person. "The Buddha" usually refers to Gautama, born at Lumbini Nepal.

Chakra – a site of energy in the body. There are seven chakras.

Cheese and Onion –slang term among medical students used for the spiral-bound Oxford handbook which is an indispensable resource. (used in UK and all Commonwealth countries).

Chiya – Nepali tea, boiled with milk and spices. The forerunner of Chai.

Chini – rough crystals of Nepali sugar.

Chowkidar – a uniformed guard.

Glossary of Terms – 3

Chautara – a rest stop. Usually a stone wall in a raised ring filled with earth into which two trees are planted, a Bo and a Pipal. Found throughout

Nepal. The one in Beni has a Sal tree. Specific trees have specific religious connotations.

Chhetri – ethnic group of Nepal, dark complexion. Historically, the warrior caste.

Cimellia - Buddhist symbol that illustrates a teaching. The eight cimellias are: double-fish, lotus, white conch, victory banner, Buddha wheel, auspicious knot, treasure vase and precious umbrella.

Dal bhaat – boiled rice served with lentil soup. The staple of Nepali diet.

Dai – older brother, used with any older male. Often used as a post-fix to the given name, as in "Ranjit dai"

Dakini – a female spirit, sometimes malevolent, that occupies a person's body. Also, a thought or concept that becomes an obsession.

Dakka cloth – brightly colored hand-woven cloth of Nepal. The best Dakka comes from Palpa district.

Daruwa Suruwal - Men's traditional outfit.

DBT – frequently used abbreviation for dal-bhaat-terkari.

Dharma – one of the pillars of Buddhism, a book of principals of practical action. "The eightfold path."

Dhoti – a cotton plaid skirt worn by men the Terai.

Didi – literally, "older sister" but used with any female older than you. In Nepali hospitals, often used to designate the Charge Nurse.

"Din me raat, rat me dat" roughly, "In daytime you see my dark skin, in nighttime you only see how my teeth shine."

Doko – a packbasket for carrying cargo. Used throughout Nepal, with a tumpline – a rope slung around the carrier's forehead.

Dorje – "lightning bolt," a symbolic handheld metal implement used in conjunction with a small bell to aid in meditation. About the size and heft of a roll of pennies.

Gajal – a musical genre which came to Nepal from Arabic lands. Also the name for kohl, a type of eye makeup used to enhance romance.

Ghee – purified butter.

Glossary of Terms — 4

Gurkha – member of elite Nepali military unit in service to UK or India or Singapore, serving as mercenaries since 1814.

Gurung – name of ethnic group found mainly in west-central Nepal.

Hajur – honorific term to address a person of higher social stature than the speaker.

Honorific – linguistic term for a system of verb conjugation which incorporates the awareness of relative social status into everyday conversation.

Hungry Ghosts – in Vajrayanic Buddhism, one of the six realms of sentient beings. "This is a metaphor for people futilely attempting to fulfill their illusory physical desires" (Wikipedia)

Istha Devi – a personal deity, assigned to an initiate, for the purpose of focusing meditation on Buddhist principles.

Janai surya – "starting a bond" an engagement party.

Janayuddha Jindabaad – slogan of Maoists which means "Long live the revolution"

Japaa – a form of puja which focuses on the use of repetitive mantras, aided by rakshya beads.

Jatra – a procession, usually involves parading a statue of the deity on a festival day.

Kali – literally, the color black. Also used as a nickname. Also a name for the Goddess of death, "The Black One."

Karma – the cumulative positive or negative credit built up during this life or a previous life.

Ke Garne – expression in wide use conveying" what to do!"

Kora – "walking meditation" to promote mindfulness. Used by all Buddhists.

Kuire – white person (never used in presence of actual white person). *offensive*

Kukri – the legendary forward-curving knife of Nepal, carried by Gurkhas but also in common use.

Kurtha Suruwal – two piece garment. Trousers plus a top which includes front and back panels or aprons that add extra modesty to the hips and buttocks.

Glossary of Terms – 5

Lama – A Tibetan monk who provides spiritual advice to the lay public.

Lassi – a drink made of yogurt and honey with spices, served as refreshment.

Lathi – a stick of four foot length used to administer a beating.

Lightning bolt – also known as a dorje. Symbol of man's virility and knowledge

Lotus flower – Buddhist symbol of femininity.

Loadshedding – rolling power blackouts used to share electricity.

Machhendranath – name of an annual festival in Patan, during which a large-wheeled cart is hauled through the city, to display the relic of the God who protects the people there.

Maoists – the communist-inspired revolutionaries. This term refers to the underground civilian guerilla combatants.

MBBS – "Bachelor of Medicine and Surgery" abbreviation for the academic degree associated with the course of medical study in Nepal and Commonwealth countries.

Mehendi – henna dye, applied to the skin in fanciful designs, a temporary tattoo.

Mindfulness – a key precept in Buddhism. Being aware of your own bodily response to simple activities. And so much more.

Mojo –. The essence of manhood which propels the life force forward. Not a Nepali term.

Momo – a meat dumpling that is steamed. Originally a Tibetan dish, now found throughout Nepal.

Mudra – one of the set of hand gestures used in classical Hinduism.

Muumuu – a Hawaiian one-piece loosefitting woman's garment that goes down to the ankles.

Namaste- a greeting used to acknowledge the divinity that exists in all fellow human beings.

Newari – a major ethnic group in Nepal, based mainly in Kathmandu but with outposts throughout the country.

NGO - Non-Governmental Organization.

Puja – ceremony of prayer.

Pakka - Hindi for "proper."

Glossary of Terms – 6

Pashmina – woven cloth made from the belly wool of a Nepali goat. Better than cashmere!

Pedicab – three wheeled bicycle. Driver pedals from a bicycle seat and passengers sit in a seat over the main axle

PLA – "People's Liberation Army" – the military wing of the Maoists. Please refer to website for more detailed backstory of civil war.

Police Force – (often "the armed police"). A military force designed to pacify the Maoist areas, given better weapons than the local police.

Raksi - homemade distilled alcohol based on rice. Very potent.

Rinpoche – in Tibetan Buddhism, a person with documented rebirth from a previous life.

Rodhi – an ad hoc kinship group of youth, particularly among Gurungs, that serves as a social unit.

RNA – "Royal Nepal Army" – the military employed by the King. Heavy weapons including attack helicopters.

Roti – bread, similar to a tortilla.

Rum Doodle - highest mountain of the Himalayan range – 40,000 and 1/2 feet.

Rundi – prostitute. (*derogatory term not used in polite company*)

Sadhu – an ascetic Hindu holy man who has renounced material goods

Sanga – one of the three pillars of Buddhism. The cohort of people with whom you share this life.

Santoshi Mata – a form of the Goddess. "The Goddess of Satisfaction" relatively new to the Hindu belief system.

Sar – "sir" usually a post fix for a respected male.

Shakti – the female goddess of pure sensuality.

Shangri-La – a legendary paradise in a hidden valley of the Himalaya described by James Hilton in the book "Lost Horizon" (1933)

Shiva- prime Hindu deity. The essence of maleness.

Sindoor – a streak of red coloring in the center part of a woman's hair that indicates she is married.

Sel roti - a type of bread made by dropping liquid dough into boiling oil, usually in a ring shape

Glossary of Terms – 7

Tandoori – a clay oven used to bake bread and other foods.

Tantra – "the third way" of knowledge, embracing direct experience of pleasures and pain. Best embarked upon under the guidance of a guru.

Tap – water source, usually one which has been improved with a spout or spigot.

Thamel – neighborhood in downtown Kathmandu where all the tourists and vagabonds are congregated, with guest houses, restaurants and bars.

Thapa – caste name for a person of the Magar ethnic group.

Third World Country – now considered a demeaning term. "Low Income Country" is more appropriate.

Thrashing – frontier justice administered by a group of men with lathis, often to the point of death.

Thugpa – a kind of Tibetan noodle soup

Tika – a mark on the forehead over the "third eye"

Topi – the small cap, usually of daka cloth, worn by Nepali men. The best are made from cloth handwoven in Palpa district, Nepal.

Tout – a self-appointed hustler who serves as a middleman in getting through some known point of bureaucratic bottleneck such as customs or the government.

Tuk tuk – small motor vehicle used to transport over short distances.

Tundikhel – parade ground; usually a large flat place in a city.

Vajrayogini – a very specific manifestation of the female Goddess, popular in Vajrayanic Buddhist worship.

Videshi – foreign person

Yak – an animal found in the Himalaya and Mongolia, domesticated for transport

Joe Niemczura

Getting Connected

The author invites readers to post a review of this book online, at Amazon, Goodreads or the book site of the reader's choice.

Send email to the author at joeniemczura@gmail.com. The author is available for Skype (Joe.niemczura1) or videoconference with book clubs or University classes in Global Health.

Resources in support of this book can be found on FaceBook, a Wordpress blog, the author's YouTube channel, and Good Reads. At these sites the reader can find info about hospitals, the Nepal Civil War, the author's work in Nepal, and Global Health. While the author does not accept friend requests from people he does not know, he invites everyone to "like" the fan page instead.

- Facebook page: https://www.facebook.com/thesacramentofthegoddess
- Wordpress blog: http://sacramentofthegoddess.wordpress.com/
- YouTube: http://www.youtube.com/user/Joeniemczura
- Good Reads: https://www.goodreads.com/book/show/19682575-the-sacrament-of-the-goddess

We Find Healing In Existing Reality

Plain View Press is a 37-year-old issue-based literary publishing house whose books are an artistic collaboration between writers, artists and editors. Over the years Plain View Press has become a far-flung community of activists whose energies bring humanitarian enlightenment and hope to individuals and communities grappling with the major issues of our time—peace, justice, the environment, education and gender. This humane, highly creative group of people combine art and social change. The poems, stories, essays, non-fiction and memoirs show evidence, that despite the relentless violence of our time, there is hope and there is art to show the human face of it Visit the publisher's website at www.plainviewpress.net.

About the Author

Joe Niemczura, RN, MS teaches nursing in the USA. Since 2007 he teaches critical care nursing in Nepal, which inspired this book. In the United States, Joe has a background in adult critical care and hospital middle-management.

This is his second book, after *The Hospital at the End of the World*, (Plainview Press, 2009), a narrative nonfiction about teaching in Nepal. Find it on Amazon in hardcover, softcover and a digital edition.

Joe is an Eagle Scout and a practicing Catholic. He can read Devanagari and hand-shear a sheep. He divides his time between Charlottesville, VA, Kathmandu, Nepal and a secluded cabin on a pond in Maine not far from the Appalachian Trail. His trail name is "Catch-Up." He has two daughters, neither of whom will discuss medical things at the dinner table. He is boring in real life.